8/13

# A Spear of Summer Grass

Center Point
Large Print

**This Large Print Book carries the
Seal of Approval of N.A.V.H.**

# A Spear of Summer Grass

## DEANNA RAYBOURN

CENTER POINT LARGE PRINT
THORNDIKE, MAINE

This Center Point Large Print edition
is published in the year 2013 by arrangement with
Harlequin Books S.A.

The text of this Large Print edition is unabridged.
In other aspects, this book may vary
from the original edition.
Printed in the United States of America
on permanent paper.
Set in 16-point Times New Roman type.

ISBN: 978-1-61173-850-6

Library of Congress Cataloging-in-Publication Data

Raybourn, Deanna.
A Spear of Summer Grass / Deanna Raybourn. — Center Point Large
Print edition.
pages cm
ISBN 978-1-61173-850-6 (Library binding : alk. paper)
1. Large type books. I. Title.
PS3618.A983S64 2013
813´.6—dc23

2013017085

For Valerie Gray,
gifted editor and maker of magic.
I am a better writer for knowing you.

# 1

Don't believe the stories you have heard about me. I have never killed anyone, and I have never stolen another woman's husband. Oh, if I find one lying around unattended, I might climb on, but I never took one that didn't want taking. And I never meant to go to Africa. I blame it on the weather. It was a wretched day in Paris, grey and gloomy and spitting with rain, when I was summoned to my mother's suite at the Hotel de Crillon. I had dressed carefully for the occasion, not because Mossy would care—my mother is curiously unfussy about such things. But I knew wearing something chic would make me feel a little better about the ordeal to come. So I put on a divine little Molyneux dress in scarlet silk with a matching cloche, topped it with a clever chinchilla stole and left my suite, boarded the lift and rode up two floors to her rooms.

My mother's Swedish maid answered the door with a scowl.

"Good afternoon, Ingeborg. I hope you've been well?"

The scowl deepened. "Your mother is worried about you," she informed me coldly. "And I am worried about your mother." Ingeborg had been worrying about my mother since before I was born. The fact that I had been a breech baby was enough to put me in her black books forever.

"Oh, don't fuss, Ingeborg. Mossy is strong as an ox. All her people live to be a hundred or more."

Ingeborg gave me another scowl and ushered me into the main room of the suite. Mossy was there, of course, holding court in the centre of a group of gentlemen. This was nothing new. Since her debut in New Orleans some thirty years before she had never been at a loss for masculine attention. She was standing at the fireplace, one elbow propped on the marble mantelpiece, dressed for riding and exhaling a cloud of cigarette smoke as she talked.

"But that's just not possible, Nigel. I'm afraid it simply won't do." She was arguing with her ex-husband, but you'd have to know her well to realise it. Mossy never raised her voice.

"What won't do? Did Nigel propose something scandalous?" I asked hopefully. The men turned as one to look at me, and Mossy's lips curved into a wide grin.

"Hello, darling. Come and kiss me." I did as she told me to, swiftly dropping a kiss to one powdered cheek. But not swiftly enough. She nipped me sharply with her fingertips as I edged away. "You've been naughty, Delilah. Time to pay the piper, darling."

I looked around the room, smiling at each of the gentlemen in turn. Nigel, my former stepfather, was a rotund Englishman with a florid complexion and a heart condition, and at the moment he looked about ten minutes past death. Quentin Harkness was there too, I was happy to see, and I stood on tiptoe to kiss him. Like Mossy, I've had my share of matrimonial mishaps. Quentin was the second. He was a terrible husband, but he's a divine ex and an even better solicitor.

"How is Cornelia?" I asked him. "And the twins? Walking yet?"

"Last month actually. And Cornelia is fine, thanks," he said blandly. I only asked to be polite and he knew it. Cornelia had been engaged to him before our marriage, and she had snapped him back up before the ink was dry on our divorce papers. But the children were sweet, and I was glad he seemed happy. Of course, Quentin was English. It was difficult to tell how he felt about most things.

I leaned closer. "How much trouble am I in?" I whispered. He bent down, his mouth just grazing the edge of my bob.

"Rather a lot."

I pulled a face at him and took a seat on one of the fragile little sofas scattered about, crossing my legs neatly at the ankle just as my deportment teacher had taught me.

"Really, Miss Drummond, I do not think you comprehend the gravity of the situation at all," Mossy's English solicitor began. I struggled to remember his name. Weatherby? Enderby? Endicott?

I smiled widely, showing off Mossy's rather considerable investment in my orthodontia.

"I assure you I do, Mr.—" I broke off and caught a flicker of a smile on Quentin's face. Drat him. I carried on as smoothly as I could manage. "That is to say, I am quite sure things will come right in the end. I have every intention of taking your excellent advice." I had learned that particular soothing tone from Mossy. She usually used it on horses, but I found it worked equally well with men. Maybe better.

"I am not at all certain of that," replied Mr. Weatherby. Or perhaps Mr. Endicott. "You do realise that the late prince's family are threatening legal action to secure the return of the Volkonsky jewels?"

I sighed and rummaged in my bag for a Sobranie. By the time I had fixed the cigarette into the long ebony holder, Quentin and Nigel were at my side, offering a light. I let them both light it— it doesn't do to play favourites—and blew out a cunning little smoke ring.

"Oh, that is clever," Mossy said. "You must teach me how to do it."

"It's all in the tongue," I told her. Quentin choked a little, but I turned wide-eyed to Mr. Enderby. "Misha didn't have family," I explained. "His mother and sisters came out of Russia with him during the Revolution, but his father and brother were with the White Army. They were killed in Siberia along with every other male member of his family. Misha only got out because he was too young to fight."

"There is the Countess Borghaliev," he began, but I waved a hand.

"Feathers! The countess was Misha's governess. She might be related, but she's only a cousin, and a very distant one at that. She is certainly not entitled to the Volkonsky jewels." And even if she were, I had no intention of giving them up. The original collection had been assembled over the better part of three centuries and it was all the Volkonskys had taken with them as they fled. Misha's mother and sisters had smuggled them out of Russia by sewing them into their clothes, all except the biggest of them. The Kokotchny emerald had been stuffed into an unmentionable spot by Misha's mother before she left the mother country, and nobody ever said, but I bet she left it walking a little funny. She had assumed—and rightly as it turned out—that officials would be squeamish about searching such a place, and with a good washing it had shone as brightly as ever, all eighty carats of it. At least, that was the official story of the jewels. I knew a few things that hadn't made the papers, things Misha had entrusted to me as his wife. I would sooner set my own hair on fire than see that vicious old Borghaliev cow discover the truth.

"Perhaps that is so," Mr. Endicott said, his expression severe, "but she is speaking to the press. Coming on the heels of the prince's suicide and your own rather cavalier attitude towards mourning, the whole picture is a rather unsavoury one."

I looked at Quentin, but he was studying his nails, an old trick that meant he wasn't going to speak until he was good and ready. And poor Nigel just looked as if his stomach hurt. Only Mossy seemed indignant, and I smiled a little to show her I appreciated her support.

"You needn't smile about it, pet," she said, stubbing out her cigarette and lighting a fresh one. "Weatherby's right. It is a pickle. I don't need your name dragged through the mud just now. And Quentin's practice is doing very well. Do you think he appreciates his ex-wife cooking up a scandal?"

I narrowed my eyes at her. "Darling, what do you mean you don't need my name dragged through the mud just now? What do you have going?"

Mossy looked to Nigel who shifted a little in his chair. "Mossy has been invited to the wedding of the Duke of York to the Lady Elizabeth Bowes-Lyon this month."

I blinked. The wedding of the second in line to

the throne was the social event of the year and one that ought to have been entirely beyond the pale for Mossy. "The queen doesn't receive divorced women. How on earth did you manage that?"

Mossy's lips thinned. "It's a private occasion, not Court," she corrected. "Besides, you know how devoted I have always been to the Strathmores. The countess is one of my very dearest friends. It's terribly gracious of them to invite me to their daughter's big day, and it would not do to embarrass them with any sort of *talk*."

Ah, *talk*. The euphemism I had heard since childhood, the bane of my existence. I thought of how many times we had moved, from England to Spain to Argentina to Paris, and every time it was with the spectre of talk snapping at our heels. Mossy's love affairs and business ventures were legendary. She could create more scandal by breakfast than most women would in an entire lifetime. She was larger than life, my Mossy, and in living that very large life she had accidentally crushed quite a few people under her dainty size-five shoe. She never understood that, not even now. She was standing in a hotel suite that cost more for a single night than most folks made in a year, and she could pay for it with the spare change she had in her pockets, but she would never understand that she had damaged people to get there.

Of course, she noticed it at once if *I* did anything

amiss, I thought irritably. Let one of her marriages fail and it was entirely beyond her control, but if I got divorced it was because I didn't try hard enough or didn't understand how to be a wife.

"Don't sulk, Delilah," she ordered. "You are far too old to pout."

"I am not pouting," I retorted, sounding about fourteen as I said it. I sighed and turned back to the solicitor. "You see, Mr. Weatherby, people just don't understand my relationship with Misha. Our marriage was over long before he put that bullet into his head." Mr. Weatherby winced visibly. I tried again. "It was no surprise to Misha that I wanted a divorce. And the fact that he killed himself immediately after he received the divorce papers is not my fault. I even saw Misha that morning and stressed to him I wanted things to be very civil. I am friends with all of my husbands."

"I'm the only one still living," Quentin put in, rather unhelpfully, I thought.

I stuck out my tongue at him again and turned back to Mr. Weatherby. "As to the jewels, Misha's mother and both sisters died in the Spanish flu outbreak in '19. He inherited the jewels outright, and he gave them to me as a wedding gift."

"They would have been returned as part of the divorce settlement," Weatherby reminded me.

"There was no divorce," I said, trumping him neatly. "Misha did not sign the papers before he died. I am therefore technically a widow and

14

entitled to my husband's estate as he died with neither a will nor issue."

Mr. Weatherby took out a handkerchief and mopped his brow. "Be that as it may, Miss Drummond, the whole affair is playing out quite badly in the press. If you could only be more discreet about the matter, perhaps put on proper mourning or use your rightful name."

"Delilah Drummond *is* my rightful name. I have never taken a husband's name or title, and I never will. Frankly, I think it's a little late in the day to start calling myself Princess Volkonsky." Quentin twitched a little, but I ignored him. The truth was I had seen Mossy change her name more times than I could count on one hand, and it was hell on the linen and the silver. Far more sensible to keep a single monogram. "It's a silly, antiquated custom," I went on. "You men have been forcing us to change our names for the last four thousand years. Why don't we switch it up? You lot can take our names for the next few millennia and see how you like it."

"Stop her before she builds up a head of steam," Mossy instructed Nigel. She hated it when I talked about women's rights.

Nigel sat forward in his chair, a kindly smile wreathing his gentle features. "My dear, you know you have always held a special place in my affections. You are the nearest thing to a daughter I have known."

I smiled back. Nigel had always been my favourite stepfather. His first wife had given him a pair of dull sons, and they had already been away at school when he married Mossy and we had gone to live at his country estate. He had enjoyed the novelty of having a girl about the place and never made himself a nuisance like some of the other stepfathers did. A few of them had actually tried on fatherhood for size, meddling in my schooling, torturing the governesses with questions about what I ate and how my French was coming along. Nigel just got on with things, letting me have the run of the library and kitchens as I pleased. Whenever he saw me, he always patted my head affectionately and asked how I was before pottering off to tend to his orchids. He taught me to shoot and to ride and how to back a winner at the races. I rather regretted it when Mossy left him, but it was typical of Nigel that he let her go without a fight. I was fifteen when we packed up, and on our last morning, when the cases were locked and stacked up in the hall and the house had already started to echo in a way I knew only too well, I asked him how he could just let her leave. He gave me his sad smile and told me they had struck a bargain when he proposed. He promised her that if she married him and later changed her mind, he wouldn't stand in her way. He'd kept her for four years—two more than any of the others. I hoped that comforted him.

Nigel continued. "We have discussed the matter at length, Delilah, and we all agree that it is best for you if you retire from public life for a bit. You're looking thin and pale, my dear. I know that is the fashion for society beauties these days," he added with a melancholy little twinkle, "but I should so like to see you with roses in your cheeks again."

To my horror, I felt tears prickling the backs of my eyes. I wondered if I was starting a cold. I blinked hard and looked away.

"That's very kind of you, Nigel." It *was* kind, but that didn't mean I was convinced. I turned back, stiffening my resolve. "Look, I've read the newspapers. The Borghaliev woman has done her worst already. She's a petty, nasty creature and she is spreading petty, nasty gossip which only petty, nasty people will listen to."

"You've just described all of Paris society, dear," Mossy put in. "And London. And New York."

I shrugged. "Other people's opinions of me are none of my business."

Mossy threw up her hands and went to light another cigarette, but Quentin leaned forward, pitching his voice low. "I know that look, Delilah, that Snow Queen expression that means you think you're above all this and none of it can really touch you. You had the same look when the society columnists fell over themselves talking

17

about our divorce. But I'm afraid an attitude of noble suffering isn't sufficient this time. There is some discussion of pressure being brought to bear on the authorities about a formal investigation."

I paused. That was a horse of a different colour. A formal investigation would be messy and time-consuming and the press would lap it up like a cat with fresh cream.

Quentin carried on, his voice coaxing as he pressed his advantage. He always knew when he had me hooked. "The weather is vile and you know how you hate the cold. Why don't you just go off and chase the sunshine and leave it with me? Your French lawyers and I can certainly persuade them to drop the matter, but it will take a little time. Why not spend it somewhere sunny?" he added in that same honeyed voice. His voice was his greatest asset as a solicitor and as a lover. It was how he had convinced me to go skinny-dipping in the Bishop of London's garden pond the first night we met.

But he flicked a significant sideways glance at Mossy and I caught the thinning of her lips, the white lines at her knuckles as she held her cigarette. She was worried, far more than she was letting on, but somehow Quentin had persuaded her to let him handle me. Her eyes were fixed on the black silk ribbon I'd tied at my wrist. I had started something of a fashion with it among the smart set. Other women might wear lace or satin to match their ensembles, but I wore only silk and only black, and Mossy didn't take her eyes off that scrap of ribbon as I rubbed at it.

I took another long drag off my cigarette and Mossy finally lost patience with me.

"Stop fidgeting, Delilah." Her voice was needle-sharp and even she heard it. She softened her tone, talking to me as though I were a horse that needed soothing. "Darling, I didn't want to tell you this, but I'm afraid you don't really have a choice in the matter. I've had a cable from your grandfather this morning. It seems the Countess Borghaliev's gossip has spread a little further than just Paris cafés. It made *The Picayune*. He is put out with you just now." That I could well imagine. My grandfather—Colonel Beauregard L'Hommedieu of the 9th Louisiana Confederate Cavalry—was as wild a Creole as New Orleans had ever seen, but he expected the women in his family to be better behaved. He hadn't had much luck with Mossy or with me, but he had no trouble pulling purse strings like a puppeteer to get his way.

"How put out?"

"He said if you don't go away quietly, he will put a stop to your allowance."

I ground out my cigarette, scattering ash on the white carpet. "But that's extortion!"

She shrugged. "It's his money, darling. He can do with it precisely as he likes. Anything you get from your grandfather is at his pleasure and right now it is his pleasure to have a little discretion on your part." She was right about that. The Colonel had already drawn up his will and Mossy and I were out. He had a sizeable estate—town houses in the French Quarter, commercial property on the Mississippi, cattle ranches and cotton fields, and his crown jewel, Reveille, the sugar plantation just outside of New Orleans. And every last acre and steer and cotton boll was going to his nephew. There was a price to being notorious and Mossy and I were certainly going to pay it when the Colonel died. In the meantime, he was generous enough with his allowances, but he never gave without expecting something back. The better behaved we were, the more we got. The year I divorced Quentin, I hadn't gotten a thin red dime, but since then he had come through handsomely. Still, feeling the jerk of the leash from three thousand miles away was a bit tiresome.

I felt the sulks coming back. "The Colonel's money isn't everything."

"Very near," Quentin murmured. It had taken him the better part of a year to untangle the mess of inheritances, annuities, alimonies and settlements that made up my portfolio and another year to explain exactly how I was spending far more than I got. With his help and a few clever investments, I had almost gotten myself into the black again. Most of my income still went to paying off the last of the creditors, and it would be a long time before I saw anything like a healthy return. The Colonel's allowance kept me in Paris frocks and holidays in St. Tropez. Without it, I would have to economize—something I suspected I wouldn't much enjoy.

I looked away again, staring out of the window, watching the rain hit the glass in great slashing ribbons. It was dismal out there, just as it had been in England. The last few months of 1922 had been gloomy and 1923 wasn't off to much better of a start. Everywhere I went it was grey and bleak. As I watched, the raindrops turned to sleet, pelting the windows with a savage hissing sound. God, I thought miserably, why was I fighting to stay *here?*

"Fine. I'll go away," I said finally.

Mossy breathed an audible sigh of relief and even Weatherby looked marginally happier. I had cleared the first hurdle and the biggest; they had gotten me to agree to go. Now the only question was where to send me.

"America?" Quentin offered.

I slanted him a look. "Not bloody likely, darling." Between the Volstead Act and the Sullivan Ordinance, I couldn't drink or smoke in public in New York. It was getting harder and harder for a girl to have a good time. "I am protesting the intrusion of the federal government upon the rights of the individual."

"Or are you protesting the lack of decent cocktails?" Quentin murmured.

"It's true," Mossy put in. "She won't even travel on her American passport, only her British one."

Quentin flicked a glance to Nigel. "I do think, Sir Nigel, perhaps your initial suggestion of Africa might be well worth revisiting." So that's what they'd been discussing when I had come in—Africa. At the mention of the word, Mossy started to kick up a fuss again and Nigel remonstrated gently with her. Mossy hated Africa. He'd taken her there for their honeymoon and she had very nearly divorced him over it. Something to do with snakes in the bed.

Nigel had gone to Africa as a young man, back in the days when it was a protectorate called British East Africa and nothing but a promise of what it might become someday. Then it was raw and young and the air was thick with possibilities. He had bought a tidy tract of land and built a house on the banks of Lake Wanyama. He called it Fairlight after the pink glow of the sunsets on the lake, and he had planned to spend the rest of his life there, raising cattle and painting. But his heart was bad, and on the advice of his doctors he left Fairlight, returning home with nothing but his thwarted plans and his diary. He never looked at it; he said it made him homesick for the place, which was strange since England was his home. But I used to go to his library and take it down sometimes, handling it with the same reverence a religious might show the Holy Grail. It was a mystical thing, that diary, bound with the skin of a crocodile Nigel had killed on his first safari. It was written in soft brown ink and full of sketches, laced with bones and beads and feathers and bits of eggshells—a living record of his time in Africa and of a dream that drew one good breath before it died.

The book itself wouldn't shut, as if the covers weren't big enough to hold the whole of Africa, and I used to sit for hours reading and tracing my finger along the slender blue line of the rivers, plunging my pinky into the sapphire pool of Lake Wanyama, rolling it up the high green slopes of Mt. Kenya. There were even little portraits of animals, some serene, some silly. There were monkeys gamboling over the pages, and in one exquisite drawing a leopard bowed before an elephant wearing a crown. There were tiny watercolour sketches of flowers so lush and colourful I could almost smell their fragrance on the page. Or perhaps it was from the tissue-thin petals, now crushed and brown, that Nigel had pressed between the pages. He conjured Africa for me in that book. I could see it all so clearly in my mind's eye. I used to wish he would take us there, and I secretly hoped Mossy would change her mind and decide she loved Africa so I could see for myself whether the leopard would really bow down to the elephant.

But she never did, and soon after she packed us up and left Nigel and years passed and I forgot to dream of Africa. Until a sleety early April morning in Paris when I had had enough of newspapers and gossip and wagging tongues and wanted right away from everything. *Africa.* The very word conjured a spell for me, and I took a long drag from my cigarette, surprised to find my fingers trembling a little.

"All right," I said slowly. "I'll go to Africa."

# 2

Quentin raised his glass of champagne. "A toast. To my brave and darling Delilah and all who go with her. Bon voyage!"

It was scarcely a fortnight later but all the arrangements had been made. Clothes had been ordered, trunks had been packed, papers procured. It sounds simple enough, but there had been endless trips to couturiers and outfitters and bookshops and stuffy offices for tickets and forms and permissions. By the end of it, I was exhausted, so naturally I chose to kick up my heels and make the most of my last evening in Paris. Quentin had guessed I would be feeling a little low and arranged to take me out. It had been a rather wretched day, all things considered. I had almost backed out of going to Africa a dozen times, but that morning Mossy appeared in my suite brandishing the latest copy of a scurrilous French newspaper that had somehow acquired photographs of Misha's death scene. They dared not publish them, but the descriptions were gruesome enough, and they had taken lurid liberties with the prose as well.

" 'The Curse of the Drummonds,' " Mossy muttered. "How dare they! I'm no Drummond. I was married to Pink Drummond for about ten minutes sometime in 1891. I barely remember his face. If they want to talk about a curse on the women of our family, it ought to be the L'Hommedieu curse," she finished, slamming the door behind her for emphasis.

With that I had given up all hope of avoiding exile and started pouring cocktails. I was only a little tight by the time Quentin picked me up, but he was lavish with the champagne, and when we reached the Club d'Enfer, I was well and truly lit.

I adored the Club d'Enfer. As one would expect from its name, it was modeled on Hell. The ceiling was hung with red satin cut into the shape of flames and crimson lights splashed everything with an unholy glow. A cunning little devil stood at the door greeting visitors by swishing his forked tail and poking at people's bottoms with his pitchfork.

Quentin rubbed at his posterior. "I say, is that really necessary?"

"Oh, Quentin, don't be wet," I told him. "This place has *swing*."

Behind us, my cousin Dora gave a little scream as the pitchfork prodded her derrière.

"Don't bother," I told the devil. "She's English. You won't find anything but bony disapproval there."

"Delilah, really," she protested, but I had stopped listening. A demonic waiter was waving us to a table near the stage, and Quentin ordered champagne before we were even seated.

Around us the music pulsed, a strange cacophonic melody that would have been grossly out of place anywhere else but suited the Club d'Enfer just fine.

As we sat, the proprietor approached. He— she?—was a curiously androgynous creature with the features of a woman but a man's voice and perfectly-cut tuxedo. On the occasion of my first visit to the club, it had introduced itself as Regine and seemed to be neither male nor female. Or both. I had heard that Regine's tastes ran to very hairy men or very horsey women, of which I was neither.

Regine bowed low over my hand, but then placed it firmly in the crook of his or her arm.

"My heart weeps, dear mademoiselle! I hear that Paris is about to lose one of the brightest stars in her firmament."

Such flowery language was par for the course with Regine. I smiled a little wistfully.

"Yes, I am banished to Africa. Apparently I've been too naughty to be allowed to stay in Paris."

"The loss is entirely that of Paris. And do you travel alone to the *pais sauvage*?"

"No. My cousin is coming. Regine, have you met Dora? Dora, say hello to Regine."

Dora murmured something polite, but Regine's

eyes had kindled upon seeing her long, lugubrious features. "Another great loss for Paris."

Dora dropped her head and I peered at her. "Dodo, are you blushing?"

"Of course not," she snapped. "The lights are red."

Regine shrugged. "A necessary artifice. One must believe one is truly a tourist in Hell at the Club d'Enfer." With that, Dora received a kiss to the hand and blushed some more before Regine disappeared to order more champagne and some delicious little nibbles for us.

Quentin shook his head. "I must admit I'm a bit worried for you, Delilah. Africa won't be anything like Paris, you know. Or New York. Or St. Tropez. Or even New Orleans."

I sipped at the champagne, letting the lovely golden bubbles rush to my head on a river of exhilaration. "I will manage, Quentin. Nigel has provided me with letters of introduction and very sweetly made me a present of his best gun. I am well prepared."

"Not the Rigby!" Quentin put in faintly.

"Yes, the Rigby." It was the second gun I learned to shoot and the first I learned to love. Nigel had commissioned it before travelling to Africa, and it was a beautiful monster of a firearm—eleven pounds and a calibre big enough to drop an elephant.

Quentin shook his head. "Only Nigel would be

sentimental enough to think a .416 is a suitable gun for a woman. Can you even lift it?"

"Lift it and fire it better than either of his sons. That's why he gave it to me instead of them. They'll be furious when they realise it's gone." I grinned.

"I can't say as I blame them. It must have cost him the better part of a thousand pounds. I suppose you remembered ammunition?"

"Of course I did! Darling, stop fussing. I will be perfectly fine. After all, I have Dora to look after me," I said with a nod toward where she sat poking morosely at a truffled deviled egg.

"Poor Dora," Quentin observed, perhaps with a genuine tinge of regret. Quentin had always been sweetly fond of Dora in the way one might be fond of a slightly incontinent lapdog. The fact that she bore a striking resemblance to a spaniel did not help. She was dutiful and dull and had two interests in life—God and gardens. We were distant cousins, second or third—the branches of the Drummond family tree were hopelessly knotted. But she was a poor relation to my father's people, and as such, was at the family's beck and call whenever I required a chaperone. She had dogged me halfway around the world already, and I wondered if she were growing as tired of me as I was of her.

She looked up from her egg and smiled at Quentin as I went on. "Dora's going to have the

29

worst of it, I'm afraid. My lady's maid quit when I told her we were going to Africa, and it didn't seem worth the trouble to train a new one just to have her drop dead of cholera or get herself bitten by a cobra. So Dora is going to maid me as well as lend me an air of respectability." She made a little sound of protest, but I kept talking. "I started her off at the salon. I dragged her to LaFleur's and made Monsieur teach her how to cut my hair." I might have been heading to the wilds of Africa, but there was no excuse to look untidy. My sleek black bob required regular and very precise maintenance, and Dora had been the natural choice to take on the job. I told her to think of it as a type of pruning or hedge control.

Quentin laughed out loud, a sure sign that the champagne was getting to him.

I fixed him with my most winsome expression. "You can do a favour for me while I'm away."

"Anything," was the prompt reply.

"I have garaged my car in London." I reached into my tiny beaded bag and pulled out the key. I flipped it into his champagne glass. "Take her out and drive her once in a while."

He stared at the key as the bubbles foamed around it. "The Hispano-Suiza? But it's brand new!"

It was indeed. I'd only taken possession of it two months before. I had cooled my heels for half a year waiting for them to get the colour just right.

I had instructed them to paint it the same scarlet as my lipstick, which the dealer couldn't seem to understand until I had left a crimson souvenir of my kiss on the wall of his office. I had ordered it upholstered in leopard, and whenever I drove it I felt savagely stylish, a modern-day Boadicea in her chariot.

"That's why I want it driven," I told Quentin. "She's like any female. If she sits around doing nothing for a year, she'll rust up. And something that pretty deserves to be taken out for a ride and shown off."

He fished into the glass and withdrew the key, wearing an expression of such wonder you'd have thought I just dropped the crown jewels into his lap. He dried the key carefully on his handkerchief and tucked it into his pocket. Cornelia wouldn't like it, but I didn't care and neither did Quentin.

Just then the Negro orchestra struck up a dance tune, something sensual and throbbing, and Quentin stood, holding out his hand to me. "Dance?" I rose and he smiled at Dora. "We'll have the next one, shall we?"

Dora waved him off and I went into his arms. Quentin was a heavenly dancer, and there was something deliciously familiar about our bodies moving together.

"I have missed this, you know," he said, his lips brushing my ear.

"Don't, darling," I said lightly. "Your mustache is tickling me."

"You never complained before."

"I never had the chance. I always meant to make you shave it off when we'd been married for a year."

His arm tightened. The drums grew more insistent. "Sometimes I think I was a very great fool to let you go."

"Don't get nostalgic," I told him firmly. "You are far better off with Cornelia. And you have the twins."

"The twins are dyspeptic and nearsighted. They take after their mother."

I laughed as he spun me into a series of complicated steps then swung me back into his arms. He felt solid under my touch. There had never been anything of the soft Englishman about Quentin. He was far too fond of cricket and polo for that.

I ran a happy hand over the curve of his shoulder and felt him shudder.

"Delilah, unless you plan on inviting me up for the night—"

He didn't finish the sentence. He didn't have to. We both knew I would. We'd spent more nights together since our divorce than we had during our marriage. Not when I was married to Misha, of course. That would have been entirely wrong. But it seemed very silly not to enjoy a quick roll in the hay when we both happened to be in the same city. After all, it wasn't as though Cornelia had anything to fear from me. I had had him and I had let him go. I wasn't about to take him back again. In fact, I rather thought I might be doing her a service. He was always jolly after a night with me; it must have made him easier to live with. Besides that, he was so lashed with guilt he invariably went home with an expensive present for Cornelia. I smiled up into Quentin's eyes and wondered what she'd be getting this time. I had seen some divine little emerald clips in the Cartier window on the Rue de la Paix. I made a note to tell him about them.

We danced and the orchestra played on.

The next morning I waved goodbye to Paris through the haze of a modest hangover. Dora, who had restricted herself to two glasses of champagne, was appallingly chipper. Paris had dressed in her best to see us off. A warm spring sun peeked through the pearl-grey skirts of early morning fog, and a light breeze stirred the new leaves on the Champs-Élysées as if waving farewell.

"It might at least be bucketing down with rain," I muttered irritably. I was further annoyed that Mossy had sent Weatherby to make certain I made the train to Marseilles. "Tell me, Mr. Weatherby, do you plan to come as far as Mombasa with us?

Or do you trust us to navigate the Suez on our own?"

Weatherby wisely ignored the jibe. He handed over a thick morocco case stuffed with papers and bank notes. "Here are your travel documents, Miss Drummond, as well as a little travelling money from Sir Nigel in case you should meet with unexpected expenses. There are letters of introduction as well."

I gave him a smile so thin and sharp I could have cut glass with it. "How perfectly Edwardian."

Weatherby stiffened. "You might find it helpful to know certain people in Kenya. The governor, for instance."

"Will I?"

He drew in a deep breath and seemed to make a grab for his patience. "Miss Drummond, I don't think you fully comprehend the circumstances. Single women are not permitted to settle in Kenya. Sir Nigel took considerable pains to secure your entry. The governor himself issued permission."

He brandished a piece of paper covered with official stamps. I peered at the signature. "Sir William Kendall."

"As I say, the governor—and an old friend of your stepfather's from his Kenya days. No doubt he will prove a useful connection in your new life in Kenya."

I shoved the permit into the portfolio and

handed it to Dora. "It's very kind of Nigel to take so much trouble, but I don't have a new life in Kenya, Mr. Weatherby. I am going for a short stay until everyone stops being so difficult about things. When the headlines have faded away, I'll be back," I told him. I would have said more, but just then there was a bit of a commotion on the platform. There was the sound of running footsteps, some jostling, and above it all, the baying of hounds hot on the scent.

"There she is!" It was the photographers, and before they could snap a decent picture, Weatherby had shoved me onto the train and slammed the door, very nearly stranding Dora on the platform. She fought her way onto the train, leaving the pack of reporters scrambling in her wake.

"Honestly," Dora muttered. Her hat had somehow gotten crushed in the scrum and she was staring at it mournfully.

"Don't bother trying to fix it, Dodo. It's an improvement," I told her. I moved to the window and let it down. Instantly, the photographers rushed the train, shouting and setting off flash-bulbs. I gave them a mildly vulgar gesture and a wide smile. "Take all the pictures you want, boys. I'm headed to Africa!"

My high spirits had evaporated by the time we boarded the ship at Marseilles. I was no stranger to travel. I liked to keep on the move, one step ahead of everybody, heading wherever my whims carried me. What I resented was being *told* that I had to go. It was quite hurtful, really. Mossy had weathered any number of scandalous stories in the press and she'd never been exiled. Of course, none of her husbands had ever died in mysterious circumstances. She'd divorced all except my father, poor Peregrine Drummond, known to all and sundry as Pink. He'd gone off to fight in the Boer War just after their honeymoon without even knowing I was on the way. He had died of dysentery before lifting his rifle—a sad footnote to what Mossy said had been a hell of a life. He had been adventuresome and charming and handsome as the devil, and no one could quite believe that he had died puking into a bucket. It was a distinctly mundane way to go.

Since Mossy might well have been carrying the heir to the Drummond title, she'd spent her pregnancy sitting around at the family estate, waiting to pup. As soon as she went into labour, my father's five brothers descended upon Cherryvale from London, pacing outside Mossy's room until the doctor emerged with the news that the eldest of them was now the undisputed heir to their father's title. Mossy told me she could hear the champagne corks and hushed whoops through the door. They needn't have bothered to keep it down. If she'd been mother to the heir she'd have been forced to stay at Cherryvale with her in-laws. Since I was a girl—and of no particular interest to anyone—she was free to go. The prospect of leaving thrilled her so much she would have happily bought them a round of champagne herself.

As it was, she packed me up as soon as she could walk and we decamped to a suite at the Savoy with Ingeborg and room service to look after us. Mossy never returned to Cherryvale, but I went back for school holidays while my grandparents were alive. They spent most of their time correcting my posture and my accent. I eventually stopped slouching thanks to enforced hours walking the long picture gallery at Cherryvale with a copy of *Fordyce's Sermons* on my head, but the long Louisiana drawl that had made itself at home on my tongue never left. It got thicker every summer when I went back to Reveille, but mellowed each school term when the girls made fun of me and I tried to hide it. I never did get the hang of those flat English vowels, and I eventually realised it was just easier to pummel the first girl who mocked me. I was chucked out of four schools for fighting, and Mossy despaired of ever making a lady of me.

But I did master the social graces—most of them anyway—and I made my debut in London in 1911. Mossy had been barred from Court on account of her divorces and it was left to my

Drummond aunt to bring me out properly. She did it with little grace and less enthusiasm, and I suspected some money might have changed hands. But I fixed my fancy Prince of Wales feathers to my hair and rode to the palace in a carriage and made my double curtsey to the king and queen. The next night I went to my first debutante ball and two days later I eloped with a black-haired boy from Devonshire whose family almost disowned him for marrying an American with nothing but scandal for a dowry.

Johnny didn't care. All he wanted was me, and since all I wanted was him, it worked out just fine. The Colonel came through with a handsome present of cash and Johnny had a little family money. He wanted to write, so I bought him a typewriter as a wedding present and he would sit at our little kitchen table pecking away as I burned the chops. He read me his articles and bits of his novel every evening as I eventually figured out how not to scorch things, and by the time his book was finished, I had even learned to make a proper soufflé. We were proud of each other, and everything we did seemed new, as if it was the first time it had ever been done. Whether it was sex or prose or jam on toast, we invented it. There was something fine about our time together, and when I took the memories out to look at them, I peered hard to find a shadow somewhere. Did the mirror crack when I sat on the edge of the bathtub and watched him shave? Did I spill salt when I fixed his eggs? Did an owl come to roost in the rafters of the attic? I had been brought up on omens, nursed on portents. Not from Mossy. She was a new creation, a modern woman, although I had spied her telling her rosary when she didn't think I saw.

But there were the others. The Colonel's withered old mother, Granny Miette, her keeper Teenie, and Teenie's daughter, Angele. They were the guardians of my childhood summers at Reveille, and they kept the old ways. They knew that not everything is as it seems and that if you look closely enough, you can see the shadows of what's to come in the bright light of your own happiness. Time is slower in Louisiana, each minute dripping past like cold molasses. Plenty of time to see if you want to and you know where to look.

I never looked in those days with Johnny. When I opened a closet and something fluttered out of the corner of my eye, I told myself it was just moths and nothing more, and I hung lavender and cedar to drive them away. When I peered in a cupboard and saw a shadow scurry past, I said it was mice and bought a cat, the meanest mouser I could find. I sent to Reveille for golden strands of vetiver and carried the dry grass in a small bundle in my pocket. It was the scent of sunlight and home, pungent and earthy and cedar-green-smelling, and I sewed a handful of it in the uniform that Johnny put on in 1914.

The uniform came back—or at least pieces of it did. Germans blew him to bits during the Battle of the Marne, and I don't remember much of what happened after that. A black curtain has fallen over that time, and I don't ever pull it back to look behind. It's a place I don't visit in my memories, and it was a long while before I came out of it. When I emerged, I chopped off my hair and hemmed up my skirts and set out to see what I'd been missing in the world. It had been an interesting ride, no doubt about it, but things had gotten a little out of hand to land me with banishment to Africa. I had handled my affairs with style and even a little discretion from time to time. But the world could be a hard place on a girl who was just out for a little fun, and I felt mightily put upon as the train churned into the station at Marseilles.

At the sight of the ship, my spirits perked right up. I had had a choice of sailing with a British outfit or later with a German one, but I had refused point blank to cross to Mombasa with a bunch of Krauts. I was still holding a bit of a grudge over Johnny and wasn't inclined to give them a penny of my money. Sailing a week earlier meant missing the closing of Cocteau's *Antigone*, but I was not about to budge. And when I saw the crew, I didn't even mind giving up the Chanel costumes or the Picasso sets. The boys were absolutely darling, each and every one of them, and for the next fortnight, I nursed my grievances in style. The deck steward made certain my chair was always in the best spot, near the sun but comfortably shaded as we moved south. As soon as I settled myself each morning, he was there with a travelling rug and a cup of hot bouillon. The dining steward dampened my tablecloth lightly so my plate wouldn't slide in rough seas and the wine wouldn't spill on my French silks. The older officers took turns escorting me onto the dance floor, and the younger ones gathered up empty bottles by the armful. We composed messages to seal inside, each one sillier than the last, and hurled them overboard until the captain put a stop to it. But he made up for it by inviting me to sit at his table for the rest of the voyage, and I discovered he was the best dancer of the lot. Poor Dodo was violently seasick and spent the entire trip holed up in her cabin with a basin between her knees and a compress on her brow.

I was feeling much better indeed by the time we sailed into Mombasa, past the old Portuguese fort of St. Jesus. I had asked the officers endless questions about the place and they talked over each other until I scarcely got a word in edgewise. I learned quite a bit about Mombasa, although my knowledge was rather limited to places that might appeal to sailors. If I needed a tipple or a tattoo or a two-dollar whore, I knew just the spots, but five-star hotels seemed in short supply. They told me if we sailed into port early in the morning, I could make straight for Nairobi on the noon train, heading up-country to where the white settlers had carved out a settlement for themselves. The captain had an uncle who had gone up-country and he regaled me with tales of hippos in the gardens and leopards in the trees. I knew a bit from Nigel's stories as well, but the captain's knowledge was somewhat fresher and he offered me his guidebook as a reference.

"Be careful with the natives," he warned. "Don't let them take advantage of you. If you need advice, find an Englishman who's been there and knows the drill. Make sure you visit the club in Nairobi. It's the best place to get a bit of society and all the news. They won't let you join, naturally, since you are a lady, but you would be permitted inside as the guest of a member. You will want to mix with your own kind, of course, but mind you steer clear of politics."

"Politics! In a backwater like this?" I teased.

The captain had lovely eyes, but the expression in them was so serious it dampened the effect. "Definitely. Rhodesia gained its independence from the Crown last year, and there are those who feel that Kenya ought to be next."

"And will England let her go as easily as she did Rhodesia?"

A slight furrow plowed its way between his

42

brows. "Difficult to say. You see, England doesn't care about Africa itself, not really. It's all about control of the Suez." He flipped open the guidebook and pointed on the map. "France, England and Germany have all established colonies in Africa to keep a close eye upon the Suez. At present, we have the advantage," he said with a tinge of British pride, "but we may not keep it. It all depends on Whitehall and how nervous they are about India." He traced a line from India westward, through the Arabian Sea, into the Gulf of Aden and then a sharp turn up the slender length of the Red Sea to the Suez at the tip of Egypt. "See there? Whoever controls Egypt controls the Suez, and through it, all the riches of India."

I picked up the long slender line of the Nile. One branch, the Blue, curved into Ethiopia, but the other snaked through Uganda and trailed off somewhere beyond. "And whoever controls the Nile controls Egypt."

"They do," he conceded. "For now, we Brits control Egypt and the Suez is safe, but matters could change if the ultimate source of the White Nile is discovered to be in hostile territory."

"Reason enough for England to hold onto Kenya," I observed.

"Not just that," he said, slowly folding up the map. "England has an obligation to the Indians who have come to settle here."

"Indians? In Kenya?"

"Thousands," he said grimly. "Now, they did their part during the war and no doubt about it. But one cannot deny that it has complicated matters here to no end. They are agitating for the right to own land, and some at Whitehall are inclined to give it them."

"That can't make the white colonists very happy."

"Tensions are running high, and you'd do well to avoid any appearance of taking sides. Not that anyone would expect so lovely a lady to trouble herself with such things," he added. I was a little surprised at his gallantry.

"Now, don't you even think of flirting with me," I warned him with a light tap to the arm. "I know you have a wife back in Southampton."

He gave me a rueful smile. "That I do. But I can still appreciate innocent and congenial company."

"So long as we both understand that the company will remain innocent," I returned with an arch glance.

He laughed and freshened my drink. "My vessel and myself are at your disposal, Miss Drummond. How may we amuse you?"

I cocked my head to the side and pretended to think. "I would like to steer the ship."

# 3

I did steer the ship, and very nearly ran her into an island, but the captain was most understanding and we parted as friends. When I disembarked with Dodo—still looking a bit worse for wear—the crew assembled to wave us off and even fired a salute. I blew kisses to them until Dodo jerked my arm nearly out of the socket.

"Delilah, must you always make such a spectacle out of yourself?" she hissed. I tried not to take it personally. She still looked peaky and clutched her basin fervently.

"It's not me, darling. The boys gathered to see us onto shore. It would be rude not to acknowledge them." I waved one last time as I climbed into the car waiting to transfer us to the station. Dodo heaved into her basin while she juggled my jewel case and a strap of books the crew had given me, all inscribed with thoughtful messages.

The town of Mombasa was just as strange and wild as I had expected, the air damp and heavy with the scent of spices and smoke and donkeys. I lifted my nose, sniffing appreciatively, but Dodo just moaned softly until we were safely ensconced on the train and pulling away from the city.

I lowered the window, letting in the fragrant spices and the tang of the woodsmoke that poured from the engines. "Here, Dodo, sit by the window and stick your head out like a dog. The fresh air will sort you out."

She did as I told her to and soon her colour came back, although that might have been the red dust blowing into her face. She sat back after a while and we passed the next hours peacefully. Dodo dozed and I watched Africa reveal itself. First came the mangrove swamps with their sinister-looking roots. They reminded me of the bayous back home, the branches twisting out to catch at a person and hold them fast. The roots thrust up through the muck, looking as if the trees had gotten up and walked around when no one was looking and had just come to rest.

After the mangrove swamps, there were acres of orchards thick with tropical fruits—coconuts and mangoes, bananas and papayas, all ripening like jewels as monkeys frolicked through their branches, plotting and pilfering like highwaymen. Beyond the fruit trees, the country opened up to wide prairie, tilting upward like an angled plate and each mile carried us higher. We crossed a few bridges I didn't like the looks of, and I liked the sound of them even less. Each one swayed and creaked in protest, and I held my breath until we made it to the other side.

We stopped at every small station on the line to fill the boilers of the steam engines, and at every station women peddlers with sleek black skin wrapped bright calico fabric about their bodies and sold wares from baskets on their heads. I bought bananas and mangoes and devoured them, licking mango juice from my hands as Dora continued to moan.

I pointed out one bridge from my guidebook as we crossed it. "This is the Tsavo bridge, Dodo. When it was built, a pair of man-eating lions spent nine months gobbling up the crew. It says here they ate more than a hundred men."

She gave a delicate hiccup and fixed me with a hateful look. "What are you reading? *The Ghoulish Guide to Kenya*?"

I waved the book at her. "It's the guidebook the captain gave me, his own personal copy. Baedeker's. Ooh, and it says that the lions would creep into camp and carry off victims, staying just close enough that their companions could hear the beasts crunching into the bones in the night."

"Stop it, Delilah. You're just as bad as you were when we were children, always reading those horrible ghost stories out loud just to frighten me."

"Don't be stupid. I read them to you because you never owned you were frightened. If you'd shown the slightest fear I would have stopped."

"I used to lock myself in the bathroom and sleep in the bathtub. Of course I was frightened," she argued. "You just liked to torment me."

"Possibly," I conceded. "Oh, and it says here

47

one of the stations is notorious for the number of man-eating lions that have roamed around it, eating the builders. The station is called Kima. That means 'minced meat' in Swahili."

"Do be quiet," she said sharply and promptly vomited into her basin.

I turned back to the view and watched Africa unrolling before me, mile after mile of emptiness under a sky as big as any in the States.

Some time later, when dusk began to fall, I heard footsteps overhead. Dora jolted awake. "What is that? An animal?"

I answered her with a peal of laughter. "No, you ninny. It's the railman lighting the lamps."

Just at that moment, a trapdoor opened above us and a cheerful Indian face peered inside.

"Good evening, *memsahibs*."

Dora gave a little scream and shrank back against the seat, but I smiled at the fellow.

"Ignore her, I beg you. She has delicate nerves."

He reached in to light the oil lamp and the carriage was bathed in the warm glow of civilisation. He gave a single nod and said crisply, "*Voi* in half an hour," before dropping the trapdoor neatly back into place.

"What does *Voi* mean?" Dora demanded.

I rifled through the pages of the guidebook before giving her a triumphant smile. "*Voi* is where we eat."

Right on schedule, the train stopped at a bungalow. Hanging outside was a hand-lettered sign proclaiming that we had reached *Voi*. In the packed-earth yard, third-class passengers crowded around picnic baskets while first-class travellers made straight for the dining room inside. The stewards were wearing pristine white jackets and serving thoroughly English food from the look of it. Dora staggered to her seat and collapsed gratefully, requesting a gingerroot tisane and waving off any suggestion of food.

Just as I had made up my mind to order a second glass of champagne, a shadow loomed over the table.

"I say, I'm terribly sorry to intrude, but there don't seem to be any empty tables."

I looked up to see that the Englishman matched his voice, rich and slow. He was good-looking in a slightly seedy way, and I liked the coolness of his blue eyes. His mouth was thin and possibly cruel, but his hands were beautiful. I smiled.

"There is a free seat at the table over there," I countered with a nod towards a trio of gentlemen tucking into bowls of muddy brown soup. "Why not sit with them?"

He didn't hesitate. "Because a beautiful woman in this place is like a long drink of cool water in the desert. And two beautiful women . . ." He trailed off, collecting Dora with his gaze. It was the rankest flattery. Dora was not beautiful.

I waved him to one of the empty chairs as he introduced himself. "I assure you, manners are far more relaxed here in Africa than back home. You needn't worry about the lack of formal introduction. I am Anthony Wickenden."

"And how do you know where home is for me, Mr. Wickenden? I might be accustomed to very casual manners indeed."

He raised a brow into a delicate arch. It was a practiced gesture and one I had no doubt he had used often and to great effect. "I think a lady of such sophistication could only come from Paris."

I clucked my tongue. "Disloyal for an Englishman," I scolded gently. "Don't you have sophisticated women in London?"

"None like you."

I took out a Sobranie and fit it into the holder. Before I could reach into my bag again, he bent forward, a tiny flame dancing at the end of his match. I leaned into him as he cupped his hands to protect the flame. I took two short drags, sucking the fire onto the end of my cigarette, my eyes fixed on his. He swallowed hard, and I blew out the match.

I sat back and crossed my legs. "Tell me about Mrs. Wickenden."

A slow smile spread over his face. "What makes you so certain there is a Mrs. Wickenden?"

"I can smell a wife a mile away, Mr. Wickenden, and you have the stink of one all over you."

He laughed, and the suave stranger disappeared. He was simply a friendly fellow looking for a bit of a chat then, and we settled to our dinner companionably. The stewards served up a succession of depressing courses—brown Windsor soup followed by boiled beef and cabbage, listlessly mashed potatoes, and tinned fruit and custard. I picked the insects out of mine and lined them up on the edge of the plate. Wickenden didn't even bother.

"You'll get used to it in time. Insects and dust will be half of every meal you consume out here." Between indifferent bites he told me a little about himself. He was on his way home to his farm outside Nairobi. He had been in Africa for many years, having come out as a boy with his parents. He had tried—and failed—to farm a variety of crops and had decided to turn his hand to breeding racehorses.

"That's what I was doing in Mombasa," he said smoothly, "looking at some fresh stock."

He was testing out the lie, I could tell, seeing how well it fit his tongue before he tried it at home. I shrugged. I wasn't his wife; it didn't matter to me what he'd really been up to in Mombasa, but even I knew it wasn't exactly a hot spot for horse-trading.

I told him about Fairlight and he leaned forward, almost dragging a cuff in his custard. "Hold on, now. You know Sir Nigel?"

"He was my stepfather," I explained. "He has very sweetly put Fairlight at my disposal while I rusticate."

"But we're neighbours!" he exclaimed happily. He had drunk the better part of a bottle of gin at that point, which might have accounted for his excitement, or maybe a new face in the Kenyan bush was just that much of an event. Either way, it was nice to be welcomed, and I told him so.

"More than welcome, my dear. You must come to dine with us at Nyama Ranch."

"Us?" I teased.

He had the grace to smile. "Yes, us. Nyama is owned by my wife's aunt. Jude and I live there with her. Sort of keeping the old girl in line, you understand. Not as young as she used to be."

Oh, I understood perfectly. Poor feckless Wickenden had gambled himself into the poorhouse with his farming experiments and had no choice but to live off his wife's money now. I wondered who was footing the bill for the racing stables.

We finished our drinks and towed Dora onto the veranda for brandy and cigars. I liked my Sobranies, but I loved a good cigar. It was like French-kissing fire. Dora had long since grown immune to my occasional indulgence, but Wickenden lit up like a boy who had just seen his first naughty photograph.

"How deliciously scandalous," he breathed. He

52

leaned close to my ear, whispering a few inappropriate suggestions, but I pretended not to hear. A steward rang the veranda bell just then, sounding the signal for passengers to board the train. Dora hurried on, but Wickenden caught my hand.

"Silly girl. We needn't go yet. It takes ages to warm those damned engines up. Unlike mine," he finished, sticking a fat, limp tongue in my ear.

I turned to smile at him as I took the end of my cigar and held its glowing tip to his trouser leg. It took less time than I would have thought. The linen of his suit was excellent quality, woven so fine the cigar burned right through and singed his skin before he realised what was happening. He jumped up, scattering sparks and swear words into the darkness.

I swayed off towards the train as he hurled a variety of names at my back. As usual, they rolled right off, and I returned to the carriage to find that the beds had been made up with fresh linen and blankets and Dora was already tucked up for the night. She had left out my night things as well as a jar of my cold cream from Elizabeth Arden. A better lady's maid would have stayed up to put away my clothes, but I had to make allowances. She was family after all. I stripped off my dress and underthings and began to wash.

"Did he make a pass?" She didn't look up from her book, but the fact that she was reading meant she was feeling better. I glanced at the title. *Meditations on the Song of Songs.*

"He did, and a clumsy one at that. No finesse at all." I dried myself and began rubbing in the cold cream.

"What did you do?"

"Burned him with my cigar."

She smothered a laugh and returned to her book as I snuggled down in the covers. The train pulled away, blasting its whistle into the long African night.

The next morning we stopped for breakfast at another of the innumerable stations, and I ate a plate of surprisingly tasty eggs with a few questionable sausages and a bowl of cut tropical fruits spritzed with lime. Dora nibbled at corn gruel and weak tea, and when it didn't immediately reappear, she added an egg and some toast.

"Do you realise that's the first full meal you've eaten since Marseilles?" I asked, helping myself to a slice of her toast.

She perked up. "Really? Do you suppose I've lost weight?"

Dora's hips were the bane of her existence. She spent most of her time slimming—a vain effort in more ways than one.

"Hard to tell in that frock," I answered, slathering the toast with passionfruit jam.

She pulled a face. "I don't suppose it's very becoming, but you know I don't really understand clothes."

I shrugged. "You're fighting a losing battle anyway, Dodo. Straight lines don't flatter your figure," I told her. Dora's shape might have been fashionable in Edwardian times, but fashions had changed and unfortunately Dora's body didn't. The pouter-pigeon silhouette which came naturally to her—heavy breasts and rounded hips—was hopelessly out of date. There wasn't a dress to be had in all of Paris that would have complemented her small waist and Junoesque curves. It was all slim seams and clinging fabrics that conspired to make her look lumpy and dull. Her hair didn't help. It was nice enough—the colour of dark honey and rippling like a windy pond when she took it out of the pins. But it was long enough she could sit on it and the roll she wore at the nape of her neck made her look like someone's grandmother. All that hair gave her a perpetual headache, too, but it just went hand in hand with her digestive troubles.

"Then there's no point to my bothering about clothes since nothing looks good on me anyway."

I didn't trouble to respond. Usually Dora had as much vanity as a dust mop, but every once in a while she got onto the subject of her own dowdiness and when it came to feeling sorry for herself, Dodo could ride that hobby horse until the paint wore off.

After we boarded the train again with the other passengers—I was amused to see that Mr. Wickenden was markedly less friendly when he was nursing a small burn and a large hangover— we set off on the last leg of our trip to Nairobi. Here the plains were vast, opening up before us like an invitation. There were clusters of bushes and in the distance I could make out moving shapes I was certain were herds of wildebeest. I pointed out to Dora the sight of Mt. Kilimanjaro in the distance to the south, just over the border in German-controlled Tanzania.

"Look at its snowy peak," I instructed her as I thumbed through the guidebook. "It's as if the mountain were wearing a clever little nightcap. It says here that Mt. Kilimanjaro used to belong to the Kenyan side of the boundary until Queen Victoria decided to smudge the border a bit to give the mountain to her grandson for his birthday."

Dora was fixed on the view. "That explains a good deal of what was wrong with the Kaiser. If the Queen of England and Empress of India is willing to redraw a map to give you an entire mountain as a birthday present, it's just a small step from there to thinking you have a right to plunge the whole world into war and kill thousands of people."

I didn't say anything, but Dora was familiar enough with my silences to know a sharp one.

"I'm sorry, Delilah. I didn't think."

I shrugged. "It's been nine years since Johnny died. I should be able to talk about the war without falling to pieces."

We were quiet a moment, then Dora sat up, exclaiming, "Zebra! A whole herd of them, running alongside the train—look, Delilah, here they come!"

Sure enough, an entire herd of zebra had apparently decided to keep pace with the train, which wasn't very hard to do. The poor old engine could have been outrun by a small child with a limp. But the zebra were making an event of it, tossing their short manes and snorting as they ran alongside. They were so close I could almost put a hand out and touch one stripy coat. Dora and I hung out the window to yell encouragement to them as they kicked up clouds of fine red dust that settled in our mouths and ears.

"We look like red Indians," I told her.

"Don't smile so much—it's getting in your teeth," she answered, smiling just as broadly.

Other passengers were hanging out as well to snap photographs or just feel the cool savannah breeze as it passed. I could smell the zebra, a horsey odour of sweat and grass and something musty riding just underneath. I was still smiling when Dora turned to me.

57

"I've often wondered—did you love any of them? The others who came after Johnny?"

She didn't look at me and I didn't look at her. Some questions are so direct the only way to ask them is sideways.

"What would you say if I told you I loved all of them and none?"

"I'd say you were dodging the question."

"Then call me the Artful Dodger," I told her.

She didn't say anything, but the sigh she gave was eloquent enough. It said she got what she expected and less than she hoped.

"Fine. You want a real answer? The truth is I have loved them all when I remembered to. But it's easy to forget."

"I don't see how."

"You close your eyes and suddenly he's not there anymore. What you loved, or thought you loved, just isn't there, and there is a man-shaped hole in your memory of where he used to be. The sad part is when it happens when he's sitting at the same table or lying in the same bed. You can turn and look at him and not even remember his name because he was just a visitor. He was a man who was only passing through your heart, and you never really made a place for him, so he just keeps passing. My husbands since Johnny have been passing men. Not a stayer among them."

"And Johnny?"

"Johnny was a stayer," I told her, wiping the red

dust from my face. "That Johnny was a real stayer."

Dodo was done asking questions then, and even if she wasn't, I was finished answering. We watched the zebra for a while, until they faded back and stood, lathered up, their striped sides heaving as they watched us move farther and farther away.

Dora reached for the guidebook. "It says here the telegraph wires are on poles that are higher than customary on account of the giraffes," she read.

"Tell me more," I ordered, and she did, reading from the guidebook until her voice was hoarse, reading until the flat, tilted plains of Africa ran us up to Nairobi, reading until I wasn't thinking about Johnny anymore but about telegraph wires and giraffes and man-eating lions grinding up the bones of the dead.

A little past noon we rolled into Nairobi, a flat town coated in red dust that looked as if it had been scooped up somewhere in India and plunked down in the middle of the African savannah. The streets of Nairobi were teeming gently with people bent on the business of civilisation. There were people of every description—purposeful Indian clerks jostling with the darker–skinned native Africans who moved with slow grace through the throng. Here and there were white faces, most meticulously guarded from the equatorial sun by double terais or *sola topees*. The white folks were the only ones who strode freely, keeping to the fitful shade of the blue gum trees that lined the street, as the Indians and Africans all stepped quickly out of their way to walk in the sun. It was nothing new to me. I had spent too much time in Louisiana watching the black folks carefully keeping out of the way of the whites.

The streets were paved and there were electric wires hanging high overhead where colourful birds perched and monkeys swung hand over hand. There were plenty of motorcars, but the streets were choked with oxcarts as well, and rickshaws scuttled by, leaving the pushcarts to trundle in their wake, slogging through mule dung and rotting fruit. The air was pungent with both, and they combined with woodsmoke and the gum leaves and the sunburned red soil to give Africa its own unique perfume. I inhaled it deeply until Dora dragged me back from the window, scolding that I would make a spectacle of myself.

I combed out my hair and powdered my nose and lacquered on a fresh coat of lipstick as we pulled into the station. I could hear a commotion on the platform, and Dodo darted a glance at me, her eyeballs rolling white.

"There can't be reporters here waiting," she muttered. "There just can't."

"There can and there probably are," I retorted.

"Oh, Dodo, I know they're a misery, but just put your head down and carry on. They'll stop when they get a picture."

I handed off everything except my handbag to her and smoothed out my silk skirt. I had decided upon white for my arrival in Nairobi and everything was the same arctic shade, from my suede shoes to the fur stole I draped over my arm. It was far too warm to wear it, but the fur was simply too sweet to pack away. I straightened my stockings and squared my shoulders as I stepped from the train, bracing myself for the onslaught of cameras and reporters.

Just as I set foot on the platform, Mr. Wickenden also emerged from the train. He gave me a cool smile.

"Miss Drummond." He lifted his hat.

"Mr. Wickenden. I hope the invitation to visit still stands. I would hate to think we couldn't be friends."

I arched a brow, and he hesitated, then grinned. "Africa's a big place, Miss Drummond, but it's entirely too small for grudges. We shall be neighbours, after all, and we must stick together out here."

He lifted his hat again and moved to offer his hand.

Before I could take it, I heard a roar over the gathered throng. It must have been a hell of a roar, too, for me to hear it over the chaos of the

Nairobi station, but in that moment everything stopped. The shouts of the porters, the wailing babies, the cries of the vendors—everything went silent and heads swivelled to the end of the platform where a pirate stood, booted feet planted wide as he surveyed the scene, hands fisted at his hips.

He wasn't a pirate of course, but that's the first impression I ever had of him and first impressions die hard. He was dressed haphazardly, with a filthy shirt tucked into even filthier trousers that were themselves tucked into a high pair of scuffed leather riding boots. His sleeves were rolled back and his collar was open, and every muscle seemed to vibrate with rage. He wore a beaten leather Stetson jammed down on his head, throwing his face into shadow. He strode straight to one of the native fellows and said something unintelligible in the native lingo. The man promptly handed over a long, slender whip. The pirate took it and walked directly to where Anthony Wickenden was still reaching for my hand. He didn't even pause before he reached out and grasped Wickenden by the shoulders and lifted him clean off his feet. He threw Wickenden to the platform. Then he raised the whip, and the first crack of it was so loud the sound echoed straight down to the base of my spine.

What commenced was the bloodiest thrashing I had ever seen in my life, and when it was done,

Wickenden was rolling on the platform, spitting blood and testing his loosened teeth.

"Goddamn you, White," he managed to say before he rolled over and heaved out his stomach. His assailant had lost his hat in the fray, and he bent to pick it up, leaning close over Mr. Wickenden as he did so. He pitched his voice low, but I heard him quite distinctly. "I saw the bruises, Tony. If you ever so much as think about touching her again, I will kill you—so slowly you will beg me to finish you off. Do you understand me?"

Wickenden spat out another mouthful of blood and gave a short groan by way of reply.

The pirate clapped his hat back onto his head and strode off, tossing the whip back to its owner without even breaking stride. There was a moment of sustained silence, and then the crowd began to move again, shouting and pushing as porters hurried to the injured man and the rest began to spread the story of what they'd just seen. A flashbulb went off in my face and some ferrety fellow asked me for a story, but before I could give him a piece of my mind, a slender gentleman appeared at my elbow.

"Miss Drummond, I presume? I'm Bates, Government House. I am afraid I must ask you to come with me." I didn't bother to protest. He had tucked my hand through his arm and towed me swiftly away.

"Delilah! Where are you going?" Dodo shrieked

63

from behind me. I shrugged, but the gentleman turned and called over his shoulder.

"Government House. You may rendezvous with Miss Drummond at the Norfolk Hotel."

He hurried me through the crowds and out of the station and down the street to Government House. I thought of invoking the name of Sir William Kendall, but decided to wait until a more opportune time. We entered through the wide doors and proceeded straight up a broad staircase of polished wood, down a few corridors and stopped outside a closed door. A pair of chairs had been arranged outside, and to my astonishment, I saw the assailant from the platform had already taken up occupancy of one of them. He looked as cool and unruffled as if he'd spent the morning totting up figures in a ledger instead of beating a man sideways.

Mr. Bates stopped and indicated the vacant chair. "Wait here, please, Miss Drummond."

He disappeared inside the closed door and I heard voices from within. I seated myself as instructed and immediately applied myself to a study of my companion. He looked out of place in the polished rectitude of the Government House, with his scuffed boots and unshaven chin. I noticed that his earlobes had been pierced, and through each hole he had threaded a small gold hoop. Pirate indeed. His hat sat on his knee while his hands rested loosely on his thighs—big, capable hands mapped with scars and calluses. His hair was a disgrace, tangled and in desperate need of a shampoo and a cut. In a gentler climate it might have been a soft brown, but the African sun had burnished it to gold, the same colour as the stubble at his jaw, and his face was weathered bronze, a web of tiny wrinkles around his eyes from squinting at horizons too hard for too many years. On one tanned wrist he wore an odd collection of bracelets, some beaded, some braided, and one slender leather thong strung with what looked like an assortment of teeth and claws. Underneath the bracelets I could see scars marring his left arm, long thin whips of white stretching from his wrist to disappear under the rolled cuff of his shirt. I shuddered lightly and looked away. Everything about the man told a story if someone cared to listen. I picked up a magazine from the table and pretended to read.

While I had been studying him, he had been returning the favour, letting his gaze run slowly from my feet to my hair and back again. "Sorry about your shoes," he said. His voice was low and a little rough, but his vowels were tidy and his accent was not English but not quite American either.

I peered down at the snowy suede, now indelibly marked with bright crimson souvenirs of the beating. I turned my ankle, looking at my foot from different angles.

"Oh, I don't know. I might start a new fashion," I told him.

"You're awfully calm about the whole thing," he remarked.

I shrugged. "Didn't he have it coming?"

He laughed, a short, almost mirthless sound, and leveled his gaze directly at me. His eyes were strikingly blue, like pieces of open sky on a clear, clear day. He looked through them with an expression of perfect frankness, and the beauty of those eyes combined with that cool detachment was powerful. I wondered if he knew it.

"He did. He beat his wife."

"And the lady is a friend of yours?"

A slow smile touched his mouth. It was an expressive mouth, and he used it well, even when he didn't speak.

"You could say that," he said.

I lifted a brow to indicate disapproval, and he laughed again, this time a real laugh. The sound of it was startling in that small space, and I felt the rumble of it in my chest just as I had the crack of his whip.

"Don't look so disapproving, Miss Drummond. I would have thought the notion of a friendship between the sexes would be the last thing to shock you."

"I see my reputation has preceded me," I said, smoothing my skirt primly over my knees.

"You've already made the betting book at the

club," he told me, holding me fast with those remarkable eyes.

"Have I, indeed? And what are the terms?"

"Fifty pounds to whoever names the man who beds you first," he stated flatly.

Before I could respond, the door opened and Bates reappeared.

"Miss Drummond, if you please, the lieutenant governor will see you now."

I rose and went to the door, turning back just as I reached it. I gave him a slow, purposeful look, taking him in from battered boots to filthy, unkempt hair.

"Tell me, who did you put your money on?"

He stretched his legs out to cross them at the ankle. He folded his arms behind his head and gave me a slow grin. "Why, myself, of course."

# 4

Inside the office, a squirrelly fellow with coppery hair—the lieutenant governor, I imagined—was scribbling on some papers and pursing his lips thoughtfully. No doubt he was keeping me waiting to impress upon me the significance of his position, so I looked around and waited for him to get tired of his own importance. After a few minutes he glanced up, peering thoughtfully through a pair of spectacles that needed polishing.

"Miss Delilah Drummond? I am Oswell Fraser, Lieutenant Governor of the Kenya colony."

I smiled widely to show there were no hard feelings for his less-than-polite welcome, but he continued to scowl at me.

"Now, I understand your stepfather has pulled a few strings with the governor on your behalf."

I shrugged. "Well, I wouldn't say—"

"I would," he cut in sharply. "And I want you to know that it won't do you any good. Not now. Sir William has found it necessary to return to England and expects to be there for some weeks. In his absence, I am acting governor." He finished this with a little preen of his mustache.

"How nice for you," I began, but he lifted a hand.

"I have no wish to spend any more time upon

this matter than necessary, so permit me to press on. I am well aware of your reputation, Miss Drummond, and I have no doubt you expect to have as grand a time here in Kenya as you have around the rest of the world. But let me speak with perfect frankness. I will not have it."

He was so earnest I smothered a laugh and put on my best expression of wide-eyed innocence. I even batted my lashes a few times, but he was entirely immune.

"I am quite serious, Miss Drummond. There are circumstances afoot just now which make it imperative that the colonists here conduct themselves with decorum and respectability. This includes you."

I gave him a winsome smile. "Mr. Fraser, really, I cannot imagine how you have come to have such a terrible opinion of me, but I assure you I have no intention of misbehaving."

"Misbehaving?" He reached for the sheet of paper and began to read from it. "Arrested for stealing a car outside a Harlem nightclub and driving it into the Hudson River. Caught *in flagrante* with a judge's eighteen-year-old son in Dallas. Fined for swimming nude in the Seine. Need I continue?"

"Those incidents were taken entirely out of context, I assure you."

"I doubt it," he returned primly. He put the sheet aside, letting it drop from his fingertips as if he could not bear to touch it. "They, and the other incidents chronicled in this report, speak to a lifetime of poor decisions and irresponsible, sometimes *criminal,* behavior. And if this were not enough, I happen to be married to a former schoolmate of yours. Annabel has been extremely forthright about your antics in Switzerland."

"Oh, dear Annabel!" I said faintly. I remembered her well. A mousy girl with forgettable features and thick ankles. She had taken immense pleasure in carrying tales to the headmistress and then gloating over my punishments. "How is she? Please pass along my regards."

He refused to thaw even at this little bit of polite flummery. "Remember what I said, Miss Drummond. These are significant times for this colony. I will not have your behavior or anyone else's coming between us and our ultimate independence from London."

"Is that why the governor has returned to England?"

To my surprise, at this he actually unbent a trifle. "Well, yes. Parliament has convened a committee to study the feasibility of permitting self-rule here in Kenya."

I remembered what the ship's captain had told me. "You mean like they did last year in Rhodesia?"

His mouth dropped open. "I am astonished that you are aware of it, but yes, that's it precisely."

"And you and the governor naturally believe

that the committee, and by extension Parliament itself, will look more favourably upon the subject of self-rule if the colonists are seen as hard-working and respectable folk."

"Quite," he said, his voice marginally warmer. "You see, with decisions being made so far away in London, it's terribly difficult to ensure that the decisions are the right ones. Take the question of Indian land ownership—" And he did. He took the question and ran with it for the better part of the next quarter of an hour. I smiled and nodded and looked deeply interested, a trick I learned from Mossy when I was five. Men always fell for it, and if you were careful enough to make the occasional "hmmm" sound they thought you were pondering deeply. This freed you to think of stockings or whether he was going to try to kiss you. Not that I wondered the latter about Mr. Fraser. One look at those thin damp lips would have been enough to put me off kissing forever.

At last he finished, and he rose, bringing the interview to a close. "So you see why it's so very important that you behave yourself, Miss Drummond. And in that vein, I think it best if you proceed to Fairlight without delay."

"Without delay? But Mr. Fraser, I had thought to spend a few days in Nairobi, meet the members of the club, that sort of thing."

He shook his head. "Out of the question. In fact, I have arranged for you to be taken to Fairlight

71

first thing tomorrow morning. You will, of course, be welcomed at the Norfolk Hotel for tonight only. Please oblige me in this."

I hesitated, and then it occurred to me that with the governor out of the colony, Fraser was the most powerful man around. It might not be such a bad thing to have him in my debt.

I shook his hand again and said, in an appropriately sober tone, "Very well, Mr. Fraser. I shall take your excellent advice. You may rely upon me."

I saw the flicker of doubt in his eyes and knew that Annabel would be getting an earful that night. I took my leave then, passing the scruffy villain from the platform on my way out. Before the door shut, I had just enough time to hear Fraser say, "Blast you, Ryder, what have you done now? Couldn't you have thrashed the man on his own property instead of the middle of Nairobi station with a hundred witnesses?"

The pirate gave a laugh as the door closed behind him, and I left, adjusting my fur and frowning at the blood on my shoes. So much for decorum and respectability. All I had done was step off a train and got my knuckles rapped for it while the great white hunter knocked a man's teeth out and was clapped on the shoulder. Men!

I found Dodo waiting at the Norfolk. She had already checked in and unpacked what we needed for the evening. She clucked and fretted over my ruined shoes while I tidied myself up and told her what Mr. Fraser had had to say on the subject of my arrival in Kenya.

"That's the price of leading a notorious life," she said, primming her lips as she sponged at my shoes.

I blew out a smoke ring and lay back in the bath. "I prefer to think of it as energetic. What do you fancy, Dodo? Shall we wear something inappropriate and scandalise the rustics tonight?"

"We shall not. I have already ordered dinner to be served here in our rooms, and our transportation will apparently be here immediately after breakfast, which is also to be served in private."

I pulled a face at her. "I'm not a leper, you know. Notoriety isn't contagious."

She didn't reply, and why would she? We both knew it wasn't true. Notoriety was indeed contagious. If you were a carrier, decent people didn't care to spend time with you lest they come down with it. Infamy was an infection most folks could do without, even if the price for it was living a very small and colourless life. They were beige people in a beige world, and Dora was one of them.

But she had been a swell sport about being dragged off to the wilds of Africa. I could give her an evening of good behavior.

I rose from the tub and dried myself off, dusting thoroughly with rice powder scented with mimosa. I pulled on my favourite Japanese kimono—raw peacock silk embroidered in silver—and slid my feet into satin mules. I unpacked the phonograph and opened a bottle of gin.

"We can have a party, just the two of us," I told Dora, and by the time dinner was served, she was wearing the window curtain as a Roman toga and an open handbag on her head in place of a crown. She was cataloguing dolefully the men she had loved and never kissed, and didn't even stop when the waiters began piling dishes on the table. They served up a lovely dinner and I tipped them lavishly as Dora started in on Quentin.

"He has the handsomest mustache. I always wondered what it would be like to kiss a man with a mustache."

I refilled her glass. "You ought to have asked him. He might have obliged you. Quentin is a very obliging fellow."

It was proof of her advanced state of intoxication that she even considered it. She shook her head, then put both hands up to stop her head from moving.

"No, I don't think so. I seem to remember he's married."

"To Cornelia," I supplied, ever helpful.

"But that doesn't ever stop you." She seemed genuinely mystified.

I shrugged. "I got there first. I have a prior claim."

She struggled a moment to count on her fingers. "No, that isn't right, it isn't right at all. He was betrothed to Cornelia when he met you."

"I didn't say I got to his heart first, Do. I got *there* first," I explained with a pointed look at her crotch.

She shrieked and pulled her toga even tighter, although I don't know why she bothered. She had tied it over her clothes and was as safe as a vestal virgin, especially in my company. I had several friends with Sapphic proclivities, but I never joined them. I always liked to be the prettiest one in the bed, so I stuck solely with men. Of course, Misha had come damned close to beating me on that score. He had had the face of a Renaissance angel. I always suspected that was one of the reasons our marriage had failed.

"You were the smart one," she told me, staring into the contents of her glass as if she wasn't entirely sure where the gin had come from. "I should have got it over early. Now it's too late. Things have probably grown shut. You know, *inside,*" she wailed, commencing to weep into the bread basket. "And you don't even feel the sin of it, do you? You don't even care that it's so wrong, so criminally wrong."

She continued to sob. I rose and slid my hands under her arms and hefted her up. For her bulk, she was surprisingly light on her feet. It was almost like handling a child, and she curled into my shoulder as I helped her to her bedroom.

"You're tight, Dora. No more gin for you."

She nodded and immediately groaned. "Why does this hotel have spinning rooms?"

"I think it came with the gin, darling."

"Oh, that makes sense."

I pulled the covers to her chin and turned out the light. "Nighty-night, Dodo."

"Oh, I'm not sleepy," she announced before turning over and promptly letting out a howler of a snore.

I returned to the table and pushed the food away. I poured myself another gin and lit another cigarette. After a minute I got up and turned out the light and stepped out onto the private veranda. It was late, and Nairobi had settled into the uneasy sleep of a town that straddles the edge between here and there. I could hear an animal cry in the night, a shriek that unsettled my blood. The moon was waning, but the stars shone high overhead, slanting silver light over the slumbering town. Somewhere nearby a monkey chattered in the trees and a drunk was singing a maudlin song in mournful French. I ground out my cigarette and took in a deep, long breath, drinking in Africa, strange and wonderful Africa. And as the stars winked out, one by one, I took myself off to bed and slept the dreamless sleep of a traveller.

# 5

The next morning I woke to find Dora creeping around the suite, finishing the packing. She looked like hell and moaned gently from time to time as she folded and organised. The porters brought breakfast and I helped myself to the full English while Do sat nursing a weak cup of coffee, a wet handkerchief tied about her brow.

I shook my head. "Do, I hope you're not going to be difficult in Africa."

"Difficult?" Her voice was hollow, as if she were speaking from a great distance.

"You take things too seriously, you always have. You ought to have some fun here, kick up your heels a bit. You're only young once, you know."

I dunked a bit of toast into my egg and Dora's face went green.

"I'm sure I don't know what you mean. I ought to go see about the bags."

She fled with the handkerchief pressed to her mouth and went down to supervise the loading as I finished up, taking my time with a second cup of tea. I stopped by registration to settle the bill and collect a packed lunch basket. A charming young man in livery trotted out to the curb with the hamper and added it to the mound of baggage piled on the walk. Parked next to it was an absolute heap of a vehicle. It had clearly started life as an ambulance and God only knew what sins it had committed to have fallen so low. It was pocked with rust and scarred with solder marks from where fresh bits of scrap metal had been used to bandage its wounds.

As I watched, the driver jumped out and began to instruct the porters on where to shove the bags and I recognised him instantly. He was wearing exactly the same clothes as the day before, which didn't surprise me. He had probably slept in them. I stepped up and fixed my brightest smile.

"I didn't realise you offered chauffeur service," I said sweetly.

He turned and pushed his hat back a little with his forefinger. "Only one service of many, Miss Drummond."

"That truck looks like it's being held together with spit and a prayer."

To his credit, he smiled. "It'll do." He nodded toward the pile on the curb. "I see you've come well prepared for roughing it."

I shrugged. "I'm a girl who likes nice things," I told him with the faintest emphasis on the word *nice*. "You haven't told me your name."

He removed his hat and inclined his head in as courtly a gesture as I had ever seen. "J. Ryder White."

"And I detect by your accent you aren't English,

but I don't think you're a fellow American either, Mr. White."

"I go by Ryder. You've got a good ear. I'm from nowhere and everywhere, but I was born in Canada."

"A Canadian! How delightfully rustic," I remarked in the same honeyed tones. "Tell me, are you housebroken?"

His mouth twitched, but he didn't smile. He bent to the pile of baggage and selected a long, narrow case chalked with indecipherable symbols from the Mombasa customs house. "I see you've come fully armed, Miss Drummond." He flicked open the latches and threw back the lid. Whatever he had thought to find, the contents surprised him.

"You're not serious. Did a friend send this with you as a practical joke?"

"I assure you, I am perfectly acquainted with that weapon."

He hefted the Rigby and smiled a crocodile's smile. "Princesses shouldn't try to slay dragons. Leave that to the knights."

"And the peasants?"

He laughed aloud at that and replaced the Rigby, snapping the case closed. "Oh, I think we're going to have fun."

"Don't bet on it," I told him, baring my teeth.

I moved aside to let him get on with the business of loading his monstrous vehicle. Dora was standing at the passenger door and I went to shove her in. She shook her head desperately.

"I need the window," she whispered, pleading.

"Oh, for God's sake, when will you learn to hold your liquor?" The question was rhetorical. Dora got tight on a thimbleful of sherry and I had poured half a bottle of gin down her. The least I could do was give her a chance to be sick discreetly. I sighed and clambered into the wreck, settling myself in the middle while Dora crammed herself up against the door.

"Stop moaning, Do. We haven't even started moving yet."

"Maybe you haven't," she retorted. She closed her eyes and slumped, her head angled out the window. A moment later a shadow fell over her face.

"Miss?" Ryder's voice was gentler than I had yet heard it. Dodo lifted her head like a dog sniffing the air. He smiled at her and handed her a tin cup. "This might help."

She took an experimental sip. "Oh. *Oh.* What is it?"

He shrugged. "Cure of my own making. Pawpaw juice, ginger, a few other things. Just keep drinking. I've got a flask full of it."

She stared up at him, her expression worshipful. "Thank you."

I slanted him a look and he smiled over her head at me, then lifted his hat and actually bowed to Dora. "Anytime, miss."

A moment later he was sliding into the seat next

to me until his thigh touched mine. "Shove over, princess. I've got to work the gears."

I moved over as far as I could and gave him another sweet smile. "And where is my morning libation?"

"You're not hungover," he pointed out.

"I'm not hungover," Dora put in as forcefully as she could. "Ladies do not imbibe to excess. I am merely overtired."

"Of course," Ryder said soothingly. He winked at me and I folded my arms over my chest. Dora had her eyes closed again and was sucking hard on the cup.

"What did you put in that?" I demanded.

He leaned a trifle closer than absolutely necessary, his voice low. "Exactly what I said. Pawpaw juice, ginger. And half a bottle of gin."

"That's what got her into this in the first place."

He shrugged. "Best cure for a hangover is to get drunk again. Believe me, I wouldn't do this drive sober if I could help it. She'll thank me later."

"Yes, but will I?"

His only answer was a laugh and a crash of gears.

"You *are* the driver arranged for by that nice Mr. Bates from Government House, aren't you? I should hate to be abducted and not know it."

"You are my passengers. Paying passengers," he added meaningfully.

Dodo opened her eyes and reached for her bag.

I slapped her hand. "Don't you dare. Not until he's seen us safely to Fairlight. He might just dump us in the desert and then where would we be?"

He flicked me an amused glance. "The desert? Princess, where do you think you are? This isn't the goddamn Sahara."

With that he gunned the engine and we roared off, away from Nairobi and the last vestiges of civilisation.

We drove for a little while in silence as he negotiated the traffic out of Nairobi. It was surprisingly busy—donkey carts and rickshaws jostling with sleek new automobiles and pedestrians laden with bundles of fruits and firewood. He did point out a few of the local landmarks, including the Turf Club and Kilimani Prison and the Japanese brothel, but I didn't ask questions and Dodo was too busy nursing her "cure." I stared out the window, watching as the shabby little bungalows that dotted the outskirts of Nairobi fell away. The *murram* road stretched upwards now, carving its way through the wilderness, a wilderness that hadn't changed since Eve went dancing in a fig-leaf skirt. The soil was as red as good Georgia clay, and here and there a flat-topped thorn tree shaded the high savannah grasses. As far as the eye could see there was nothing but land and more land, an emptiness so big not even God himself could fill it. The miles rolled away and so did my bad mood, and when the first giraffe strode gracefully into view, I gasped aloud.

Ryder stopped the vehicle and gestured. "She's got a foal." I peered into the brush behind the giraffe and noticed a tiny version, teetering on impossibly long legs as it emerged. The mother turned back with a graceful gesture of the head and gave the little thing a push of encouragement. They came closer to the truck and I saw it wasn't tiny at all—it was frankly enormous, and Ryder eased down the road, slowly so as not to startle them.

"Why did we leave?" I demanded. "I would have liked to have watched them."

"Second rule of the bush. Never get too close to anything that has offspring."

"What's the first rule?"

"Food runs. If you don't want to be food, don't run."

I smiled, expecting him to laugh, but he was deadly serious. His eyes were on the road, and I took the opportunity to study him a little more closely than I had the day before. He had tidied himself up a bit, even if his clothes were disreputable. His jaw was still rough with golden stubble, but his hands and face were clean. He had strong, steady hands, and I could tell from looking at them there was little he couldn't do. Mossy always said you could tell everything you needed to know about a man from his hands. Some hands, she told me, were leaving hands. They were the wandering sort that slipped into places they shouldn't, and they would wander right off again because those hands just couldn't stay still. Some hands were worthless hands, fit only to hold a drink or flick ash from a cigar, and some were punishing hands that hit hard and didn't leave a mark and those were the ones you never stayed to see twice.

But the best hands were knowing hands, Mossy told me with a slow smile. Knowing hands were capable; they could soothe a horse or a woman. They could take things apart—including your heart—and put them back together better than before. Knowing hands were rare, but if you found them, they were worth holding, at least for a little while. I looked at Ryder's hands. They sat easily on the wheel and gearshift, coaxing instead of forcing, and I wondered how much they knew.

They had known pain; that much was certain from the scars that laced his left arm. He had been lucky. Whatever had dug itself into his arm hadn't wanted to let go. They were long, raking white scars, like punctuation marks, dotted here and there with a full stop of knotted white scar tissue where whatever it was had hung on hard. Some men might have covered them up, rolled down their shirtsleeves and pretended it hadn't happened. Others would have told the story as soon as you met, flaunting those scars for any Desdemona who might be impressed. But Ryder didn't even seem conscious of his. He wore them as he did his bracelets—souvenirs of somewhere he had been. I could have asked him, but I didn't. I liked not knowing his stories yet. He was a stranger, an impossible and uncouth one, but a stranger nonetheless. And there is nothing more interesting than a stranger.

I decided to let him keep his stories and give me only the mundane things that didn't matter. "So, you were born in Canada. Whereabouts?"

"Quebec."

I lifted a brow. "Really? You don't sound Québécois."

"Left when I was a year old. My father and I travelled up and down the Mississippi and then west to California. Ended up in the Klondike by the time I was six."

"That's quite a lot of travelling for a young boy. What did your father do?"

"As little as possible," he answered with a wry twist of the lips.

"And what did your mother have to say about this? Did she like being dragged around at his whims or was she afflicted with wanderlust as well?"

"She died before we left Quebec." He said the words easily. They were just words to him. We might have had the loss of a parent in common, but not what we had done with the emptiness. Not a day went by that I didn't think of Pink and how different my life would have been if he'd lived.

"Were you raised without a female influence, then?"

"There was an Algonquin woman who travelled with us. She took care of me and my father, although I'm not sure I'd exactly call her female. Her mustache was thicker than his."

"How did you end up in Africa?"

"My father got lucky. He struck gold, and he worked it until the claim played out. By then he said the Klondike was getting too crowded and too cold. Africa was empty and hot. We landed here when I was twelve. Been here mostly ever since."

"And what do you do here?"

He shrugged one solid shoulder. "This and that—lately quite a bit of guiding. I lead safaris. I have a little place on the coast where I grow sugarcane, and I own a few *dukas*."

"*Dukas*?"

"Shops—each one is a general store of sorts. The closest thing you'll find to civilisation out here. The post gets delivered there and people will come for a drink and to catch up with the neighbours."

"God, it's the end of the earth, isn't it?" I asked. Africa had seemed a great adventure when I was sitting in a Paris hotel room. Now the reality of it intruded, vast and unsettled, and I felt very, very small.

He flicked me a glance, his expression unreadable. "It won't be so bad, princess. You'll see."

Suddenly, I sat bolt upright, staring out the windscreen, all thoughts of exile gone. Stretching before me was the most spectacular thing I had ever seen in my life, and even those words cannot do the memory of it justice. It was the Great Rift Valley, spanning the view from left to right, slashing the surface of the earth in a crater so vast no man could see from one end of it to the other. Deep in the heart of this great continental divide the grasses waved, an immense green carpet dotted with animals the likes of which I had seen only in picture books and travelogues. A tiny herd of elephants looked infinitesimal from our lofty height, and when Ryder stilled the engine, I heard nothing but the long rush of wind up from the valley floor. It carried with it every promise of Africa, that wind. It smelled of green water and red earth and the animals that roamed it. And there was something more, something old as the rocks. It might have been the smell of the Almighty himself, and I knew there were no words for this place. It was sacred, as no place I had ever been before.

"My God," I breathed. "How big is it?"

"Four thousand miles from the upper reaches of

Syria to the depths of Mozambique. The width varies, sixty miles wide in some places, but here it narrows. Just about twenty miles across."

"It's the most amazing thing I've ever seen." I shoved Dodo, who roused herself to look, blinking hard.

"How high are we?" she croaked.

"About six thousand feet."

Dodo whimpered and clutched at the seat. "Best close your eyes until we're down," Ryder told her kindly. She nodded and pressed her handkerchief to her eyes, leaning as far back as she could. He turned to me, his expression challenging.

"What about you, princess? Man enough to watch?"

"Drive," I told him, gritting my teeth.

He laughed and crashed the gears into second to start the descent. I missed the Hispano-Suiza's suspension desperately as we bounced and jounced our way down the twisting slope. The smell of overheated metal filled the air, and by the time we descended, the brakes were so hot and slick they were barely catching at all. We skidded to a stop at a stream and Ryder parked the vehicle, turning off the engine to let it rest. The only sounds were the ticking of the hot metal and the rushing of the stream and Dora's faint wheezing.

Ryder glanced down pointedly, and I saw that I had been clutching at his leg. I moved my hand instantly, but he merely smiled.

"It's over, Dora," I snapped. She roused herself as Ryder jumped from the vehicle.

"Where are you going?" I demanded.

He reached into the back and lifted a can. "Water. After a ride that hot, you have to fill the radiator. Remember that if you ever do the drive by yourself."

He stepped around the vehicle and I made to follow. "Stay inside," he ordered. "There's wildlife around here and you don't know what you're doing."

I opened my mouth to argue when he raised a hand, silencing me with a gesture as imperious as a Caesar's.

There was a low snuffling sound, and then a crash as something enormous moved in the bushes beside the stream. Ryder stepped carefully backward, his eyes never leaving the shivering bushes.

"Hand me my gun."

I twisted, reaching into the gun rack behind me. "Which one?"

"The biggest. It's already loaded and the safety is on. Just pass it over."

I did exactly as he told me. "Good girl," he murmured. "Don't make any noise or any sudden movements. You can't make it back up that hill, the engine's too hot. If anything happens to me, drive like hell straight down the road until you come to a *duka*. The storekeeper will know what to do."

*"If anything happens to you?"* I hadn't known it was possible to shriek in a whisper, but I managed it. Dora was cowered against the seat, peeping over her handkerchief and pulling so hard on the flask I thought she was going to suck the finish off the metal.

"It's probably a buffalo," Ryder explained. "They don't much like people, and if I have to take him, I'll have one shot. He'll be out of that cover too late for a second. If I miss, don't stay to watch. It won't be pretty."

His tone was so calm, so matter-of-fact, we might have been discussing what he wanted for dinner rather than whether he would live or die. He hadn't looked at me once. His whole attention was directed toward the coming reckoning. He was on the far side of the vehicle, and with his gaze fixed firmly on the bushes, it was easy to slip into the back and retrieve the Rigby. The ammunition was close at hand, and I took out two rounds, my fingers slick with sweat against the cool metal. There was no point to taking more. I wouldn't have time to reload. I slid the cartridges into the rifle and closed the breach. I moved soundlessly to stand behind Ryder. He never moved his head, but he must have seen the shift in the shadows. His own rifle was lifted to his shoulder, one eye closed as the other sighted down the gun.

"Get back on the other side of the car. I want you

to shoot from cover. Wait until you have a clear shot," he instructed softly. "He's coming head-on. Aim between the eyes. I'm taking the heart."

There were a dozen things wrong with that, but I didn't argue. I moved back to put the vehicle between us, using the hood to brace my arm. I cocked both barrels of the rifle and waited. It felt like the end of time and back again before the branches shivered hard and parted. What came through was the size of a small house, big and black and relentless. He was solid as the earth, and his eyes were narrow and mean. He paused for a moment, and I saw the sweat gathering on Ryder's shoulders, soaking his shirt as he held the gun steady, waiting, waiting for a chance not to shoot.

But the buff didn't oblige. It put its head down and gathered its strength, pushing off to run straight at us.

Ryder was wrong. He did have time for a second shot. His first was fast and hot and straight through the thick shoulder of the buff into its heart. I put one round into its forehead, and before I could recover from the punch of the recoil to sight the next shot, Ryder had put a second bullet into the same spot. The buffalo sat down heavily on its haunches and flopped forward, coming to rest inches from Ryder's boot. I crept around the car, one round still in the chamber. I held the gun out to Ryder.

He didn't take it. "No need. He's finished," he

told me. We stood watching as the mean, piggy eyes went blank and soft and glassy. I was panting hard, and a trickle of sweat ran down the hollow of my spine, puddling in the curve of my bottom. I put a hand to my forehead and pushed away my fringe, letting the air cool my face. Little beads of perspiration rolled off my neck. I was damp and trembling all over, and my legs had second thoughts about holding me up.

Ryder looked at me closely. "You all right?"

"Yes." The lie was easy.

He glanced at the stillness of the buffalo. "Damned good shot, princess." He reached down and dipped a finger into the buffalo's blood. He pressed the finger to my brow, marking me.

"First African blood," he said gently. "It's a hunter's custom out here."

He unloaded my Rigby and put the guns away. Dora was weeping quietly into her handkerchief in the car, and he said something consoling to her in soothing tones. Then he came to where I still stood, staring down at the vast emptiness of the buffalo's corpse.

He took me by the hand and led me to the stream. He took a handkerchief from his pocket, and the sight of that small square of plain linen brought hot tears to my eyes. It ought to have been a Gypsy bandana, filthy and smelling of cheap perfume. But it was as white and clean as any my grandfather carried.

He took off his hat and knelt at the stream. When he bent his head I saw that his hair curled a little at his neck, and the bareness of his neck and the sweetness of that curling hair nearly did me in. He dipped the handkerchief into the stream and passed it over my face, wiping away the blood and the sweat, diluting my tears. "It's all right, princess," he said softly.

If I had leaned into him, he would have held me then. But I didn't lean. I just sat on a rock, letting him clean me. "You're a fool," I told him. "You should have shot from cover as well."

He didn't say a word. He merely crouched at the stream and washed the blood from the handkerchief, wringing it out until the water ran clear.

"You put yourself between the buffalo and us to give us a chance to get away if it charged," I accused.

He swivelled on his heels. "That's my job. The clients' safety comes first."

"And if it's a question of us or you, it must be you?"

He shrugged. "Like I said, that's the job."

"It's a damned stupid way to earn a living."

He reached into his pocket and pulled out a cigarette case. He extracted two cigarettes and lit them, drawing deeply until the tips glowed hot. He handed one to me and I took it. It wasn't black and sleek like my Sobranies, but it would do. My hand shook a little, and he pretended not to notice. The cigarette case was slim and silver, sterling from the look of it. A tip from a wealthy client, no doubt. Most likely a woman.

"Why do you do this? Haven't you any education?" The words were needle-sharp and chosen to prick.

He pulled thoughtfully on his cigarette. "I have as much education as any man needs."

"Not if you have to risk your life just to haul stupid rich people around to shoot at animals."

"Well, the rich are the only ones who can afford to pay me."

He was smiling and I threw the remains of my cigarette at him. He ground it out slowly under his heel and reached a broad hand to help me up. I took it.

"Come on, princess. It's time to get you on the road."

I rocked a little on my heels. "I think I'm going to faint."

"Don't you dare," he ordered through gritted teeth.

He made to loop an arm around my waist, but I batted him away. "I can walk on my own, thank you."

I pushed off and made my wobbly way back to the truck, scrubbing uselessly at the bloody streaks on my white dress and shoes. I looked like a walking wedding night.

Dodo rushed from the truck as I approached. "Delilah! Darling, are you all right?"

"Quite," I said with an artificially bright smile.

And then I slithered to the ground in as graceful a heap as I could manage.

I came to a few minutes later, my cheeks stinging and gasping for air as something toxically alcoholic was being forced between my lips. I shoved it away.

"I am awake, thank you," I said coldly. Ryder shrugged and took a swig from the flask he'd been shoving in my mouth.

"Your loss. It's single malt."

I rubbed at my cheek. "Did you *hit* me?"

He shrugged. "It seemed called for under the circumstances."

He moved away then, leaving Dora to help me up. "I have a vinaigrette somewhere, but Ryder said he could bring you to faster."

"I'll just bet he did," I said, testing my jaw. "It's going to bruise."

"Not at all," Dora assured me. "It was really just a tap, I promise."

I took her word for it, although the pain in my cheek said otherwise, and I heaved myself into the truck. I turned to speak to Ryder.

"Get us to Fairlight. Get us there as quickly as humanly possible. And then go. I think I've seen quite enough of you for now."

He smiled. "Pity you feel that way."

I thought of the extremely arrogant bet he'd made at the club and felt a stab of satisfaction that at least I was making him eat his own heart out.

"Really? And why is that?" I asked sweetly, prolonging the pleasure of the moment and his humiliation.

He turned to face me. "Because I live at Fairlight." He leaned closer, so close I could see the yellow flecks in the blue of his eyes. "Howdy, neighbour."

# 6

We drove on in silence. Dora slept, mouth open, snoring gently as she cradled her flask. I made no move towards the luncheon basket and neither did he. He seemed content to drive forever on roads that stretched off to nowhere. The *murram* gave way to straight dirt, but that didn't slow him down. My grandfather always swore it was better to drive as fast as possible on a dirt road because you were halfway through the next bump by the time you felt the first. Ryder seemed to believe the same. We flew down the road, raising a cloud of dust that must have been visible for miles across the savannah.

Ryder didn't say a word, but his silence was comfortable. He wasn't upset in the least. My silence was different. Mine had sharp edges and a thorny underbelly, and my biggest annoyance was that he didn't seem to notice. I had planned to punish him with it, but if he didn't even care, there wasn't much point. I finally sighed and asked the inevitable.

"How much farther?"

He shrugged. "Nobody measures miles in Africa. Journeys are measured in time—a two-day walk, a four-hour drive. But it depends on the roads. When the rains have come, it can take two days to get to Nairobi. It's dry just now, so we'll only be another half hour or so."

I resorted to my stocking flask then, taking discreet sips at first, but subsiding eventually into the deep pulls of an accomplished drinker. I felt only a little better as we approached Fairlight. There were no gates—or rather, there were, but they were rusted, hanging limply from broken hinges.

"I do hope this is not a sign of things to come," I muttered darkly, but Ryder said nothing. He wore a grim smile I did not like, and I soon realised why.

The estate was, in kindest terms, a wreck. The fences were broken, offering a gap-toothed smile to the savannah beyond, while the house itself was long and low, squatting with its back to the drive. It was built of solid stone and handsome enough, but the trim was chipped and peeling and the boards of the veranda were warped. I alighted from the truck without a word and stood, overcome by the awfulness of it all. From the overgrown bushes to the torn curtains at the windows, the entire place lacked care. I thought of the sketches in Nigel's diary and could have wept. It was like being shown a photograph of a winsome orphan one meant to adopt, only to arrive and find the child had rickets and a snotty nose and was dressed in rags. I felt my shoulders sag as I stood, rooted to the spot.

Of all emotions, disappointment is the most difficult to hide. Rage, hatred, envy—those are easy to mask. But disappointment strikes to the heart of the child within us, resurrecting every unsatisfactory Christmas, every failed wish made on a shooting star. And I made no attempt to hide it. The journey had been tiring, the company less than enjoyable, and the various stresses of the day had finally taken their toll.

I turned to find Ryder watching me closely. "You might have warned me."

"It seemed kinder to let you hang on to your illusions for a little while longer."

I gave him a chilly look. "I'm afraid I haven't any cash on me. You will have to ask Dora for what we owe you. Good day."

He gave a snort. He strode forward and took my arm. "Come with me."

I had little choice. The hand on my arm was firm and for a moment it was delicious to give myself up to being bossed around. He led me up to the veranda and around the house to where the property overlooked the edge of a large green lake. The sun was dipping low to the ground, brushing the last of its warm rays over the shimmering surface, and turning the waters to molten gold. A flock of flamingos rose suddenly, flashing their gaudy feathers in a pink farewell as they departed. Across the lake a hippopotamus wore a crown of water lilies draped drunkenly over one eye and munched contentedly as a light breeze ruffled the lake water. I took a deep breath and saw, for just an instant, the Africa I had thought to find. Then, in a violent burst of crimson and gold, the sun shimmered hotly on the lake and was gone, sinking below the horizon, leaving only purple-blue shadows lengthening behind.

"There's no such thing as evening in Africa," he told me. "Now the sun is down, you'd best get inside. There's no moon tonight, so the lions will be out."

I turned to face him. "Are you saying that just to scare me?"

"No, I'm saying it to save you. You strike me as the type of woman just stupid enough to go for a walk in this country and get herself eaten."

I thought for a moment then shrugged. "You're probably right about that. Thank you for this," I said, waving a hand toward Lake Wanyama. "It is truly lovely."

"Africa is a complicated place, Miss Drummond. It's the most beautiful place on earth and the most dangerous. Don't forget that."

"I won't," I promised.

He hesitated. "You have staff in the house. They aren't worth much, but they do know how to find me. I have a *boma* about ten minutes' walk from here. If you need me, send one of the houseboys. Do not try to find me on your own under any circumstances."

I nodded. "Understood."

"Good."

Still he did not leave, and the strange twilight created an atmosphere that was oddly intimate. "It was kind of you to show me the lake at sunset."

A quirk of the lips was the nearest he came to a smile. "I just didn't want to see you give up so fast. It doesn't suit you."

And with that he turned and strode away into the gathering darkness.

Dora called to me then and I joined her on the front veranda. An assortment of servants had emerged from the house and were shuffling towards the pile of baggage, haphazardly taking as little as possible before scuttling into the house with it.

"Is there any sort of organisation?" I asked her. "Anyone in charge?"

She shrugged. "I asked, but they don't seem to understand English."

"Of course they understand English. You there, yes, you with the turban. Are you the boss?"

He shook his head and pointed to a cottage some little distance away. The place was dark and shuttered, and after a lengthy conversation involving more hand signals than words I discovered that the farm manager lived in that cottage but was not presently at home.

"It seems we are not expected," I told Dora. "I suppose Mr. Fraser's insistence on my departing

Nairobi so suddenly has caught the staff on the hop. We weren't scheduled to arrive for almost a week yet," I reminded her. I turned back to the fellow in the turban. "May we go inside at least instead of standing out here getting devoured by insects?"

I swatted at the various things trying to suck my blood and the fellow understood me at once. He gestured for us to follow and we entered Fairlight at last. I gave a sigh of relief. It wasn't as bad as I had feared based on the outside. Of course, candlelight makes everything look nicer, and I realised Fairlight was not wired for electricity. There were candles and paraffin lamps instead.

"How very nineteenth-century," I murmured. "Is there food?" I mimed eating.

He nodded and waved us through. The entry hall, panelled in some very nice tropical woods, gave onto a pleasant drawing room with a broad fireplace with a mossy velvet fender. The dusty parquet floors were scattered with moth-eaten hides of various animals, and trophy heads hung on the walls, staring with blank, glassy eyes. Feathers were spilling out of the armchairs, but at least they looked comfortable, and I sank into one with an audible sigh.

He disappeared down a service passage and reappeared a few minutes later with a tray.

"Soup," he said, pointing to the tray. There was no soup to be found, but there was a mixed rice dish with bits of unidentifiable meat and curry spices, some roasted potatoes, flatbreads and more boiled eggs.

"By the time we leave Africa, I'm going to be clucking," I told Dora.

"Don't complain. At least you know a boiled egg can't poison you," she said, peering suspiciously at the meat.

I was too ravenous to care. I forked in the food as fast as I could, and I was happy to find there was a rice pudding for dessert and happier still to find the supply of booze. I poured us each a nightcap and we stretched out by the fire.

"I'm so tired I don't think I can get up to go to bed," Dora said at last.

"I know." I eyed the oozing sofa with distaste. "You realise we will have to do something about this place. If we're going to be in exile for months, we cannot live like savages."

"Hush," she said, her eyes closed. "They'll hear you."

"No, they won't. And they don't think of themselves as savages. Besides, I wasn't talking about them. It's one thing to live in a hut with a leopard skin for a blanket because you don't know better. It's entirely different to live in these conditions and do nothing to improve them," I told her, plucking a loose feather out of the upholstery.

"Tomorrow," she promised, her voice drowsy.

She began to murmur her prayers, but I kept talking.

"We'll make a list," I said, warming to the idea. "It will be nice to have a project. And Nigel will be very happy to know the place is being spruced up. Materials might be an issue, but labour should be cheap."

Dora's only reply was a snore, and I lay awake, watching the shadows on the ceiling. We never did get up and go to bed. My first night at Fairlight was spent drinking on a mouldering sofa in a house that wasn't mine, listening to the sounds of a darkness that was darker than any I had ever known.

The next morning I awoke to find Dora poking me in the shoulder and an assemblage of various native fellows standing in a line, staring at me curiously.

"What the devil is their problem?"

I tried to roll over, but Dora stopped me. "Well, you do look a bit of a fright."

I sat up and took inventory. Crumpled silk dress stained with red dust and Ryder's fingerprints on the sleeve. Shoes caked in mud and buffalo blood. Empty flask on my lap, and I knew without even looking in a mirror that yesterday's maquillage would be smeared everywhere.

"Say no more. Is there hot water?" I croaked.

"After a fashion," she said. She pushed a cup of hot coffee into my hands. I detested coffee and she knew it, but it did the trick. I drank it down and lurched to my feet.

She showed me to the bathroom and I turned back to face her. "Is this a joke? Dodo, I count seven different kinds of insects, including a spider that may well be poisonous."

"Spiders are arachnids," she corrected.

I slammed the door in her face and applied my bloody shoe to the lurkers in the bathtub, eradicating all, except one little scorpion that dodged behind the toilet. I flung myself into the hot water and scrubbed, grateful that she had unpacked my French-milled soaps and a proper washcloth. After I was clean and dry and had washed my hair, I felt a pinch better.

Dodo had laid out a particularly fetching frock of green-and-black figured silk with green suede shoes, and as I put them on I wondered if they'd make it through the day. This country was hard on shoes, I thought ruefully. The white suede pair covered in Anthony Wickenden's blood had been burned by the Norfolk staff, and the white silk ones soaked in buffalo blood would be next. I could have cried.

I emerged from my room looking vastly improved and feeling famished. Dora had found the dining room and there was toast, proper toast, with oranges and boiled eggs and some sort of meat that fought back when I poked it with a fork.

"Make a list, Dodo. First order of business—find a cook."

Mercifully, she remembered the untouched picnic hamper from the previous day and we fell on it like Mongols, tearing into the parcels only to find flatbreads hardened to the consistency of rocks and some fruit that lay limp and apologetic in the bottom of the basket. There was a clutch of boiled eggs there as well, and some sort of potted meat I wouldn't have touched if you'd offered me a palace on the moon.

When the meager meal was finished, we took a tour of the house led by the turbaned fellow whose name, as unlikely as it seemed, was Pierre.

"Surely that can't be right," I murmured to Dodo. But the name gave me an idea, and I turned to him. *"Parlez-vous français?"*

His face lit up. *"Oui!"* And then he burst into a volley of rapid and fairly grammatical French. In a very few minutes I learned everything I needed to know about him and about the situation at Fairlight. Dora, whose French limped along at its most athletic, had been left far behind. She waited for me to translate.

"Pierre was educated at a mission school not far from here. French Benedictine nuns who taught him their own language and a smattering of Latin, but no English."

"Latin?"

"That's what the man says. He remembers Nigel

quite well, although he was merely the houseboy at the time. Since then he's grown and married. Two wives, although he hopes to add a third soon."

"Goodness," Dora said faintly, but I noticed she was looking at Pierre with heightened interest. His features were arresting, more akin to those painted on an Egyptian tomb than what one would expect to find in sub-Saharan Africa. His nose was sharp and beaky and his skin the colour of polished walnuts. He was tall and stately and moved with such peculiar grace, he would have put any Paris mannequin to shame.

"He's Somali and Christian—good for us because it means that, unlike a Mohammedan majordomo, he'll touch pork and alcohol."

"Well, that covers your nutritional requirements," she put in.

She wasn't wrong. I related the rest of what Pierre had told me. "There's a farm manager, a fellow called Gates. He has a wife and a pair of children, but they're away for a few days. There's a cottage down the road that Fairlight lets to an artist from New York, and farther on is the *boma* where Ryder lives. They are our nearest neighbours. He said we should expect people coming from farther afield as soon as they realise we're here. Apparently newcomers are fresh meat."

I gave her a wolfish smile and she turned to Pierre and asked him in her halting French if she might see the garden. Since she always believed that volume was at least as important as vocabulary in making herself understood, she stood a foot away from Pierre, repeating, "*LE JARDIN. COMPRENEZ-VOUS? LE JARDIN?*"

He looked to me and I nodded, taking myself off to the kitchen. At least, I went to where I thought the kitchen might be. Instead it seemed to be a sort of butler's pantry with an assortment of cloudy crystal and cracked china and a long table, and I realised Fairlight had been built along the same lines as Reveille with the kitchens outside the house. It made sense for several reasons, the most important of which were the heat and the risk of fire. In the butler's pantry there was a door leading outside and I headed out and down a short path to a separate building. I could smell something that might have been food, but I almost hoped wasn't.

I tapped at the door and entered immediately. I have regretted few things so quickly in my life. The smell was repellent. Old grease and rotten vegetables formed the base note. Over it hung the sulfurous reek of old boiled eggs, choking out almost everything else. Almost everything.

A plump old man, the cook, I had no doubt, hunched at the hearth, smoking. I could smell unwashed flesh and soiled clothes, but something besides, something sweet and heavy.

I clapped my hands and the old man peered at

me, struggling to focus through a cloud of dense and familiar smoke.

"What's the matter, Grandpa? Ganja got your tongue?"

I grabbed up a broom and advanced. He got to his feet and started gabbling away in one of the native tongues. I brandished the broom.

"No wonder the food is so disgusting. You've probably kept the best of it for yourself. Get up!" He had prostrated himself at my feet but rather spoiled the effect by giggling. I poked him lightly with the broom. "Get up, I said. Now get out." I fumbled in the pocket of my dress, rather surprised to find anything there. "Here's a pound. Take it in lieu of wages and don't come back."

He took the money and started jabbering again, rubbing his fingers together as if he wanted more.

"Not likely," I told him roundly. "You're lucky you got anything. You could have poisoned us with the trash you served. Now get out." I lifted the broom and he scurried away, so quickly he left his smouldering cigarette behind.

I lifted it and sniffed. Then I took a deep drag and held it.

"Delilah!"

Dora stood in the doorway, her tone heavy with disapproval.

I exhaled slowly. "I found the cook." I held up the cigarette. "This is why he wasn't up to par.

Quite good stuff actually. I haven't had any with this much kick since Harlem."

She reached out and took the cigarette and ground it out on a hearthstone, scattering the remains of the butt over the rock. "Honestly, Delilah. This isn't a party."

"I'm celebrating getting rid of that foul cook. I gave him a pound in lieu of wages."

She choked. "Do you have any idea how much money that is to these people? He'll be robbed and killed before he even gets home."

"Serve him right for keeping that meat," I said, pointing to a slab of mutton that was heaving with maggots.

Dora picked it up with a pair of tongs and threw it out the door. She returned and surveyed the rest of the kitchen. "It's completely foul. The entire place will have to be turned out and scrubbed before we can eat anything."

"You sound defeated."

"No, I'm just wishing I hadn't ground out that cigarette," she told me.

I laughed. "That's the spirit. It really was good. I wonder where he got it."

She gave me a reproachful glance. "That's quite enough of that. I was only joking, you know. Such things are sinful and wrong. Besides, Aunt Mossy expects me to keep an eye on you."

I lifted a brow at her and she went on. "She took me to luncheon in Paris and we had a lovely chat.

I didn't think I ought to tell you before, but I suppose it's time. She's quite keen that you really settle down, Delilah. She thinks you need purpose, direction. And she thinks that this may be the best opportunity for you to find it."

"The best or the last?"

"Both."

We stared at each other a long moment, then I gave her a small smile. "Not yet, Dodo. Not just yet. Now make a list of what you want done and Pierre will organise some boys to do it."

"Where are you going?"

"For a walk. Africa beckons."

I changed my clothes, leaving off my printed silk frock for a pair of riding breeches and tall boots and a man's silk shirt. It had been Misha's. After his death I had taken more than the Volkonsky jewels. Misha always had gorgeous taste in clothes and he had been slender as a Grecian faun. I had hauled armfuls of his shirts to the tailor to have them taken in, and I wore them carelessly, open at the throat with the sleeves rolled to the elbow. They reminded me of the soft cotton shirts I had worn during the hottest dog days in Louisiana. Of course, Misha would never have worn anything as pedestrian as cotton. He had dressed with flair, buying only the very best materials. I wasn't surprised his shirts had outlived him.

I started off down the path Pierre had pointed

out, heading towards the savannah. The air was cool, touched with the faintest tang of woodsmoke and dung, but the sun was warming the earth, sending up the fragrance of fresh soil. The farm had once thrived growing pyrethrum, I remembered, a crop related to chrysanthemums. The flowers were pressed for their oil, a pungent substance used in pesticides. Only a few of the fields were still in production. Most of the farm had fallen fallow and the disused fields were now long stretches of earth that had surrendered once more to the wilderness. Here and there thickets of acacia had grown up, sheltering birds and small twittering creatures that sent up an alarm as I walked. I had only gone a few yards when I realised I should have brought a gun. A gun, a club, even a stick would have been smart. But no, I had charged into the African bush with nothing more than a silk scarf to defend myself.

"Idiot," I muttered. But I pressed on. The path was wide and level and the going was easy. I stepped around a scorpion that raised his tail in challenge and sent a flock of pretty little deer vaulting away. At least I thought they were deer. They were most likely some form of gazelle, and I regretted again not having brought a gun. I had heard gazelles were excellent eating, and even if they weren't, they had to be preferable to the teeming mutton the cook had left behind.

After a while, the ground rose a little. Just past

the slope of a slender hill it fell away again to reveal a cottage nestled in a grove of acacia trees. The doors and windows were thrown wide, and I knew from the smell of turpentine that I had found the artist's cottage.

I called as I approached and after a long moment a fellow emerged, shirtless and wiping his hands on a rag. He stared as I came near, and suddenly gave a loud whoop.

"Delilah!"

He vaulted down from the veranda and scooped me up into a bear hug.

"Hello, Kit. My majordomo said there was an artist from New York here. I didn't dare hope it might be you."

"Well, it is. My God, it must be a mirage. I cannot believe you are here. Let me look at you."

He pushed me away and looked at me with his critical artist's eye. "A few years older, but my God, it doesn't show. That face! Straight out of Praxiteles. The shoulders of a goddess. And those breasts—" He put out his hands and I slapped them away.

"Come now, darling. It isn't as if I haven't seen them before."

"You haven't seen them in six years. And they've been married since you last saw them."

"But I imagine they are still spectacular."

"Naturally. Now invite me in for lunch and a drink and we'll catch up properly."

He looped an arm over my shoulders and led me in. "Welcome to my little kingdom, my queen."

I stepped into the cottage and inhaled sharply. "Kit, they're wonderful."

Kit had been a bit of a disappointment in New York. He was the eldest son in a family as famous for their blue blood as their black account books. His father had refreshed the already overflowing family coffers with smart investments in railroads and steel, but Kit had turned up his patrician nose at both. Instead he had dabbled, pursuing his art with only a little less verve than he pursued his women. A particularly nasty divorce case where Kit had been cited had put an end to that. His mother had taken ill over the scandal and his father had shipped him off to Kenya with an allowance and his paintbrushes and instructions not to come back unless he wanted to kill her for good. I had lost touch with him—all of the old crowd had. But I had always thought of him fondly. He was thirty-five and more of a boy than any man I had ever met.

And he was strikingly handsome, with bright yellow-gold hair and a pillowy, sulky mouth made for kissing. He had a pair of warm brown eyes that could melt the dress right off a girl, and a body that made you glad to be a woman. He had done a few years of sculpture study and rumour had it that all the humping marble about had given him the physique of a minor Greek god. I had made it my business to investigate the rumours and all I ever said on the subject was that they hadn't done him justice. Not by half. We had had a splendid time together for six weeks. Then I had been off to London and he had found himself another distraction. It ended—as such things ought to—with mutual affection and something that was almost, but not quite, warm enough to be regret.

I had been genuinely sorry to hear he'd been shipped off to Africa, but now that I saw his work, I realised it might well have been the making of him. His paintings were enormous, reckless things, barely containing his passion within the boundaries of the canvas. He had taken Africa as his muse and subject and every piece depicted either landscape or dark faces. They were interesting faces, too, full of character and mystery, and the closer I looked the more I wanted to.

I stepped back and saw him watching me with an expectant expression.

"They're rather good, aren't they?"

"They're brilliant and you know it. I'd buy the lot if I could," I told him truthfully.

"I'd let you if I could," he said with a smile. "There's a fellow named Hillenbrank who means to open a gallery in Nairobi. He's promised me a show when he gets it off the ground."

It was a small thing, a gallery exhibition in a backwater like Nairobi, particularly for an artist who had shown in New York. But Kit was happy and I was the last person who would rain on that particular parade. Like most artists, he was prone to dark moods and sulking fits, and I was practiced at tap dancing around them.

I smiled widely and slipped my hand in his. "You deserve it, darling. They're *important*."

*Important* is the magic word with artists, the "open sesame" that causes them to drop their guard and let you inside. They all want to think that they are contributing something to humanity, bless them, and nothing fuels their creative fire like believing they will sign their names in the history books with daubs of oil paint. Still, I meant it. There was something truly moving about his art, a sureness to his technique that had not been there before and a newfound confidence in what he wanted to say. And I wanted to listen.

He fixed a wretched lunch we didn't eat and made up for it with a sturdy batch of gin-and-tonics.

"The tonic water keeps malaria at bay," he told me.

"Really?"

"No. It's something the Brits made up to justify drinking enough gin to stagger a sailor. But it sounds good," he added with an impish smile.

He reached for me then and I didn't put up much of a fight. Some men want a lot of resistance; it makes them feel like conquering heroes. But others, like Kit, are content with a token refusal. I said no, but his hand was already inside my shirt, and I didn't say it again. I had forgotten about his hands. They might have been leaving hands, but while they hung around, they were damned good at what they did. We tried a few old favourites and a couple of new things, and by the time we finished, we were both sticking to the sheets. Africa was hot and still that afternoon and I was happy to drowse with a gin in one hand and a cigarette in the other.

"God, I had forgotten how good you are at that," he said. "Why did we ever stop seeing each other?"

"I left for London to go to a wedding."

"So? That shouldn't have stopped us."

"I was the bride."

He laughed and reached for his own glass. His other hand was tucked behind his head, showing off his chest to excellent advantage. He was a brilliant poser, always settling into a position designed to accentuate the long, handsome lines of his body, as if an invisible life class hovered nearby, charcoal in hand, waiting to capture his likeness. He turned his face so it was in three-quarter profile.

"What happened to that husband?"

"Divorced. He's my lawyer now. And there's been another since him. A Russian prince who died on me before I could get my divorce."

"Poor darling Delilah. Unlucky in love," he murmured into my hair.

I got up then and went to the ancient gramophone by the window, wearing nothing but the black silk ribbon at my wrist. I sorted through the recordings before slipping one onto the machine. I wound it up and dropped the needle on "The Sheik of Araby." I suddenly felt a little jangly and the music suited my mood.

"Tell me about this place," I instructed him. "I want to hear about the neighbours and what you do for fun."

"Well, you'll be the belle of the ball if that's what you're worried about," he said with a grin. He knew me too well. "The king and queen, appropriately enough, are Rex and Helen Farraday. They own a place a little farther up in the hills. He's trying to ranch cattle but the poor brutes keep dying off. British, of course. They came out here and set up as the reigning pair and so far everyone is happy to let them."

"I know them. Friends of Mossy's—although I think Helen is a bit younger. Rex danced with me at my coming-out party. Quite dashing and perfectly tailored."

"Still is, although how he manages in this heat, I cannot understand," Kit said, his mouth a little rueful. I dropped a kiss to keep it from turning outright petulant. He reached for me, but I danced away and went to change the record.

"Keep talking. Who else is here?"

"There's a doctor named Stevenson, a missionary named Halliwell who lives with his sister, a very upright and tightly buttoned sort. She won't approve of you at all." I pulled a face and he went on. "Then there's Gervase Pemberton and his Spanish wife, Bianca."

"I know them, too. He's cadaverously thin? Claims to be a poet? I met them in Paris. Is she still pretending to be a dancer?"

"God, yes. It's horrifying. If I have to sit through another one of her fan dances, I'm going to fling myself into the mouth of the nearest crocodile. He damaged his lungs during the war, so they came here to live off a bit of family land that no one wanted. She's bitter and he's grim. They're perfect for one another."

"Sounds like it."

His eyes sharpened. "Did you bring that pet cousin of yours along? What was her name?"

"Dora. Yes, I brought Dodo. Why?"

"I always thought I'd like to take a crack at her. Prim girls sometimes conceal the most surprising secrets."

I laughed. "Not Dodo. She's a virgin, you know. And a very good Christian."

"Oh, never mind, then. I do prefer a girl who knows how to participate," he said with a leer at my bottom.

He reached out again and this time I let him

119

catch me. When I was buttoning up afterwards, we fell to talking about the locals again.

"What do you know about the fellow who drove me out here? Ryder White. He may well be the most uncouth man I've ever met."

I expected Kit to agree but his expression turned sober. "Uncouth, but entirely sterling of character—one of the best. I hate him."

"Because you can't measure up?"

"Precisely. The natives adore him, and he's bedded all the best-looking women for a hundred miles. I don't need the competition."

I thought of Ryder's violent defense of one woman in particular. "I presume you know the Wickendens? I watched Ryder horsewhip Anthony Wickenden in the Nairobi train station yesterday."

He threw back his head and laughed. "Did he, by God? Wish I'd been there to see it. I might have gotten in a few licks myself. Jude Wickenden is the handsomest woman in Africa by a long shot, at least until you arrived," he corrected quickly. He nuzzled my neck by way of apology for the slight. "She was married once before and her husband disappeared into the bush during the war. She went to live with an aunt who happens to be crazy as a bedbug. When Jude had the fellow declared legally dead, the aunt threatened to shoot her. They live in the same house now, but they don't speak. The old woman still goes out into the bush looking for the husband who disappeared."

I thought of all the young men who hadn't come back from the war in Europe and I understood. "Sometimes it's difficult to accept that they're gone without a body to bury." I thought of the shreds of Johnny's uniform and pushed them out of my head.

Kit shrugged. "She's Jude's aunt, not his. You'd have thought the old girl would have taken Jude's part. Still, poor Jude was out of the frying pan and into the fire. Wickenden's a drinker."

"Aren't we all?"

"But I'm a delight when I drink," he said, raising his glass and pressing a lingering kiss to my neck. "Wickenden's a mean one. Slaps her around, which she says she can handle herself, but this last time he worked her over pretty hard. Left bruises in all the wrong places. Ryder takes it upon himself to look after her. He loves to play Lancelot to damsels in distress."

He raised his glass then and drained the last of the gin. His eyelids began to droop. The heat, the liquor and the exertion had taken their toll. His hand went slack and the glass rolled gently to the mattress. I dropped a kiss to his beautiful, sulky mouth and tied my silk scarf around one of his wrists, hitching it firmly to the bedpost. I saw myself out.

# 7

I returned to Fairlight to find Dora supervising a crew of young men as they scrubbed the kitchen. She threw up her hands when she saw me and joined me on the veranda for a sundowner.

"It's impossible. I can't get them to understand that one doesn't clean with dirty water and the soiled rags must be changed for new ones. All they're doing at this point is moving the filth around. At least I found an assortment of tins that look safe enough. I told Pierre to have them opened and heated up for dinner."

"Told Pierre? In what language, pig Latin?"

"Pantomime. If nothing else my skills at charades should improve vastly from living here. And I haven't the faintest notion what's in the tins. The labels have all come off, so it will just be a sort of surprise potluck."

"Drink more and it won't matter," I suggested. She hesitated and I waved the bottle at her impatiently. "For God's sake, Dora, it's just a drink. Don't be such a goose."

With reluctant fingers she held out her glass for a refill. My bad influence was beginning to take hold, I decided. "Where did you get off to? I began to think a lion might have carried you away."

I gave her a loaded smile. "Our tenant is none other than Kit Parrymore."

She choked on her gin and it was a full minute before she could speak again. "You're joking."

"I would never joke about that body," I said, stretching my arms high overhead.

"Oh, Delilah, you didn't!"

I shrugged. "It was either that or eat his cooking for lunch. And he's a rotten cook."

"What is he doing in Africa?"

I told her and filled her in on the neighbours while I was at it. When I finished, she passed me an envelope.

"This came while you were fornicating with the neighbour."

I took it and lifted a brow. "Don't be poisonous, Dora. Hmm. Heavy stationery. Someone likes expensive paper." I sniffed. "And jasmine perfume. God, it smells like a French whore rolled herself in the envelope."

I pulled out a note and squinted at the scrawl of green ink, then passed it to Dora. "I can't make it out. What does it say?"

She peered at it, holding it this way and that like a cryptographer studying a particularly tricky cipher. "Apparently Helen Farraday is delighted you've come and would like to host a little dinner in your honour to introduce you to the neighbourhood."

"When?"

"Tomorrow."

"She doesn't let grass grow under her feet, does she? But then she never did." Mossy had used her as an object lesson when I was making my debut of how one ought *not* to behave. Helen had come out when I was still in pigtails and Mossy was changing husbands as often as she changed her knickers. A Chicago heiress, Helen had taken one look at the pickings in the windy city, loaded up her meatpacking money and headed for London. She wanted an Englishman, someone with blue blood and a five-hundred-year-old name. She'd gotten neither with Rex. His family money had come the generation before and left with it, too. But he was charming as the devil and twice as handsome. Mossy always said he was the best dancer she'd ever met, and he could have had his pick of a dozen girls. Why he chose Helen was anybody's guess, although Mossy suspected he'd been intrigued by the gossip that Helen was a nymphomaniac who had seduced three of her tutors and one of the housemaids. Of course, the money wouldn't have been much of a deterrent, and from all accounts the marriage had been happy enough. There was infidelity of course, but since it was on both sides, nobody had reason to complain.

Dora tucked the note back into the envelope. "Will you go?"

"Of course. And you're coming with me."

"I wasn't invited," Dora said pointedly.

I shrugged. "Since when has that ever stopped me? Helen must not realise you're here or she would have included you. I'll write and let her know. Besides, Kit will be happy to see you. He asked after you today."

"Did he?" If the light had been better, I was quite sure I would have seen her blush.

I slept a little better that night, probably for being in a bed at last. Dora had done a marvelous job of settling me into the master suite. I gave her Mossy's old room even though it boasted a prettier bed and a frilly little dressing table that she wouldn't even look at twice, much less actually use. But Nigel's suite had bookcases and a view of the lake, and it suited me just fine, particularly when Dora hung the fresh mosquito netting and checked under the bed for scorpions.

"All clear," she informed me as she scooted out from under the bed. She was brandishing a Chinese slipper, prepared to do battle with any creepy-crawlies. She rose and tightened the belt on her robe. "I'm just across the hall if you need me in the night."

Dora always slept within calling distance. It was more for peace of mind than anything else. I seldom needed her, but it made me feel better to know she was around if I did. Sometimes when the nightmares got too bad and I couldn't sleep I would give her a shout and we played gin rummy.

It was an ongoing game, and she was ahead of me in the tally by five thousand points, but I hoped to make it up eventually. I suspected she was cheating, but I never could figure out how.

"Good night, Do."

She left and I turned over, watching the stars shimmer to life over the lake. I wondered if the lions would be out, and that led me to think about Ryder White. And before I knew it, I slid into sleep.

I woke up to a painfully bright morning and Dora carrying in my breakfast tray.

"Good morning, Delilah."

"Dodo," I croaked. I waved at the window. "Pull those curtains, will you? No sun should be that bright at this hour."

"It's nearly eleven," she said. She busied herself putting out towels and running the bath, every brisk move a reproof for my slothfulness.

"I suppose I overslept," I said contritely. "But there's nothing much to get up for, is there?"

"There are callers, actually. They have been here since daybreak."

"Callers? What sort of callers?"

She gave me a pinched look. "Local folk."

"Local folk? You mean Africans?"

"That's exactly what I mean."

"Well, good grief, what do they want with me?"

Dora bit back a smile and adopted a lofty tone. "They seem to be suffering from various ailments. If I understand Pierre correctly, it is their belief that the lady of the house can provide them with succour."

"Succour? Do, it's too early for practical jokes."

"See for yourself."

"Are you serious? There are really natives here who expect me to play Florence-bloody-Nightingale?"

"Language, Delilah." She poured out the tea, but I bounded out of bed. I washed and dressed in record time, and was out the door before the tea even had a chance to cool. And there they were. Twenty, maybe thirty of them. Dressed in lengths of fabric wound up in various ways with necklaces and bracelets of beads strung onto copper wires. Some of them had bandages, others had crutches. Some clutched sick babies and others their own stomachs.

I was aware of Dora at my elbow and I muttered out of the side of my mouth at her, "It looks like Saturday night at Bellevue."

Seeing them up close had sobered her. "I suppose we could do something," she said doubtfully. "We don't have much in the way of medicines, really. Do you think they'd like some bromide salts?"

They were staring at me, but not expectantly. Their expressions were blank, the faces of people who had spent their hopes too many times in all the wrong places.

I turned to Dora. "Fetch whatever medical supplies we have, and bring a few extra sheets we can tear up for bandages."

Just as she dashed off, Ryder appeared, sauntering in without a care in the world, whistling a tune with his rifle slung over his shoulder. I held up a hand. "Don't even think of staying unless you mean to help."

He surveyed the scene. "Playing at being the Lady with the Lamp, are we? I wouldn't have thought the role suited you. Mind you don't accidentally amputate something you shouldn't."

Something had riled him, but I couldn't imagine what and I didn't care to try.

"You can either help me or you can get lost. I don't particularly care which."

He thought about it, but after a moment he turned and signalled to a young man who had followed him up the path. The fellow was a native African, tall and slender like the people who sat in my garden, but the resemblance ended there. He wore a sort of toga of scarlet cotton and his hair was plaited into long, intricate braids that had been reddened with ochre dust. Long strings of beads hung across his chest and wrapped around his wrists, and he carried a tall spear. When he rested it was on one leg, the other tucked up like a stork, and his gaze was solemn and watchful. He helped Ryder move a table outside and together they carried hot water and tore up sheets and generally made themselves useful.

I surveyed the contents of the first aid kit while Ryder filled me in.

"They are Kikuyu. Word travels fast in the bush, and to these people white women mean medicine. There's not an Englishwoman out here who doesn't dispense castor oil and antiseptic on her front porch."

"I thought my farm manager had a wife. Why doesn't Mrs. Gates take care of this?" I asked, scrubbing irritably at the table with a moderately clean rag and a bucket of hot water.

"Gates doesn't believe in spoiling the workers. He thinks their native remedies are good enough."

"Clearly not," I snapped. I took a deep breath. "Very well. What do I need to know about the Kikuyu?"

"They're farmers, mostly, with some black-smithing ability. It's their handiwork you admired on my truck," he added with a smile. "But they really are quite skilled. They can fashion whatever you need—keys, knives, that sort of thing. The one thing they can't do is fight. They're rotten warriors, and that's why they're so attached to the white farms. They work the fields for the whites and tend their own *shambas*—smallholdings," he added when I gave him a questioning look. "When the British started settling this area, it meant the

Kikuyu weren't getting slaughtered by the Masai and the Somali anymore. They still skirmish, but nothing like what they used to get up to. You'll be treating mostly accidents and quarrels and stomach upsets and worms, not the effects of tribal warfare, if that's what you were afraid of."

"I'm not afraid of anything."

He was still laughing when I motioned for the nearest woman to come forward. She placed a small child on the table and I looked her over. She was getting enough to eat; her muscles were sleek and her ribs weren't visible. But her eyes were listless and a loose, dirty bandage drooped from one arm. I didn't even have to look under it to know what the smell meant.

Gingerly, I peeled away the filthy bandage to find a small suppurating wound. I rummaged through the travel case Dora had fetched but there was nothing besides the usual assortment of tweezers and lint and antiseptics and digestive aids. Certainly nothing like a scalpel. I turned to Ryder.

"Give me your knife."

He reached into his pocket and pulled out a clasp knife. "How did you know I had a knife?"

I took it from him and pulled it open. "Your kind always does."

I held the blade in the fire as long as I dared, and when it was red-hot, I gestured for the mother to hold the child fast. I stuck the blade into the wound and the pus ran freely. The child screamed, but the mother was firm, holding her tightly and murmuring words of admonishment as I worked. The tissue was still wholesome, and I worked fast, pressing a little to encourage the pus to drain faster. The thick yellow fluid mingled with blood, and I wiped carefully, peering at the wound. I took tweezers from the case and went back in, emerging a moment later with a long thorn. I held it up to show the mother and she smiled broadly. Her teeth were white and beautiful, although she was missing a few. The child had quieted completely and did not fuss, not even when I pressed the sides of the wound again to make the blood flow freely. I wanted to make certain the gash was clean, and as the blood ran fresh and bright, I held a cloth over the top to staunch it. After it clotted, I applied an antiseptic powder and bandaged it firmly.

I turned to Ryder. "Can you explain to her that the bandage must be kept dry and clean? I want to see the child back tomorrow."

He stared at me, a hard appraising stare, and after a long moment, he nodded. He gabbled something at the mother and she ducked her head shyly at me. "*Asante sana.*"

"What did she say?"

"She thanks you."

"I probably ought to learn a few words of Kikuyu," I mused.

"She wasn't speaking Kikuyu, and I guarantee you wouldn't be able to learn it even if she were," he returned. "But most of them speak Swahili and the up-country version is easy enough to pick up."

"Up-country version?"

"It's a coastal language," he explained. "The Swahili spoken down near Mombasa is more formal. Everybody who speaks Swahili up-country uses it as a second language and knows just enough to get by. It's crude, but effective."

Rather like the man himself, I thought sourly. "Tell me again what she said. Slowly."

He sounded out the words for me and I repeated them. "What response do I give her?"

"Just tell her *karibu*."

I turned to the woman. "*Karibu*."

She smiled again and shuffled off with the child who was sending me venomous looks. I didn't much blame her.

My eyes fell on the bags of flour that Dora had cleared out of the kitchen to throw away. Suddenly it seemed like an obscenity to get rid of anything that might be useful to these people. I summoned Pierre and addressed him in rapid French.

"Sieve that flour to get rid of any weevils and then make flatbreads. That will be quick and filling. And if there's any fat that isn't rancid, make certain to work some of that into the dough.

They need feeding up. See if there's any powdered milk for them, too."

Dora went with him and I turned to Ryder.

"There ought to be vitamin drops in the milk and a teaspoon of castor oil to build them up," I said to Ryder. "Could I find such things in Nairobi?"

"Yes. And at my *duka* if you don't want to wait for a trip to town."

"Good. Consider this an order. And I suppose I ought to get a milk cow."

"One of the natives might sell you one or you could try Rex Farraday's herd."

"Thank you—" I broke off. Ryder was staring hard at me again, and it was unsettling. "What?"

He shook his head. "People don't surprise me. You do."

"You obviously don't have much experience with Southern women. My great-grandmother held her plantation against the Union navy when it sailed up the Mississippi from New Orleans, shelling every Rebel house along the way. I come from hearty stock."

He took an appraising look at my slender body and snorted. "Where did you learn to bandage like that?"

"War hospital in London. I worked as a nurse for four years."

He was silent a moment, then said in a calm, flat voice, "Three years in the Royal Flying Corps, Squadron 26."

"Yes, well, if you think we're going to trade war stories and become fast friends, you're quite mistaken. I don't need a battle buddy."

"No, but you do need a guide. You don't know this country yet. I'll be back this afternoon to take you into the bush and teach you some more Swahili."

Before I could reply, he shouldered his rifle and beckoned his friend, the tall warrior with the spear.

"This is Gideon. He's a Masai. He will stay with you to finish up." Before I could reply, he shouldered his rifle and disappeared.

"Like a bloody ghost," I muttered. I turned to the warrior. "Do you speak English?"

He smiled, a dazzling smile, and I noticed his teeth were missing on the bottom as well.

"Of course, *memsahib*. I learned at the mission school."

"I thought the nuns only taught French."

"The nuns left and the English came. I learned to speak English there and to know the stories of your Bible." He stepped forward, shifting his weight as gracefully as a dancer. "Ryder has gone. I will help you now. I speak Maa—my own language, your English, Swahili and a few of the other dialects. I am a learned man."

His slender chest swelled with pride and I smiled at him. "Very well, Gideon. Let's get started."

Dora was moving quietly through the group, dispensing cups of powdered milk and pieces of flatbread still steaming from the pan. They ate and drank and waited to be seen.

I summoned the next patient, and for an hour straight I worked, treating blisters and burns and stitching up the occasional slash wound.

"What is that from?" I asked Gideon softly.

"It is a wound from a *panga*, *memsahib*."

"A *panga*? What is that? Some sort of animal with tusks?"

Gideon threw back his head and laughed. "No. A *panga* is a knife." He reached into his toga and pulled out a long, wicked-looking blade that was slightly curved. It reminded me of a machete, and as I stared at it, I realised what he had said.

"You mean someone did this on purpose?" I asked, gesturing to the scalp I was stitching closed.

"Sometimes men must fight one another," he replied with a shrug.

I thought of the consequences of the fighting I had seen, the rivers of blood, the broken bones, the scarred lungs and shattered minds. "No, they mustn't, Gideon. They just do."

# 8

I finished up with the last patient just as the milk ran out. I went in the house and washed my hands and collapsed onto the bed. Dora found me there a moment later. She was carrying a plate of thin beef sandwiches.

"You ought to eat. But first you need to change your shirt. It's a disgrace." I looked down. Misha's heavy silk was stained with blood and pus and oil and the powdered red ochre the Kikuyu rubbed into their hair. I sniffed at it.

"It's a peculiar smell, don't you think? But not completely unpleasant."

"Don't romanticise it. It's foul." She rummaged in the wardrobe searching for a fresh shirt. She threw it to me and carried the filthy one away between her fingertips.

I rolled away from the plate of sandwiches. My stomach was strong, but not quite strong enough to spend the morning as I had and still want luncheon. I had lost weight during the war, too. Too many operating theatres, too many torn limbs and broken bodies. As a volunteer nurse I shouldn't have seen any of it. I should have been rolling bandages and reading aloud letters from home and pouring cups of tea. But war doesn't care about "should haves." One of the surgeons noticed that I had steadier nerves and better hands than most of the seasoned professionals. After that he'd made a point of requesting me. I think he thought he was doing me a favour. I was sick three times during my first operation—an amputation that took off a young infantryman's leg and nearly cost him his life in lost blood. But every time I was sick I wiped my mouth and crept back until the surgeon put that whole leg into my hands and told me to get rid of it. It was heavy, that dead thing in my hands, and I could feel the weight of it still if I closed my eyes and put out my arms. I felt the weight of all of them, every young man who slipped under the ether and didn't come back, every officer who put on a brave face but clutched my hand until the bones nearly broke. I remembered them all. And in the darkest nights, when the gin didn't bring forgetfulness and the hour didn't bring sleep, I counted them off like sheep, tumbling dead over fences in a beautiful green field dotted with poppies.

I woke with a start. I had drifted off thinking of the boys who had never come home again and I had dreamed of them. I was disoriented for a moment, and when I heard a man's voice my heart began to race. It was a full minute before I remembered that Ryder was coming to collect me.

I dried my cheeks and brushed out my hair. For good measure I added a slick of crimson lipstick and tied on a silk scarf. I was feeling a little more like myself by the time I joined Ryder and Dora in the drawing room. It was absurd. Dora was plying him with cups of tea as if she were presiding over the tea table in a vicarage in Bournemouth while Ryder lounged in one of the easy chairs, looking like an overgrown panther. The teacup was ridiculously small in his hands, but he held it gently, and when he spoke to Dora his voice was low and courteous.

"Would you like to come, Miss Dora? Every settler ought to know the country."

Dora flapped a hand, and seemed to pink up a little under his gaze. "Oh, I hardly think so! I'm not at all outdoorsy, you know, except for gardening. I do enjoy puttering, and it seems as if everything grows so well here. The hibiscus and gladioli are practically rioting, they're so overgrown and the roses want some very serious pruning. I mean to have a look at what might be done to the patch between the house and the lake, if Delilah doesn't mind."

"She doesn't," I said from the doorway. I looked to Ryder. "You're wasting your time. Dodo is too much a lady to go bushwhacking."

The gallant thing would have been for him to remark that I was too much a lady, too, but of course he didn't. He merely gave me a slow look and rose to his feet. He was too big in that room. His very presence seemed to suck out all the air. I waved my hand impatiently.

"Let's get on with it if we're going."

He handed the cup to Dora and gave her a courteous nod of the head. "Thank you for the tea, Miss Dora."

"My pleasure, Ryder. And if I am to call you by your Christian name, I think you must do the same with me. From now on, it's just Dora."

She pinked up again and I resisted the urge to roll my eyes.

"As you like, Dora," he said easily. "I'm sorry you won't come, but at least promise me you won't walk around without an escort. You've got watercress down by the lake, and elephants love the stuff. It wouldn't do to surprise one. Make Pierre go with you. He's useless, but if he sees an elly he'll shriek and wave his arms enough to give you time to get away."

He gave her a twinkling smile and she laughed. I strode out without looking backward and nearly ran into Gideon on the veranda. He was standing, one leg folded up, looking like an abandoned toy. "Gideon, why didn't you get tea?"

Gideon merely shook his head and stepped off the veranda, heading for the path that led away from the house. Ryder fell into step beside me.

"Did I offend him somehow? Did Dora insult him?"

"No, she was very courteous. She offered to send Pierre out with tea, which confused him."

"Why? Don't the Masai drink tea?"

139

"Not in a white man's house. They aren't vicars and bank clerks, for God's sake, taking afternoon tea in the drawing room. They drink milk and cow's blood and if they find a taste for it, some of them drink liquor."

"Cow's blood?" I said faintly.

He started to explain and I held up a hand. "Not today. I've seen enough blood for now."

"That's Africa, princess. Besides, a Masai warrior would never take nourishment from a white woman's hand. It's degrading."

I opened my mouth to debate the point, but Ryder held up a finger. "Don't shoot the messenger. It's their way and it isn't my place to change it."

I lapsed into silence, but only for a moment. "Well, you've certainly made an impression on Dora. She's never chatty with strangers. Why are you so nice to her?"

He paused and his pause was heavy. He was feeling for the words. "She's a nice lady," he said finally.

"Is she your type?" I teased.

He didn't smile. His expression didn't even flicker. "I don't have a type. Now be quiet. You'll never learn anything about the bush if you keep flapping your jaws."

I sulked for the next quarter of an hour. Ryder led the way, and I noticed his walk as he moved through the bush, low-hipped and loose, as if he and the earth belonged to each other. It was the walk of a confident man who knows exactly who he is and doesn't give a tinker's damn if anybody else does.

We walked past Kit's cottage but the place looked empty and I was a little relieved.

"Looks like your boyfriend is out," Ryder said coolly. His face was in profile, and I noticed his nose. It was strong and straight, a no-nonsense nose. But the nostrils were flaring just a little, and I realised the coolness was just a pose. He had been good and irritated since that morning, and suddenly I knew why.

I surveyed my fingernails. "He isn't my boy-friend."

"Fine. Your lover is out."

I laughed. "Word travels fast out here."

"There are two kinds of white people in Africa. Those who work and those who fornicate. Kit's the latter."

"Which are you?"

He turned his head and smiled then, a slow smile that might have been an invitation under other circumstances. "Both. I'm the exception."

"I'm sorry you lost your bet," I told him. "But let that be a lesson to you, Ryder. I'm no man's foregone conclusion."

To my surprise, that didn't seem to put him off. If anything, the smile deepened, and for the first time I saw the hint of a dimple in his left cheek. His eyes were bright. He was enjoying the game as much as I was. He took half a step towards me, but just then Gideon, who had been walking some yards ahead, halted and raised a hand. He made a series of gestures and Ryder immediately stepped sharply behind me, his back pressed to mine. He cocked his rifle.

"What's wrong?" I muttered under my breath.

"Fresh lion spoor," he replied softly.

"And you're behind me? My hero."

"Lions tend to hunt in pairs or small groups and when they do, one always circles around behind. Now shut up." His head swivelled as he scanned the grasses near us. Gideon moved cautiously forward. After a moment Gideon straightened and called out something in rapid Swahili.

"What did he say?"

"All clear. The lions already fed. There's a zebra carcass just in that thicket. Keep your voice down, though. They're probably resting not far away."

I crept along until we came to a point just above a dry gulley where Ryder stopped to take a drink. He offered me a pull on his canteen, but I waved him off. I went to Gideon, motioning for him to give me a drink from his goatskin. He smiled his broad smile as he handed it over. I took a deep draught and nearly choked. It was blood mixed with milk, both of them warm and thick. The stuff coated my tongue and I willed myself to swallow it down without gagging. I wiped my lips on my sleeve, leaving long streaks of pale blood on the fabric.

"Christ," I muttered. "A girl cannot have nice things in this country."

I handed the goatskin back to Gideon and he smiled again. "*Asante*," I said.

"*Karibu, Bibi.*"

"What does *Bibi* mean?"

"It is a respectful word that means *madam*. It may also mean other things."

"Such as?"

"Such as *grandmother* or a lady who has no husband. Africans always give nicknames to the white settlers. It is our way."

Behind me Ryder snickered. "What do they call him?" I asked, jerking a thumb towards Ryder.

"That is *Bwana Tembo*. *Bwana* means *sir*."

"And what does *Tembo* mean?"

"*Tembo* is elephant, *Bibi*."

I turned to Ryder who was barely concealing a smile. "They call you Sir Elephant?"

He capped his canteen and flashed me a wicked grin as he stood up. "Yep."

I stood toe-to-toe with him. "Exactly why do they call you Sir Elephant?"

His gaze dropped to my mouth. He lifted his hand and ran his thumb across my lower lip. He held it up for my inspection. "You missed a spot." He wiped the drop of blood onto his trousers. I heard the cicadas then, their sound shimmering in the air around us, beating against my ears, or maybe it was just the sound of my own pulse.

"You didn't answer my question."

"Oh, I expect you'll find out one of these days." He turned away then looked back, a grin tugging at the corner of his mouth. "Oh, and, just so you know, they call Kit *Bwana Tausi.*"

"What's a *tausi*?"

"It's a peacock. It means they think he's all mouth and no trousers. Let's go."

I had to give the man credit; he knew how to play a good game. I could see how his rustic charm could be devastatingly effective under the right circumstances and with the right girl. Pity for him he didn't realise yet I was the wrong one.

But there was nothing he didn't know about the African bush. By the time he had walked me around and back to Fairlight, I knew the major landmarks, how to calculate my position and when the most dangerous times for lions were. He showed me the *luggas*—empty riverbeds thick with foliage and little caves—the preferred lair of the leopard. He cautioned me about the buffalo, which could hammer me flat, and the snakes that spat venom and the ant-bear holes where I could snap an ankle and a thousand other horrors until it all ran together in my head and I wondered aloud if there was any place on earth as dangerous as Africa.

"Not that I've found," he replied cheerfully.

We approached Fairlight from a different path than the one we had taken out, and Ryder stopped as we reached the gate.

"You'll be safe enough here. The path leads through those Christ-thorn bushes and opens right up onto the lawn. Just remember what I said about never going out without a weapon and a guide."

If he realised I had walked to Kit's unattended, he didn't let on and I wasn't about to rat myself out. "If I'm not supposed to go walking alone, why did you bother to teach me anything at all?"

"Because you can't really ever depend on anybody but yourself."

"In Africa or in life?" I asked mockingly.

"Both. Now get inside. I'll be back tomorrow with the supplies from the *duka*."

Before I had a chance to protest his peremptory tone, he was gone. The garden was full of cool green shadows and strange birdcalls. I put out a hand and felt it catch on a thorn. It was Eden before the fall, lush and promising and full of sharp dangers. I made my way through the bushes and out onto the lawn. Dora was snipping some overgrown bougainvillea and humming.

"I was just beginning to worry. We'll have to hurry if we're to be ready on time for the Farradays' party." She peered at my shirt. "Is that blood?"

"And milk. Apparently it's Africa's answer to the cocktail."

• • •

I dressed in white that evening. Nothing is more luxurious in a hot climate than white, and I had a backless number from Patou that was begging for an outing. I sat stripped to my French silk knickers while Dora applied *poudre de riz* with a lavish hand and a swansdown puff. When she had powdered me from face to feet, she helped me into the scrap of fragile white silk. With it I wore Shalimar and scarlet lipstick and the black silk ribbon at my wrist. Dora was nicely turned out in one of the watery greens she preferred for evening wear, and we were just putting the finishing touches on our toilettes when Rex Farraday arrived in style. He was driving a butter-coloured Rolls-Royce and the engine purred like a big cat as he left it running. He bounded up the front steps of Fairlight, dashing in his formal black, his arms open wide.

"Delilah Drummond, what a delight to have you here!"

He enfolded me in a careful embrace. Rex was always one to appreciate an ensemble. He drew back and studied me. "I don't know how you do it, but you don't look a day older than the last time I saw you and it must be going on seven years."

"Nearer to ten, but you are sweet. And handsome as ever! I do love the silver at your temples. Very distinguished! Rex, do you know my cousin, Dora?"

He was equally charming to her, but then Rex was a sort of purveyor of goodwill. Everyone felt better around him. Men sat a little straighter and fancied themselves heroes while women touched their hair and toyed with the idea of taking him to bed. He was not the most notorious playboy, but he'd been known to follow an interesting opportunity if it shimmied by in a tight silk dress. He just had a knack for making friends. He was the sort of man who could get himself elected head of the social committee in Hell.

"Would you like a drink, Rex? I'm afraid the wine cellar's not actually stocked, but we at least have gin and champagne."

"Tempting, my dear, but Helen is far too excited about seeing you. If I delay even a moment, I'll never hear the end of it. Shall we?"

He shepherded us out to the car.

"Half an hour's drive should see us there. We're just up the valley from you," he informed us as he slid behind the wheel. The interior was sinfully soft crimson leather, and I sank gratefully into it, happy that Africa could offer some comforts. Rex seemed to intuit my thoughts. He laughed.

"Yes, dear Delilah. Africa is not entirely uncivilized."

"It's a fascinating place," I told him truthfully, "but you have to admit it is a bit rough around the edges."

"I shouldn't think that would bother you. Didn't

I hear you were brought up on a ranch in Wyoming or Montana or some such place?"

"Louisiana," I corrected sharply. "And it wasn't a cattle ranch. It was a sugar plantation an hour outside New Orleans. We had opera, for God's sake."

At that he threw his head back and laughed. "Of course, Fairlight isn't exactly the best introduction to the comforts we have." He sobered a little. "It's a shame, really. Finest piece of property in the valley, and it's being run right into the ground. Still, I think you'll find plenty here to amuse you," he added, opening the throttle. We raced down the road, sending up showers of red dust in our wake.

# 9

Helen screamed when we arrived, throwing her hands into the air and rushing out to meet us. I wasn't even fully out of the car before she wrapped her arms around me and crushed me to her. It was a painful experience. Helen always was bony as a brook trout.

"Darling, you could have knocked me down with a feather when Mossy cabled to say you were coming—the veriest feather!" she said in her breathy, little-girl voice. I noticed her years of living with Rex had smoothed out her Midwestern accent to something that wasn't quite on English street but at least knew the neighbourhood. "Come right in and have a drink and meet the others."

She merely waved as I introduced her to Dodo, but Dora was accustomed to being an afterthought. Rex very correctly engaged her in polite conversation about the weather while Helen monopolized me.

She pushed a drink into my hands and towed me to the centre of the room. Clapping her hands for silence, she threw an arm around my shoulders.

"My darlings, this is why we have all gathered here tonight, to welcome dear Delilah. Her mother is one of my very oldest friends." She placed heavy emphasis on the word *oldest* so everyone would understand that Helen was in no way ancient enough to be my mother. "She's come to join our merry band, so you must all make her feel quite welcome."

The guests raised their glasses and Helen sketched a little bow, somehow making my moment almost entirely about herself. It was a quintessentially Helen performance. She was a classic upstager, always seeking the spotlight even if she had to swipe it from someone else. But I hadn't grown up Mossy's child for nothing. I stood perfectly still, making certain I was positioned so the warm glow of the lamps would illuminate me, a figure in unrelieved white except for the crimson mouth and the sharp black ribbon to match my bob. I was creating an art study with myself as the subject, a *chiaroscuro* self-portrait that demanded nothing more than to be looked at. With her bright blue silk and unruly blond curls, Helen didn't have a prayer. I moved my eyes slowly around the room, resting them for just a moment upon each face, caressing, inviting, but so coolly they might have imagined it.

Within seconds the men had all detached themselves and lined up for introductions. Helen looked a trifle put out, but she linked arms with me, probably in the spirit of "if you can't beat them, join them." She smiled warmly at the first comer.

"This is our resident medical man, Bunny

Stevenson, a brilliant doctor and thoroughly lovely man. No, don't blush, Bunny darling, it's entirely true."

He was about Rex's age, but not wearing it quite so well. Whereas Rex's laugh lines and silver hair were nicely balanced by a hard body and sinuous grace, the doctor was slightly inclined to *embonpoint*. A beard camouflaged what I suspected might be a softly doubled chin, but his handshake was warm and firm.

After him came a gentleman in a kilt accompanied by a woman in a dingy white gown pinned with a tartan sash. "Our local missionaries," Helen said with a trifle less warmth than she had shown for the doctor. "Lawrence Halliwell and his good sister, Evelyn." I shook hands with them both and forgot them almost immediately. I had little use for missionaries, particularly the ones who took on mission trips to godforsaken places and then dressed up for dinner parties. It whiffed of hypocrisy.

Following them was a lugubrious figure I recognised instantly. "Gervase, how nice to see you again. And Bianca, how brave you are to wear so much scarlet. I would never have the nerve." Gervase Pemberton, the grim poet, and his tawdry Spanish wife. The comment on her cheap red silk dress was unkind, but she had behaved very badly at the last party I had invited them to in Paris. She had disappeared to the powder room and emerged

151

wearing nothing but a string of pearls down to her nethers. I was no prude; I believed in having fun as much as the next girl, but giving away the farm to every Tom, Dick and Harry in the room was just common.

Kit Parrymore was next, and beside me Helen purred a little. "Kit, you naughty monkey. I think you've already welcomed Delilah quite thoroughly to Africa."

He leaned near and brushed a kiss to my ear. "How word does travel," I murmured.

"It's the natives," he whispered back. "They know everything and they tell it all."

"I'll remember that." I gave him a demure look and he stepped back to let another fellow through. This one was sporting a face full of fresh bruises and some rather impressive cuts.

Anthony Wickenden held my hand a moment too long. "I must apologise for bleeding on your shoes in Nairobi. They were in the wrong place at the wrong time. This is my wife, Jude."

He drew forward a woman who might have been the loveliest creature I had ever seen if she'd given a damn. She would have done any show-room in Paris proud, and I could imagine her dressed in the latest fashion, leaning on the arm of a duke as she swept into the opera house. But instead she was here, in a colonial backwater, and the closer I looked, the more provincial she seemed. Her hair was badly cut and styled even

152

worse. It had been crammed hastily into a snood and she was wearing an evening gown that looked as if it had come out of the closet of a plump octogenarian and altered badly. A moment later, I realised why.

Behind her was her aunt, presented as Sybil Balfour. "Call me Tusker," she ordered, thrusting out her meaty hand. She was wearing a gown very similar in cut to Jude's, only this one was straining at the seams. Jude's had been awkwardly taken in and it hung badly on her tall, slender frame. Tusker was half a foot shorter and almost twice as wide, although her bulk seemed to be entirely muscle and when she shook my hand I would swear I heard the bones crack. "Welcome to Africa."

"Thank you so much," I said to her, and then to the company at large, "Thank you all for such a warm welcome."

Helen beamed at us, then at Rex's gentle cough, remembered to introduce Dora as well. We nibbled on tiny hot sausages and made small talk as Rex handed around fresh drinks.

"What's this?" It was a champagne glass, but the liquid inside was foaming instead of bubbling. I peered at the murky colour.

"That is a Black Velvet, champagne with stout. Not a very pretty cocktail, I admit."

"It looks like somebody tried to bottle evil." But I had drunk worse. I took a sip and rolled it on my tongue. It was creamy and heavy and musky. "Not bad."

He gave me a wink and moved on.

As soon as we'd finished our drinks, Helen whisked everyone into the dining room. "Now, I realise we're odd numbers—only six men for seven women, so one of you gentlemen will have to take on two ladies," she said with a waggish expression.

"Thirteen at table," Bianca said darkly.

"Don't be absurd, Bianca. That's a peasant superstition," Helen returned sharply. Meanwhile, Rex had solved the problem quite neatly by offering an arm each to Dora and to me and making it seem as if we were doing him a tremendous favour.

The table was set as beautifully as any in England—in fact, the entire house might have been spirited over by fairies, and I placed myself firmly in Helen's good graces by telling her so.

"Oh, you are sweet!" she said breathily. "I designed it, you know. Well, I helped Rex. He's so clever," she added with a coo down the table in his direction. "We shopped for months in Paris and London to get just the right furnishings. Wait until you see my bathtub—pink quartz! So audacious it was even featured in *Tatler.* Of course, it took ages to have it all shipped over, but it is absolutely my dream house, right to the last detail." She promised to give us a tour later, and then dinner was served.

The food was good and the wine impeccable, but something seemed slightly off with the company. There were undercurrents of tension I didn't quite understand. In any close group of people there are bound to be secret resentments, and this group was closer than most. With the exception of Ryder and a few farming families, they represented the whole of white society in the little valley. There would be unspoken alliances in such a gathering, and doubtless unspoken annoyances as well.

But little things could fester in the African heat, and I wondered if any small thorn prick had been left to turn septic. I watched Bianca's small dark eyes following Gervase with a feverish intensity. When she touched him, there was ownership in those caresses. I also saw Jude and her aunt Sybil work hard not to exchange a single word the entire evening. I was only a little surprised Jude was still living with her husband after he had beaten her. I had known my share of women mistreated by their men. But they were all tormented creatures, with eyes like caged animals and a tightly wound intensity that burned them inside. Jude was different, cool as a mountain lake, and I suspected she stayed with Wickenden because his beatings couldn't really touch her. Perhaps that was *why* he beat her. Some men can only stand to be ignored for so long before they have to do something about it.

The soup was handed around by native servants wearing red fezzes and long white robes. They gave us little cups of consommé, and I dipped in my spoon, sighing in pleasure as I tasted it.

"The secret is eggshells," Helen told me. "That's how you clarify it. I'll give you the recipe for your cook."

Dora snickered into her soup, but I thanked Helen politely. Talk then turned to kitchen help and servants in general and how difficult it was to put together a competent staff.

"Of course, the language problem always gets in the way," Helen said. "I can spend an entire morning trying to make them understand exactly what I want and end up with nothing more than a headache for my pains!"

"Why don't you learn some of their language?" I asked.

The table went quiet for a moment, then erupted in laughter.

"You are optimistic, Miss Drummond," the missionary Halliwell put in, not unkindly. "In any given household, there may be a Somali or Egyptian who speaks French or Arabic, a number of local tribesmen who speak their own languages, and some coastal folk who speak Swahili. Is a householder expected to learn all of these tongues just to be master of his own home? Far better for them to learn a little English, don't you think?"

His argument wasn't unreasonable, but it put my back up just the same. Before I could respond, Gervase looked up from the plate of duck that had been put in front of him.

"Typical clergyman," he said lightly. "Would it suit you best if they were all speaking Latin and begging for the Host?"

Mr. Halliwell's gentle expression did not falter. "Not at all. I accept that not all of them will be saved, but I live in hope, Gervase. As I live in hope that you, too, will come into the fold."

Gervase rolled his eyes toward me. "Lawrence cannot bear having an atheist in the herd."

"On the contrary," Halliwell returned quietly. "I consider you to be a testimony to God's faith that whatever questions you might raise, I am sufficient to answer."

Bianca's eyes flashed. "He does not require your answers."

"Now really, Bianca," Miss Halliwell said, putting her fork down. "There's no call to be rude just because Lawrence is doing his job."

"His job?" Bianca's upper lip curled a bit. She wasn't a particularly attractive woman, but she did scorn well.

"Yes, his job," Miss Halliwell said firmly. "And furthermore—"

"Oh, will the lot of you shut up before you give me indigestion?" Sybil Balfour spoke up sharply. She reached down under the table and pulled out a tiffin box which she proceeded to fill with the contents of her dinner plate.

"Sybil, darling, you do a better job at hostessing my parties than I do!" Helen said, almost sincerely. She looked to me. "Sybil has a frightful cook. He prepares everything out of tins and even then he's a menace. How many times has he poisoned you now, Sybil?"

"Seven," the older woman put in promptly. She motioned to the doctor who reluctantly gave up half of his portion of duck for her tiffin box.

"If he's so awful, why do you keep him?" I asked.

Sybil shrugged. "Obligation. I saved his life once. Nasty business with a snake. Anyway, he believes he's indebted to me and won't leave. He thinks he's a fine cook, and I haven't the heart to tell him otherwise. If it weren't for the leftovers from Helen's dinner parties, I'd never get a decent meal at Nyama."

I passed her my dinner roll for her tiffin box and she gave me a gruff nod.

Dessert was a fig gratin, and with it came small glasses of Sauternes, the pale gold wine gleaming under the soft lights.

"Château d'Yquem," Helen said. "I ordered it when I thought Ryder might be coming, but he begged off. Always out adventuring, we never know if he'll turn up or not. He sends his regards to everyone."

If anyone thought it strange that Ryder and Wickenden should be expected to meet socially so soon after the railway station thrashing, no one said a word. Wickenden went on quietly consuming his food, chewing quite slowly, perhaps because of the molar Ryder had knocked out. Only Sybil showed a reaction, a tiny smile she could not quite suppress. Jude looked as remote as ever, and I wondered if she was even grateful to Ryder for what he had done.

"Probably out with the Kukes again," the doctor put in.

I looked up and Rex smiled at me. "Ryder is famous in these parts for his devotion to the native tribes. Although I think you've got it wrong there, Bunny. He's a Masai man, through and through."

The doctor shrugged. "As if one needed to know the difference."

"I'm surprised anyone could confuse them," I offered. "There are Kikuyu and Masai both at Fairlight and they don't look at all alike, not really." The Kikuyu were shorter, with rounder faces and limbs for the most part, while Gideon was tall and slender, his muscles long, his face fine-boned.

"Perhaps not," the doctor conceded, "but they are all troublesome devils."

I glanced about the table to find mixed reactions—boredom from the women, studied nonchalance from the men and a glimmer of warning from Dora not to start trouble. Kit alone was watching me with something like amused anticipation. It was the same expression I'd seen on my grandfather before he headed out to watch a cockfight.

"If they're troublesome perhaps it's because white people brought the trouble to them."

Mr. Halliwell put down his fork. "An excellent point, Miss Drummond. Certainly the arrival of whites in the colony has changed the balance of power. But there were always conflicts, always warfare and bloodshed amongst these people. Why, even during our Great War, the Masai and the Bantu fought a vicious war that is still talked about. It is our duty to show them another way."

"Bloody nonsense," the doctor said, raising his glass to drink deeply. It was his fourth and the more he drank the more his hands shook. I made a mental note to stay healthy while I was in Africa. There was no way I wanted those plump trembling hands anywhere near me. "They've no understanding and no capacity for understanding. The kindest thing is to keep them in a place where they can be watched over by those who know best and left to sort out their own troubles." He turned to me with a sly look. "I think you Americans had the right idea putting your natives onto reservations. It's worked out well enough for you lot, hasn't it?"

I ignored him and directed my attention to our

host. "You've been here the longest, Rex. Do you agree that we have a moral duty to civilize the natives? Or do you think they ought to be pushed onto reservations?" I asked.

He paused and when he spoke, his answer was thoughtfully crafted. "I think the question of duty is one for men in comfortable London meeting rooms to debate. Out here there is only the truth."

"And what is the truth?" I persisted.

"That Africa is a hard place, a very hard place. But it is full of promise, a land of such immense beauty and possibility that every man is a new Adam. Those who have lived here for centuries have lived simply, too simply. The land is not managed, and because of this, disease and animals take their toll upon the population and poverty runs rampant. We can fix that and we must if the whites are to thrive here. We are the builders of empire, my dear. We bring roads and schools, medicine and good food. We have the power to save the lives of children and, if we're lucky, to put a few pounds in the bank against a rainy day. We can make a better life for everyone in Africa, and we need not choose to be either saints or devils to do it," he added, looking from the doctor to the missionary. "We are but men, the sons of Seth, inheritors of this vast new Eden, this little paradise."

It reeked of Shakespeare, but it was a good speech altogether. The doctor raised his glass high and shouted, "The sons of Seth!" slurring only slightly on the *s*'s.

Everyone else joined in the toast, and when it was drunk, Helen waggled a flirtatious finger at her husband. "And don't you leave us out, Rex. It's not just the men who will make over Africa. We women have a role to play, too."

"Of course you do, my darling," he said with a fond smile. "For without the inspiration of woman, what man has ever accomplished anything?"

She simpered at this piece of gallantry and in the wake of it, I turned to Rex again.

"Speaking of the role of women, I'd like to buy a milk cow."

He raised his brows. "Fancy starting your own dairy herd? Do you know anything about cattle?"

I shrugged. "What's to learn? They all have four legs and give milk and when they don't you can shoot them and eat them for dinner."

Bianca gave a little scream and covered her mouth with her hands, but Jude Wickenden laughed aloud, the first sound I had heard out of her all evening.

Rex smiled, his laugh lines creasing handsomely. "Dairy cattle take quite a bit more attention than beef cattle. I have an excellent book on starting a dairy herd if you're interested, although I'd be more than happy to sell you as much milk as you could possibly need for your little household."

"Oh, it isn't for us. It's for the Kikuyu labourers."

The room went silent. Even the music from the gramophone seemed suddenly softer. Everyone's eyes fixed on me, and I could have guessed what they were thinking. Only the doctor dared say it aloud.

"You'll spoil those devils if you give them milk. They can get their own and if they can't, well, it's nature's way, isn't it? Culling the herd."

Rex ignored him. "In that case you'd be better off with a few head of native cattle. They'll be more resistant to disease and the locals will like the milk better. It has a more pungent taste than what our European dairy cattle give. Take my advice and get a boy to tend them as well, preferably a Masai. I can arrange it with one of the natives if you like."

I don't know what made me resist. It would have been simpler just to leave it in Rex's hands. But before I could do the easy thing, my mouth interrupted. "Thank you, but I think I'll try it on my own first."

Anthony Wickenden snorted into his glass, and Sybil Balfour shot him an evil look.

"Glad to hear it," she boomed at me from her end of the table. "Too many women come out here and forget they've got brains of their own." She looked from Bianca to Helen, and the latter gave a bright peal of laughter.

"Guilty as charged, Sybil. I don't do anything but set a nice table and make sure the guest room is made up for travellers."

"I know precisely what you do," Sybil shot back, and I saw that Rex was watching them both closely.

"I am practicing my hostessing for when I'm first lady of Kenya," Helen said, wrinkling her nose at Sybil.

I looked at Rex. "Do you have aspirations to be governor?"

"Governor!" It was Anthony Wickenden, talking with a little difficulty through his swollen lips. They seemed to have stiffened up during the meal. "He means to be president."

I looked curiously at her, but Rex merely waved a hand. "Helen, I think it's time to cut Anthony off," he said with a twinkle. He turned to me. "Our great hope is that London will extend to Kenya the same status it has conferred upon Rhodesia—that of a free nation."

"I heard some talk about that as I was coming in. Isn't that why Governor Kendall is in England right now?"

Rex nodded. "Yes, pleading our case before the Parliamentary committee. We are every bit as educated and devoted to Africa as the landowners in Rhodesia, and we fought just as hard in the Great War to support the mother country. We deserve our shot at self-determination."

"It sounds like a reasonable enough request. Will they grant it?"

"They are politicians," Gervase said bitterly. "When were politicians ever reasonable?"

Rex was more generous. "Now, Gervase, that isn't entirely fair. They listened to the Rhodesians and they responded. We can only hope they do the same for us."

"They might if it weren't for the bloody Indians," the doctor interjected.

Yet again I ignored him and turned to Rex as he explained. "What the doctor means is that during the Great War, India supported England, as you must know." He hesitated, touching only lightly on my own involvement in that terrible time. "There are a great many Indians here, running shops, building railways. They are almost all merchants or labourers. But they want to own land, and under the current laws they cannot. India is pushing the government in London to grant them ownership rights and to keep Kenya as a crown colony. Naturally, we oppose this."

I remembered what the ship's captain had told me as we approached the teeming harbor at Mombasa. "But if they are business owners surely—"

I hadn't even finished before the doctor cut me off. "One cannot expect an American to be sensible about these things!"

"Yes, we know nothing about colonies and revolution," I said sweetly.

Rex threw back his head and roared with laughter. "Hoist with your own petard, Bunny." He covered my hand lightly with his own. "I'm glad you're taking an interest in what will become of us. I know you don't mean to stay forever, but I do hope we will have the pleasure of your company for some time to come."

He removed his hand then, but the warmth of it lingered on my skin and when I looked up, Helen was regarding me thoughtfully.

Kit rose then and lifted his glass. "To both of our enchanting new additions," he said, graciously including Dora in his salute. The rest of the company joined in and Dora and I clinked glasses merrily across the table. I sipped deeply from the Sauternes, thinking that if Rex could run a country as well as he could stock a wine cellar, Kenya wouldn't have a thing to worry about.

Rex rose. "And another toast, to Bianca and Gervase, who are leaving us tomorrow. Safe journey, my friends."

Everyone drank, and I turned to the Pembertons. "Where are you bound? Safari?"

Bianca's only reply was another curl of her lip, but Gervase was more forthcoming.

"We're going down to the coast. Our place is farthest up the valley, and the altitude isn't good for Bianca's blood pressure. Once a year we take a rest and go down to sea level."

"Ryder has a house in Lamu," Helen put in. "It's

a divine old ruin, once the palace of an Arab slave trader! It's terribly haunted by ghosts and djinns and that sort of thing, but it's perched on the loveliest spot overlooking the ocean. It makes for a wonderful escape, and Ryder is a dear about loaning the place to any of his friends desperate to get down to sea level."

"He must be a popular fellow," I said mildly.

Helen gave a peal of laughter. "Oh, my dear, he's legend! If you'd stayed in Nairobi any longer you'd have heard some of the stories."

"Most of them far too scandalous for a respectable dinner table," Miss Halliwell put in, her lips prim.

"Oh, he isn't as bad as all that," Helen said, flapping a hand at her. "He's just high-spirited. For instance," she said, turning her attention to me, "every year at Christmas everyone gathers at the club. It's a wonderful time, so many people from all over the colony meeting up with old friends, the parties, the dances! Well, at one of the formal dinners, everyone was having a marvelous time when all of a sudden, the club steward comes in shrieking something about a lion out in the street."

I lifted a brow. "A lion. *In* Nairobi?" I glanced around the table, but Rex was nodding.

"There was. A young male. Nasty piece of work, too."

Helen picked up the tale, breathless and wide-eyed. "Well, everyone was so stunned, they just sat like statues, they simply couldn't move! But not Ryder. He got up and walked straight to the nearest gun rack, took down a rifle and strode right into the street and shot that lion dead!"

Rex leaned near. "The story made it as far as the English papers because he was wearing full evening dress at the time."

I gave him a little push. "Now I know you're teasing."

"Not at all," he protested. "I'll dig the clipping out after dinner."

Good as his word, after we'd adjourned to the drawing room for a little dancing to the gramophone, Rex appeared at my elbow with an album, a sort of scrapbook of the colony. There were pages devoted to the races and the Christmas festivities in Nairobi with photographs of smiling people and newspaper clippings detailing the silly pranks they played on one another, some of them straight out of the schoolroom. But here and there were other clippings, sober reminders of lives lost too early, death notices and mentions of accidents and misfortunes.

"A hard place, your Africa," I said softly.

Rex gave me a gentle smile. "But worth every life it takes, and so many more."

"You really love it here, don't you?"

The elegant silvering brows rose. "Of course. I know you don't understand that yet. How could you? Africa is brutal, but you will come to love her, in spite of the brutality. Perhaps even because of it."

He turned the page then and pulled out a loose clipping. He handed it to me with a smile. There were two photographs with the article. One featured the lion, stretched out on the bar of the Norfolk Hotel, dripping blood onto the polished wood. Everyone was packed around it in their evening finery, raising glasses in a toast to the narrow escape they'd had. Only Ryder was absent. The second photo was of him on his own. He was wearing his evening clothes, and was only half-turned towards the camera, as if someone had called his name and he had lifted his head in response.

"He wouldn't let them photograph him with the lion," Rex told me. "Thought it was all the most awful palaver. I don't even think he kept the claws off that one."

"The claws?"

"Oh, yes. Bit of a tradition of his. Every big cat he takes, lion or leopard, he takes a claw or tooth to put onto a bracelet he wears. Not as a trophy, mind you. He says it's to remind him that every life out here counts for something and shouldn't be forgot. Oh, dear. Bunny seems to have found the single malt. Do excuse me."

He took the album with him but the clipping was still in my hand. I looked down at the photographs, the laughing, lively faces crowded around the atrocity of the dead lion. There was something faintly obscene about it, and I was absurdly glad that Ryder hadn't been a part of it. Then I thought of the bracelet he wore, each tooth or claw representing a different animal he had killed, and I shivered a little.

"What's the matter? Goose walk over your grave?" Kit's voice was warm in my ear.

"You try wearing a backless evening gown," I said, turning quickly. "You'd shiver, too." I dropped the clipping to the table behind me and tucked my arm into his. "Come dance with me. I seem to remember your form is as good on the dance floor as it is in other places."

He laughed and swung me into his arms.

# 10

The next morning Dora hunted me down when I was having a bath to talk about the house.

"It's really in deplorable shape," she said, arranging my toilet articles on a tray and primly averting her eyes as I soaped up. "Most of the books are riddled with worms, there are moths in the upholstery and white ants seem to be devouring the wallpaper."

"Take it down. I hate wallpaper."

"But it isn't our house," she pointed out. "It's Sir Nigel's."

"Nigel has let it go to rack and ruin," I reminded her. "The whole place needs a good turning out and to be scrubbed from top to bottom. Let's make a list."

She fetched pencil and paper and by the time we were finished with projects—wood to be polished, floors to be scrubbed, baths to be disinfected, beds to be turned out—it ran to three pages of Dora's tidy little handwriting.

"Now make another," I ordered her. This list was purely for me. I had her outline my plans to keep dairy cattle for the workers and plow under a few of the struggling old pyrethrum fields for growing vegetables. "And chickens," I added. "There ought to be chickens for fresh eggs. That means building a henhouse and a secure pen. Do lions eat chickens?"

She blinked at me. "Good heavens, how would I know?"

I stood up and she turned away again, applying herself to the list. "But that means purchasing lumber and wire and nails . . ." She trailed off, writing busily.

"Not necessarily. We haven't prowled through the outbuildings yet. The barn alone is probably stuffed with old junk. We might find what we need there."

"We'd better," she said grimly. "What you're talking about will cost money—money we don't have."

I shrugged as I towelled myself dry. "I'll think of something."

"You usually do."

After breakfast I was pleased to find the little Kikuyu mother with her child sitting outside in the shade of the veranda, waiting for me. I removed the child's bandage gently and was satisfied to find the wound healing nicely with no sign of fresh infection. I redressed it and mimed that she was to continue doing as she had done. She nodded, smiling her beautiful calm smile.

Suddenly, the smile faltered, and I realised she was looking over my shoulder. Behind me stood a man I hadn't met before, and as soon as I turned, he pulled off his hat.

"Miss Drummond! I cannot tell you how sorry I am I wasn't here to welcome you properly to Fairlight. My wife and I had taken the little ones to the sea for a bit of bathing."

He gestured towards a pale woman—unlikely in this climate—and a pair of unwholesome-looking children. The woman nodded and the children simply stood silent, the boy picking enthusiastically at his nose while the little girl stared at me and breathed through her mouth.

"You must be Mr. Gates," I said. I didn't bother to extend a hand. I had no desire to touch any of them and I was highly put out that he hadn't been here to receive us.

"I am, I am. And this is Mrs. Gates," he added unnecessarily. "And our boy, Reuben and our daughter, Jonquil."

Jonquil! It was a surprisingly exotic name for such an ordinary child. No doubt they'd taken one look at the boy and pinned all their hopes on the second child. I thought of asking if the children were simple-minded, but it seemed unkind.

"I would like to discuss the state of the farm with you, Mr. Gates. Kindly make yourself available this afternoon."

His skin had been burned to umber by the African sun, but under the tan his colour was sickly, and sweat rolled from his brow. The tic of a tiny muscle near his eye kept a regular beat. He was nervous.

"Of course, Miss Drummond. Although I did understand from Sir Nigel that you were here for rest and relaxation. We certainly don't intend for you to wear yourself out with things you needn't trouble over."

And there it was. The sharp metallic scent of his fear was in the air. I could smell it in his sweat, and I smiled, making quite certain it didn't reach my eyes.

"Mr. Gates, I do not find rest to be relaxing. I like to be busy and I think here at Fairlight there will be much to keep me occupied."

The wife darted a glance at her husband and tightened her hands.

He gave me a fawning smile. "Of course, of course. I do understand. And naturally whatever I can do to help . . ."

He let the sentence trail off, but I pounced.

"Actually, you can. I want to know if there is scrap lumber on the premises. I want to build a henhouse. You can organise some labourers to put it together."

"A henhouse?"

"For chickens," I said slowly.

"Yes, I understand." He was getting rattled. There was a slight edge to his voice now, a resentment he couldn't contain anymore, and I saw the wife shift another quick glance at him. I had no doubt he took his bad moods out on her. She looked like the sort of woman who was accustomed to catching the rough side of a man's tongue. Of course, I couldn't blame him. Her cringing made me want to slap her myself. "You want to keep chickens?" he asked.

"Yes. And I want the barn cleaned out and a pasture staked for a few dairy cattle. When that's sorted, I want to plow under the two fields closest to the road. The pyrethrum crop is nearly unsalvageable there. The land looks exhausted. We can buy loads of manure from the Masai and till it in and plant it with vegetables and maize to make our own *shamba*. Between the milk and the eggs and the fresh vegetables, we should get these people looking a far sight healthier."

"You mean to feed the farmworkers?"

"I do. And I have a mind to take a closer look at the pyrethrum crop as well. This much land under planting ought to yield a far better amount than I saw reported in the farm books."

He held up a hand. "Miss Drummond, I must insist that you let me handle this. Farm work is man's business."

I snorted. "Not where I come from. My great-grandmother is past ninety and still she manages a sugar plantation that runs to twenty thousand acres. She tends cattle, delivers babies, keeps the books and she cracks the whip on anybody who gets out of line, including her six sons. Now, I would like to know more about Fairlight and I think you are the man to tell me. So, why don't you plan on meeting me this afternoon and we'll sort some things out?"

I smiled again and walked off before he had a chance to reply. Around the corner, Ryder was waiting on the veranda. He was settled into one of the planter's chairs, his booted legs resting comfortably on the long arms of the chair.

"Good morning. I see you've been getting acquainted with the help."

I shook my head. "I dislike that man, and those children look like they ought to have been drowned at birth. But I don't want to talk about the walking farce that is the Gates family. You're late. The Kikuyu have been and gone."

He rose and pointed toward the tins of powdered milk stacked on the veranda. With them were a large bottle of castor oil and another of vitamins, and a fresh tin of antiseptic powder.

I prowled through the pile, happy to find sacks of dried beans and rice as well as a wide basket of fresh produce, onions and gourds mostly.

"Well done," I told him, brushing back my fringe. "What do I owe you?"

He stood the barest inch too close. "Consider it a housewarming present."

"I think I'll pay my own way. What do I owe you?"

He smiled then and eased back a step. "I'll tally it up later."

"If you're sure. I'd hate for you to lose any

more money on my account," I said sweetly.

He would have been a good poker player. I had beaten him at his own game, and he didn't like it much, but there wasn't a damned thing he could do but swallow it whole.

Just then Gideon appeared, carrying another tin of powdered milk. "Good morning, *Bibi*," he said in his lightly accented English.

I raised my brows and he gave me a broad smile. "You would say '*Habari za asubuhi.*'"

He repeated it half a dozen times before I got the pronunciation right, but eventually I got my tongue around it. "Very good, *Bibi*. Now, I have heard that you would like to purchase a cow. *Bwana* Ryder and I will take you."

"Gideon, I think Mr. Bell wouldn't have bothered with the telephone if he'd had any experience with the marvels of the African bush. Yes, I would like to buy a cow, a very fine Masai cow."

He shook his head. "This thing is not possible, *Bibi*. A Masai will not sell his cow."

I thought of a peculiar Hindu gentleman I had met in London. We had spent the better part of an otherwise deadly dull dinner party chatting about India and his curious beliefs as I lapped up a steak and he pushed vegetables around his plate. The light came on.

"I understand. Cows are sacred to Masai."

Gideon gave a hoot of laughter. "No. Cows are

money, *Bibi*. They are worth far more than whatever you could think to exchange for them. But the Kikuyu keep cattle, too, and they do not respect the cattle as the Masai. They will take your money."

"Lead on," I told him.

He shouldered his spear and we walked together as Ryder fell in behind us. I remembered much of what he had told me the day before and I pointed out various plants to Gideon, trying out their Swahili names. A warthog ran across the path. "*Ngiri*," I said triumphantly.

"*Ngiri*," Gideon affirmed.

I smiled at him, and when he smiled back I felt a curious tug. It wasn't just a smile from a handsome man. I collected those like other women collected air to breathe. This was something altogether different. There was a gentleness in Gideon, a simple way of looking at the world. He was unencumbered by the silly and the trivial. There was nothing petty about him. His world was bound by death and blood, and life itself was short and sharp as a thorn, cheap as dirt and as precious as diamonds. It is a rare thing to find a man who wears his pride without vanity, but Gideon was such a man. I wanted suddenly to know everything about him, to drink up everything he knew to the last drop. Fate had given him the gift of serenity, and I envied him bitterly.

I looked sharply away and he went on, reciting

the musical words of Swahili for me as one might teach a child. "This is how you say 'fire' . . ."

Cattle-dealing in Africa is the same as the world over. We found a Kikuyu willing to sell a few cows and their calves, and after poking into their mouths and feeling their udders, Gideon negotiated a price. There was much discussion I didn't understand and much staring on the part of the Kikuyu children. They were a little awed by a Masai warrior, but a white woman in trousers was really something.

When we were finished, Ryder and Gideon talked a moment before Gideon turned to me.

"You must have a boy to watch your cattle. I know such a boy. Would you come with us to where I live?"

I accepted, and we set out on what turned out to be a long and dusty walk.

Ryder seemed to have recovered a little of his good humour and as we trudged through the bush, Gideon spoke. "*Bwana*, this is a thing that I know . . ." It was a game they played when they were out walking, Gideon told me. It always began with one of them saying, "This is a thing that I know," followed by some truth, a fact or bit of philosophy. Then the other took his turn, either arguing the point or contributing something of his own.

"Would you care to play, *Bibi*?" Gideon asked.

"I will start. This is a thing that I know—that the droppings of two animals will disturb the cattle—the lion and the ostrich."

"The lion I can well believe, but the ostrich? Really?"

"Oh, yes," Gideon assured me. "The ostrich is no friend to the cattle. Now, you must tell us a thing that you know."

"Very well. This is a thing that I know—that Ryder saved my life by shooting a buffalo on the drive to Fairlight."

Ryder's head came up sharply, and Gideon stopped. "*Bwana*, how big was this buffalo?"

Ryder didn't look at him, but kept his eyes fixed on mine. I watched his Adam's apple bob as he swallowed hard. "The spread of the horns was over four feet."

"That is very, very big, *Bwana*," Gideon pronounced. "It is an excellent thing that you saved *Bibi*'s life."

Still Ryder didn't look away. "We saved each other," he said quietly. Then he turned sharply on his heel and stalked away.

Gideon and I followed, and Gideon called ahead. "*Bwana*, this is a thing that I know—that you carry many poems in your mind. Will you speak one for us?"

Ryder shook his head, never slackening his pace. "Not now."

I leaned closer to Gideon. "He writes poetry?"

180

"Oh, no, *Bibi*. He remembers the poems that other men have written. He carries them in his head, and sometimes he speaks them."

I couldn't quite take it in. I stared ahead at the broad back, the rifle slung over his shoulder, the glint of gold in the rings in his ears. "No, really. Ryder recites poetry?"

Gideon nodded. "And the periodic table of elements. I have learned only as far as rubidium. I have much left to know."

I was still trying to get my head around the idea of Ryder with a head full of poetry and Gideon learning the periodic table when we arrived at a small village so primitive it was like something out of the Stone Age. A wide-open area under some acacia trees had been cordoned off with great bundles of thorn.

"To keep the cattle safe from the lion," Gideon informed me.

I nodded. "It makes sense. I ought to do the same around the pasture I'm clearing at Fairlight."

"The barn will be all that is required, so long as you have a good boy to watch the cows," he said. "A good boy who will not fall asleep and let the lion steal in and take what does not belong to him."

He led us into the enclosure of the *boma* and to a mud hut. It looked black as pitch inside, and Gideon stood in the doorway, calling respectfully to the occupant. After a moment there was a dry, shuffling sound, like the rustling of autumn leaves, and an elderly man came to the doorway. He was wearing the Masai toga—which Gideon had told me was called a *kanja*—and several slender leather thongs looped about his neck. They were beaded, as were the heavy ornaments in his ears, and perched on the tip of his nose were a pair of thick, round spectacles, giving him the look of a curious owl. In spite of the warmth of the day, he was wrapped in a sort of cloak of long, greyish fur.

He lifted his hands to Gideon's strong shoulders and spoke to him in rapid Maa. Gideon returned the greeting, and the old man did the same to Ryder, holding his head briefly in his withered hands. Gideon turned to me.

"*Bibi*, this is my *babu*, my grandfather. He is a respected elder amongst my people."

Ryder was at my side. "The *babu* speaks only a little Swahili, but he will understand your greeting of '*shikamoo*.' A respectful way to address him is as *Mzee*."

I bowed my head to the small, leathery man. "*Shikamoo, Mzee*."

He raised his hand in a gesture very similar to one a priest might make. "*Marahaba*."

"He thanks you for your respectful greetings," Gideon told me.

The grandfather invited us in and Gideon led the way into the hut. The first thing I noticed was the stench. It was like walking into the deepest corner of a barn that hadn't been cleaned in a century. There were mixed odours of mud and dung and smoke from the cooking fire, which had only a small hole in the ceiling for ventilation. A woman moved around with a battered pot and after a moment we were served calabashes full of bitter, milky tea that smelled and tasted of woodsmoke. I was only relieved it wasn't more blood and milk, and I took it gratefully as we seated ourselves around the fire.

Gideon and Ryder chatted with the grandfather while I looked the place over. A Spartan might have found it bare. There was a cowhide pallet in a corner and a small shelf for cooking utensils. And that was it. Just a few square yards of beaten earth, walls of mud and dung, and a roof of woven grasses. But Gideon's *babu* seemed content, and as the conversation wore on, Gideon informed me that his *babu* was a comfortably wealthy man for a Masai. He had many cattle, fine cattle, and he was proud of them. Ryder explained to him that I had just bought cattle myself and the *babu* responded with a burst of chatter.

"He wants to know if you have experience with cows." Gideon was suppressing a smile, and I figured the old fellow was testing me. The Masai might not make a practice of selling cows, but Gideon had explained that they believed every cow on earth was theirs by divine right.

183

I fixed the *babu* with a firm but respectful gaze. "I am experienced, *Mzee*. My own *babu* is also a man who owns many cows."

"He wants to know how many," Ryder related.

I told him the number and the old man dropped his head into his hands, shaking it and moaning a little.

Gideon laughed. "He says that is a very great number, a greater number than any Masai owns. He says your *babu* must be a man of extraordinary good fortune. And this good fortune must have fallen to you as well. He is happy that the cows will be entrusted to you and he says that my young brother has his permission to come and tend your cows for you."

"Your brother? Is he here now? Can I meet him?"

"Moses is at the mission school today," Gideon said proudly. "He is very smart and he is good at his lessons. But I will bring him to you soon and you will have a good boy to mind your cows."

We chatted longer, drinking our foul tea and communicating through sign language and Gideon. It was the nicest tea party I had had in an age, and I sighed a little as I dusted myself off when we rose to leave.

Gideon's *babu* stopped at the doorway and shook his head as he looked at me.

"What?" I turned to Ryder.

"He says there is a spirit that follows you—a sad

man with eyes that are grey, like the sky during the long rains. Do you know such a person?"

I could not speak so I merely shook my head.

The *babu* spoke again, more insistently.

Gideon interpreted. "He says it is so. The man with the grey eyes wears a uniform, like a soldier or policeman, and he watches you, *Bibi*. My *babu* has powerful magic. He can banish the spirit if you wish."

"Don't bother," I said bitterly. "He can't hurt me anymore."

Ryder and Gideon walked me back to Fairlight. This time Ryder walked ahead, his shoulders set and his jaw hard. Something was needling him, but I couldn't imagine what. I left him to his thoughts and chatted with Gideon. He told me about his plans to marry when he was no longer a warrior.

"It is our way, *Bibi*. A warrior, a *moran*, has work to do. He works hard for many years, from the time of his circumcision when he becomes a man and puts away his childish ways. Only when his work is finished and he becomes an elder is he permitted to take a wife and have children."

"And you have a young lady in mind?"

He looked a little bashful. "I do. I think her father and mother will be happy for us to marry."

"Do you get on well together?"

He nodded. "She is strong and smart and will build a fine house and bear many sons, I think."

He paused then added, "She is very quiet. I do not know what she thinks of. But perhaps a warrior is not meant to know the thoughts of women."

"Is she pretty?" I teased him.

His expression was sober, but I noticed his eyes smiled even if his mouth did not.

"Pretty like the first sunrise after a deep rain," he said.

"A poetic sentiment, Gideon. Have you told her that's what you think of her?"

He shook his head. "A warrior should not speak so freely of such things to women. I should not have told you."

"Some things ought to be said. Tell her. I promise she won't be quiet if she knows how much you admire her."

"I should talk to this woman? Tell her my inmost thoughts?"

"Yes. Trust me, Gideon. I've been married three times. I know what works and what doesn't."

"Three times! And you are a widow? All three of your husbands are dead?"

"No. Just two. The second one is still alive back in England. I divorced him."

He shook his head again. "It is a bad thing to put away one's husband, but sometimes it must be done. Did he mistreat you?"

"Not in the way some husbands do. He didn't beat me."

"Was he given to drink?"

I smiled. "Not as much as I am. It was a matter of trust. He thought I betrayed him."

"Betrayed him?"

"He thought I was unfaithful to him with another man."

Gideon clucked his tongue. "This is a bad thing, too."

"Not always," I advised him. "But in this case my husband was wrong. He believed gossip and lies over my word. And since he could not believe in me, I left him."

"Did he learn that you were innocent?"

"When it was too late. And I wouldn't take him back then because I am stubborn and proud and because we would have failed at being married eventually. But it was a lesson to him. We are great friends now because he knows he can trust me completely."

"Why do you not marry him again?"

"He has another wife. And children now."

"Fine sons?"

"One. And a twin daughter."

"Daughters are good. Daughters care for the cattle and build the houses and take care of the ones who need them."

"And what do warriors do?" I asked with a smile.

He smiled back. "We protect, *Bibi*. It is what we do."

# 11

When we reached Fairlight, Ryder turned down the path to his *boma* without a backward glance. Gideon walked me into the garden where the clergyman Halliwell was standing chatting with Dora.

"Look, Delilah, Mr. Halliwell has brought us oranges!" she said, brandishing a basket of bright round green fruit.

"Our African oranges are green," he explained. "My sister thought you might enjoy them. She bought a bushel only this morning and wanted to be a good neighbour. Hello, Gideon," he said, a trifle more slowly. "I hope you've been a help to Miss Drummond." He turned to me. "Gideon was educated at our mission school. One of the brightest youngsters to come through our doors."

He had a fatuous smile, as if it never occurred to him that a fully grown Masai warrior ought not to be spoken to as if he were of no more significance than a lapdog. There was a casually dismissive air about his attitude.

"Gideon has been most instructive," I said sharply. "He took me to meet his grandfather."

Halliwell gave me a gentle shake of the head. "Tread with caution, Miss Drummond. Native ways are inscrutable to a mind that loves Jesus."

"Well, I never claimed to love Jesus, Mr. Halliwell. In fact, we're barely acquainted."

Dora cut in swiftly. "Where are my manners? Mr. Halliwell, will you join us for some tea on the veranda?"

He agreed and I turned to Gideon. He was watching me closely, and as the clergyman moved away with Dora, Gideon pitched his voice low. "Do not wear your anger like a mask, *Bibi*. His kind are simple as children. They cannot help what they do not know."

I gave him a broad smile. "I know you will not accept food or drink from me, but there is a fellow working in the kitchen. I hope you will take something from him before you make the journey home again."

He nodded and gave me a wave as he headed to the kitchen. I joined Dora and Halliwell on the veranda. Dora passed me a glass of lemon squash with a warning glance. I rolled my eyes at her, and took a seat, stretching out my booted legs onto the arms of the planter's chair as Ryder had done.

"It's lovely country for walking, isn't it?" Halliwell offered. I thawed a little then, and we fell to discussing the countryside. "Of course, one must always be careful of the wildlife, but it gives a fillip of excitement to one's existence, I find. Danger lurks around every thornbush here. I am always telling Evelyn to be cautious when she goes out to paint."

"Is she an artist?" Dora inquired politely.

"After a fashion. She does like to try to capture the landscapes here, so different from our native Kent. But she makes no claim to talent like Mr. Parrymore."

"Kit's talent is extraordinary," I agreed. "He has developed tremendously as an artist since the time I knew him in New York."

Halliwell sat forward eagerly. "His paintings are so full of life, of vibrancy—don't you find? They almost seem to have a pulse, they are so alive."

Dora sipped at her lemon squash while I lit a cigarette. "You surprise me, Mr. Halliwell. I wouldn't have expected a clergyman to feel so strongly about art."

He laughed. "I admit I do not have the same calling as many of my fellow men of the cloth. It was a decision of my parents' making. We were brought up on a small estate outside of Canterbury. Our elder brother was the heir, of course, and Evelyn and I were made to follow the plan our parents laid out. I was sent into the church and she was to keep house for me. But our first love was always art. Alas, I was never given proper tuition in the subject, so my technique has never developed. Evelyn received some very rudimentary training from a drawing master for a few months. I'm afraid that is the extent of our formal education," he added, his expression rueful.

I could tell Dora was about to say something pointlessly soothing, so I cut in.

"Why didn't you run away?"

He blinked, like a rabbit just up from his hole. "I beg your pardon?"

I took a long pull on my cigarette just to heighten the moment. "Why didn't you run away? Take your life in your own hands and make what you wanted out of it?"

He stared at me for a long minute, no doubt as mystified as if I had been speaking Mandarin.

At last he laughed again, apparently deciding I was harmless and perhaps a little mentally defective. "My dear lady, what a question! How simple you make it sound and how impossible."

"Difficult," I corrected. "Not impossible." Dora stirred beside me, and I didn't have to look at her to know she was wearing her disapproving expression. That's what I always found so tiresome about the English. The long list of Things That Must Not Be Said.

"Not impossible," I repeated. "You simply had to make up your mind to do without your parents' help. Say goodbye to their money and you say goodbye to their interference."

"You are serious," he said slowly.

"As a grave. Nobody should have to do what they don't want just because some moneybags relative makes it so. Purse strings are puppet strings, Mr. Halliwell. They can be cut."

Dora couldn't take it anymore. "She's joking, of course, Mr. Halliwell," she said soothingly. "She doesn't actually believe that or she wouldn't be here herself."

It wasn't like Dora to air the family's dirty linen, but my reasons for being in Africa were common knowledge. It was, however, a symptom of her annoyance with me that she mentioned it.

"Oh, I believe every word of it. I just happen to be a hypocrite." I bared my teeth at Mr. Halliwell in a crocodile smile. "I like nice things and I would be less than useless with a job."

"A job!" He reached for his handkerchief and passed it over his brow. "I should think not. No properly brought up young lady should have to work for money."

"I suppose Evelyn toils away at the mission school purely in hopes of a heavenly reward?"

Dora jumped to her feet. "Mr. Halliwell, have I shown you the changes I'm making to the garden? I should love to have your opinion. No, no, bring your drink. It's too hot to go walking without some refreshment." They left the veranda, but not before she gave me a backward glance that would have scalded milk.

I settled back into my chair to finish my lemon squash and cigarette. I had bought a cow, terrorized the farm manager, and offended the neighbours, I reflected. Not bad for a morning's work.

● ● ●

My afternoon meeting with Gates was less than productive. He had apparently decided on a tactic of unctuous cooperation—at least on the surface. Whatever I suggested he approved enthusiastically, and then a few minutes later, he would casually drop in every reason why what I wanted wasn't feasible. Then I would remind him who had the whip hand and he would fall in line before starting the whole process over again. It was exhausting, but by the time I'd finished with him, he had set a few of the Kikuyu to reinforcing the barn and building a rudimentary henhouse.

I was arguing with him over the size of it when Ryder appeared with a small dead antelope of sorts draped over his shoulders. "Dinner," he said.

"Thank God. We haven't gotten around to replenishing the stores and it's been nothing but flatbreads and boiled eggs."

He carried the antelope to the kitchen while I dismissed Gates, who scurried off with ill grace.

"I don't think he likes you much," Ryder observed.

I grinned. "Good."

Ryder didn't answer my smile. "Be careful. He can be a nasty piece of work."

"Does he beat his wife like your friends do?"

"Anthony Wickenden is not my friend," he said flatly. "And no, that's one sin you can't drop at Gates' door. But he does like to harass the Kukes."

"Why specifically the Kikuyu?"

"Because I've told the Masai to stay out of his way."

"He would treat them worse?"

"Everybody does. The Masai are the lowest on everyone's list, white or African."

"But why?"

"You saw how they live. Mud huts and cow's blood to drink. It doesn't get more primitive than that."

"Ryder, I am accustomed to indoor plumbing, feather beds, vintage wines and fast cars. This is all primitive to me."

He grinned again. "*Touché*. Now, let's finish getting your storeroom sorted."

But rather than heading towards the house, he took the path leading to the road.

"Where are we going?"

"To my *duka*. What I brought was for the Kikuyu. Now it's time to lay in supplies for you. I have everything you need. Including chickens."

He wasn't exaggerating. The little shop was almost an hour's walk from Fairlight, but well worth the journey. A tin roof housed the shop and its deep porch, and on the porch in the shade of that tin roof, a small, plump Indian man with a turban sat at an elderly sewing machine. The fabric flew through his hands as he worked the treadle, and a small monkey perched on top, supervising. When we approached, the man jumped up and shouted into the building as he came to greet us.

"Mr. Ryder! And the lady of Fairlight!"

"Makes me sound like something out of Tennyson," I murmured to Ryder.

Ryder introduced me properly to Mr. Patel and the fellow pumped my hand and bowed several times as he escorted us into the building. It was far more than a shop; it was Ali Baba's cave. The walls were crammed to the ceiling with boxes and barrels and tins of food and supplies, while the counter was hung with a sign proclaiming it was an official post office. A small bar ran along one wall, and tucked in a corner were a few small rattan chairs fitted with chintz cushions. More chintz had been hung over the narrow doorway that separated the shop from the living quarters behind. Mr. Patel yelled through the curtain and in a moment a slender Indian woman wearing a pink sari appeared with a tray of glasses and a plate of small pastries. She was small, not quite my height, with heavy black hair that she had bound into a plait that swung like her hips whenever she walked.

Mr. Patel introduced me to his wife and told her to serve us. The glasses were full to the brim with very sweet tea and the pastries were stuffed with pistachios and drizzled with honey. She handed them out in turn with a smile that showed pretty white teeth against her dusky skin.

"Delicious," I told her. I didn't know if she spoke English, but she smiled anyway and hurried back through the curtain. The monkey had a glass as well and he drank politely, wiping his mouth after every sip. I looked up and saw that the curtain was very slightly parted, and only the gleam of one dark eye showed through. It wasn't focused on me, though. It was fixed unblinkingly on Ryder.

Mr. Patel, who never seemed to stay still for more than a minute, bounded up and dashed behind the bar. When he returned, he handed me a thick stack of envelopes bound with a bit of rough twine.

"The post!"

"Rajesh fetches the post from Nairobi," Ryder explained, "but it doesn't go any farther. You have to come here to collect it or to send a letter. If a telegram arrives, Rajesh will send one of his sons out with it on the motorcycle."

"Your sons?"

"Yes," Mr. Patel said, smiling widely, "I am blessed with three strong boys. Almost fully grown."

I thought of the slim, youthful Mrs. Patel and wondered how that was possible.

"The first Mrs. Patel died last year, very sad," Mr. Patel told me, his voice pitched low. "I have taken a new bride to be mother to my sons and to bring me happiness. This is the Mrs. Patel you have met, my jewel."

I flicked a gaze at Ryder who was studying his boots nonchalantly.

"How nice for you," I told Mr. Patel. "And you have a motorcycle?"

"Oh, yes! Very reliable and very fast."

I scarcely heard him. I was too busy thinking about his jewel and wondering if he knew what she got up to when he was off in Nairobi. I flipped through the stack of mail, noticing the return addresses. "Mossy, Nigel, Quentin. Bless them. And there are several for Dodo, too. She'll be thrilled."

I tucked the letters into my pocket, savouring the anticipation of reading them over a long cool gin and tonic. We chatted with Mr. Patel until the pastries were nothing but sticky crumbs on a plate. I spent the next hour scouring Ryder's shelves for anything and everything we might need at Fairlight. It added up and when Mr. Patel presented me with the total, I was horrified.

I turned to Ryder. "I'm afraid I don't have any money with me."

"It's useless out here anyway, at least on a daily basis. It will just go on account, settled quarterly. Rajesh, put it on the Fairlight account." Mr. Patel opened a battered green ledger and began to make a tidy notation.

"Who pays for that?" I demanded.

He flicked a glance to Mr. Patel who looked

faintly embarrassed. "It is the responsibility of the estate to settle the account."

"When is the reckoning?"

"Quarterly, *memsa*."

"And did Gates settle the account for the last quarter?"

"I regret to say this is not so."

"How many quarters is the estate in arrears?"

He traced his finger lightly down the page of his ledger. "Six, *memsa*."

I turned to Ryder. "Six quarters? For a year and a half, Fairlight hasn't paid its bill?"

He looked away. "These things happen."

"These things do not just happen, and that's a damned poor way to run a business. Mr. Patel, how much is the total?" He named a sum which made me suck in my breath. "I would like for you to prepare a report, please. Itemize the bill so I can see precisely what has been purchased by the estate. I will get you your money."

He perked up considerably then. "As you wish, dear lady. I will have the bill prepared and delivered to Fairlight at the earliest possible opportunity."

"And it is to be put into no one's hands but mine, do you understand?"

He gave me a slow wink. "We are conspirators, *memsa*."

"Exactly. And did you write down my chickens?"

Ryder raised a hand. "You refused before, but

I would like you to have a welcome present."

"Thank you. You're such a wretched business-man I should refuse, but I think Fairlight owes quite enough just now." To my surprise, Ryder laughed at the barb.

I made arrangements with Mr. Patel to have everything delivered and waved goodbye. When we emerged, I was surprised to find the shadows had grown long.

"Don't worry. There's plenty of time to get you home," Ryder said. It was a little disconcerting how easily he read my thoughts. We walked along in silence for several minutes until he stopped and pointed at a tree. A bright yellow bird was busily constructing the most peculiar nest I had ever seen. It was shaped like a teardrop and hung from the branch like some exotic Christmas ornament.

"How beautiful," I breathed.

"It's a golden weaver bird. The male builds a nest for the female he admires to come and inspect. If she doesn't like it, he tears it apart and builds a new one."

"What if she doesn't like the second one?"

"Then he builds another."

"And if she doesn't like that one?"

"He builds another. He will keep doing everything in his power to make her happy until she finally relents."

Ryder was looking at me, but I kept my own gaze firmly fixed on the bird.

"It might be simpler if he gave up and found a female that was easier to please."

"He isn't interested in simple. He wants what he wants. No matter how much trouble she is and no matter whether he even understands it himself."

He walked on then, leaving me to hurry along in his wake. He didn't speak again until we reached the fringes of the garden at Fairlight. "I left the antelope with Pierre for dinner, but it's only a small one. There isn't enough to feed everybody in your house. Come home with me. I'll feed you supper and bring you back afterwards."

I should have said no. It would have been the wiser course. But then, I wasn't any more interested in wise than Ryder was interested in simple. Besides, I was curious as to how he lived. He was a mass of contradictions, moody and thorny one minute, charming as the devil the next, and I wasn't sure which of those men was the real Ryder White. One of Mossy's altruisms was that a man can fool you in public, showing whichever face he likes, but his home doesn't lie. His home tells more truth than his tongue ever will.

We walked to his *boma* through the deepening shadows, and just as we reached his little establishment, the sun gave one last brilliant shimmer of red-gold and sank away beneath the horizon. There was a purple-blue stillness that lasted for the space of a few minutes, and then rolled away under the gathering darkness.

Ryder took me in through the hedge of wait-a-bit thorn and into his mud-and-wattle *rondavel*. It was snug and small, but outfitted for most of the essential comforts. There was a tiny table with two chairs, a shelf for plates and cups and a single pot. A bottle of whisky rested there, single malt from an expensive distillery. He had a narrow bedspread with a colourful coverlet and a small trunk, which I presumed held the rest of his wardrobe. There wasn't much, but what there was was good. Everything was of excellent quality, as if he'd chosen only the very best of the very fewest things a man could live with. He hefted his rifle to a gun rack over the door and set to work preparing the food. His cooking fire was outdoors and two acacia stumps served as seats. The air grew colder as the evening wore on, and he tossed me a blanket. It was a length of the stuff the Masai wore, bright scarlet and surprisingly soft. I wrapped it around myself and sipped at my whisky while I watched him.

Some men can't do women's work without looking foolish, but Ryder wasn't one of them. I suppose it was because he was so fully masculine that even if he'd dressed up in a frilly apron and passed me a *petit four*, he still would have knocked down every man I'd ever met for sheer maleness. I think he knew I watched him. He seemed aware of everything I did whether his eyes were on me or not. I had no sooner taken the last sip of my drink than he poured another. I took it along with the plate of food he handed me. I was ravenous, and the stew, thick with meat and spices and squash, was delicious. There was flatbread to soak it up, and I ate like a field hand. We stayed outside to eat, enjoying the warmth of the fire, and I glanced up once in a while to watch it flicker over his face. He seemed entirely relaxed, like a big cat after it's been fed and groomed and has nothing better to do than flick its tail as the world goes by.

I cleared my throat. "You are an exceptionally fine cook. I ought to offer you a job."

He laughed. "I learned in the Yukon. Not many women in the camps there and I was too small to be much good at mining."

"I can't believe you were ever small," I said, my lips twitching slightly.

"Don't start flirting with me now. I won't be accountable for my actions," he said. His tone was light, but the cool blue of his eyes had warmed. Some men have a trick of looking right through you, as if your clothes were something to stop everybody but them from seeing into you. Ryder was one of them.

"I thought you said you would see me safely back to Fairlight."

"And I will. Just as soon as you've finished eating."

I felt an odd little stab of something like

disappointment and a far sharper pang of annoyance. I wasn't accustomed to indifference. I thought of slim Mrs. Patel and the pang turned sharper. I had expected a proper attempt at seduction, something overt and easy to rebuff, something that would give me a chance to put him firmly in his place and keep him there. But he wasn't playing by the rules. Instead of rushing me, he'd merely left himself open, wanting me to do the work for him. It was a subtle strategy, and I had to give him high marks for it, no matter how grudgingly. He had baited the trap, but whether or not a willing woman fell into it was entirely up to her. If she didn't, there was nothing to forgive, nothing to excuse. He'd merely offered dinner and conversation. But if she made a move to take him to bed, I had no doubt he'd rise to the challenge so fast she wouldn't even have time to realise he was the one calling the shots. The beauty of this approach was that the average woman would never even recognise it as a deliberate seduction. She might even, given a little judicious manipulation, come to think of it as entirely her fault. But I wasn't average—not by half, and it would be child's play to push him past the limit of his control.

I put on my softest smile, the one that sat in my eyes and looked up through my lashes, inviting and coaxing and promising things I might or might not give.

"Weren't you supposed to be trying to seduce me? I seem to recall you placed a bet regarding my virtue."

He shrugged. "That's a bet I've already lost. I knew I should have placed a side bet on Kit." He shook his head and sighed. I felt my annoyance creeping higher.

"And it doesn't bother you?"

"What? That you've slept with Kit Parrymore?" He threw back his head and laughed. "If I thought I would suffer in comparison to Kit, I would walk out into the bush and shoot myself for the vultures to eat."

"Big talk," I said flippantly.

He surged up then, pulling me with him. His hands were tight on my upper arms and his face half in shadow. I could feel the sheer power of him, like a force of nature, and I heard the blood beating swift and steady in my ears. My lips curved into a smile. Child's play, indeed.

His hands bit into my flesh, hurting, and the pain felt good. That pain was power. It meant I had pushed him just that step too far and he was giving me what I had already given him. I parted my lips.

"Sin with me," he murmured, lowering his head.

At the last second, I turned and his lips grazed my jaw, touching hard bone instead of the soft mouth he'd been looking for. He pulled back, confused, and the smile I gave him this time was for me alone.

"You didn't really think it was going to be that easy, did you?"

He dropped his hands as quickly as if I'd burned him, and maybe I had. My blood was molten, and I could smell brimstone on my breath. He stepped back, putting the cool evening air between us.

"Didn't anybody ever teach you it's dangerous to play with fire?" His voice was hoarse and his hands were flexing, opening and closing on empty air instead of me.

I tilted my head, smiling. "You're a real piece of work, Ryder White. You wager on my wreck of a reputation while you're busy screwing half the women in Kenya, including poor Mr. Patel's little jewel. Tell me, does he even suspect?"

"Probably not. Husbands can be remarkably shortsighted when they want to be."

"Oh, that's not unique to husbands. Now, we're going to see quite a bit of each other while I'm here, so let's get a few things straight. I do what I like with whomever I like, and I don't give a tinker's damn what anybody thinks about it. But I'm not just a carnival prize you win for putting your ball in the hole, and I'm nobody's notch on a bedpost. I don't belong to anybody but myself and I am never a sure thing. So, you keep your libido in check and stop sniffing around my skirts. Because it's not going to happen."

He folded his arms over his chest and stared at me. The firelight warmed the dark gold of his hair, reddening it as the shadows passed over his face and back again. Any other man would have apologised and smoothed the moment over, patting his dignity into place with soft hands and softer words. Not Ryder. He smiled slowly, and there was a flash of cruelty there, a flash he was happy to show me before he sat it down in the corner and made it behave.

"You understand that we're alone out here, don't you, Delilah? There's not a soul within screaming distance, nobody to hear you, nobody to help you. I could violate you sixty different ways and throw you out for the hyenas to have their way with before anybody ever even noticed you were gone."

The words were dangerous, but the voice was low and soft and coaxing, mixing me up until I wasn't sure whether to believe his lips or his eyes. My pulse was coming hard and fast as he put out a hand and wrapped a lock of my hair around one finger. He pulled slowly until my head came forward. He didn't lay a hand on me aside from that one finger, just that one finger, pulling me closer and closer until my mouth opened. I had had men use their whole bodies to seduce me, and their minds and fortunes, too, but never just one finger, coaxing me closer until that one finger was all I could think about. I felt his breath pass over my lips, felt the warmth of his mouth as he almost but not quite touched me, holding himself just out

206

of reach. I leaned forward, thinking how much I'd like to pin his ears back with my knees.

"Have it your way, princess," he said, whispering the words across my skin, raising gooseflesh as they passed. "We'll see who caves first."

With that he unwound his finger and stepped away. My legs were shaking as he went into the *rondavel* for his rifle.

I nearly choked on the words, but I managed to say brightly, "Thank you for your hospitality. Dinner was delicious."

He didn't respond. He merely led the way home, pausing only once when we heard a loud rasping noise, like someone sawing wood.

"Leopard," he murmured, his lips annoyingly close to my ear. His chest was pressed to my back. There was a slow, deep rhythm beating behind it, and I stood still, feeling his heart drumming evenly. He wasn't scared, and because he was there, neither was I. We stood very still until he felt it was safe to continue, and in a remarkably short time we were back at Fairlight. He left me in the garden.

I hesitated, one foot on the veranda. "Ryder," I started, and only later was I glad he interrupted me. I never did figure out what I might have said to him.

"For Christ's sake, woman. Don't stand there mooning about. This is Africa. Go inside before something eats you."

I went.

# 12

I slept poorly that night. The moon was small and lopsided, like a child's balloon being slowly inflated. But still it poured its silky light into my room, and I lay awake watching it move the shadows across the bed. I heard the nightjars singing in the garden and the crickets serenading one another, and under it all the occasional low rasp of the leopard. When I did sleep, my dreams came fast and sharp, like a moving picture running at too high a speed, jerking from one scene to another. I could not remember them in the morning, but when I woke my pillow was wet.

That afternoon my cows arrived. Gideon collected them from the Kikuyu and walked them to Fairlight. He brought with him a boy who walked with a limp, leaning on a crutch. He might have been ten or twelve, with a slender build and a solemn face. He stared at me as Gideon made the introductions.

"This is my brother, *Bibi*. He is called Moses."

"Hello, Moses."

"My brother Moses does not speak, *Bibi*, but he hears perfectly, and he is very good with cattle. It is a great responsibility to care for your cattle, and Moses will do an excellent job."

"I'm sure he will. Thank you, Moses," I said, turning to the boy.

He looked startled at that. I suppose most whites didn't bother thanking Masai for anything, but Gideon instructed him where to take the cattle and turned to me.

"He will sleep in the barn with the cows, *Bibi*. Perhaps occasionally, when his work is finished and the cows are safe, he may go home and see our *babu*."

"Of course. Whenever he likes."

"No, *Bibi*. It is for you to say."

"I think we are about to have our first argument, Gideon." I smiled to show I wasn't serious, and to my relief, his face split into a wide grin.

"You are joking with me."

"Yes, I am. I really am quite happy for Moses to go back home whenever he is needed so long as the cattle are secured. What about his schooling?"

"Most Masai never go to school. Moses has already learned much more than many of our people. He is happy to have a job that will pay him money." He hesitated, and although he said nothing, I sensed there was more.

"Gideon?" I made the word gentle, coaxing.

He took a breath, his voice pitched low as he leaned on his spear.

"*Bibi*, I worry for my brother. His leg is weak and he cannot tend cattle as Masai do, walking many, many miles every day. Without this, he cannot be a man of importance in our tribe, and he will not marry. It is a very bad thing for a man not to marry and have children. It is not our way for a man to be alone."

"I see. And by earning a wage, he can contribute?"

The tension in his face eased.

"This is true, *Bibi*. And I would not tell you an untruth. If I say that Moses is good with cows, he is very good indeed. He does not speak, but he can whistle and he has a sense for what they need. They like him. Your cattle will be in good hands."

"I never doubted it. You really think this will help him?"

"Yes, *Bibi*. He will earn money, and in time he will buy his own cows and then a girl will be happy to marry him and give him children because he will be a man like others."

"Very well. He can skip school and tend the cattle and he may visit your *babu* whenever he likes."

He gave me a nod. "I will tell Moses of this. He will come to you before he goes to make certain it is your wish."

"Fine."

He paused. "Is there anything else you would have me do?"

I shrugged. "Nothing I can think of. I suppose you will be off with Ryder, hunting."

"No, *Bibi*. I am to remain here."

I lifted a brow. "To do what?"

Gideon shuffled a moment. The Masai do not like to tell untruths. Neither do they like to admit something distasteful, but then no man likes to tell a woman something that might annoy her.

"Gideon?"

"I am to watch over you, *Bibi*."

"I do not require watching over."

"Regardless, *Bibi*, this is the thing I have been given to do."

I kept a rein on my temper and thought the matter through. I liked Gideon. Ryder had set him to watching over me, which I deplored, but that was my issue with Ryder, not Gideon. I nodded.

"I understand. It's not your fault Ryder is a high-handed arrogant jackass."

"I beg your pardon, but this word I have not heard. What does 'jackass' mean? Is it like 'son of a bitch'?"

"I'm assuming you didn't learn that phrase at the mission school?"

"Oh, no. *Bwana* is very fluent in bad language."

"No doubt. And no, 'jackass' isn't quite as bad as 'son of a bitch.' It just means someone who gets on your nerves."

He nodded, his expression serious. "A woman could love a jackass. She could not love a son of a bitch."

"Many have tried, Gideon. Many have tried."

• • •

Gideon put himself to work finishing the fencing in the small pasture where I had elected to keep the cattle. The huge Masai herds roamed over vast tracts of the savannah and scrubland, but a few dairy cattle would be far easier to keep penned near the house. Moses moved among the skittish cows, petting them and humming an odd little tune. From time to time he gave me a wide smile, very like his brother's, and I carried lunch out to them, leaving it on a rock for them to find since they didn't like to eat directly from a woman's hand.

As I walked back to the house, I saw the rising dust cloud on the horizon, and in a very few minutes Mr. Patel arrived in his motorcycle, his turban half-unwound and fluttering behind him and his motoring goggles coated in red dust. His sidecar was packed tightly with all I had ordered and a cage of traumatized chickens was lashed to the top. His monkey had ridden pillion, and as soon as he stopped it launched itself at the nearest tree, chattering angrily.

"Then why do you insist on coming, you diabolical creature?" Mr. Patel demanded, raising his fist. He climbed off the motorcycle, shaking out his robes and winding his turban firmly about his head. He pulled the goggles down to his neck and smiled.

"*Memsa*! I have brought your things. And would

you like to buy a monkey? I could give you an excellent price."

"No, thank you, Mr. Patel. Would you like help with all of that?"

"Absolutely not! A lady should not sully her hands," he insisted. Dora emerged from the house then and I introduced them.

"Dora, this is Mr. Patel. He's the nearest thing we have to Harrod's out here. Mr. Patel, this is my cousin, Miss Brooks."

Patel bowed with a courtly flourish as Dora inclined her head. "How do you do? I'll show you where to put all of that if you'd like to follow me."

He trotted off, shouldering the cage of chickens as if they weighed no more than a pillow. Well, they were mostly feathers, I supposed with a shrug.

I had just turned to follow them when I saw another cloud of dust approaching. I shaded my eyes and stayed to watch, waving as I saw Rex's buttery Rolls coming down the drive.

"Hello, Rex. Goodness me, but it's like Grand Central around here today."

He stepped from the car and dropped a friendly kiss to my cheek. "Hello, my dear. I was on my way to Nairobi and thought I would stop in and see if you needed anything from town."

"That's terribly neighbourly of you. We're fine. Could I interest you in a drink to speed you on your way?"

He grinned. "I oughtn't. I'm going to be frightfully long on the road as it is, but a man can only resist so much temptation."

"Am I temptation?" I teased.

The smile deepened. "More than any woman has a right to be," he said lightly. "A gin and tonic if you don't mind."

"Of course not. Let's have them on the veranda. The house is filthy enough without me tracking half the savannah inside."

He followed me up to the veranda and I poured. He took his first sip and something seemed to roll off him then, some hidden weight that had bowed him down.

"Everything all right, Rex?"

He struggled with himself. Whatever was on his mind, he was itching to share it, but something stopped him. He merely gave me another of his remote smiles and sipped at his drink.

"Have it your way," I said with a shrug. "But you're always welcome here if you need a friendly ear."

He drained his glass and put it down with a loud crack. I jumped a little and he clamped a hand over mine. He didn't look at me, but his hand stayed where it was, covering mine as he drew in a deep breath. He let it go, surrendering something.

"I wish I could tell you. I wish I could tell you everything," he said, his voice sharp.

I put down my glass. "You can, Rex. Of course you can. We're friends, aren't we?"

"Are we?" He looked at me as if seeing me for the first time. "Yes, I think we are. I think I could tell you anything."

"Then do. Clearly something's troubling you. Get it out and you'll feel like a new man," I promised him.

His smile was back, smaller and more tentative than before. "Is that really how it works? I think you must be more American than English to suggest it. We're good at bottling things up, holding them so tightly we can't let them go even when we want to."

He didn't say anything more and I sat back with a shrug and picked up my drink.

"This place breaks my heart," he said finally. "It is so beautiful and so vast and so untouched. There's nothing ahead but destruction if something isn't done about it. Someone has to protect it. Someone has to love it enough to try."

"Are you talking about Africa or Fairlight?"

The smile was still small, still tentative. "Both, I suppose. I've offered to buy Fairlight, you know. More than once. But Sir Nigel is sentimental, too attached to the place to let it go. I can't blame him. I feel that way about all of Africa."

He fell silent again and I went back to my drink. He rose then and put out his hand, pulling me to my feet.

"I think I might actually feel better."

"I can't imagine how. I didn't do anything."

"You let me sit and just be. That's a rare gift for a man. You have no idea how rare."

He dropped another kiss, this one markedly warmer, to my cheek and left, his step lighter. Dora appeared just as he drove away.

"Was that Rex?"

"It was." I poured her a gin and tonic of her own and handed it over.

"What did he want?"

"To have a moan about an unrequited passion. Apparently he's in love with Africa and she doesn't love him back."

She kicked off her shoes. "Mr. Patel has stacked everything in the storeroom, and retrieved his vile little monkey. He just left. I managed to get Gates to finish the henhouse just in time for the chickens. They're not settling in at all well. The hens are all huddled together in the corner, whimpering, and the rooster is making a nuisance of himself by trying to escape."

"Just make sure you warn them, the first one to wake me at dawn is going into the cookpot."

She saluted wearily. "Aye, aye, Captain."

It wasn't the rooster that awakened me at dawn. It was the shouts of the Kikuyu, keening and wailing as they gathered in the garden. I shoved my arms into a kimono and hurled on my slippers, falling over Dora as we threw back the locks and hurried outside. All the Kikuyu farmworkers were there, clustered around a group in the centre who were carrying something on a blanket. As we got closer, they set it onto the ground, and it took me a moment to realise what I was looking at. The body was small and so broken I could only recognise bits of it. I saw the white bandage, grubby and torn and a handful of shredded skin attached to small braids. The feet were entirely intact, the little white bones snapped just above the ankle, and there were long white femurs, cracked open, the marrow lapped. Above the ululations of the Kikuyu, I heard another sound, a high, gasping shriek that went on and on.

I turned to Dora and shoved her head down onto my shoulder, shielding her eyes and muffling her scream. After a moment she stilled and pushed away from me to be sick in the bushes. I moved forward to the mother who had collapsed onto the ground. She was tearing a bit of bougainvillea into shreds in her fingers. I covered her hands with my own.

She looked up at me, and the word came out flat and dull between lips that were stiff with shock. *"Simba."*

I nodded. A shadow fell over us, and I looked up to see Gates, struggling into his shirt, the broad fish-belly white of his torso gleaming in the early morning light.

"A lion has killed her child."

He nodded. "You can tell from the bites. Lions like big muscle. That's why the thighs and buttocks are gone. They don't bother with the smaller bits," he added, pointing toward the tiny feet.

I swung around on my heels. "Shut up. Shut up. Shut up." Each word was punctuated by a slap to his legs.

His eyes were round as he stared from the mother to me, comprehension slowly dawning. "Are you worried about her? These Kukes don't speak English, Miss Drummond. There's no need to tiptoe around their feelings. Besides, if it wasn't lion or leopard or snake, it would have been disease or fire. They don't always have the best luck keeping their children alive," he finished with a shake of the head.

I rose, putting one hand to the mother's head as I did so. I turned to the Kikuyu and addressed them in halting Swahili. I asked if the lion had been killed, and they shook their heads. After a great deal of pantomime, it became clear that this was why they had come. They wanted to show me the lion's work and take back with them a promise that it would be taken care of. I turned to Gates.

"Did I understand them correctly? They expect us to hunt down the lion and kill it?"

He nodded. "They could do it themselves, but

it's dangerous work and they aren't allowed guns. It's easier for a white man to do it."

"Fine. Then you will do it."

He blinked rapidly. "I don't think so, Miss Drummond."

"You just said—"

He held up a meaty hand. "I said it was easier for a white man to do it. But not this white man. I'm a farm manager, not a hunter. It's not in my job description. Now, I've been accommodating since you arrived, Miss Drummond, very accommodating, and I've done many things that weren't strictly speaking my responsibility. But I draw the line here, I do draw it here. I am a family man. What would become of my family if I died trying to kill a lion that wasn't my place to kill?"

He was sweating, but his expression was smug. He had me. I couldn't force him to risk his life to kill a man-eating lion. But I knew exactly who would do the job.

I said whatever words of comfort I could manage in Swahili and the Kikuyu accepted my promise that the lion would be dealt with. Dora turned away as they gathered up the blanket with its small, broken burden. I watched them leave then turned to Gates.

"You're entirely correct, Mr. Gates. You are a farmer. So get back to your plow and I'll talk to you when this is over."

He slunk away and I headed into the house to

dress. By the time I finished, Dora had seen to breakfast and I choked down a piece of toast and a cup of tea before I stood up.

"Wrap a few sandwiches for me, Do. I've got to find Ryder and I don't know how long I'll be gone."

She opened her mouth then clamped it shut again as the man himself stepped onto the veranda.

"Didn't I tell you not to go looking for me?" he asked, his mouth quirked up. "You don't listen very well."

"Oh, thank God you're here."

He raised his brows. "That's a greeting a man could get used to," he said, settling himself at the table.

"May I offer you some breakfast?" Dora asked kindly. "There are plenty of eggs and we've toast and tea and some lovely preserves."

She loaded a plate for him while I stewed. "This isn't going to be a social call, Ryder. I need you to go kill a lion."

He held up a hand. "I know all about your lion. That's why I'm here."

"Oh. Well, in that case, we ought to discuss terms."

Dora rose and murmured something about making more tea as Ryder fixed me with an amused look. "Terms?"

"Yes, the terms of your employment."

He laughed aloud. "Princess, you can't afford me, so let's just dismiss that idea right now."

"How do you know what I can afford?"

He smiled, the lines at his eyes and mouth crinkling gently. "Because I know what I charge and it's generally only royalty and Rockefellers who can match my prices."

"Name it," I challenged.

He did and I stared at him as he loaded a second plate with eggs from the chafing dish.

"Jesus Jiminy Christ, Ryder, if that's how much you make you ought to be feeding me breakfast."

He grinned. "Told you."

"How on earth do you get away with charging that much?"

He shrugged. "People are always willing to pay for the best."

I snorted. "I see modesty doesn't number among your virtues."

"No, but honesty does. I am a damned good hunter, princess, but I hate guiding for other people. I figured if I charged outrageous prices people would stop hiring me and I could do whatever I liked, but it hasn't turned out that way."

"No?"

He forked in a bit of egg and followed it with half a piece of toast. "It turns out that charging astronomical prices only makes people want you all the more. Apparently it offers *cachet*," he said, tipping his head to the side.

"*Cachet* aside, you're right. I can't afford that. I could buy a flat in Paris for that kind of money."

"So I'll do it for free," he finished.

I narrowed my eyes at him. "Why?"

He sat back and folded his arms. "What's the matter? Don't like the idea of being beholden to me?"

"As a matter of fact, I don't."

"Then come with me. I charge half as much to get rid of man-eaters if someone else takes the shot. You'll only be half-beholden to me then."

I hesitated for all the right reasons. And I accepted for all the wrong ones.

"Fine," I said, putting out my hand.

He took it in his and shook it slowly. He was still holding on to it when Dora appeared with a fresh pot of tea. I jerked it back and she put on a deliberately blank expression.

Ryder rose and thanked her. "I'm going back to my place to put a few things in order. I'll be back after luncheon and we'll head out then."

When he left, Dora looked up sharply from the teapot. "I don't see why you must do this. Surely Sir Nigel never intended—"

"Nigel isn't here," I reminded her.

She went on patiently. "Even so, if he knew, I cannot believe he would want you to risk your very life over such a thing."

"Such a thing?" I kept my voice gentle. "A child is dead, Dora."

She winced. "I know. And I don't mean to sound uncaring—"

"Then don't."

Her pale complexion flushed deeply. "I say, that isn't fair. I take an interest in their welfare, a healthy interest," she said, stressing the word *healthy.* "But I think it shows a strange sort of arrogance to involve oneself so deeply in their affairs."

"Arrogance?"

"Yes," she said, two spots of colour still high on her cheeks. "We are not meant to understand them, Delilah. Their ways are simply too different. The role of the white in Africa ought to be a simple one—to set an example of learning, of civilisation, of good management."

I let her ramble on in that vein for a few minutes before I stopped her with an upraised hand and a thin smile.

"I've heard it before, Dora. You forget, I was brought up in a place not terribly different from this. The blacks do their work, the whites count their money—at least that's what most people think. The reality is quite different. There has to be understanding on both sides. And it begins with not being afraid of them."

The hot colour ebbed. "That isn't fair."

"Isn't it? I see how you draw back when you have to speak to an African."

"That isn't because of their skin," she returned

hotly. "I'm simply unaccustomed to giving orders. It makes me uncomfortable."

"You do well enough back in England. You bawl out the butcher if the chops are too fatty or tear a strip off the boy at the garage if he tries to charge too much to mend a puncture on your bicycle. You've no trouble speaking your mind to them."

"Of course not! They're—" She broke off, setting her lips stubbornly. "Oh, never mind. But I still say it's wrong, it's very wrong for you to mix with them as if you were friends. You ought to hold yourself above them to set the very best example you can."

"I'm nobody's best example," I reminded her. "Anything else?"

"Yes, in fact, there is. He's a good man, Delilah." She didn't say his name, but there was no mistaking who she meant.

"Is he? I'm not sure I would know a good man if I saw one."

"Then take my word for it. He is a good man."

I shrugged. "If you say so. But you probably don't know the half of it."

"I'm not talking about local gossip. I know he's a bit of a philanderer and his morals are unique."

I snorted, but she went on, her cheeks heating up again. "Laugh if you like, but there's something fine about him. Underneath the wildness, there's something pure."

*Pure* might have been the last word I would have chosen to describe Ryder White, but Dora did have a point. I decided not to tell her about his threat to violate me and feed me to the hyenas. Her illusions were too pretty to shatter. Besides, for all I knew she was right.

She broke a piece of toast to bits and threw it out into the garden.

"What did you do that for?"

"There's a tortoise living under the veranda. He likes toast."

I rose and she put her hand to my arm. "I know you think I'm a fool, but I mean it, Delilah. Don't hurt him."

I thought of the miserable bet he'd made about getting me into bed. If I did hurt him, it would only be fair. He'd drawn first blood.

"I'm not sure I could," I told her.

"Then you're not half as smart as I gave you credit for," she said, releasing my arm.

"Go feed your tortoise, Do," I told her as kindly as I could. "And leave my life to me."

True to his word, Ryder appeared after luncheon, Gideon trotting quietly behind. I had prepared as best I could, packing a small bag with necessities and making sure my guns were clean. I left Dora in charge of Fairlight, or at least, as in charge as she could be with Gates around. Moses waved goodbye from the pasture where he stood with the cattle, saluting his brother. Gideon lifted his spear in farewell and we were off.

We hiked down the Nairobi road some distance toward Rex's place then turned abruptly down a narrow track of beaten earth.

"Where are we going?" I asked Ryder.

"Nyama Ranch. I need to see Tusker before we set out. We'll need some men, and she'll probably want to come along. She loves a good lion hunt."

"She makes a habit of hunting lions?"

"Don't look so surprised. She breeds racehorses, and lions are her biggest nuisance. She doesn't bother with them until they come in and bother the horses. Same with leopards."

I shuddered.

"What's the matter, princess? Lost your taste for this? You can turn back now. I'll have Gideon walk you home."

"Absolutely not. That thing is a man-eater and I want to see it taken care of. It's just easy to forget."

He slowed a little, slanting me a curious look under the brim of his hat. "Forget what?"

"How vicious this place is. How life can just turn on a dime. My mother breeds horses, too, you know. She has a fine stable in England, and she says a hundred different things can kill her stock. She worries about bad water and bad food and hoof-and-mouth, but the one thing she doesn't ever have to worry about is some damned cat clawing her horses to pieces in the middle of the night."

"True, but does she have all this?" he asked, sweeping an arm out to take in the country before us. The flat savannah stretched for miles, dotted with thornbushes and acacia trees as it ran up to a tall purple escarpment in the distance. A herd of elephants grazed at the foot of the escarpment, heavy grey shadows moving in the bushes. Over it all, a dome of vast blue sky rose so high I got dizzy just looking up at it. Ryder moved on then, not waiting for an answer. I slowed to walk with Gideon. I smiled at him.

"You seem in very good spirits, Gideon. For a man that usually means a woman, but I'm guessing for a Masai man, it means a lion."

"You begin to understand us, *Bibi*," he said, returning the smile with interest.

"Gideon, I hope you don't think me rude, but may I ask about the gap between your teeth? I've noticed most of the natives here have it."

He put a finger to the space where his two lower teeth ought to have been. "They are pulled when we are very small children. Then when our second teeth come, these also are pulled. It is so we may be fed if we are sick with the lockjaw."

It made perfect sense; it was actually a rather clever solution to the problem of tetanus. Most people who got it starved to death because they couldn't take in food. Pulling the teeth at least meant there was a way to nourish them until the fever passed and the jaw muscles unclenched.

"But Moses' teeth haven't been pulled."

It was as if a shutter came down over his eyes. "No, *Bibi*. It was his mother's wish that he be left as he was born."

"Why? If he gets tetanus, he'll almost certainly die."

"His mother would not mourn," Gideon said, his tone edged in bitterness. "She is an unkind woman and her heart is closed. She does not love her son as she should."

"You mean she's content for him to die? Is it because he won't speak?"

"No, *Bibi*. It is because of his leg. He was born with a twisted leg, and she was beaten very badly by our father for adultery. He said all of his other children were born straight and tall, and this child must not be his. His mother was very angry and her anger has turned against her son."

"Was she telling the truth? Or had she committed adultery?"

"Both, possibly. She was caught with one of my brothers in age. This is a very bad thing. A woman may lie with her husband and sometimes with the men who were circumcised with him. But to lie with a man from another age group is a very bad thing indeed. My father beat her when he caught her. She says Moses is his son and already growing inside her when she lay with the other man and that it was my father's beating that caused him to grow a twisted leg. My father beats her for saying such a thing."

"You mean they're still together?"

He shrugged. "She is very lovely. My father drinks *moratina* and forgets why he hates her. Then he drinks more and remembers again. They fight very much, and my father has sold his cattle to buy *moratina*."

"What is *moratina*?"

"Honey beer. It makes him forget how to be a good man and he raises his stick to his younger children. Most of them are out of his house now. The girls have married, bad marriages, because they had few cattle to take to their husbands. And the younger boys get up to much mischief and are often beaten by the *morani* for their disrespect. He has not taught them to speak with dignity and to be useful. He has taught them only to despise others and so they are despised. Only Moses is free of him."

"How?"

"One day when our father was drinking much *moratina*, I stood over him as he lifted his stick to Moses. I told him for every blow he struck my brother, I would strike one upon him. I am taller than my father," he said with a small, sad smile. "My father was frightened of me and he shoved Moses into my arms and said he would be as my son now and I would have the care of him. I took him to my mother's father, my *babu*. He is a very good man, *Bibi*. He opened his home to the child of his daughter's husband's other wife, and this is not often done."

"Your *babu* is generous."

Gideon's brow furrowed. "Yes, but he grows old, *Bibi*. And when he dies, his cattle will be given to his sons and daughters, as they must be. There are no cattle for Moses. This is why I am happy Moses has work. He will be a man with cattle because of you."

We walked on then and he pointed out the tracks of the tiny mice that lived on the plains and the soft swirl left by a passing snake. He gave me the leaf of the *leleshwa* and crushed it into my palm so the sage-smell of it would fill my nose. He lifted a tiny bone from the dust and explained that it came from the spine of a porcupine, and he taught me to hold myself very still to watch the antics of a small black bird that leaped and swayed.

"The white settlers call this a widowbird, but it is not a lady bird. It is the male. For most of the year he is grey and plain, but once a year his feathers change and he looks as you see him now."

It seemed impossible that this bird could ever be plain. His plumage was glossy black and the feathers of his tail swept into a long train that he carried behind him with kingly dignity. As we watched, he capered and danced, all the while singing an elaborate song and flapping his wings for emphasis.

"That is his dance to bring a lady bird so they can marry," he told me.

I peered into the bushes. "I do not see another bird."

"Then he dances for you, *Bibi*," he said with his broad, gap-toothed smile. "You are welcome in Africa. Africa wants you here."

And as we walked through the warm sunlight of that afternoon, I believed it.

# 13

We reached Nyama at teatime, and I was surprised to see Kit happily devouring sandwiches.

"Delilah!" he called through a mouthful of crumbs. He rose and pressed a kiss to my cheek. Ryder shot us both a cool look then moved to sit next to our hostess. Jude was on his other side, sipping slowly at a cup of tea.

"Afternoon, Tusker," Ryder said, helping himself to a plate. "Hope you don't mind, but we're after a lion. I need to collect my gear and I could use a few of your boys as bearers."

She waved him to a chair. "Anytime. You know that." She turned to me. "So, Miss Drummond. Your first lion hunt. I hope you won't turn soft when the time comes to shoot. They're beautiful monsters, lions, but monsters they are and don't mistake it. They'll just as soon tear you to pieces as look at you."

I thought of the broken bits of flesh that had been carried into my garden on a blanket and pushed the sandwiches aside. Jude poured me a strong cup of tea and handed it over. "There's whisky if you need a stiffener," she said. Her voice was cool, but there was recognition in her eyes. She understood something of facing down new horrors, I realised.

"I've half a mind to go with you," Tusker announced. "It's been ages since I had a good break from this place. I'd like to feel the wind in my hair again and get out there."

"Then pack up," Ryder told her. "I want to leave tonight."

She shook her head. "Not if you're after the lion that ate the Kuke child at Fairlight. It's been seen on the other side of the *lugga* at the edge of my property. The moon's still a bit too dark to try that at night. Best to start first thing in the morning. Don't worry, I'll put you up tonight and give you a proper feed before we leave tomorrow. Jude can look after Nyama while I'm gone."

To my surprise, Ryder agreed. He turned to Kit. "Coming with us, Parrymore?"

There was an unspoken challenge in his voice, and Kit must have heard it. He lifted his chin and smiled. "I don't think so, old boy. I think the hunting is plenty good right here."

He slanted Jude a mischievous look and she ignored him, as inscrutable as some Eastern goddess. She merely sat sipping at her tea while Ryder's eyes narrowed at Kit.

"Watch your mouth, Kit. Do you think talk like that will do her any favours if Wickenden hears you?"

"I shouldn't think that would bother you. If Anthony gets out of line, it will just give you an excuse to thrash him again. After all, everyone knows how much you like to play the hero."

"Or I could just eliminate the problem at the source," Ryder said, his voice soft with menace.

Kit hesitated, his *sang-froid* slipping slightly. Ryder saw it and smelled blood. He smiled, baring his teeth as he sat back in his chair. He folded his arms over his chest, the scars on his left arm chillingly apparent in the bright afternoon light. Kit's eyes fell on them and he looked quickly away.

"Men are such children," Tusker said to me. "Really, I've seen male lions mauling each other with more subtlety."

Jude laughed suddenly, and I wasn't sure at whom. "Come on, Kit. Say goodbye. You were just leaving."

"Oh, was I?" But he obeyed. "Goodbye, all." He paused at my chair and bent over me. He swept my hair away from my ear and pressed a kiss to the hollow just below it. "Be safe out there. Don't let anything eat you that shouldn't."

He left laughing, and I lit a cigarette. Ryder made a short remark about checking his gear and stalked away, shoulders very square. Tusker sighed as she watched him go.

"Ryder's a dear boy, but it's rather like keeping a pet panther in the drawing room to have him around."

"Do he and Kit always go at it?"

Tusker put her hands through her cropped grey

hair. "Ryder puts most men's backs right up. He doesn't mean to, but look at the fellow. He's like something out of a myth, covered in battle scars and women throwing themselves at him. It makes other men nervous. And he takes it all in his stride, the women wanting him and the men hating him. Nothing touches him, not really."

"What happened to his arm?"

Tusker reached for the whisky. She poured a healthy shot into both of our cups. "Drink up, child. It's almost cocktail hour anyway."

She took a deep sip, closing her eyes as the whisky ran down her throat. "God, that's good. We owe those bog-Irish a medal for that. What were we talking about? Oh, yes, Ryder's arm. Leopard."

"A leopard did that?"

She nodded. "He was guiding a Scandinavian prince—it wouldn't do to say which one because the story does not reflect well on his people, but I can tell you he was a Dane. Anyway, they were stalking a black leopard that had killed several Masai cattle. It was the sort of hunt he's led a hundred times without incident."

"But not this time," I prompted. I sipped at the whisky and raised a brow. Ryder apparently wasn't the only one with a taste for single malt.

"This one was a brute, big and fast. Ryder tracked it for his prince, but the prince only winged it, a glancing shot on its flank, just enough to make it good and mad. It turned to charge at them and the prince stood there and pissed himself."

"Good God." I took another deep swallow. "Then what happened?"

"Ryder stepped in front of him. He only had time to get off a single shot, but the prince shouted and the cat turned, so the shot wasn't true. It hit the leopard in the leg just before it landed on Ryder. He managed to get his left arm down its mouth and he held it with his right hand. It clawed and struggled, but it was the only chance Ryder had. If he'd let go, it would have killed him for certain. His only hope was to suffocate it. So he kept shoving that arm down its throat and squeezing with the other as it mauled him."

I shoved the cup aside. The whisky was sour on my tongue. "How did it end?"

She shrugged. "The cat bled out or Ryder suffocated it, he never knew which. But they lay on that ground for almost half an hour, eye to eye, just staring at one another and waiting for one of them to die. He told me later it was the most spiritual experience of his entire life. He saw God in that leopard, and God let him live, Miss Drummond."

I didn't speak.

"He knows death and he knows God. Most men are too afraid to look either one in the face and he's walked right up and shaken hands with them. It makes him special and it makes him stupid."

I roused myself. "Stupid?"

She flapped a hand. "That business in the station with Anthony. He shouldn't have whipped him, at least not publicly. It's bad form for a white man to be lowered so much in the eyes of the Africans. Could cause trouble. There are far more of them than of us. If we start letting them lose respect for us, for any of us, it could have consequences."

"Speaking of consequences, will he face any for assaulting Mr. Wickenden?"

She laughed, a deep belly laugh. "Child, the lieutenant governor told him off for doing it in public, but believe me, the government doesn't care about family squabbles."

"Family squabbles?"

She poured more whisky into my cup.

"Didn't you know? Ryder is my nephew. Now finish your drink. My cook is appalling and dinner will be foul. Much better to be drunk by the time it's served."

I sipped at the whisky and thought of what Ryder had said to me that first afternoon, my assumption that he had been defending a paramour when he thrashed Anthony Wickenden. But Jude was his cousin, and I thought of his casual greeting to her when we'd arrived. I could smell attraction on a man. I knew what it meant when his eyes were hot, and I knew that it meant more when he never looked at a woman at all, keeping his need bound up and secret. Ryder and

Jude had been perfectly comfortable with one another; they talked with the ease of siblings. But why had he been so needled by Kit's presence?

I thought of Kit's warm lips on the skin of my neck and I took another sip of my whisky. Tusker was watching me closely.

"I suppose you're also going to tell me that he's a good man and not to hurt him," I said sharply.

She laughed again. "You couldn't, Miss Drummond. To hurt a man you have to hit him in his heart and Ryder doesn't have one. Oh, he can be kind, but he doesn't really let anyone or anything in. You see, he was married once, years ago. And losing her changed him. He closed himself off. One can't blame him, of course. It's quite a common reaction. He thrashed Anthony as much for the family name as for hurting Jude. He's loyal and he's strong, and he's put up a wall so high you can't even see to the top of it. Take my advice and don't even try."

"Thanks for the warning," I told her, arching a brow.

"I like you, Miss Drummond. In fact, I like you so much I'm going to call you Delilah."

"By all means."

"And I'm going to give you a piece of advice."

"Oh, dear."

She snorted. "Pay attention to your elders, child. We have the wisdom of the ages within us."

"Very well. What advice do you have for me?"

"Don't risk your happiness on a man with a stone for a heart."

Her lip trembled for a moment, and I wondered about her own happiness. She seemed hugely content with her lot in life, mistress of a vast property in a beautiful wilderness, doing work that she loved. She ought to have been happy. But something softened her mouth, making it vulnerable.

I covered her hand with my own. "Don't worry about me, Tusker. Ryder may have a stone heart, but mine's diamond. And there's nothing on earth harder than that."

For all its spaciousness, Nyama lacked guest rooms. Ryder pitched a tent in the garden, Gideon slept underneath a tree, and I shared with Jude. Anthony had gone to Nairobi, and the evening was a pleasant one. Dinner was every bit as foul as Tusker had warned. I pushed gristly meat around my plate and drank a bottle of excellent red wine to fill in the empty spaces.

"Don't worry," Jude murmured as she passed me a bowl of grey peas, "her camp cook is the best in Kenya. You'll eat well on safari at least."

It was the longest comment she made the entire evening. She was full of cool reserve, and I was rather surprised when she offered to let me share her room so I didn't have to sleep outside.

I thanked her and she shrugged. "Bath is that

way if you want to go first. Just save me the water. I'm not fussy."

I scrubbed up quickly and scrabbled in my bag for a fresh set of white silk underthings. Jude dressed herself in what I can only think must have been one of Tusker's old nightdresses, voluminous pink flannel and worn nearly through.

I gave her a look as she climbed into bed with me and she shrugged again. "It's comfortable."

"It's vile. You really ought to do something with yourself, you know. You're quite the loveliest woman I've ever met but you dress like a farmhand."

"I am a farmhand," she said, giving me a lop-sided smile.

I pulled out my nail buffer and began to polish my nails. "Have it your way. I never have any luck getting Dora to spiff herself up either."

"I just don't see the point." Jude settled herself on her side, watching me buff. "I spend all day with horses."

"And all night?" I asked pointedly.

She gave me a cool look. "Anthony doesn't seem to mind the way I look. As he is so fond of saying, all cats are black in the dark."

"I know it's none of my business, but he's a cad. You have to know that. Why do you stay with him?"

She laughed then, and there was something like

pity in it. "Do you really think I'm any better? If he's a cad, I'm a whore. We're well-suited."

"I'm not just talking about adultery, Jude. You're both grown up. Whatever you get up to in other people's beds is your own business. I mean the other."

"The hitting?" She rolled onto her back and stretched. "I feel sorry for him sometimes. He just doesn't know any other way to reach me."

"He hits you and you feel sorry for him?"

"He loves me more than he's ever loved anything in his entire life," she said, relating the words in her cool, passionless voice. "All he wants is to touch me, to move something inside of me so that I will love him back. And I can't. I give him silence and pity and sometimes it's just too much for him. He hits because it's the only way he can get a reaction out of me."

"And bruises are better than kisses?"

"Something like that. Haven't you ever seen a small boy trying to get his mother's attention? He'll tug at her skirts and call her name, and if she ignores him, he'll just get louder and louder, poking and pinching until she sees him. That's Tony's problem. I can't see him, and no matter what he does, he can't make me."

"Why hasn't he tried to get back at Ryder for thrashing him in public?"

"Because he knows I'd kill him. That's the difference between us," she told me, her eyes wide and untroubled. "Tony gets mad and he goes hot, he lets it burn him up. My rage is cold, the sort that would poison his dinner or put a cobra in his bed and watch him die."

"Would you kill him? Could you?"

"Probably not. But Tony thinks I can and that's enough. He's quite good company, really. He keeps me from thinking too much. And most of the time he's happy he married me because it gives him something to work for, making me love him back."

"If you don't love him, why did you marry him?"

The silence between us was so heavy it took on its own form, like a third person in the room. Finally, she broke it, weighing her words like stones.

"I suppose it was because he loved me. And it had been a very long time since anybody looked at me like I was the most important thing in the world."

"My husband died in the war, too," I told her. I turned away and put aside my buffer. She blew out the lamp and we lay in the dark, watching the sliver of moonlit shadow move over the ceiling.

"My husband didn't die in the war." Jude's voice was small in the darkness. "I think he's still alive somewhere. Only he doesn't know how to find his way home again."

"I thought he had been declared dead."

242

I felt her shoulders shrug into the mattress. "That's the courts. Just because the law says it's so, doesn't make it true."

"What if you were right? What if he did come home and he found you married to Tony?"

"I was his first," she said dreamily. "I will always belong to him. That's how I know he isn't really dead. Tusker knew it, too. She used to go out searching for him, and when I had him declared dead and married Tony, she was furious with me. She still doesn't talk to me if she can help it. I'm glad. When she's silent, it makes it easier for me to be silent, too."

I did not know what to say. Silence and sorrow mingled in that house, and I suddenly felt a thrust of pity for Anthony. I couldn't imagine what it would be like to live with these two women who both pined for a ghost who might still be among the living.

"I shouldn't have married Tony," she went on. "I know that now. I was angry and tired and I had been waiting for so long. I just wanted to be loved again."

She turned away, the mattress creaking under her, and I knew the conversation was over. She might have cried. I heard a brief snuffling, and then felt a shudder as she relaxed into sleep. I lay awake, watching for ghosts, but whether I expected to see hers or mine, I couldn't have said. I thought about my Granny Miette and I wished she and Teenie and Angele had been there to cast a circle with black salt and holy water to keep the spirits at bay. I couldn't remember the protective incantations she had taught me, and I didn't have a gris-gris bag or a white candle. All I had was a prayer to Our Lady of Prompt Succour whispered into the darkness that shifted and sighed around me.

I slept deeply and late and by the time I awoke, breakfast was almost over and the garden was teeming with porters. Gideon pointed out the differences between the Kikuyu and Turkana and Swahili and Samburu.

"The Samburu are most like the Masai, and they, too, speak Maa, but they plant crops and this is unlike the Masai," he explained. I could see the resemblance. Both tribes were tall and slender, although no one who had seen the two could reasonably mistake one for the other. The Masai might have been the poorest, but they carried themselves like kings.

He went on. "You see there, the fierceness of the Turkana? The rest of us carry the *panga*, but the knife of the Turkana is different." What I had taken to be a peculiar sort of bracelet was in fact nothing of the sort. The Turkana bent blades to wear as bracelets, the sharp edge facing out and protected by a slim piece of leather. "The Turkana are quick to fight," Gideon warned me. "And they bargain very hard. The Swahili come from the coast and are smaller men, but they carry heavy loads."

Sixty pounds was the limit for each porter's load by law, but a good headman would insist upon the porters carrying very near to it. Tusker had already explained that the porters would not respect a white hunter who paid well and expected too little. In return, they demanded two things: a leader who would stand his ground and who could shoot well. Failure in either respect could cause a fatal loss of respect among the men, and it was not unheard of for disenchanted bearers to simply walk away from a hunter they did not like, leaving him to make his way back—if he could find it.

"Of course, that won't be an issue with Ryder. They fight like cats to be chosen," she added, nodding toward the squabbling porters. Ryder waded into the fray and they stilled at once. He spoke quietly and within minutes had sorted out who would be coming and who would be left behind. He appointed a headman to keep the various porters in order, and I tilted my head toward Gideon.

"Why not him?"

Tusker shook her head. "The other tribes won't stand for it. Ryder has tried, and even he's found it to be more trouble than it's worth. No, he'll take Gideon as his personal guide and they will work together, but the headman will have to sort out the others, a full-time occupation, believe you me."

"If it's so difficult to keep the tribes in order, why not just choose them all from a single group?"

"Fatal," she said flatly. "They band together and turn on the whites. There was a hunt went out a dozen years ago that took nothing but Kikuyu. There was some dispute over the payment. By the time the hunt was finished, the Kikuyu had taken the white hunter back to their village to stake him out and let every villager piss in his mouth. Since then folk have mostly mixed up their bearers. Damnation! Just realised I forgot the grouse paste," she said. She lifted her voice to bark an order in Swahili and one of the porters hurried to retrieve the tins.

Tusker supervised the loading of the liquor and first aid supplies into the safari car, a battered old Ford that had been fitted for rough travel. The rest of the gear was portioned out for the bearers to carry, and Tusker ordered a cage of chickens to be lashed to the top of the car.

"Fresh eggs on safari," she said, rubbing her hands together. "And if they won't lay, chicken *fricassee*."

She nodded to my guns. "Hope you're prepared to use those."

I lifted a brow. "It seems a bit much firepower for a single lion."

She guffawed, thrusting her hands into her hair. It stood up in tufts over her head. "Silly child. We

246

have to feed the porters. That's the real reason Ryder let me come along. It's damned hard to hunt a man-eater and feed the bearers as well. We'll have to shoot enough game to keep them well fed. It's the law, you know."

"I didn't, actually."

She patted my arm. "Never mind. You'll soon catch on. Mind you shoot what they like, though. A happy crew makes for a happy hunt, and if you give them eland more than two days running, you'll have the lot of them ducking behind the *leleshwa* bushes to shit in a row. Fatty meat, eland is," she advised me.

She walked away then, and Ryder appeared at my elbow. "Getting the lay of the land from Tusker?"

"She's a unique character," I said faintly.

"Not in Africa. But then Africa attracts all kinds."

I followed him to where the cooking fire for breakfast had just fallen to grey ash. "She was telling me that I will be responsible to help feed the porters."

He bent to scoop some ash, sieving it through his fingers into a small leather bag. "Yes, you will. Did she warn you about eland?"

"In graphic detail."

"Well, she's not wrong. Stick to antelope and you'll be fine."

He scooped another handful. "What are you doing?"

"Ash bag. It's to help tell which way the wind is blowing when it's too soft to move the grass."

"If it's too soft to move the grass, how do you know it's blowing at all?"

"I don't, but a lion will. If we're on the wrong side of the wind, he'll be gone before we ever see him or we'll get the business end of his teeth."

My gaze fell to his arm, the long white streaks of scar cording the brown muscle of his forearm. "Tusker told me," I said, nodding toward his arm. "I can't imagine living through something like that."

He tied off the bag and straightened, dusting his hands. "No doubt she made it sound heroic." He smiled. "Don't be impressed, princess. Everybody out here has scars. Mine just happen to be on the outside."

By the time the safari car was packed and the bearers loaded, the sun was riding high, casting short shadows over the grassy savannah. Ryder directed the hunt towards the *lugga* where Tusker said the lion had been seen. He had already visited the kill site to see the pug marks in the soft soil and talk to the Kikuyu. We were hunting a young male, large and fit and unpredictable, he had warned. He roamed the dry riverbed, scrutinizing the sign as Tusker and I kept a watchful eye out for leopards. The headman directed the porters to rest and Gideon took the other half of the *lugga*.

After a lengthy consultation, they pointed us west, toward Lake Victoria and Uganda in the far distance.

We set off, Tusker driving the safari car and Ryder and Gideon walking. Some of the staff, including the cook whose duties exempted him from carrying anything, clung to the outside of the car as Tusker bounced them around the long plains. The others stretched out in a long line, singing songs in their various tongues as we wended our way westward.

I walked between Ryder and Gideon carrying my .22. The Rigby was far too much gun to carry for any length of time, but the .22 was manageable, although I noticed Ryder sending me sidelong glances to make sure I was holding up.

We came to the first river, a narrow crossing, but deep and tricky for the Ford. The porters came forward with sticks and rocks and began to hurl them into the water. The green water received them then suddenly began to heave like a pot coming to the boil. I saw a flash of teeth and tails as crocodiles thrashed their way out of the water and onto the sandy bank. They were hideous, like something prehistoric with their flat, dead eyes and their broad bodies. They ought to have been slow, but they weren't. They hurled themselves awkwardly onto one another, fighting for space as they fled the water.

The headman kept a watchful eye on them as he

waved Tusker forward. The car crossed, stately as a dowager, and behind her the porters hurried, each treading hard on the heels of the man in front. Gideon followed, and suddenly only Ryder and I were left. One of those scaly monsters opened his mouth and a small white bird hopped inside, pecking delicately at the morsels lodged between the monstrous teeth.

"Come on, princess. Before the crocs go back in and decide you look tasty."

He took my hand and waded forward. I put one foot in front of the other, but my body moved of its own accord. My mind had pushed everything aside except those eyes, those hungry, waiting eyes that never blinked. If I had been alone, I would have stood there in the rushing green water and let them take me. But Ryder never let go, pulling me forward and keeping me so close to him that both of my hands were tucked under his and resting on his hips. We climbed out the other side and I pried my cold fingers from his.

"Thank you," I murmured.

He smiled. "They're just crocs. Not dangerous if you know what to do."

"But I don't know what to do," I pointed out.

"That's why you have me."

He set a brisk pace after that, and I was glad. The speed and the golden light that spilled around us warmed me up. A small herd of zebra stopped grazing at our approach and lifted their noses. The porters began to sing again, and the miles unwound slowly behind as we walked. Ryder's eyes kept to the middle distance, softly focused to show him where the ground might have been disturbed. He stopped from time to time to consult with Gideon and between them they kept the lion's tracks before us. Sometimes the marks disappeared into the tall grass and we veered in a different direction, but always the lion had corrected back almost due west, taking us into the lengthening sun.

We stopped for a cold luncheon and began to walk again after the porters had rested. As we walked, Gideon raised his voice. "This is a thing that I know—Ryder knows the poems of Mr. Whitman."

For a moment I thought Ryder was ignoring him, but then he spoke. "'Passing stranger! you do not know how longingly I look upon you, you must be he I was seeking, or she I was seeking, it comes to me as of a dream, I have somewhere surely lived a life of joy with you . . .'"

He went on, reciting the rest. I had read Whitman. Mossy had bought me a copy that my Granny Miette had promptly confiscated and burned upon my arrival in Louisiana on the grounds that it was indecent. But I hadn't thought it indecent. Whitman was real; Whitman was passion. Whitman was aching and bruising and wanting and having. Reading him was like a long drink of cool water on a hot day at noon.

" 'I am to see to it that I do not lose you.' " Ryder finished. I did not have to look at him to know he had shifted his gaze. He wasn't staring at the pug marks then or looking for ant-bear holes or stray snakes.

Gideon spoke first. "I do not remember this poem of Mr. Whitman's. What is it called?"

" 'To a Stranger,' " I said quickly. I glanced at Ryder and his mouth curved into a slow smile.

"Familiar with it?"

"Yes." I tried not to think of the words on his lips. *Breast* and *beard* and *hands* and *body*.

Gideon spoke again. "I think that I like best the 'Song of Myself.' Will you say this one, *Bwana*?"

Ryder turned back to the tracks cutting through the long grass and began to speak. We walked on, each step marked with a syllable of the poem, the words slipping gently into my ears, music for our journey. Some words passed quickly, but others, whole phrases, clung to my skin. " '. . . every atom belonging to me as good belongs to you . . . I lean and loafe at my ease observing a spear of summer grass . . . A few light kisses, a few embraces, a reaching around of arms . . .' "

He continued on through the first five stanzas, each word a murmured invitation. There was enticement in that poetry, metaphors that passed from his lips to my ears as surely as any kisses. The poem had been written to shock, to strip away pretension and artifice, and leave nothing but naked souls behind. His voice caressed the words, not a practiced orator's voice, but a man's, low and rumbling gently over the African plains. Gideon walked solemnly, enjoying the poem as entertainment, but I shivered with each step, creeping closer as he dropped his voice lower with each stanza. It was seduction by poetry, and if we had been alone, I would have taken his hand and pulled him close, putting my mouth to his and drinking every word.

But we weren't alone, and just as he finished the fifth stanza, he stopped, raising his hand. He turned, silhouetted starkly against the dying sun.

"We'll make camp here," he announced.

"But there's an hour of daylight left," I protested. My knees were shaking and my ears buzzing with the sudden stopping.

He took off his hat and ran a hand through his hair. "We camp here," he repeated. "The porters need time to set up the tents and start the cooking fires." He slanted me a curious look. "What's the matter, princess? Haven't had enough yet?"

I didn't answer him, and he didn't seem to expect me to. He moved to stand in front of me. "Delilah," he said softly.

I didn't move away. "Yes?"

I looked into his eyes, wondering how they could possibly be so blue against the wide black pupils. He tipped his head down, then raised his hand, drawing one finger down my cheek. I shivered and leaned forward. He put his lips to my ear, grazing the curve as he spoke. "You need to go shoot some fresh meat."

My head snapped up. "I beg your pardon?"

"The porters need to eat. I don't waste my shooting permits on bush meat. Get going. Gideon will point you in the right direction."

He crossed his arms and stood with his feet planted wide apart, a pirate Colossus, grinning at me. I swung around and stalked away, knowing he was watching me with every step.

# 14

I shot a sizeable antelope for the cooking pot, and the men smiled their appreciation. The cook made it into some sort of stew with gourds and onions and they devoured it by their own fires, one for each tribe. They had piled their fires high with green matter causing them to smoke heavily, driving away the insects that would have plagued them. They would sleep under the stars, but two tents had been pitched on level ground, one for me and another for Ryder. Tusker refused to sleep in a tent, choosing the car instead.

"No, thank you," she said when I offered to share. "I have had quite enough experience of snakes in the bush. It makes me drink just to think about it. A nice day's hunting and no sooner do you fall asleep than something comes slithering into your tent to bed down between your legs. No, thank you, indeed."

Ryder's mouth was twitching hard, and I looked away so as not to laugh. Tusker excused herself and I rose from the fireside, wrapping a length of Masai cloth about my shoulders. Gideon had presented it to me before trotting off to make a bed for himself under the trees, and I was glad of it. Nights on the plains could be cool.

"Delilah," Ryder called as I reached my tent. I paused.

"Yes?"

He looked up from where he lounged, hands laced behind his head, legs crossed at the ankle.

"You might get scared," he said evenly. "There are noises in the bush, scary things with teeth and claws that go bump in the night. You might need protecting. I could help with that."

"Don't worry," I said sweetly. "I have my gun. If I hear anything coming toward my tent, I'll just shoot first and worry about what it might have been later."

He was still laughing when I shut myself in my tent.

The next morning we picked up the track again and it veered sharply south. Ryder was quiet, his mood solemn, and Gideon must have sensed it. He didn't ask for poetry and I doubt he would have gotten any if he had. Ryder grew even quieter as we approached an outcropping of rock. Gideon fell back with the headman and the porters and together they kept to the track. Only Ryder struck off, heading straight toward the rocks. I followed him, and he slowed, matching his pace to mine. I did not ask where we were going. The rocks rose straight before us, grey and weathered, the only real landmark in this part of the savannah.

We stopped at the foot and I saw where a cross

had been carved roughly into the rock. Ryder took off his hat as we moved close. He passed his hand over it, tracing the lines, first down, then across. He laid the flat of his hand over the stone, palm to rock, and remained that way for several minutes. Then he gave a great sigh and backed away to stand next to me. His hand brushed mine, but he did not reach for my fingers.

"Is this where your wife is buried?"

The question seemed to surprise him. "Eliza? No. This is my father's grave."

"Why is he here and not the churchyard?"

"Because this is where I killed him."

He clapped his hat back onto his head and swung around to rejoin the group. I strode after him, matching him step for step. "You can't just say something like that and walk off, you know. What happened?"

He took in a deep breath then blew it out slowly. "Elephant attack. He was hunting and got too close to a cow, the biggest female I've ever seen. Each tusk was two hundred pounds and he wanted the ivory for a trophy." His jaw was set as he told the story, grinding out the words as if each one hurt to give. "He slipped as he made the first shot. She was on him before he could fire again. I shot her twice and she rolled to the side, but it was too late. She'd already torn him open from neck to groin. It was just a matter of time."

"So you shot him to put him out of his suffering."

"You can dress it up to sound noble, but the ugly truth is that I put a bullet straight between his eyes. I did it because he asked me to." His gaze had gone flat and cold. "He wanted to do it himself, but she had crushed his fingers. He couldn't pull the trigger on his own revolver."

I shook my head. "Don't tell me any more."

"You asked, princess. Don't you want to hear it all? Don't you want to know that we fought just before he took that shot? I told him she was too close and he didn't need another damned trophy. I called him an old fool. Those were the last words I said to him, you know. He asked me to kill him and I did it and I forgot to tell him I was sorry. I forgot to tell him I loved him. I forgot to tell him that everything I know about being a man I learned from him. I forgot everything I should have said, and then he was dead and it was too late. It will always be too late."

I slipped my hand in his, and that small touch seemed to release something within him. The coiled tension eased, and his shoulders lowered. His jaw softened and he took out his handkerchief and handed it to me.

"Don't you ever carry your own?"

I shook my head and wiped at my eyes. I held it out, but he shook his head. "Keep it. I like to think of you owning something of mine."

He dropped my hand then and we walked back to the others who were still filing slowly across the wide African plain.

Late that afternoon we were walking sluggishly, full after a good lunch and feeling the pull of the warm sun towards the occasional shadow of an acacia. Suddenly, Gideon began speaking rapidly in Swahili to Ryder who bent swiftly over the tracks. Ryder turned to me, smiling broadly.

"We've got him and another. He's found a mate."

There in the soft soil, next to the pug marks of the large male, were the smaller prints of a female, sometimes bounding ahead, sometimes circling flirtatiously behind. Ryder explained that we had to move forward cautiously until we found them.

"You don't want to sneak up on a mating pair," he told me. Gideon took out the ash bag and sifted out a handful to toss lightly into the air. The wind was favourable and we moved forward, signalling to the porters and Tusker to stay behind. They began to set up camp as we followed the lions.

We heard them before we saw them. Just past a little rise, the land dipped down to a small *lugga*. There was scant vegetation, just a few thorn-bushes and an acacia, but there was some shade and it was here that the lions had decided to copulate. Gideon circled slightly to the left and made a series of swift hand signals while I stayed with Ryder.

"We won't go any closer and we won't take him now," he said, his mouth against my ear.

I shrugged slightly and he put a finger to his lips then gestured for me to watch. The lioness had apparently just decided to succumb. She was crouching low, flicking her tail back and forth under the lion's jaw, teasing him. With a low roar he flung himself forward, covering her as she dug her claws into the earth. He bit her neck, holding her down in submission as he pushed himself into her. She gave a little mew and turned her head, nuzzling at him. He was monstrous, a solid thing of muscle and bone and sinew and far larger than I had expected him to be. Even at a distance, I could feel the ground shake with the violence of his thrusting.

All at once, it was over. The lioness turned on him, letting out an impatient roar and lashing his nose with her claw. Blood spurted from his nose and he snarled at her as she whipped her tail, giving a low growl in response. They fought, first one lunging, then the other, and occasionally rolling around, raising a cloud of dust to powder them both. Then just as suddenly as they began the fight, it was finished. The male shook his head, the blood running freely from his nose. The female crept near, licking it, nuzzling. He turned his head, aloof to her attentions. She moved past him, graceful as a dancer, tantalizing him with the tuft at the end of her tail, again flicking it gently under his chin. He growled and she turned to walk past again, sinuous, inviting. He lowered his head and she moved past a third time, shifting her hips. At a sound from him she crouched, moving her tail aside as he lunged to cover her again.

Ryder touched my arm. "Best go while they're occupied," he murmured. We crept away and he signalled to Gideon to meet us at the encampment.

"If you're sure that's the man-eater, why didn't you take him?" I demanded.

"Oh, I'm sure. He's missing a toe on his back foot. No mistaking him."

"Again, why didn't you take him?"

Ryder's lips twitched. "I thought instead of a last meal he might like a last—"

"Never mind," I said.

He laughed. "Relax, princess. He is our man-eater and we'll get him tomorrow. But he'll be mating with that female for the next two days. I just thought I'd give him a chance to get cubs on her before I shot him."

"You think more lions are a good thing? When they eat people's children and cattle?"

He swung to face me. "I'm not a scientist, and I'm not a historian, but I can tell you those lions were here long before we were. And they won't be here much longer if everybody starts treating them like vermin. Now, I've got no problem taking out a lion that's a nuisance. But just because he's a man-eater doesn't mean his cubs will be."

"But they might," I pressed.

"Then I'll kill them, too. Happy?"

"No! You are the most contradictory person I've ever met—a white hunter who doesn't like to hunt?"

He sighed. "Delilah." The softness of my name stopped me in my tracks. He was looking at me, really looking, as if the strength of that looking could teach me to understand him. "I've been doing this a long time. I saw what happened in the States when people were given free rein to hunt buffalo. There used to be millions of them roaming the plains. Now they're gone, vanished into nothing, and with them went all the tribes that used to survive on them. It's a whole way of life that just isn't there anymore, and that's a tragedy. It's more than a tragedy, it's a crime, only no one is ever going to swing for it. The one thing Roosevelt did right was to create protected parkland and preserves. Maybe, just maybe, some of the kind of wilderness I grew up in will survive. But there's nobody to do that here. It's all too new, too much chaos and too much arguing. Nobody is putting aside parkland and nobody is protecting the way of life that's been here for thousands of years."

He took a step closer, his tone urging. "Don't you see? Those zebra we saw yesterday are part of something bigger, a huge migration that moves over these plains in a vast circle every year. First the wildebeest come, then the zebra, then the small gazelles. There's a rhythm to it, a rhyme and a reason that makes you believe in a god when nothing else will. And when people stay out of it, the system works just fine. Some of the hooved stock are lost to the lion and the leopard, but most aren't. Most survive, and so do the cats, and so do the people who live out here. It works, at least it did until the white folks came in and started taking it apart. Now there's only so much time left until it's all undone."

He stopped and drew a deep breath. "The odds are long that the lioness will even conceive. And if she does, most of the cubs probably won't even make it to adulthood. But if one does, then I will have undone what I have to do when I kill that man-eater. I can bring everything back into balance, and when this place goes to hell, when there's nothing left on this plain but memories and regrets, it won't be all my fault. Can you understand that? Will you understand that?"

He was standing so close I could see the gold flecks in the blue of his eyes. I opened my mouth, but he turned. "I shouldn't have preached. Come on. Let's see what Tusker rustled up for dinner."

Tusker's cook produced a marvel of a meal, and while Ryder went to the porters to discuss what would happen during the next day's shoot, Tusker and I lounged by the fire with pink gins. The nightjars were calling and the crickets sang as the

263

ripening moon rose. Tusker threw her head back and inhaled deeply.

"Breathe in Africa, child. It's the most revivifying place I have ever been."

"Did you grow up here?"

She gave a short, barking laugh. "God, no. I was brought up in England, a proper little debutante, making my curtsey to the Prince of Wales and filling in my dance card. I broke out as soon as I could. Told Balfour I would marry him if he took me right out of England. It was an escape plan, you see."

"Escape?"

"From all of it, the expectations and the decorum and the polite smiles hiding vicious tongues. I'd had my heart broken, you see. Fell in love with the wrong chap and he crushed me right down to the bedrock. Nothing left but humiliation."

"And Balfour picked up the pieces?"

"He did. A good fellow, was Balfour. For a poofter."

She took a long sip of her cocktail and I blinked at her. "He was a homosexual?"

"Oh, as flouncy as they come! But I didn't care. It meant he would never bother me in the bedroom, and that's all I wanted. So I married him and he brought me here. We got on quite well together. Poor dear, he always had schemes for making money and none of them ever worked.

But we rubbed along together and we were happy enough."

"What became of him?"

She flapped a hand. "Same thing that happens to all of us, dear child. He got dead." She took another deep drink. "It was blackwater fever that took him. A nasty business, that. It comes after you've had malaria too many times and it can kill you. A man can only withstand so many bouts of blackwater fever before his body just gives out and he drops dead. Poor Balfour died his first go-round with it. But Ryder is stronger stuff. I imagine he'll make it through another time or two before he goes." She frowned at her glass. "I think I need topping off. What about you, dearie?"

I held out my glass and she poured. "What did you mean about Ryder? He's sick?"

"Not now. Got the constitution of an ox. But he's had blackwater fever three times. No man lives through five."

"Is there any way to prevent getting it?"

She shrugged. "Kill all the mosquitoes? It's the mosquitoes that cause it, you see. It starts with the malaria. Just after the rains, when the weather is warm and damp, he takes precautions. Usually heads up to the hills, gets up too high for the mosquitoes to be a nuisance. But there are no guarantees. Oh, don't look so grim, child! He doesn't think twice about it most days. And why should he? Out here you can be right as rain and step on a cobra and that's it, your number is up and you're singing harmony in St. Peter's choir."

She fell silent and I glanced to where the men had gathered around their fire. They were listening intently to Ryder, plucking ticks off their legs and flinging them into the flames.

"It must be nice for the two of you to have one another out here. Family, I mean."

"Oh, that. Well, it was an accident, pure and simple. I'd lost touch with his father after he left home. Ran off at seventeen, Jonas did. Always a flighty boy. There's a streak of wildness in the family, you know," she added with a wink and a nod. "But he always wanted to see the world, and see it he did. I wasn't altogether surprised when he landed here. Of course, if you're English and you want wilderness, there aren't many spots left, are there? All the cast-offs and vagabonds make it through Mombasa at some point. When I heard Jonas was there, I cabled him and he came up. I was surprised to find he had a boy. None of us had known about him. And that brought troubles of its own, of course."

"Troubles?"

"Our elder brother, Miles, had inherited the family title. Nothing at all impressive, just a baronetcy with no money and little land. But Miles hadn't had children of his own yet, and Ryder was heir presumptive. Miles insisted on having him sent to England to be educated.

Ordinarily, Jonas wouldn't have agreed, but he'd just been through a bad patch health-wise. Feeling a bit of his own mortality, the Grim Reaper's long shadow, all that rot. So he sent Ryder to England, much against the boy's protestations, I can assure you. He spent two terms at Rugby and was sent down for fighting. Miles decided to find a private tutor and that was even worse. The boy ran away and it took a fortnight to find him, living rough on Dartmoor, of all places."

"I can believe it," I said, smiling into my glass.

"Yes, well, that was enough for Jonas to regain his sense. He brought Ryder back to Africa and Miles did what he ought to have done and found himself a wife and started making his own heirs."

"I take it Ryder isn't the heir anymore."

"God, no. There are now seven between him and the title, and that is perfectly fine with him. He'd sooner hang than live in England. He said the whole country is too damned small. Gave him claustrophobia."

"It can be a little stifling," I agreed.

"What about you? Where do your people come from?" she asked suddenly.

"Here and there. My father was a Devonshire Drummond and my mother is a L'Hommedieu from Louisiana."

"Devonshire? I remember dancing with a Devonshire Drummond at my coming-out party. Thick as two planks nailed together but a damned fine dancer. And quite good-looking. All the Devonshire Drummonds are handsome and stupid."

"That sounds about right."

"What are the L'Hommedieus like?"

"Stupid and handsome."

She laughed her barking laugh again. "Do tell."

"Well, not stupid precisely, but doggedly attached to the old ways, come Hell or high water. My grandfather L'Hommedieu was the youngest colonel in his cavalry regiment."

"A military man, eh? Nothing wrong with that."

"He was a Confederate."

"Ha! Backed a losing side. Shame. Ah, well. It happens to all of us now and then. I presume your people are Creoles. You've a look of them with that black hair."

"Yes, dark as the devil and twice as wild, my grandmother always says."

"Blood will out," Tusker agreed. "The first thing you learn in breeding horses and it holds true for people as well. That's why you've got to bring in fresh blood."

"So my mother preaches. But there are a dozen other stables in her part of the county. It must be more difficult for you to get fresh stock."

She fixed Ryder with a pointed stare as he came near. "Tell him that. My racehorses are pedigreed, but I breed others, too, also fast as the wind. They're tidy little earners, but someone refuses to go and get me new stallions."

Ryder snorted. "That's because the last time I went, it nearly cost me my manhood."

Tusker let out a peal of laughter, holding her sides. "Oh, it's true, my dear," she said in response to my skeptical look. "The best horses in the world are bred in Abyssinia, but it's impossible to trade for them. I bet Ryder he couldn't bring me back an Abyssinian stallion and pair of mares without getting himself caught and castrated."

"Castrated?" I stared at Ryder.

"The penalties for horse thieving in Abyssinia are a bit extreme," he admitted.

"You rode all the way to Abyssinia to risk castration?"

"Of course not," he said, giving me a slow smile. "I walked."

I shook my head as Tusker went off in gales of laughter again. She wiped her eyes on the hem of her shirt. "I thought for certain the boy was dead. He was gone weeks, *weeks*. He finally came limping back leading a string of the most beautiful horses you've ever clapped eyes on, Delilah. Each one of them was worthy of an emperor. That trip was so dangerous, it was written up in the book at the club."

"And greatly exaggerated," Ryder put in. "I didn't kill three lions. Just one." He rubbed a finger over the braided bracelet at his wrist. I leaned closer.

"A souvenir?"

He held up his wrist. "He was after the horses. Killed one before I could get him, but I thought a bit of his mane might make a nice memento." The hair was black as a starless night.

"I didn't realise they came with black manes." I touched the hair. It was springy and thick. My fingertip brushed the pulse at his wrist, and for a moment we locked eyes.

"Anything with black hair is trouble for me," he said. His tone was light, but his expression was serious. A nicer woman would have felt sorry for him. A kinder woman would have put him out of his misery and taken his hand and walked him back to her tent. A sweeter woman would have let him spend the night.

But I'm none of those things. So I rose and said good-night and went to bed alone.

The next morning we woke before sunrise. The lions were still mating. The sounds of their copulating rolled over the plains, and the porters scurried about with a new urgency. Today was the day they'd been waiting for. A kill, a good meal, and the start of the journey home with their families and a hefty tip waiting at the end.

Ryder checked the weapons and he and Gideon and I set out after breakfast. I hadn't eaten, but Ryder shoved a packet of sandwiches at me and told me to carry them. I took my rifle and ammunition and followed him across the grass and down to the *lugga* where death waited.

The lion had paid for his pleasure. She'd given him a beating; open cuts laced his nose where she had lashed him. Her own back was marked with foamy pink froth from his mouth where he'd held her, sometimes ungently. Ryder had gone over the procedure while he ate. When they separated, we were to take the male and leave the female if possible. He explained that she might charge, but it was a chance we were going to have to take.

We settled into the bushes and began to wait. We waited all that morning and into the afternoon, sitting so still that it felt as if we had never known how to move at all. The sun rose overhead, burning off the early morning cloud and casting short shadows. Hunger came and went again, and still we waited. At last, as the afternoon was drawing to a close, the lion finished mounting her for the last time. She lashed at him and he crouched and rolled on the ground. She hadn't meant it. She stretched and wandered a little distance to the stream to drink and then she simply walked away, tail held high, no longer interested in him.

Just then, the male caught sight of something, or perhaps he smelled us.

He rolled back onto his four massive paws, lifting his enormous head and moving slowly toward us. Gideon lifted his spear and Ryder and I shouldered our rifles.

"Got him?" Ryder asked coolly.

"Yes." The trigger was cold under my finger.

"He's yours. Take him."

My belly rolled. I didn't want to do this. I would never have done this. This was destruction, something that felt criminal and wrong. The lion moved closer, never hurrying, secure in his own size, his own ferocity. His amber eyes surveyed the bush, and I saw that they were yellow around the pupils, just like Ryder's.

"Princess?"

"I have him," I said. My voice shook, but my hand was steady. The lion gathered himself then, and gave a roar so loud the ground trembled under my feet. The sound moved from the earth up into my legs and spread through my belly and my heart and lodged in my throat. I could feel it still when I pulled the trigger and the roar of the lion and the roar of the gun and the roar of my own voice were the same.

The lion stopped, stuttered a step, then kept coming. I fired again, and this time he gave a whimper and rolled onto his side. Ryder told me to reload and cover him as he moved out from the bushes. My hands were slick, and the bullets rattled in my palm.

"I will cover him, *Bibi*," Gideon said softly, his spear arm ready.

I nodded and stuffed the bullets into the chamber, cocking the gun. Ryder motioned me forward.

"He's done."

"I don't want to see him. Do I have to see him?"

"He's your trophy."

"Leave him there. I don't want him touched. The hyenas can have him. And that's not why I killed him. You know that."

"Doesn't matter to him," Ryder pointed out. He bent to the bloody business with his knife, and rose a moment later. He walked back and opened my hand. He pressed something hard in the palm and I looked down. It was a tooth, as long and broad as a man's finger. It was sharp and gleaming white through the blood. It was warm in my hand. He gave me a tuft of its mane as well, and I shoved the two trophies into my pocket.

Ryder turned to Gideon. "Any sign of the female?"

"No, *Bwana*. She ran at the sound of the guns."

"Good," Ryder told him.

"Yes, I am relieved," Gideon said with his gap-toothed smile.

We turned and began to walk back to the camp. I felt nothing, no fear, no euphoria, nothing but an odd, incomparable lightness. I could have floated away just then, and only the weight of that tooth in my pocket held me down.

"Why are you relieved?" I asked suddenly.

Gideon turned to me. "The female is very deadly and very dangerous, and if she decided to avenge her mate, she could harm *Bwana*. And then perhaps I would have to kill her myself."

"You don't want to kill her?"

"No, *Bibi*. I have killed nine lions. That is enough."

"Nine is a very great number," I agreed.

He shook his head. "It is too great a number. For a man to kill more than nine lions, he has taken more than his share, and he will suffer very bad luck, *Bibi*. Very bad luck indeed."

# 15

We returned to the cheers of the men just as Tusker was returning with her bearer. He carried a reedbuck slung over his shoulders and in one hand he held the stomach, stuffed with the internal organs and sewn shut. The cook went to work and the porters brought water, filling a canvas bath in my tent. I cleaned myself first, scrubbing off dirt and sweat and blood, surprised to find that I didn't look any different. I spread my fingers and stared at the clean skin and immaculate nails.

"No perfumes of Araby needed to clean this little hand," I murmured.

"Talking to yourself? Ah, well, at least you're assured of intelligent company," Tusker put in. She thrust only her head and hand through the tent flap as she offered me a glass. "Champagne. It's tradition."

She vanished and I sipped at the champagne. It was marvelously cold, and when I joined them at the fireside for dinner, I told her so.

"It's the wicker," she said, nodding toward the narrow woven bottle covers. "We just put the bottles into them and sink the whole mess into a river or stream. Keeps the bubbly nice and cold. Let's pop another cork, shall we?"

In fact, we popped three more and in the end

only Tusker and Ryder and I were left at the fireside, each with our own bottle.

"Glad to see you ate a good dinner," Tusker said, hiccupping gently. "Ryder thought you might have been upset at killing that lion. I walked over to see the body. The vultures had made a start but he was a big brute."

"It had to be done," I said faintly. I took another deep swig from the bottle and the bubbles tickled my nose.

"You did well," Ryder said softly. He was sitting opposite me, the fire flickering between us. His eyes were warm.

"I must admit, Delilah, I did worry you might lack bottom," Tusker put in. "I thought you might turn and run or at least make Ryder shoot the bloody thing. Glad to see you're made of sterner stuff."

"So I've been tested and found not wanting?" I said lightly.

"Something like that," Tusker replied. Ryder said nothing, but his expression was unlike any I had seen on his face before. There was something marginally softer there, something almost vulnerable. "Women out here fall into two camps," Tusker went on. "Those who are worth everything and those who are worth nothing. There is no in-between. And those who are worth everything are rare as hen's teeth. You've got bottom," she said, lifting her bottle.

I sipped again. Ryder was still watching me.

"I don't know how much bottom I have," I said slowly. "I didn't want to pull that trigger. I still don't want to."

"That's what makes you worth something," Ryder said, his voice barely audible over the crackling of the flames. "You didn't want to, and you did it anyway because it was a thing that had to be done."

"I should have left it to you."

"You couldn't have. It was your battle, not mine. The lion made sure of that when he killed one of your Kikuyu."

"They're not my Kikuyu," I returned, my voice sharper than it needed to be. Tusker upended her bottle, sucking the last of her champagne.

"The minute you set foot on Fairlight they became yours," Ryder countered. "Whether you like it or not, they're your responsibility. And you know it, or at least your bones and your blood do. Otherwise you never would have taken that lion yourself. You protected your own people because that's what we do out here. You're becoming one of us."

"One of you?" I echoed. "Your sense of humour is better than I thought because that's a damn good joke. I'm not one of you. I'll never be one of you."

"Of course you will," Tusker put in, hiccupping again. "Just takes a bit of time, that's all. By this time next year—"

"This time next year I won't be here. I'm not staying. I was never supposed to stay. I'm here to serve out a sentence and nothing more. As soon as I make parole as far as my family is concerned, I'm taking the first steamer out of Mombasa."

Tusker snorted. "You've already got a taste for Africa, child. You won't be satisfied with anything less. Europe, America, even the Orient. They're all pallid and bloodless, full of people who've had all the fire and spirit leached out of them. Is that what you want?"

"Yes," I said coolly. "I want to wear silk shoes without getting them bloody. I want to eat without swallowing as much red dirt as I do food. I want to go to bed without worrying about ants or scorpions or snakes trying to have their way with me. And I want to be in a place where children don't get chewed up just because somebody turned their back."

Ryder said nothing as I spoke. He just took another long drag off of his bottle.

"Well, children, I'm turning in," Tusker said, rising unsteadily to her feet. We said good-night to her and she lurched off toward the car.

"Will she be all right?"

Ryder gave me a half smile. "I've seen her take down an elly twice as drunk as she is now. She'll be fine."

We rose as well and Ryder put a hand to my

shoulder. "Stay inside tonight, no matter what you hear. If that lioness decides to come sniffing around, it could be dangerous."

"Fine," I said. I turned to go, but before I had made it a dozen steps, Ryder was at my side.

"What the hell did I just tell you?"

"To stay put once I turned in. I haven't turned in yet," I pointed out reasonably.

His voice was harsh. "You saw what one of those things can do to a human. How damned stupid do you have to be to go wandering around?"

"I'm not wandering around. I just need a moment alone before I go into the tent," I told him. "I drank a bottle and a half of champagne."

"For Christ's sake," he muttered. He took me hard by the hand and dragged me into the bushes. "Go there."

"I think not," I said, folding my arms. I stood toe-to-toe with him, refusing to budge.

"Women," he said finally. He circled around to a thick bush and struck it several times with the flat of his hand. An irritable porcupine wandered out, shooting him resentful glances as it waddled away.

Ryder indicated the bush with a flourish. "Behind there. I'll wait here by the tree, until you finish. Then I will personally escort you to your tent and tie it closed. Deal?"

"Fine." I did what I needed and hurried back. He

was resting a shoulder against the tree, and when I approached, he didn't move.

"Ryder?"

He pointed upwards, and I stood next to him, watching as the moon emerged from behind a narrow cloud. It was still weak, but it was enough to silver the whole of the African savannah, washing everything with cool light. In the distance I could hear the men still talking at their fires, their voices low and sleepy as they settled down for the night. Far in the distance I heard the lioness give a long, low howl and it sounded like mourning.

I looked up at Ryder to find him watching me. I put out my hand, running my fingers over the scars on his arm. He sucked in his breath sharply, but didn't move. The night breeze stirred a little, rustling the leaves around us, and the air was thick with the sage scent of the *leleshwa* and the sharp green brightness of the tiny violets we had crushed underfoot.

I put the flat of my other hand against his chest. I stepped as close as I could, pressing myself to him, thigh to thigh, belly to belly, ready for him to make the next move.

I didn't have long to wait. He grabbed both of my wrists and pushed me, slamming my back against the tree, pinning my arms high overhead. I was stretched taut as a bow. My legs shook and he shoved his thigh between them, holding me up.

I said his name and he lowered his head. Any other man would have kissed me. Ryder didn't. He pushed himself hard against me, filling the space so that there was no me, no him, no tree, no separateness. He put his face close to mine, his nose at my temple. And then he inhaled, slowly, tracing his way down from my hairline. He circled my ear, lingering at my neck, and nuzzling a moment before moving lower. My arms ached and my thighs hurt and I wanted it to go on forever, until the end of the world burned us up into ash that would scatter on the wind over the savannah.

He buried his face between my breasts and then lifted his head again, still sniffing me like an animal. His hands were bruising my wrists, but I wanted them tighter. I pulled, and he growled, pressing me farther into the hardness of the tree behind. He wasn't gentle or sweet or easy, and I wanted him so badly that the wanting was a thing apart, driving everything I did. I would have clawed off my own flesh to get rid of it, and I wanted him to know it.

His face was pressed to my neck and I turned my head, putting my mouth against his temple. He reared back as if I'd scalded him, then shoved his body even further against mine, punishing, stretching my arms further. "Yes," I said, half sobbing.

He shook his head. "No."

He let go of me then, releasing me so fast I

slipped to the ground. My legs and arms were boneless, useless things. I sat hard, staring up at him.

He put out a hand, then quickly pulled it back as if touching me would scorch him. "Sorry, princess. I can't take the chance."

"What chance? You were willing enough before. What's changed?"

"Everything. You're leaving."

"You knew that." I put my hands flat against the dirt and pushed. I managed to stagger to my feet, dizzy and aching. I pulled a cigarette from its case and lit it, my hand shaking so badly that I dropped three matches before I managed to kindle a flame.

"I thought you might change your mind after you spent some time here."

"Well, I won't." I took several long pulls off my cigarette before I spoke again. "You're just full of surprises," I said finally.

"Don't make me talk about it. I can't explain it."

"No, I don't think you can. I ought to be insulted. I don't get turned down very often. But this isn't about you not wanting me, is it? I'm a big girl, Ryder. I know when a man wants me. And I know you want me so badly right now it's taking everything you have not to throw me down right here. You don't even have to tell me I'm right. I can see your hands shaking. I know you're hard for me."

I had meant it as a jibe, but his face was serious.

282

"You think it's the first time? I'm used to this by now, Delilah. It takes nothing these days. The sound of your voice, the smell of your perfume. Hell, you don't even have to be around. All I have to do is think about you and I'm so ready I could take this damn place apart rock by rock just to get to you."

"Then why didn't you do anything about it? You're not the only one suffering, you know."

"Don't," he ordered.

"That's it? That's all I get? You'll let me get you good and ready, but then you won't use it to repay the favour? Naughty, naughty, Ryder. Didn't anyone ever teach you it's not nice to be selfish?"

His hands were clenching and unclenching on his thighs. "I don't hit women," he said, half to himself.

"But you'd like to," I went on, softly. "You'd like to put something into me, and if it isn't going to be what we both want, why not your fist?"

I ground out my cigarette on my boot and stood close to him. I picked up his hand, that closed, fisted hand, and I opened it, coaxing the fingers to spread wide. His palm was open and flat, vulnerable, and I pressed my mouth into it, nipping lightly with my teeth.

He clapped his other hand to the back of my head, shoving it upward until he found my mouth. It wasn't a kiss. It was an assault, and I hurt him right back, biting his lip. I tasted juniper and blood and

I twisted my hands in his hair, pulling him closer.

I wasn't surprised when he broke the kiss. He twisted away, and grabbed both my hands in his.

"Delilah," he said, and there was pleading in his voice.

"It's all right," I told him. "I'm done. I won't push it any more."

He released my hands. I put one to the front of his trousers, cupping hard.

"I just wanted both of you to have something to think about when you're lying awake tonight."

I turned and walked back to my tent. I had had the last word. It wasn't much consolation, but it would have to do.

Much later, long after the moon had set, I awoke, my heart slamming into my ribs. I sat up, straining my eyes, and could just make out a shadow beyond the flap of my tent. It did not move, but I heard a low, carrying howl. The sound came from some distance away, and I watched the still shadow crouching in front of my tent.

Over the howl came a series of unearthly cries, shrieks that could only mean one thing: the hyena had found the lion. I listened to them until I couldn't stand it anymore. My hands were knotted in the sheets, and it took everything I had to unclench them. A line of sweat beaded my hairline as I heard them, snarling and snapping as they dismantled the body. It seemed to go on for hours, those maddening, horrifying sounds as they broke the lion apart, and all the while the shadow in front of my tent never moved.

I moved to swing my feet over the edge of my cot and the frame gave a tiny squeak of protest. The shadow shifted.

"I'm here, Delilah. Go back to sleep."

I put my head back down to my pillow, but it was hours before I slept again. And all through that long night he stayed there, watching over me, saying nothing as he peered into the darkness that pressed against us like a living thing.

The journey back to Fairlight was uneventful. Tusker was nursing a modest hangover and the men were jubilant. They sang songs, filling the savannah sky with their chanting, and sparing the rest of us the burden of conversation. We cut directly across the countryside, saving a day and reaching Tusker's ranch by teatime. I walked with Gideon and it was companionable, our silence, unlike the prickly thing that had sprung up between Ryder and me. He did not look at me, not until we had left Tusker at Nyama and he had taken me back to Fairlight. He unloaded my gear and stood, arms at his sides.

"I will have to arrange for your fee to be sent from Nairobi," I began.

"Forget it," he said, his mouth angry. "This one was on the house."

"That's very kind of you."

"I'm not kind and we both know it. I do what I want for my own reasons."

"Fine. You're not kind and I'm not grateful. Is there anything else?"

"Yes." He pushed his hands through his hair. It was rough and unkempt, but it had felt like raw silk in my fingers. "I'm leaving. I'll be gone at least a month. I've got a short safari to guide for a client coming out of Nairobi."

"Safe journey, then."

"Goddammit, Delilah—" He broke off. "Never mind. I'm leaving Gideon behind. He'll keep an eye on you and on Fairlight."

"I don't need a nursemaid, Ryder. Not even yours."

"No, but you could probably use a friend. He'll know where to find me if you need me."

Before I could say a word, he grabbed me by the back of the neck, kissing me hard. It was over as soon as he began, and when he released me he looked angrier still, as if kissing me had been something he had done entirely against his will.

"I know exactly how you feel," I murmured. He stalked off without another word and I turned and went into Fairlight, now empty and small. But whether I was thinking of the house or myself, I couldn't say.

After that, things settled into a routine. I spent my mornings patching up the Kikuyu and Masai at

Fairlight while Gates hid his resentment and did what I told him for the most part. While I was away, Dodo had started a complete overhaul of the house from top to bottom. She had the house scrubbed, and hauled the carpets and curtains outside to the garden to be beaten. She set four boys with cricket bats to them, and the cloud of dust and insects they raised nearly choked us all. The floors were waxed and polished and the silver rubbed until it shone. Every window was cleaned with vinegar and sheets of newspaper, and when she was finished the house seemed lighter, shedding its coat of filth and neglect.

The kitchen was overhauled as well, and Pierre found a proper cook, an elegant Somali named Omar. He wouldn't touch pork, but his skills made up for the lack of bacon at the table. Pierre was delighted with the changes and I presented him with a dashing new red fez to replace his old one. He even went so far as to serve dinner one evening wearing white gloves, but I told him it was a ridiculous affectation in Africa and he took them off. He sulked for a while, only perking up when I promised him a raise. Dora pursed her lips and looked disapproving, but she said nothing. She had worked her fingers to the bone on the house. The entire place shone like a new pin, and I told her so.

"Why, thank you," she said, looking a little startled. "I have actually rather enjoyed it. Not all of it, mind you. There were days only stout British resolve got me through. But it looks rather lovely now, if I may say."

"You may. The slipcovers you made for the drawing room were an inspired choice."

She had ordered yards of a glazed black chintz with a pattern of falling autumn leaves and I had wiped out the rest of that quarter's allowance from the Colonel to pay for it. The black kept it from feeling too feminine and the falling leaves somehow evoked the warm colours of the African landscape. She had broken half her nails on an elderly sewing machine she'd unearthed before she found that Mr. Patel could run up anything in half the time for pennies an hour. It was a useful discovery considering the fact that we had each managed to ruin most of the clothes we had come with. Insects, stray nails, thornbushes—all had taken their toll, and Dora had finally resorted to having Mr. Patel make half a dozen housecoats to put over her own clothes while she worked. I hadn't bothered. I had gotten into the habit of wearing riding breeches and Misha's shirts every day, my fashionable Paris frocks packed away in cedar and lavender until an evening entertainment or trip to town presented itself.

Aside from Kit, we had seen little of our neighbours. I made a point of walking over to visit him a few times a week for obvious reasons. He had decided to paint me, and after he fed me lunch and took me to bed, he would get up and stand in front of his easel, the sunlight warming his bare skin. He committed me to the canvas, first with a soft pencil, then with a palette and paints, frowning from the image to me and back again. He had positioned me sitting up against the headboard, the sheet draped carelessly at my waist, a cigarette dangling from my fingertips. I was at an oblique angle, something like *La Grande Odalisque*, so there was nothing objectionable on display, although I knew objections would be made in any event. I didn't much care. Kit was a talented artist, and I quite liked the idea of hanging on some collector's wall, or better yet, in a museum, naked for the world to see. I turned my face so that my gaze would be directed at whoever viewed the painting, and Kit gave a little shout of exultation.

"Perfect, my darling! Hold that expression. Chin down just a fraction—there. Don't move. And whatever you're thinking about, don't stop. That expression is precisely what I want. It dares the viewer to look away. It will make them feel as if they are naked instead of you."

I couldn't wait to see it, but Kit was superstitious. He always made me dress and leave straight after so I couldn't peek. He was excited about it, more than the lovemaking itself. Most days he rushed the sex to get to the painting, and I should have been a little miffed. But I always made sure I got what I came for, and if he didn't, well, he had the painting to console him. He said it was going to be the centrepiece of the Nairobi show, and he chattered like a monkey while he worked. Most artists liked silence while they painted, but not Kit. He wanted to talk so long as I listened and didn't move too much. He twittered on about how small the art world was and how one successful show anywhere would be his ticket back in. He talked about the contacts he still had in Paris and New York, and how the Berlin art scene was beginning to hop. He talked about Barcelona and Chicago and Rome, all of his hopes and ambitions.

He talked about people, too, mostly our neighbours, and he gave me a wicked look as he began to catalogue the women he'd had since he'd arrived in Africa. I wasn't surprised he'd bedded Jude and Bianca, but the fact that he'd slept with Helen came as a bit of a shock.

"I would have thought her a little old for you," I said, careful not to move my mouth too much.

He gave a short bark of laughter, like a hyena. "If Helen likes to put it about, who am I to stop her? The trouble is that Rex isn't enough for her. Oh, it's not his fault. She said he's enormous and very skilled with it. But our Helen likes variety."

"So she *is* a nymphomaniac. Poor Rex. Do you think he knows?"

"Oh, he knows. And between you and me, I think he's almost proud of it in a strange way. Rex likes to have the best and most beautiful and Helen's little adventures prove that other men want what he has. Besides, his driving passion is politics. He tolerates her lapses and she tolerates his ambitions. It seems to work fine for them. More than fine—they are not a couple I would want to come between."

"Perhaps. It still seems a little sad."

"Why? Don't tell me the scandal of two continents believes in fidelity," he said with a mocking twist of his mouth. Why had I never noticed how thin his lips could go?

"Three continents, actually. You forgot about that time in Buenos Aires. And yes, I do believe in fidelity. Not to you, of course," I added with a malicious smile. "But I have always been faithful to my husbands until they either died on me or the marriage broke down. I have never deceived a man I promised to love until death."

He said nothing for a minute. He was too busy painting furiously. Then he peered around the canvas. "I had a letter from my sister. She said the Paris gossip mills were working overtime when your Russian prince died. Word is you might have had a hand in it. Did you?"

"No," I said slowly. "But he asked me to. He gave me his revolver. It belonged to the last tsar of Russia, you know. It was a beautiful little piece, but lethal enough. I just couldn't pull the trigger. A better wife would have done it." I thought of

Ryder's choice under the same circumstances. It was strange that we had something like that in common. It made a bond between us even though we had answered the call quite differently. He was stronger than I was. Or maybe he had just loved his father more than I had loved Misha. You had to love someone completely to be willing to destroy them.

The paintbrush clattered to the floor. "Jesus Christ."

I took a deep drag off my cigarette. "Well, you did ask," I said evenly. "That was the last time I saw him. I put the gun to his head and my hand was shaking. And I thought of how many times I had stroked that hair and brushed it and clutched it as I screamed his name. And I couldn't make myself squeeze the trigger. I walked out and left him there, knowing he wanted to die and that I didn't love him quite enough to help him do it."

He didn't attempt to retrieve his brush. He just stood there and stared at me as I talked.

"Why did he want you to do that? Was he that upset about the divorce?"

I laughed, but it didn't sound like a laugh. It sounded like a sob, something dry and brittle rattling between the bones. "I've never broken any man's heart badly enough to kill him, Kit. He had cancer, the painful, sly kind, wedged down deep in his bones. There was nothing the doctors could do. He wanted to go out on his own terms before things got worse. He had been shooting himself with morphine, but it had gotten so bad that it was barely knocking the edge off the pain. It was time."

"What happened after you left?"

I shrugged. "Misha found the courage I had misplaced. He put the gun into his mouth and pulled the trigger and ruined a yard of expensive wallpaper at the Ritz. They billed me for it, the bastards."

Kit put down his palette and walked slowly to the bed. "I don't even know how you live with a story like that."

"Easy. Like every bad thing that's ever happened to me, I lock it up and don't think about it. And once in a while someone asks, and I take my pain out and pass it around for other people to look at. It's like a glass eye or a wooden leg. It shocks them and it gives me a gruesome little thrill to inflict it on the unsuspecting."

He shook his head. "You have always been dazzling—the life of every party, the glamour girl who dances until dawn."

"Well, I am. But I'm dancing on broken glass. I'm Miss Havisham's wedding cake, Kit. A frothy, expensive, mice-eaten confection. I'm the Sphinx's nose, the fallen Colossus. I'm a beautiful ruin, and it's time that has done the deed."

To my astonishment, he reached out and held me then, and after a moment I let him.

He put a finger to the black ribbon at my wrist. "I've always wondered what you're hiding. Makes you even more mysterious, you know."

"What do you think is under there?"

He gave me a devilish smile. "I think it's a tattoo from where you were marked with Creole voodoo as a child. Or were you branded for thievery, like Milady de Winter?"

"You've read too many Gothic novels. It's just a ribbon, Kit."

"I like my version better. More interesting," he said, closing his eyes and pulling me nearer. I relaxed against him and almost let myself go.

That's the danger of locking away your pain. It makes it hard to be human again, to let someone hold you just for the sake of being close. And before things got too comfortable between us, I slipped my hand between his legs and he forgot about consolation. Instead he thrusted and grunted and when it was done, he rolled over and fell asleep almost instantly. I sat up in the sticky sheets and smoked another cigarette. I had almost let down my guard with Kit. He was wild and creative and unpredictable. But there was another side to him as well, an unexpected sweetness that was dangerous. He was fickle as the wind, unreliable as spring sunshine. It would never do to invest my hopes in him. There was no bedrock in Kit to build on. I couldn't let myself get too fond of him. I dressed quietly and slipped away.

# 16

The rest of that month brought surprises. The first was how much I grew to like Tusker Balfour. She appeared at Fairlight one morning covered in red dust from the road, pushing a bicycle with a flat tire.

"Had a puncture just beyond your gate," she said by way of greeting. "Don't suppose you'd run me back?"

"Of course. Ryder left me his pitiful excuse for a truck. We can throw your bicycle in the back. But you must have lunch first."

She accepted so speedily I wondered if the puncture might have been a ruse to get inside the gate. She needn't have bothered. The code of the African bush was the same as that of Creole hospitality. If a neighbour appeared, you fed and sheltered them and got them where they needed to be without question or mention of payment.

We sat down to a dish of curried chicken and rice and a few tasty accompaniments, including an orange sponge cake that Omar was ridiculously proud of. He had split it and filled it with custard, then sprinkled the whole thing with rosewater and presented it with a flourish. Tusker unashamedly ate three pieces.

"Damned fine cake. However much you're

paying that fellow, best double it if you don't want Helen to lure him away. She's the worst servant poacher hereabouts."

"That doesn't seem very neighbourly."

Tusker shrugged. "That's Helen. She's all right, I suppose. Bit fluffy-headed, but no real harm in her."

Faint praise, indeed. She went on. "Where's that cousin of yours?"

"Dora? Off attempting a landscape of the countryside. She was so worn out after over-hauling the house, I told her to start taking time to kick up her heels a little. For Dora that means a sketchbook and a new sponge cake recipe. She and Evelyn Halliwell have struck up a friendship based on art and gardens, I think. And Kit helps them with the rudiments of their work from time to time."

She shook her head. "I have to wonder what you're thinking."

"I beg your pardon?"

She sat forward, her expression earnest. A tiny bit of custard clung to one lip, trembling a little as she spoke. "You have character, a backbone. Oh, it may wobble from time to time, but it's there. Like my niece, Jude. You can do better than Kit Parrymore. He's handsome, I'll grant you that. But he's soft inside. No spine of his own. You'll end up carrying him, and it will break you. You'll regret him."

"Only if I'm stupid enough to rely on him," I countered.

She gave a sharp yip of laughter. "Well, that's a relief. At least you see him for what he is."

"It would be difficult to see him for anything else. Kit isn't like most men. He makes no secret of his shortcomings."

"True enough." She picked up a dish of pistachios and began to crack them idly. "For instance, did you read the piece in the latest issue of the *Standard*? There's a juicy little item about the pair of you. All about how the centrepiece of his coming show is a painting he's doing of you—a nude."

"Is that right?" I lit a cigarette and blew a smoke ring while she played with her pistachios. *Crack. Crack.*

"It said the painting will be the latest in a long line of scandals for you. And then it proceeded to list them."

"I'm surprised the good people of Nairobi have nothing better to read about than my little peccadilloes."

"Kit said it would be the making of his career."

I stopped halfway through blowing another smoke ring. It fluttered away like a stillborn angel. "Kit was quoted?"

"Lavishly." *Crack. Crack.*

"Bastard," I said softly. I stubbed out the cigarette. "Well, I shouldn't have expected any different from him. In my experience, all artists would sell their own mothers for a bit of publicity."

She yipped again and I respected her for not trying to say something consoling. I reached out with my napkin and wiped the custard off her mouth. "If you're going to sit there cracking pistachios, at least eat them."

She crunched a few and slipped the rest into her pocket. "For my new filly. Special treat."

"How did you get the name Tusker?"

"When I was newly married, I went on safari with Balfour. I killed an elephant with one shot, and me not nineteen. It was the talk of the colony—or the protectorate, as it was then. I was even written up in the *Standard* for it. The governor himself sent me a letter of congratulation. But I didn't realise the elephant was a mother. She had a calf that had got separated, and when I killed the mother, I orphaned the calf. I cried all the way home. Balfour had taken the tusks and I took the tail. The calf followed along, trailing the smell of its mother's blood. Balfour said we ought to just shoot it, but I wouldn't let him. I fed it and taught it to use its trunk and what plants to eat and how to scratch itself on a tree. I even shot a leopard that sprang at him and tried to take him when he went to drink. Years passed and that elephant followed me everywhere. He grew the most beautiful set of tusks you ever saw—a hundred and fifty pounds if they weighed an ounce. And when he was fully grown and ready to mate, I walked him out into the bush where he could live out his life with his own kind."

"A sweet story," I said.

She cracked another pistachio. "Oh, not so sweet. Hunter took him a month later for those tusks. Just carved them right out of his head and left him there. He died not a mile from my house. I think he might have been coming back to see me." She ate the nut slowly. "That's why I'm peculiar about ellies."

"Peculiar?"

"Ask anybody. They'll tell you I'm mad, but I'm not. It's just that I can't bear to see the tuskers hurt. They're so big that people forget how gentle they are. And how much like us."

"Elephants are like us?"

"More than most any other animal I've ever seen. They live in families, and when one dies, the others pay their respects. They grieve. I've seen them do it. And I've seen them keep on mourning for years afterwards. They'll go miles out of their way just to pass a place where one of their own died, and their memories are always green. They are the gentlest creatures on earth if you know how to handle them. But that sentiment gets me into trouble."

"What sort of trouble?"

"I'm banned from Government House, for

starters," she said with a mischievous grin. "I wanted the governor to sign a mandate creating a sanctuary for them and banning elephant hunting. Of course, he refused. So I took a leaf from the suffragettes' book. Chained myself to his desk."

"I don't imagine that pleased him."

"Not by half. It took them almost a day to find bolt cutters big enough to sever the chain. I looked like the world's biggest paperweight." She laughed at the memory. "Ryder understands. I think he's the only one who does."

"Odd that he would, since his livelihood depends upon hunting them."

She snorted. "Ryder is tricky as the devil and twice as clever. He always manages to guide his clients to shooting problem animals that ought to be put down anyway—man-eaters or a cat that has taken to preying on Masai cattle or Kikuyu goats. He tells them a good yarn about how vicious the animal is and how everyone else is too frightened to track it. Then he and his boys guide them right to it and when the client shoots it, Ryder has the natives stage a big scene with dancing and a feast. The hunters are carried around like St. George after the dragon and everybody's happy. The only one who pays is Ryder since he slips the natives something to cover the expense of the feast."

"That *is* clever. I'm surprised the clients are quite that stupid."

"They shoot animals for fun. They aren't exactly the brightest stars in the firmament," she said, cracking another nut. "No, they are no match for Ryder, but it won't matter. He'll get himself killed one of these days and the fun will be over."

"By an animal?"

"Or some idiot with a gun. There's a page on it in the betting book at the club. Quite a number of viable options. Could be a jealous husband or some criminal he's horsewhipped. Could be a disgruntled client or a jilted woman. Or it could be his driving. He's a trifle reckless. Of course, he has been known to walk right up to a lion, so I suppose that could always be a possibility. Then there are cobras and wildfires and epidemics and tribal rebellions and blackwater fever and envious guides and lightning on the savannah. It's a dangerous place, our Africa—for man and beast."

The days were surprisingly peaceful. Sometimes I walked out with Gideon to see the wildebeest moving in long dark shadows across the plains. Other days I simply lay on the sofa in the drawing room, smoking Sobranies and thinking. Dora had given up her art lessons with Kit and spent her time pottering about the gardens, working the soil from dawn to dark. I didn't mind. There was a glumness to her that seemed to blunt the edge of whatever good mood I might have enjoyed. She had gone grey and dull, and when she retired early, I just turned up the gramophone and sang along without her.

And every morning I went to see Moses. I started checking on him soon after I came back from the lion hunt, and it wasn't long before it became a habit. Each morning I finished breakfast and wrapped up several pieces of toast in a cloth. I walked out to the pasture, taking in deep breaths of cool, clean air. There was always the tang of woodsmoke and cow, good earthy country smells. And Moses would be waiting, lifting up his head and giving me a shy smile as I approached.

I shared the toast with him and he always wrapped up the last piece to save for later in the day. He took his meals at the back door of the kitchen, and I had warned Omar that he was never to be turned away if he asked for more. His favourite was toast dripping in honey.

One morning as we sat and watched the cattle grazing gently, a bird flitted by. It was a nondescript little bundle of grey-brown feathers. Only the white tips of its tail caught the eye as it dipped and rose on the wind, but Moses was excited. He tugged at my arm and dragged me to my feet. He hurried after the bird, beckoning me to follow.

We trotted quickly beyond the pasture and down into a *lugga*, and I cursed myself for not bringing along a rifle. Moses had only his cowherder's stick for protection. But he plunged on, running now, and only occasionally checking to see if I was keeping up.

The bird flew out of the *lugga* and flashed its tail as it darted a little distance farther out on to the savannah. A single tree stood there, and the bird made straight for it. Moses was right behind, and when I finally joined him, breathing hard and sweating like a field hand, he pointed up, smiling happily.

The tree was a wild fig. Gideon had explained the brutality of the wild fig. It grew up around another tree, wrapping itself so closely that it suffocated its host. At first glance, a wild fig looked whole, but inside the host tree was rotten, and this one held within its decayed heart a honeycomb. Bees buzzed gently around us. Moses bent swiftly and gathered a handful of grasses. He fashioned these into a twist and motioned for me to give him matches. A moment later the makeshift torch was smoking hard, the green grass burning slowly. He moved cautiously forward, humming a song of his own making. The bees continued to circle, but none came close to him. He wedged the burning grass into a knothole of the tree and used his stick to break off a piece of honeycomb. He lifted it, dripping with golden honey and placed it carefully onto his saved piece of toast. When he was finished, he scraped a hole in the ground to bury his burned grass. He hummed another few bars of his song for the bees and turned to me, smiling his sweet smile.

We walked a little distance away so as not to disturb the bees, and he broke off pieces of the honeycomb to share with me. I sucked the honey from the beeswax. It was warm and thick on my tongue and I tasted the sharp edge of something green and herbal before it was submerged into the sweetness. Moses finished his honey and chewed the beeswax and I gave him mine to save for later. He laughed at the honey on my chin, and I thought about the mother that had given up on him and the father who had disowned him and I hated them both.

It was a slower walk back to the pasture. Moses was limping now, resting heavily on his stick, but determined to return to his herd. He took his cows very seriously, and when we reached the pasture, he was very proud to show me that one of the cows I had bought was carrying.

"Make sure she gets extra care," I told him. "She'll be the foundation of our herd."

He smiled again and headed into the pasture to hum a special song to her, a song that would make her calf grow strong and her milk come sweet.

It was only after I walked away that I remembered I wouldn't be staying long enough to see it born.

There were other walks with Moses after that, and long mornings spent listening to him sing his wordless songs to the cattle and telling stories to each other with our gestures and words scratched into the dirt with his cowherder's stick. Sometimes Gideon joined us, and sometimes the three of us walked into the bush to see a baby giraffe or to gather honey for the table. Besides my outings with Gideon and Moses, Tusker called twice a week for lunch, Mr. Patel came to bring mail and packages, and I spent long hours on the veranda, nursing a drink and catching up on my reading.

I was falling into the African rhythm of life, a slow and steady pace that meant one day was sometimes very like the next until the seasons changed and brought an entirely new world. Tusker talked of the short rains that would come in November and the wild Christmas extravagances at the club in Nairobi. She talked of the growing tension between the settlers and the government, and she taught me much about the natives. She had a soft spot for the native girls, lamenting loudly the fact that so many of them were circumcised.

"Goodness knows I never had much going on in that way, what with marrying a poof, but a woman ought to at least have the option of getting her cork properly popped," she said roundly.

"Of course they all justify it by claiming it stops the women from wandering off."

"That's absurd. It certainly didn't stop adultery in Moses' mother's case."

She shrugged. "Bush logic. You'll get nowhere arguing the point. Jude has tried."

"Jude disapproves as well?" I was intrigued. Tusker mentioned her niece occasionally, as if prodding a scar to test the tender flesh beneath.

"I should say so. She got into a flaming row one day with one of the tribal elders about it. They'll come around in time, I've no doubt. That's how it always happens. We civilize and educate them and teach them how to read and write and tie their shoes, and in the process we rob them of everything that makes them who they are. And we call ourselves saints for it."

I said nothing. Tusker could warm to a theme, and one of her favourites was the role of whites in the colony. But she was contrary. I had seen her argue both sides of the coin just to spite her opponent. The truth was she cared, passionately, about the native tribes. She respected their wisdom and their ways. But she was still Englishwoman enough to rebel against the most savage of their customs. I pitied her a little. She wanted her illusions, but they had been stripped away long ago, and she saw the natives the same as she did everyone else: not as she wanted them to be, but as they were.

I raised the subject of circumcision with Gideon the next day. To my surprise, he did not seem embarrassed.

"It is tradition," he said simply. "It has always been the Masai way."

"It has not been the way of Masai to learn English. To read and write. And yet you do these things. You go to our schools, you take our medicine. Why not this?"

He held up a hand. "The elders did not understand this at first and they fought against changing our ways. But these changes are for the better."

"It would be a good change not to mutilate your women."

"Perhaps. And if that is so, then this change will come to us in time as well."

"Do you really think so?"

He smiled. "Of course, *Bibi*. Adapt or die. It is the way of nature."

I stared. "What did you just say?"

"Adapt or die. It is the essential principle of Mr. Darwin's philosophy of natural selection. Surely you have heard of him."

"Yes, I have. I'm just surprised the school taught you about Darwin. He isn't precisely popular with the religious crowd."

"Oh, the school did not teach Mr. Darwin. That was *Bwana Tembo*."

"Ryder discusses Darwin with you?"

"Of course. He is well-read upon the subject, *Bibi*. The hours can be long out in the bush. To talk softly passes the time."

"And Ryder talks about Darwin." I shook my head. "That man surprises me even when he isn't here."

Gideon smiled again. "It is good to be surprised."

"That it is, Gideon. That it is."

After that, I threw myself into working on the farm. The pyrethrum crop was failing. The rainfall earlier in the year seemed to have established the plants, but the irrigation system that carried water from Lake Wanyama was insufficient. The plants were withering where they stood, and no matter how much I bullied, Gates merely shrugged and said that some crops were a dead loss and if they couldn't be sustained by the trickle of lake water, they wouldn't be hardy enough to last until harvest.

I read all of the farm books I could lay my hands on trying to discover a solution, but it wasn't until we had been at Fairlight for some weeks that Dodo appeared during one of my morning clinics, flushed and agitated. It was a distinct improvement on her recent moods. The longer we stayed in Africa, the sulkier she became and she should have known better. Dora didn't have a mouth made for pouting.

"Delilah, you must come and see this."

I didn't look up. I was extracting a jigger, a nasty little worm that liked to burrow underneath the toenail causing a painful infection. The only remedy was to extract it slowly, in tiny increments, otherwise it would simply break off and fester and the toe would turn necrotic. The

Kikuyu farmhand was observing it all with quiet resignation. It was the fourth I had extracted from him and no matter how many times I tried to give him shoes, he refused. Of course, being African and innately courteous, he never refused outright. He took the shoes, thanked me profusely, then sold them as soon as he was out of sight of the house.

"In a minute, Dodo. I'm working a jigger."

She crossed her arms and waited, saying nothing, but her foot tapped out an impatient rhythm as I worked.

I fished out the nasty creature and dropped it into a jar of kerosene. The Kikuyu smiled and nodded and I packed the gaping toenail with antiseptic powder and bound it up. I handed him the shoes with a firm look and he nodded, putting them on before he left this time.

"Thank God for that," I muttered. I washed my hands and allowed Dodo to lead me towards the fields.

"Where are we going?"

"There's another field I found. It's part of the farm, but there's a *lugga* that divides it from the rest of the estate."

I stopped in my tracks.

"Dodo, we can't cross the *lugga* without protection. And if you have been doing so, you're even more witless than I thought."

I returned to the house for the .416, checked it

was loaded and tossed a pair of extra rounds in my pocket. It wasn't the best choice for walking around. For starters, it was too damned heavy. But I couldn't take the chance that a buffalo might surprise us in the *lugga*, and if there was one thing I had learned about the bush, it was better to be overarmed than under. When I rejoined Dodo, she was looking around furtively. In the distance some of the farmworkers were moving listlessly through the pyrethrum, picking off bugs and nipping the worst of the damaged leaves.

"Be discreet," she murmured. I rolled my eyes, but I followed her as she slid through the tall grass. I kept an alert eye on the grasses, looking for any telltale disturbances that would indicate the presence of a big cat. The wind was circling then, and I reached down for a handful of dry red earth and tossed it up lightly. It carried away from the *lugga*, which made me feel marginally better. If anything were hunkered down there, it wouldn't smell us on the wind. It wasn't an ash bag, but it would do, and Dora seemed highly impressed with the trick.

I hefted the rifle as we approached the *lugga*, but nothing stirred. There was no acrid scent of lion or leopard. I had learned that the bigger cats smelled strongly of urine and blood, particularly if they'd recently marked or fed. It was possible to track them by scent alone although it took a gifted tracker to do it.

We moved swiftly across the *lugga* and emerged into the opening in a field. It was another of the sad pyrethrum fields and I turned to Dodo with a shrug.

"So? It's another few acres of a poor crop that ought to be plowed under."

"Look again."

I moved into the field, pushing past the first several rows of pyrethrum, and straight into something quite different.

I turned back to Dodo. "You must be joking."

"No. *Cannabis sativa.* Hundreds of plants. The pyrethrum is only the border, no doubt for camouflage."

I walked farther into the field, pushing the plants apart with my hands. They were springy and green, and I wasn't surprised to find extremely good irrigation equipment functioning perfectly.

"That bastard." I turned and strode back to the main part of the farm. I think Dodo followed, but I never turned to look. A lion could have carried her off for all I cared. All I could think of was Gates.

I found him outside the barn, harassing Moses. He raised his hand and slapped the boy just as I rounded the corner.

I didn't bother to call his name. I merely lifted the heavy rifle and shot the ground at his feet, blasting a hole into the dirt. Clots of red earth sprayed upwards. He jumped straight into the air and spun around.

"Are you out of your mind, you stupid bitch?" he demanded, his face flushing red. Spittle flew from his mouth when he spoke, and Moses stared from him to me with undisguised horror.

My shoulder was aching from the recoil, but I seated the butt of the gun again and sighted him. "Pack up. Take your ugly wife and your nasty children and get off this property."

He took a single step in my direction and I fired again, this time just nicking his boot. "You're barking mad!" Gates howled.

"Shut up. I didn't even hit you. But I will the next time." I reloaded and cocked the rifle yet again, but this time I aimed directly for his heart.

He curled his lip. "You think you can get away with killing me?"

"I don't plan to kill you," I said, dropping the barrel to his crotch.

He moved then, scurrying in the direction of his house. I glanced at Moses who was breathing hard.

I cocked my head. "Moses, get back to the cows. I will have a look at your head as soon as Mr. Gates is gone."

He nodded and trotted back to his cows. Dodo rounded the corner then, holding a hand to her side. "Heavens, I've the most awful stitch. What is it? What's happened?"

"I have given Mr. Gates his notice," I informed her. "I just have to finish evicting him."

I walked slowly toward his house and by the time I arrived, he was emerging with his wife and children and a pair of hastily packed cases. "I trust we can return for the rest of our things," Gates said, his eyes icy as he faced me.

"You trust wrong."

He moved toward me and I lifted the rifle meaningfully. He grabbed his wife hard by the arm and threw her into the car, shoving the children after. He left in a cloud of dust, his arm extended out the window in an obscene gesture. His son was offering me the same gesture in the rear window and I obliged by returning it.

"Delilah, really," Dodo murmured.

"He started it."

I turned on my heel and went straight to Moses. He had only a small cut on his head. I looked him over carefully, but he seemed fine, probably better than I was. My shoulder throbbed and I could barely lift my arm over my waist.

"Moses, was that the first time Mr. Gates hit you?"

He shook his head.

Wincing, I put both my hands on his shoulders and looked him squarely in the eye. "Moses, you work for me and no one else. Nobody, and I mean *nobody,* has the right to mistreat you. If anyone does, you come directly to me, do you hear? You are my responsibility, and I won't let anyone hurt you."

He ducked his head a moment then slipped a small beaded bracelet off his wrist. It was blue and white, like many I had seen in their village, worked in an intricate pattern with a slender and distinctive green stripe for contrast. It was primitive but somehow as elegant as anything I'd seen in Paris. He pressed it into my hand, and before I could say a word he had vanished. I slipped it onto my wrist, admiring the chic exoticism.

"He won't thank you for that when you're gone," Dora said, her tone edged with something green and spiteful.

"Shut up, Dora. I've had my fill of you. You've been like this for ages now. If you hate Africa so much, go home. Nobody will miss you."

She lifted her chin and for a moment I thought she was going to yell. I would have liked her better if she had. Instead she tucked her chin down again and withdrew into herself, a small dull wren with a wretched attitude.

"I'm sorry you think I've been difficult. But I'm not wrong. Not about that boy. Not about anything."

And she turned on her heel and went to serve lunch.

# 17

The next morning I instructed the farmhands to plow the field of cannabis under and reroute the irrigation pipes to the struggling pyrethrum crop. Gideon shook his head and looked mournfully at me, but he would say nothing beyond, "This was not wise, *Bibi.*" He disappeared then, and I walked out to the fields to make sure the farmhands were doing as instructed.

I was standing propped against a tree and watching them when Rex strode up behind me. He was dressed for town with a lightweight suit and a freshly shaven chin.

"Good morning, Rex."

He didn't bother with a greeting. "I came to see if you were all right."

"Surely you didn't walk all the way from your farm dressed like that."

He didn't smile. "I'm on my way into Nairobi. I left the car on the road." He paused, his eyes searching my face. "You haven't answered. Are you all right?"

I smiled. "It would take a bit more than an oaf like Gates to rattle me. I'm just sorry I wasted two bullets making my point. Those rounds are damned expensive."

His expression relaxed then, and he even

attempted a small smile. "I'm glad to hear it. I hate you living here so unprotected."

"I can take care of myself, Rex."

"That's what I'm afraid of." He stepped forward and laid his hands on my shoulders. "Delilah, things are changing. Things I can't discuss just yet. I wish I could talk to you, tell you everything. But that just isn't possible. I can only say that you are important to me, terribly important. And your safety is paramount."

If that little speech was meant to comfort me, all it did was muddy the waters. And to add to the confusion, he suddenly bent his head and kissed me on the cheek, hard and quick.

He released me and turned on his heel, striding back in the direction he'd come. I stood staring after him, trying to figure out what the hell had just happened.

Dora walked over. "What was Rex doing here?"

"Making certain we were all right."

"By kissing you?"

"So you saw that, did you?"

"It was difficult to miss." She gave a little sigh. "Delilah, he's married."

"I know that," I told her, my voice sharp with indignation. "I didn't kiss him. He kissed me."

"I didn't see you push him away." I didn't answer. "Would you have if he had continued?"

"I don't deal in hypotheticals," I said loftily.

"Delilah, really. You can't go on like this, doing

whatever you like with no thought to the consequences. One of these days someone is going to get very badly hurt in your little games."

Her blood was hot for once. Her hands, her capable, quiet Dora hands, were balled into fists at her sides, and she was flushed.

"You shouldn't let your temper get the better of you," I told her. "It makes your complexion go blotchy."

She took a step forward. "I mean it, Delilah. You can joke all you want and pretend nothing is serious. But other people have feelings, too, you know. And those feelings can run quite deep."

I folded my arms. "Whose feelings are we talking about? Helen's? Because Rex seems to be fairly far down on her list of people to do these days. And if he comes sniffing around me, maybe it's because he's a little lonely, have you ever thought of that?"

The colour in her face ebbed a little. "What are you saying? Have you started an affair with Rex already?"

"Of course not." My teeth snapped hard on the words. She was pushing me past even my endurance. "And I don't intend to. We're just friends— not that it's any of your business. But if I did, I don't think it would be the worst thing anyone has ever done. They have an open marriage."

"People always say they have an open marriage when they're trying to justify their adultery."

"What do you want from me, Dora? You know what I am. You've known me longer than anyone and you know I do as I please. Leopards don't change their spots."

I walked away from her then, leaving her to oversee the destruction of the cannabis field. I could feel her eyes boring into me as I left.

We didn't speak the rest of that day, but in the evening a messenger came with a handwritten invitation from Helen. I shoved it back into the envelope but not before Dora had spotted the handwriting.

"Is that a summons?" she asked coldly.

"She's having a party tomorrow and I am invited."

"Just you?" There was an ugly note of triumph in her voice and I knew she was hoping that Helen planned to put me straight about any possible involvement with Rex. Of course, I wasn't planning an involvement with Rex, but it was easy to see how our friendship could be misconstrued. True, he was older, but still handsome and with a vitality that could easily put men half his age to shame. And Rex was solid as Stonehenge. He was established, with an air of command that put him head and shoulders above most men. Kit paled in comparison, and although my afternoons with him were deeply pleasurable, even pleasure palls when it has nothing else going for it. As for Ryder . . . I pushed all thoughts of him aside, as I had been doing since he left on safari. There was no point in thinking about Ryder. No, Rex was a friend. Under other circumstances, he could have been more, but I was behaving perfectly well where he was concerned. It irritated me to no end that Dora refused to see that. I didn't like having to explain myself to anyone, least of all a wet rag like Dodo.

I smoothed the envelope and slipped it into my pocket.

"Yes. Just me."

The next evening Kit came to collect me before the party. I was still dressing when he arrived, tying on my black silk ribbon. I wore Moses' bracelet to add a touch of the exotic, and I had varnished my nails a poison-green to match my beaded dress. My dancing shoes were walking sin—the highest heels I owned and designed to make a man look twice. Kit gave a low whistle as he stood in the doorway of my bedroom.

"Didn't anybody ever tell you it's bad manners to invite yourself into a lady's boudoir?"

He held up the dangling ends of his bow tie. "I never was very good with these things. Help."

"You're thirty-five, Kit. How have you never managed to learn how to tie a bow tie?"

He shrugged. "Rebellion against the establishment. Besides, I usually wear a cravat. Much less fuss and you can always tie someone up with it," he said, leering a little.

I slid the tie out from under his collar. "And you think you can't have fun with a bow tie? Fine, I'll teach you how to tie it. But pay close attention."

I propped my foot on the dressing stool and slid my dress up slowly. I slipped the tie behind my thigh and brought the ends forward.

"Now, you see how one end is longer than the other? Bring that across, and over and up from behind. Like this."

He put out his hand and I slapped it away. "Mind your manners. Pull the ends nice and tight, as snug as you can. This is where it gets tricky, so pay attention." I shifted the short end into position and wrapped the long end firmly around it. "Pretend it's a butterfly and hold the two wings together," I instructed, pinching the two loops tightly in one hand. "Now, you see the hole back here? All you do is push this bit all the way through. Then drop your hands. The wings will fan back out and you just have to give them a little tweak. Nothing to it." I turned my thigh this way and that for him to admire my handiwork.

He reached out again and I slapped his hand a second time. "Naughty, naughty." I untied the bow and draped it over his shoulder. "Your turn."

I spun him around to face the mirror and raised my hands under his arms to help him. It took him the better part of ten minutes to get it right and four more smacks to the hand, but he mastered it and stepped back, preening a little as he shot his cuffs over a sharp gold wristwatch I hadn't seen before. The art business must have been improving, I decided.

"Quite dapper," he said. "But I still say you're a cold little tease to do that to a man and not lend him a helping hand." He took my hand in his and laid it flat against his belly. He began to slide it lower down, his eyes never leaving mine.

Just as I touched the button on his trousers, I lifted my hand away. "But now you have something to think about during dinner."

On the way out, I poked my head into the drawing room, but Dora was busy eating her heart out and sticking things into a scrapbook. She didn't look up when Kit and I walked through, but I could feel her thinking about us.

"Good evening, Dora," Kit said. There was a note of laughter, barely suppressed in his voice. Dora flushed deeply and murmured a greeting.

"Have fun with your glue pot," I called as I slammed the front door. I fairly ran to the car and threw myself in. The night was warm and Kit drove fast, racing the moon as it rose high and full over the landscape. The house was ablaze with lights, and one of the native servants opened the door to us.

"*Memsa* will receive you in the bath," he said, escorting us to Helen's suite. I darted a glance at Kit, but he merely smiled. The servant tapped and opened the door without waiting. The famous pink quartz bathtub was filled nearly to the brim with rose-scented water. Helen was stretched out, her white breasts and knees rising over the foaming water, an aging Aphrodite.

"Darlings! I'm so glad you could come. Help yourselves to a drink."

There was a drinks tray set up on her vanity and Kit poured us each a stiff gin. The Pembertons, newly back from the coast, were already there. Gervase was standing in the corner nursing his glass while Bianca sat on the closed toilet, fiddling with a silver syringe.

"Dear Bianca, always so clever with a needle," Helen said with a malicious laugh. Bunny Stevenson perched on the edge of the bath, playfully flipping water at Helen's nipples. She splashed water back on him, soaking his shirtfront until she subsided into gales of laughter. It seemed forced, that laughter—brittle and hectic—and I wondered if she had helped herself to Bianca's drugs.

"Well, if I'd known we were dining in the bathroom, I wouldn't have bothered to do my hair," I said coolly. "The humidity will wreck it."

Helen waved a soapy hand. "Never fear, darling. We're finished up in here. Let's have dinner, shall we?" She rose and the doctor handed her a towel. She didn't bother to dry herself. She wrapped her wet body in a peignoir of pale pink silk dripping in marabou feathers. The damp patches turned the fabric transparent and clinging.

She put an arm through mine like a gossipy schoolgirl sharing confidences. "I am passionate about history. Did you know French queens and courtesans received their guests in the bath? And Regency belles used to dampen the chemises they wore under their dresses to show off their figures. I'm just paying homage to history," she insisted before indulging in another fit of laughter.

I didn't bother to answer her. I doubted she would notice. She ushered us into the dining room where I was surprised to find Mr. Halliwell looking only a little uncomfortable. Helen sidled up to him, pressing her breasts against his arm.

"I'm so glad you came, Lawrence. I was afraid that after last time, you might be afraid to," she said. She pulled a feather from her sleeve and tickled him with it. I glanced at Kit, but he merely shot me a mischievous look, and I realised he must have known what sort of mood Helen would be in before we arrived. And not telling me about it was payment in kind for teasing him with the bow tie.

We had just started on the soup when the door opened. "I do hope I'm not too late."

I looked up and for a split second forgot how to breathe. I had never seen Ryder in anything other than his bush clothes. He cleaned up well. His hair was slicked back and much darker. The always-present five o'clock shadow had been neatly barbered off, and he was dressed impeccably in a black evening suit with starched shirt. Only the gold earrings in his ears gave him away for the pirate he was. He slid into the chair next to me and I saw the tiny thread of dried blood just beneath his ear where he had nicked himself shaving. I had a sudden urge to put out my tongue and taste it. He swivelled his head then, and I dropped my eyes. The servants jumped to bring him a plate of soup.

The others greeted him, but I applied myself to my soup. After a moment, the conversations broke off into smaller groups, and he leaned close, his lips near enough to my ear to raise gooseflesh. "I hear you've had some trouble."

"Nothing I can't handle. Did you get your bag?"

He flashed me a brilliant smile. "And a tip big enough to buy another *duka*."

"Good for you."

But in spite of his successful trip, I detected an edginess to him. He seemed watchful, and occasionally, I noticed his eyes flicker quickly to Helen and around the table again, as if waiting for something. The atmosphere was heightened somehow with Rex gone, and I did not put it down entirely to Helen's odd mood. The men drank heavily, particularly Kit, who seemed determined to drink himself into a stupor before the cheese course. Gervase began to recite some of his gloomy poetry, this one about a man in love with the corpse of a girl he once knew, and Bunny kept kissing Helen's arms as she tried to eat.

Across the table from me, Bianca's pupils were huge in the candlelight, and I thought of the Renaissance beauties who dilated their eyes with belladonna to make themselves more alluring. It didn't really do Bianca any favours. She was talking more than usual, her colour high and her voice sharp. She caught me looking at her and peered across the table.

"What's that you're wearing? Is that native jewellery?" She rose up out of her chair and leaned across the table, putting one knee into her plate as she tried for a closer look. I held up my wrist and she shrieked a little. "How primitive! Do you mean to start a new fashion?"

I shrugged as Gervase put an arm around her waist and coaxed her back into her seat. "Maybe. I liked the line of green beads in it with my dress, and I thought it made for an unusual touch."

"Very becoming," Helen said. I was about to explain that the beads were unique to the Masai in Gideon's village, but before I could open my mouth, Bianca had started throwing bits of her bread roll at Lawrence Halliwell.

I rolled my eyes at Ryder. "Food fights?"

He continued to eat calmly as a chop bone whizzed past his ear. "I would have thought that was right up your alley."

I gave him a cool glance. "Not really. I prefer more grown-up kicks."

He didn't reply, and the food fight fizzled to a stop just as soon as it started. Bianca's shrieking laughter turned maudlin, and by the time dessert was served, she had reached for her needle again, this time injecting herself openly at the dinner table. Helen remonstrated with her.

"Bianca, really! Don't indulge too much. The numbers are uneven as it is. We shall want every woman at her best." Bianca was either not in the mood to play Helen's games or she was too far gone to pay attention. She rose from the table and began to dance one of her flamenco measures, clicking her fingers instead of castanets and flapping her shawl around like a great clumsy bird.

Helen shot me a conspiratorial wink, and before I could work out what she meant, the servants cleared the table and left the long expanse of polished wood bare. Helen rose and plucked five feathers from her sleeve. "There are five gentlemen and three ladies, so I'm afraid we shall have to be a trifle creative."

She placed a feather in front of each man. "Each man will blow his feather across the table into the lap of the woman of his choice. She must go with the man whose feather first lands in her lap," she instructed. "The guest rooms have all been made ready for you, and if you feel like inviting one of the remaining two gentlemen to watch or join in, feel free. Round two will begin with a sheet game in two hours!" she finished gaily.

She rang a little crystal bell and the men began to blow. Bunny was puffing his cheeks so hard I was surprised he didn't have an apoplexy right there. He was blowing his feather towards Helen, and she was smiling benignly at him. Kit blew once on his and collapsed in a fit of giggling, far too drunk to finish. To my horror, I saw Gervase and the reverend engaged in a pitched battle aimed in the same direction—mine.

Just as Gervase's feather hovered on the edge of the table, Ryder rose and dropped his feather in my lap. "She's mine," he said, grabbing my arm and pulling me from my chair.

"That's cheating," Gervase protested, but we were already out of the dining room and heading for the front door. He threw me into his truck and gunned the engine.

We drove for a few minutes before I turned to look at him. The moonlight rested on his features, but even that silvery light couldn't soften them. He was angry.

"Why do I have the feeling that you'd rather have your hands around my throat than that steering wheel?"

He slammed on the brakes, sending up a shower of dirt and pebbles in our wake. He cut the engine, and the only sounds were the ticking of the hot metal and the soft cricket song.

"Do you want me to take you back?"

"Of course not. In fact, I quite appreciate the rescue. It was not at all the sort of evening I was expecting."

"What did you think would happen?"

I weighed my options then chose the truth. "I thought she was going to tear into me because of Rex. She might resent our friendship."

Ryder's eyes were inky black in the fitful light. "Helen's too subtle for that. Her best revenge would be to get you to one of her little parties and then tell Rex all about it. You were a fool to go."

"How was I supposed to know?" I demanded. "And if you were so concerned about it, you could have warned me when you first arrived instead of waiting until things got going to mount your white horse and carry me off."

"I had to know."

"Know what?"

"If you wanted to be there. You didn't seem uncomfortable. For all I knew, you were fully aware of what was about to happen and were more than happy to participate."

"With Gervase Pemberton?"

"Don't sound so scornful. It's possible."

"It is *not* possible. As difficult as it might be for you to believe, I do have standards. And Gervase definitely does not meet them. Neither does going off with random men. I prefer to get my kicks with people of my own choosing, thanks very much."

"You can understand my confusion," he returned nastily. "You're sleeping with Kit. That doesn't say much for your standards."

"Oh, you are a fine one to preach to me. From what I hear, you've taken a turn on every ride in the colony. Clearly you knew what to expect tonight," I finished triumphantly.

"Yes, I've been there before," he admitted, and whether he meant to one of the parties or inside Helen, I wasn't sure, and I definitely didn't want to know.

"Sauce for the goose," I reminded him. "And furthermore, you don't have a claim on me, remember? I can go where I like, when I like, and I don't see what business it is of yours."

"Fine," he ground out, his jaws clamped tight. "I'll take you back there."

He reached for the gearshift, but I had had enough. "Oh, for God's sake," I muttered. I swung myself onto his lap, straddling him. I pulled his jacket down and off his arms and yanked off his bow tie. I opened his shirt and shoved it down to his wrists and left it there, binding him just enough to make him feel it. He opened his mouth, but before he even said a word, I had his trousers unbuttoned and my hand inside.

It wasn't pretty and it wasn't gentle and anybody who watched would have thought we

329

were trying to kill each other. Maybe we were. I pushed and rocked and clawed at him, frustrated as I had never been that there was bone and sinew and muscle between us, and he answered right back, bruise for bruise and scratch for scratch. Bodies suddenly seemed like too much trouble when all I wanted was to consume him—or let him consume me, I didn't much care which. I wanted to be burned up until there was nothing left but a small pile of grinning, ashy bones. I wanted to take him apart with my bare hands until I got right down to the core of him, something perfect and whole that I could carry away in my pocket and never turn loose of.

I lit a cigarette as we drove back to Fairlight. He kept one arm tightly around me, so I put the cigarette to his lips while he took a deep drag. I smoked the rest of it, and when we arrived at Fairlight, I took the last puff.

"Delilah—"

"You're not stupid enough to think we have to talk about this, are you?"

"No. I know nothing's changed. You are who you are. And that wasn't about me, not really. You were scratching an itch and I was weak enough to let you."

The words were bitter, but his tone was smooth. My hand shook a little as I ground out the cigarette on the sole of my shoe.

He went on. "I'm leaving again in a few days to

take a trip up to Lake Macheo for some shooting and fishing. I won't be back for a week."

As I got out of the truck my heel crunched down on something. The little Masai bracelet Moses had given me. It had gotten torn off, although which one of us had done it, I couldn't say. I picked it up and slammed the door, leaning in the open window. The inside of the truck smelled like burned tobacco and my perfume and the salty, sweaty smell of us together. Handfuls of beads from my dress shimmered on the seat and floorboard like glittering confetti.

"Safe travels," I said lightly.

He stared at me for a long minute then shook his head. "It can't happen again, Delilah. It won't."

"For such a big man, you seem awfully afraid."

"You have no idea."

"Why? Why do I scare you so much?"

He put one fingertip to my heart. "Is this where you notch the marks? One scar for each of us until there's nothing left to feel with? You've put walls a mile high and a mile thick and nothing is going to batter them down."

"You're a fine one to talk about walls."

"Mine have cracks, princess. And that's the trouble. If I let you, you'll bring the whole god-damn thing down around my ears."

"And you can't have that?"

"No," he said flatly. "I can't. There are some women and some places that get under your skin,

331

through the blood and right down into the bone itself. And they never leave. Africa has already done that for me. I don't need you there too."

"How poetic." My voice was low and smiling, but I felt chilled. He was thinking in the same metaphors that I did. And a man who spoke the same language was a dangerous man. "Maybe that's our problem, Ryder. We're just too damned much alike."

He didn't say anything, and I realised there was no point.

I gave him my most dazzling smile. "Try not to think about me when you're gone. Distractions can be deadly out in the bush."

He lunged toward the door and I danced backward, fleeing into the house. It was too late for anyone to have waited up, so I got myself ready for bed. I didn't bathe. I stripped off my ruined dress and kicked it into the corner. The bracelet went into the jewel box on my writing table—next to the cold cream I didn't bother with. I crawled straight into bed, far too wakeful for sleep. I felt like I had gripped an electric wire and couldn't let go. I lay awake for hours, watching the shifting shadows through the mosquito netting. I must have slept at some point. It was full daylight when I woke, and when I did, my skin still smelled like Ryder.

# 18

The next morning Gideon appeared. Again Ryder had left him behind to watch over me, and again I was glad of it. I shouldn't have been. I should have been outraged that he thought so little of my ability to take care of myself. But Gideon was the nearest thing Ryder had to a best friend; being with him meant being with Ryder, in a way. And if I stopped to think about how badly I wanted that, I would have scared the hell out of myself, so I didn't. I didn't think about the feel of him, on me and in me, and I didn't think about what that night might mean. I packed that thought as far away as I could, folding it into a trunk in the back of my mind and slamming the lid shut. There were plenty of other thoughts to keep that one company.

"*Habari zu asabuhi, Bibi,*" Gideon said.

"Good morning to you, too."

"I have come to ask a favour."

I stared at him. Gideon never asked me for anything. I raised a brow.

"My *babu* wishes to see you. Will you come to the village with me?"

"Of course. We'll take Moses so he can see your *babu* as well."

I told Dora we were leaving and she ignored me. She had pointedly left the wreck of my dress bundled into the corner of my room, but my shredded stockings had been carefully washed and hung up in my bathroom. It was her way of expressing her disapproval—without words, but not at all silent. That gesture spoke volumes about her disdain. She didn't ask who I had been with, and I didn't volunteer. As near as I could tell she was still speaking to me as little as possible, and I slammed the door again on my way out just to get some noise in the house.

"*Memsa* Dora is unhappy," Gideon observed as we started towards the pasture.

"Not exactly. You see, *Memsa* Dora doesn't approve of me, and that actually makes her quite happy indeed. She likes to be better than me at something."

"I do not understand, *Bibi*."

I blew out a sigh and breathed in the cool purple air of the morning. "*Memsa* Dora has always hated me a little. We were children together. Our fathers were cousins. When I went to my *babu*'s house in England, Dora was always there. But as we grew older our situations changed. My family had money and Dora's did not. She resented me for it."

"Is that all?"

"No. My life has been a difficult one, but it has been exciting, Gideon. I have loved men and they have loved me back. I am written about in newspapers and I have travelled the world. Dora's life in comparison is very small. She has spent most of her time in a tiny village in England while I gallivanted around."

"Gallivanted?" His brow furrowed. Across the pasture Moses stood, singing softly to the cattle as they grazed peacefully around him.

"It means I travelled a lot. I had fun. I've *lived.*"

He smiled. "Your life is like mine, then. I have seen much of the world around my village and I have had fun. I, too, have lived."

He was serious. He had probably been no farther than a hundred miles from the village where he'd been born and he'd walked every step of it, but he considered himself a well-travelled soul.

"I have seen many things and I have had great friendships," he went on. "But Moses has not. He has stayed in our village, and his life, like *Memsa* Dora's, has been very small."

"Then you understand what I mean."

He shook his head, his beads clacking gently. The sound reminded me of my grandmother's rosary. She told it twice a day, every day, praying on her knees in the rose-scented smoke of the incense she burned in her bedroom. The servants even whispered that when they washed her pillowcases there was always a faint halo scorched into the linen.

"I do not understand at all, *Bibi*. Moses and I are very different, but we are brothers. And I would never be angry with him for something that he

335

has, nor would he be angry with me. He sits in my heart, and I sit in his."

I swallowed hard. "That's as it should be, Gideon."

"Then perhaps you will try to make up whatever quarrel it is that you have with *Memsa* Dora," he advised quietly. "It is not good to carry anger inside you. It makes for a heavy journey."

He turned and raised his arm. Moses raised his in return, a broad smile crossing his face.

"I'll try, Gideon," I promised.

The walk to the village was easy in the cool morning air, and when we arrived, their *babu* was sitting outside to receive us. Gideon and Moses went through the usual ceremonies, and I waited my turn before bowing my head. "*Shikamoo, Mzee.*"

"*Marahaba.*"

"*Asante*," I replied. And that was the end of our Swahili. The *babu* said something to one of the women loitering about and she went into the hut, appearing a moment later with the usual calabashes of milky, smoky tea. I smiled my thanks and sipped.

The *babu* turned to Gideon and began to talk rapidly in Maa and I waited for the translation. The *babu* was folded in his long brown-grey fur cloak. I had asked the last time and Gideon explained it was a hyrax cloak, the pelt taken from a quizzical-looking little rodent with round ears.

They were rather sweet but with vicious, unforgiving teeth. Tusker told me she'd kept one as a pet until it had taken a nip at her ear and pierced it for her.

After a long exchange, the *babu* sat back and waited for Gideon to translate. He fanned himself gently with a fly whisk fashioned from a zebra tail, scattering the insects that had gathered. His little round eyes peered out from behind his thick spectacles. He watched me closely as Gideon spoke, as if to make sure every last word was passed along.

"*Babu* says that he has heard of the brave manner in which you dealt with *Bwana* Gates."

"How did he hear that?"

Gideon grinned. "I told him. He says that *Bwana* Gates is an evil man, and such evil leaves a mark behind it. The mark of his evil still lingers here."

The sun was high overhead, shedding long golden shafts of light. Perspiration from the walk beaded my temples, but I shivered. Granny Miette and Teenie and Angele had known evil and had worked to cast it out when it crept near. They always said that some evil can never be thwarted, no matter how hard you try or how far you run. It will find you if it wants to.

But I couldn't imagine Gates was as evil as the *babu* believed or that he would do me any serious harm. He was a bully, and I had bullied him back.

"Please thank your *babu* for his concern, and tell him I will be careful."

He repeated my words to the old man, but as soon as they were spoken, the *babu* shook his head firmly. He reached into his cloak and pulled out a small leather bag. It was sewn with a complicated pattern of beads on copper wire, and it smelled of smoke and earth, of cooled sweat and aging flesh, like the old man himself.

He pressed the bag into my hands.

"What is it? Some sort of jewellery?" I turned it over in my palm and felt knobbly bits inside—a few pebbles, something that rustled like leaves, and another something that felt suspiciously long and hard in its slenderness. A bit of bone?

"It is a charm of protection, *Bibi*. My *babu* is very good friends with the most powerful *laibon* in our tribe," he added with a measure of pride.

"*Laibon*? What is that? Some sort of witch doctor?"

"A *laibon* is a man with powerful magic. My *babu* asked and he has made this for you."

I nodded toward his neck. "I see you have one, too."

"As does Moses. My *babu* says this thing is necessary."

I shrugged and tied the thing to my belt loop and tucked it into a pocket. "Is that good enough?"

The *babu* peered closely through his spectacles, giving a grudging nod. He wasn't entirely pleased but he finally told Gideon it was good enough, and I was glad. I had no intention of wearing the smelly thing so close to my nose. It could live in my pocket and I only hoped Dora wouldn't complain about the odour when it was time to do the laundry.

"I'll keep it, but only to make the *babu* happy. Gates is a bully. Once you show them what you're made of, they turn tail and run." I bowed my head to thank the *babu.*

He lifted his hand to my head, pressing it for a long moment in a priestly gesture. He turned back to Gideon.

"*Babu* says that the gentleman in the uniform still follows you, but he walks with Death, *Bibi.* Death is his friend."

I said nothing and drank more of the vile tea. I wasn't surprised Death was his friend, considering the fact that I had buried him a decade before.

The *babu* went on, his voice rusty, like an old accordion.

"*Babu* says this man watches you, but Death waits for another man to join him."

Still I said nothing, but my hand shook as I lifted the gourd.

"*Babu* says you are strong, like a Masai woman, and this is good."

"Why? Does he need someone to build him a house?" I said brightly.

He repeated the joke and to my astonishment,

the *babu* wrapped his arms about his slender body, wheezing.

"*Babu* laughs. He does not wish for a house, *Bibi*. He says you are strong in spirit, and this is a good thing. You will have sorrow to bear. It is good to have a strong back for this."

I rose then and paid my respects to the *babu*. He laid his blessings upon us and we left, turning our steps towards the path back to Fairlight. Every step I thought of Johnny and the man Death was waiting for. And I thought of Ryder, out in the bush, where a broken leg or a snakebite or a fever could kill a man between breakfast and lunch.

A few days after Helen's party, Rex appeared. He looked a little haggard after his trip to Nairobi, but he refused all offers of food or drink. Dodo, who was still nursing a snit, disappeared discreetly, leaving us alone in the drawing room. He sat next to me on the sofa and draped his arm casually near my shoulders as he closed his eyes.

"You look exhausted. Are you sure you won't have something?"

He opened his eyes then shook his head as if to clear it. "No. Being here helps."

"What happened in Nairobi?"

"Disaster," he said, clipping each syllable sharply. "The governor is planning his return from England. He's giving up."

"You mean no independence for Kenya?"

"That's precisely what I mean." His lips thinned. "Everything I have worked for in the past fifteen years, and he is willing to let it slip through our fingers. It's his health. He isn't strong enough to keep up the fight."

He looked shattered, and I put a hand to his. "I'm sorry."

He clasped it a moment then released it.

"I'm sorry. I know I haven't a right to burden you with my troubles. I ought to go directly home, but Helen—" He broke off, then cleared his throat. "She was different when we met, you know. Wild of course, just like you." His lips curved softly. "I thought Africa would settle her down. Instead it seemed to make her worse. Every time I suggested leaving, she would threaten to kill herself. I couldn't bear to see her suffer anymore. I do still love her, you see. I love her so very, very much," he added with an apologetic smile. "So we struck a bargain. We would stay and she would try to make herself a proper wife when I needed her to. When I was off on business in Nairobi, she would be free to do as she pleased. I had no idea how bad she'd got until a few years ago when I came home early and found—"

He broke off again, and I gave him an innocent smile. "I can imagine."

"Can you? I don't know. Poor Helen. She always manages to choose badly. I came home that time to find her injecting herself with

341

Bianca's syringe and holding up a sheet with holes cut into it so the gentlemen of the neighbourhood could expose themselves for the ladies to compare."

So that was the sheet game I had missed. I wasn't sorry.

"She apologised, of course, and sent everyone away. She even tried to behave after that. But discretion is a bit too much of a stretch even for someone as limber as Helen. It's only a matter of time before she slips up again, drinks too much or takes those foul drugs, or starts an affair with a neighbour. It's so damnably lurid."

He closed his eyes again, his hand very still on the sofa between us. He wore no wedding ring, not even a pale strip of unmarked skin broke the tan of his finger. He gave a long sigh and opened his eyes. They were blue, and yet so unlike Ryder's. Ryder's were the sea, unpredictable and changeable. Rex's were a steady, cool northern sky.

"She's not long for this world, you know," he said suddenly. "She can't keep on at this pace. Her heart or her liver will give out. She's already on medication for both. No one here knows, but the doctor in Nairobi is keeping her alive."

"Rex, I'm so sorry."

"I've had a long time to come to terms with it. She's like a child, you know. A spoiled, lovely child, a glorious, magical creature I can't quite believe has ever been mine. I don't know what I shall do with myself when she is gone."

Again, I covered his hand with my other one, and this time he didn't pull away.

"You're a sweet child," he said, touching my hand to his cheek. A sudden glimmer of life came back into his eyes. "You should stay with us. I think you would be happy in a new, free Kenya."

I chose my words carefully. "I thought you were giving up on that dream."

He smiled, and something stirred behind his eyes as he dropped my hand. "I do have one card left to play. It hasn't been formally announced yet, but I have it on good authority that the Duke and Duchess of York will be paying us a visit next year."

"Will they? And will that really help your cause?"

"It's early days yet, my dear, too early to say," he said dismissively. "But the king's second son could be a powerful ally, and I have hopes the duke may be persuaded to see reason where others have failed. If we are successful, well, the future could be a dazzling one for us."

I opened my mouth, but he shook his head. "I shouldn't have said anything. But yours is remarkably soothing company, Delilah. You have been a wonderful comfort, my dear," he finished lightly. He rose. "I must go, but if at any time you need me, you have only to say."

He didn't say another word, just gave me a sad, meaningful smile and went on his way, closing the door softly behind him.

That night I awoke suddenly, although I couldn't say why. The crickets were singing in the garden, but the nightjars had gone quiet. I waited for a sound, but there was nothing—no crashing in the bushes that meant a hippo was wandering through, no shrill laugh from the hyenas. Nothing but the high, insistent chirp of the insects and a feeling that something was wrong. I lit a cigarette and waited. The full moon was veiled in cloud and the only light was the glow from the tip of my cigarette, winking like a firefly. Still I waited, but nothing happened and after a while I stubbed out the cigarette and rolled over in the dark.

It was the shouts that awakened me the second time. Omar the cook raised the alarm, shouting for Pierre, who shouted for me. I threw on my clothes and shoved my feet into my boots without stopping to fasten anything properly. I ran outside and found them, lying in the complete stillness that only death can bring. Their throats had been torn and their feathers were scattered around the little chicken run.

"What did it?" I demanded. "An animal? *Une animale?*"

Pierre pointed to the locked run, replying in

344

unsteady French. "An animal cannot walk through fences, *madame*."

He was right. I inspected the perimeter of the run and there wasn't a single hole or bent section of wire. It was solid as the day it had been constructed. I dusted off my hands and instructed the cook to pluck them and salvage what he could to feed the farmhands.

He backed away, holding his hands in front of himself as if to push me away.

"What is the trouble?"

Pierre looked from the cook to me. "No one will eat the chickens, *madame*. They have been touched by bad magic." The words in French had a chilling grace. *Mauvaise magie.*

"Bad magic? Don't be daft. The damage was done by a human with a key and a grudge and I think we all know who that is."

Pierre shrugged. "A man can command bad spirits to do his bidding."

"No spirit did this. It was a man," I insisted. But Pierre and Omar would not be budged. They refused even to touch the chickens, and I had to find one of the hardier Kikuyu to remove the carcasses and burn them. It was the only way to cleanse the bad magic, Pierre insisted, although he added that the services of one of the local witches would not go amiss.

I cursed under my breath, but suddenly I realised that it was fully dawn. The sun had finished rising, a great ball of blood just over the horizon. And there was no noise from the cattle, no persistent demands to be milked, no encouragement to Moses to turn them out to pasture.

"No!" I shouted, setting off at a dead run.

I smelled the blood before I opened the door to the barn. The floor was awash with it, and I slipped as I ran inside. The cows were silent lumps of flesh, already rotting, but something in that barn still lived, I realised. I threw myself down on the floor next to Moses and felt his throat for a pulse. It was there, thin and thready as a bird's. Uneven, but it was there. I checked him for broken bones and injuries and found a vicious wound to his head. His blood had mingled with that of the cows, and I gathered him up and moved him out of that dark place that smelled of death. I carried him out into the open, collapsing just as Gideon walked up. He had brought firewood, and the smile faded from his face as he opened his arms and dropped the load of it to the ground. He ran, hurdling over the pasture fence as if it were no more than a bush. He took his little brother into his arms.

"He needs a doctor, Gideon. A proper doctor. I can't fix this. I don't have enough experience with head wounds."

Gideon's expression hardened. "No, *Bibi*. There has been enough of white men in this. I will take him to our *babu*."

346

He rose with Moses, limp in his arms. "Gideon, this isn't a matter of magic. No incantations can fix this. He needs proper medicine."

Gideon gave me a sorrowful look, as one might to a child who cannot learn its lessons.

"No, this was not magic, *Bibi*. But it was evil. And no one knows more about evil than our *babu*."

I didn't argue with him. He carried his brother down the dusty track and I ran after them, carrying Gideon's spear and watching his back for lions. It was the least I could do.

I spent the day with the Masai, watching closely as the elders worked to save Moses' life. The *babu* had summoned the *laibon*, the tribal witch, the local healer and caster out of demons. He treated the head wound, packing it with their native remedies, and prepared a series of potions to spoon into the boy's mouth. He explained the herbs and how each would help, one to keep down the swelling, one to halt the bleeding, another to give peaceful rest. I heard little of what he said. I spent most of my time thinking of Gates and how stupid I had been not to confiscate his keys when I kicked him off the property. And I thought of what I would do when I got my hands on him.

After a few hours, one of the women presented me with a tin cup of corn porridge and a gourd of hot smoky milk. I hadn't thought I was hungry, but I finished them both and felt a little better.

Gideon and I sat outside the hut and talked for hours. He told me stories of Moses and how smart the boy was, what expectations he had for his brother. We talked of his bravery and his winsome ways, his bright smile and his curiosity. And then I talked, telling him stories of my Granny Miette—how she scandalised the other white women by the dark things she sometimes did with Angele and Teenie. I told him of the *chaudron*, the sugaring cauldron big enough to hold a man, a great cast-iron beast that squatted at the edge of the cane fields waiting for the alchemy of fire and the syrup. It was a crucible, boiling down the thick syrup and filling the air with smoked sweetness.

But there were other times—times when the fire was kindled for other reasons, and the *chaudron* did darker work. It might be to visit retribution on a man who had ruined a girl or forfeited a debt of honour. It might have been to still a gossiping tongue or pay back a piece of malice in kind. Granny Miette always sent me to bed early on those nights, nights when the moon had turned its dark face to the earth, away from the things that happened in the hour after midnight. But sometimes I crept out of bed and stood in the shadows of the tea olives, as Mossy had done before me, and I saw the same rituals she had seen and I shivered even though there was no wind. I never stayed to the end. I always hurried back to my bed and burrowed under the covers, the smell of tea olives and sweet smoke clinging to my skin. And on those nights, I dreamed things that came true, grisly red things that I didn't want to know. I wanted to know them now. I wanted every one of those things visited upon Gates until he cried a river of tears so deep it would drown him. I told that to Gideon, too, and he smiled.

"Moses will be fine, *Bibi*," he told me.

"How can you be so sure? Sometimes people aren't, you know." It was wrong to say it, but there was bitterness on my tongue.

"*Babu* has told his future, and it is not his time to leave us."

I laughed rudely, but Gideon's level gaze didn't waver. "I'm sorry," I told him. I turned away. My throat was too tight to say more.

One of the women brought me another calabash of milk and I held it to give my hands something to do. Just then the *babu* emerged from his little mud house. He moved slowly and Gideon hurried to lend him a strong arm, settling him next to me on the ground. The *babu* spoke and Gideon translated.

"He says there is nothing to do but wait."

"But Moses—" I began.

To my astonishment, the *babu*'s leathery old face split into a smile.

"He says that there is nothing to do but wait, although he sees that this is a difficult thing for you. You are a woman who runs."

"A woman who runs?"

The *babu* opened the leather pouch at his neck and took out a pinch of tobacco. He worked it into a plug and began to chew, spitting expertly. Then he took off his spectacles and cleaned them on the edge of his toga. The cloth smeared them a little, so I sighed and pulled out a handkerchief. I motioned for the spectacles and he handed them over, watching intently as I polished them. When I gave them back he peered through them, then grunted his satisfaction. I gave him the handkerchief and he tucked it away with a gracious nod.

"What does he mean, a woman who runs?"

Gideon repeated the question and the *babu* launched into a lengthy recitation. Gideon listened intently then turned to me.

"He says that you learned long ago to run, to hide from the dark thing that is like the dog who is half a man."

"The *rougarou*," I whispered.

"I do not know this word, *Bibi*," Gideon told me. "What is a *rougarou*?"

"It's a bogeyman, a story used to frighten children where I come from. It doesn't exist."

But even as I said the words, I tasted the lie in them. The *rougarou* was real. I had seen him often enough. The only lie was that he looked like a wolf-man. Granny Miette was the first to tell me the story of the *rougarou*. Some Creoles called him the *loup garou*; some said he punished bad Catholics. Some even said one could become a *rougarou* by *being* a bad Catholic. Seven years of broken Lents could earn you a wolf's head, it was whispered. But Granny Miette had said those were just silly superstitions. She said everyone knew the *rougarou* came by night to steal away children who were bad, who caused mischief and made their mothers cry. The *rougarou* would roam the swamps looking for naughty children, sniffing out the tender flesh and the cindery smell of wickedness with his long wolf's nose, until he found them tucked in their beds. If you were a lucky child, the *rougarou* would eat you whole, leaving nothing but the bony feet behind. But if you were very bad indeed, if your black deeds had turned your heart to the colour of night, the *rougarou* wouldn't carry you off. He would devour only your blood, turning you into a *rougarou* yourself.

"The *rougarou* has a sense for wickedness, Delilah Belle," she murmured, her pansy-blue eyes piercing in her papery face. "He can smell it out, same as you can smell new bread or the mud in the Mississippi. You can fool your grandpapa and you can even fool old Granny Miette," she would tell me, leaning so close I could smell the odour of singed violets on her skin. "But you cannot fool the *rougarou*. His nose follows pain, same as a hound follows blood. And when he sniffs you out, you can't outrun him. You can try, *chou-chou*, you can run hard and you can run fast. But no one outruns the *rougarou* forever."

It was that moment when I made up my mind to try. I knew the *rougarou* would come for me. I had always been a naughty child. I left candles burning long into the night to read. I stole pocketfuls of penny candy when Grandfather said I had had enough. And when Mossy's mother, the bricked-up saint who never left her rooms, summoned me to say the rosary with her, I skipped every third bead because I knew God would never notice. As I grew older, my crimes grew more audacious. I swam naked in the creek, knowing the sharecroppers' sons would get whipped for watching. I stole Mossy's favourite pair of earrings and lost them at a masked ball I wasn't supposed to attend. I strapped a flask under my garters and kissed boys in shadowy gardens. I rolled my own cigarettes and smoked them under the house while I read trashy novels that Granny Miette warned would wreck both my morals and my eyesight.

The *rougarou* never came for me. I packed away the story of him like everything else in my childhood. I thought I'd gotten away with it all, but the *rougarou* keeps careful accounts. He bided his time, waiting for me, always waiting, as patient as a wolf stalking a lamb. He sniffed out not my pain but my happiness, and that was when he lunged, snatching Johnny from me. I sobbed over the pieces of his uniform that came back, and in those sobs I heard the howl of the *rougarou*. I set off running then, and I hadn't stopped running since.

"It doesn't exist." I repeated the lie stubbornly.

The *babu* shrugged.

"He says that your belief does not make this thing true or not true. It is what he sees."

"I thought he saw a man in a uniform waiting with Death," I said. "Now he sees a werewolf. I think the *babu* needs better spectacles."

The *babu* didn't understand sarcasm, or if he did, he chose to ignore it. He laughed when Gideon translated my words, treating it all as a big joke. I stood up, my face hot.

"The *babu* says that you have run all the way to Africa, *Bibi*, but you do not have to run anymore. The wolf-man cannot hurt you here."

"That's what you think," I said bitterly.

I walked off then, but Gideon followed me, and I was glad. Tears blurred my vision and I was so tired I kept stumbling into the pig holes where warthogs ran to ground. Gideon walked patiently beside me, his stride easy and loose, his spear held at the ready.

I tripped once more, and Gideon put out his hand, one fingertip barely grazing mine. It was the first time Gideon had ever touched me. I twined my fingers in his and we both stared down at the linked hands, so different, and yet were they? Strip away the skin and you would find the same bones, the same blood, the same web of nerves and tendons and everything that made a person human.

"I am sorry," I told him again, wiping my eyes with my free hand. "You are my best friend here, Gideon."

"You are my friend as well, *Bibi.*"

"You know, you might knock off the *Bibi* business and just call me Delilah."

"Such a thing is not correct."

"It is correct when people are friends. You could do it when we're alone if it makes you uncomfortable to say it otherwise."

He pondered this. "Very well, Delilah." The name sounded peculiar in his mouth, but he said it anyway, and for the first time that day I smiled.

We withdrew our hands then, and I thought of the girl he planned to marry and how simple it all was for them. And I wondered why it had to be so complicated for the rest of us.

"Gideon, tell me the truth. Is there anything that you're afraid of? I mean, really afraid, so afraid that if you think of it in the dark of the night your stomach turns to water and your heart beats so fast you can hear your own blood in your ears?"

"The lion scares me," he said solemnly. "And when I was a boy, the pinching man scared me."

"The pinching man?"

"He is like your *rougarou*, but he is a real man. In each village there is this pinching man, and it is his job to punish disobedient children. He takes the skin in between his long fingernails and he twists very hard. Mothers will say to their children, 'Be good or the pinching man will make you sorry.' I was very scared of the pinching man when I was a boy. Once I was bad, and I lost my mother's favourite goat, a perfect goat with hair that looked like new milk. A white goat is a very special thing, and this goat was to be sacrificed for a special feast. And I had let the goat wander away. This is a very bad thing, and the pinching man heard of it. He looked for me all of the day. And I spent all of the day hiding from him. First, up an acacia tree which was very uncomfortable. Then in the home of my best friend, which was unkind to him for the pinching man would have pinched him as well if he had known. Then I hid among the cattle, which was worst of all. The cows knew I was afraid and it made them afraid. They stepped on me and poked me with their sharp horns, and by the time I crawled out from the *boma*, I was covered in bruises and scratches. I had spent all day wrapped up so tightly in my fear that I could not breathe. And then, when at last I came out of hiding, the pinching man was waiting for me at my house."

"What did he do?"

"He took one look at me with the bloody

scratches and the bruises and said, 'You have pinched yourself harder than I!' "

"And did he let you go?"

Gideon smiled. "Oh, no. He pinched me twice, once for losing the goat and once for making him wait. But this is a thing that I know—to live with fear is not to live at all. A man will die every moment he is afraid."

"So you mean I should face down the things that scare me? Stare down the *rougarou* and walk right up to the pinching man?"

The smile deepened. "I think that Africa is making you wise, Delilah."

I sniffled and regretted the loss of my handkerchief. I rubbed my face on my sleeve, wondering what the habitués of the Club d'Enfer would make of me if they could see me.

"Then let's go back and see how Moses is. We will wait together."

# 19

After several hours there was no change in Moses' condition and Gideon took me back to Fairlight. He left me at the garden gate and I went into the house alone, every bone aching. Dora had left food for me and a note saying the men had disposed of the corpses in the barn and scrubbed it out and that she was spending the night with the Halliwells. I ignored the food and poured a drink and settled on the sofa and that was where Helen found me a few hours later.

I was halfway through a bottle of gin and she helped me with the rest. She had shown up with an armful of flowers from her garden and an apologetic grin.

"I suppose you think I'm terrible," she began.

I held up the bottle. "No worse than the rest of us. Do you want bitters or tonic?"

She sighed. "No. Straight-up is good enough for me. Shall I apologise formally, or are we all sorted?"

"Oh, I think we're sorted."

I had hoped that would be enough, but she went on. "Those parties, there's nothing malicious in them, you know. They're just a bit of fun."

I didn't say anything. She sipped at her gin. "Sometimes I wake up and I don't like what I see in the mirror. And one of my little soirees just makes me feel good again. You can understand that, can't you?"

I didn't like her like this, pleading, looking just a trifle too intently at me. I wanted her to be careless and a little cruel, beautiful and vivacious. That was the Helen I had always known. I didn't like seeing the cracks in the facade.

"You probably wouldn't let me drink if you knew how bad it was for me," she said with a half laugh.

"I know how bad it is. I just think a person has a right to do what she wants with her own body."

She opened her mouth, then closed it again. She drank deeply of the gin, holding it in her mouth before swallowing it down. "Thank you for that. That's the worst part of not being entirely well, you know. Everyone thinks they know what's best for you. But they're wrong. This is good for me, *living* is good for me." She hesitated. "I suppose Rex told you."

"He did."

She lifted her chin. "He's fond of you. I don't mind. You mustn't think that I mind. I won't be here forever, you know. And when I'm gone maybe the two of you—"

"Don't," I said. My tone was sharp but she merely smiled.

"What's the matter? Don't you like the thought of wearing a dead woman's shoes? You'd like the pink quartz bathtub. And don't be so quick to dismiss Rex. He's a devil in bed."

I smiled in spite of myself and she laughed aloud. "Oh, I do love talking to you, Delilah. You're one of the few people I know who is genuinely incapable of being shocked. I mean it, you know. I don't mind about Rex. He's a good man. I like to think that he might not be alone when I'm gone. It's being replaced while I'm still here that I mind."

I leveled my gaze at her. "I'm afraid I don't know what you're talking about."

"Kit Parrymore," she said succinctly. Her smile faltered, but she pasted it firmly in place. Only her eyes pleaded. "I know it's a bore, but I really am quite fond of him. Don't take him away from me, will you? I get such a kick out of misbehaving with him, and you know, darling, I've so few kicks left."

I said nothing. She rose. "That gin went right through me. Point me to the bathroom and then we'll open another bottle and show these natives how it's done."

I waved her in the direction of my room and she disappeared. She was gone a long while, but I didn't follow her, and when she returned, I was glad I hadn't. There was fresh powder on her nose and her eyes were rimmed in pink. It would take a crueler woman than I had ever been to poke that. She poured us each a fresh glass and settled in for a long evening. We talked about Mossy and old friends; we put on the gramophone and danced a wobbly foxtrot. We toasted the moon and when she left, it felt as if the light had gone out of the room. There had always been glamour to Helen, real glamour, and I lifted my glass to her as she fired up her engine and stomped hard on the accelerator. The room was empty and cold without her, without Dodo. I wound up the gramophone and finished the gin. When it was done, I went to work on the whisky. It was almost dawn before I fell asleep on the sofa, and when I woke it was to Ryder putting a hand to my throat.

"What are you doing?" My voice came out as a hoarse croak.

"Checking for a pulse. You look like hell."

"Feel like it, too." I sat up. I was still wearing the clothes I had worn when I had found Moses in the barn. They were crusted with blood and stained with dirt. My hair was snarled and my fingernails were packed with earth and dried blood.

Ryder put out his hand. "Come with me."

I didn't even bother to ask where we were going. He put me gently into the truck and drove away from Fairlight. He could have driven us off a cliff at that moment for all I cared. I had assumed we were going to his little *boma*, but he took a different road, and after a while he parked the truck behind a cluster of bushes next to a small lake. We walked a little distance away into a *lugga* and from there into a thicket of trees. Tucked up against one was a narrow ladder, and he motioned for me to climb it. I did, feeling as if my legs and arms didn't belong to me. They were disjointed as my mind, and I wasn't sure how I managed to make them work except that Ryder was directly behind me, urging me upwards.

At the top of the ladder I found a platform with a short railing and a canopy of tightly woven leaves and fronds. A makeshift bed was there as well as a small metal camp trunk of supplies. Ryder told me to sit and rummaged in the trunk, emerging with flatbread and a sharp white cheese. There was biltong as well, a local specialty of meat soaked in vinegar and spices and then dried, and some fruit that was too soft but still sweet. He made me eat, and when I was done, he turned me around.

The tree house overlooked the lake, the view completely unobscured, and from the short distance we could see every creature that came to drink. A lioness was lapping at the water's edge while a group of zebra on the opposite side watched her warily. She ignored them and wandered off, her indifference apparent in every step.

I sat transfixed for hours, watching every little drama that played out there. The warthogs that shepherded their little piglets with their tails held aloft like banners. The hippo that strode firmly to the centre of the lake and submerged only to rise munching contentedly as a cow on her water plants. And the giraffes, stepping with stately intention towards the edge, lowering their heads and splaying their legs. One of them ventured towards us, nibbling at the leaves around the tree house until she was so close I could touch her. I put a finger to her hide, surprised to find it felt like horsehair. She looked like velvet from a distance with her elegant patchwork coat. She looked at me then with her enormous doll's eyes and blinked slowly. She seemed to nod in greeting, then turned away to make a graceful exit.

There was nothing that day that I didn't marvel at. And when the air grew hot and the animals sought shade and rest, I began to talk. I told Ryder things I had never told him, never told anyone. I told him about Johnny, and the fact that I had loved him and how it had surprised me and frightened me to love anyone that much. I told him about burying the pieces they had sent home to me, and what it had meant to be a widow at twenty. I told him about the men since then, those I had loved and those I had not. I told him about the things I was ashamed of, and the things I regretted, and I cried until my eyes were so swollen I couldn't see him. He held me as he might hold a sick puppy, tenderly, asking nothing.

He handed me a handkerchief and said little. His hand stroked my hair, working out the snarls, and when I was finished and could say nothing more, he fed me again and told me to lie down. He covered me with the thin scratchy blanket and lay behind me, holding me against his body. I fell asleep and slept so deeply and so long that when I awoke the stars were out, shimmering as if someone had flung a handful of broken glass across a velvet tablecloth. I counted them until dawn began to streak the eastern sky, pink and gold shot across the horizon.

Ryder awoke then and pointed to the lake. The animals were stirring, some like the lions just coming in from a night's hunting. Others, like the gentle giraffe, had never been to bed at all, preferring to stand like sleepy sentinels throughout the night. And still others, like the monkeys, were rising with the dawn, chattering in the trees in conversation with the birds.

"I don't even remember what I told you," I said as he handed me a cup of cold tea. He smiled, and there was something seraphic about that smile. Seraphs were angels, but warriors, I remembered from my catechism classes. They brought absolution and vengeance, an uneasy combination, but a magnificent one.

"It's not important. It's only important that you finally said it."

"Possibly. I know my psychoanalyst would say

so. Of course, I've been seeing him for five years and he's never managed to fix me."

"Why do you need to be fixed?"

I smothered the urge to laugh. "Weren't you listening last night?"

He shrugged. "We're all broken, Delilah. That's what Africa does. She either attracts people who were broken in the first place or she does the deed for you. This is no country for softness."

"I don't see that you're broken. You seem whole enough."

"Then you haven't looked closely."

"You mean the women?" He shrugged again.

"Stop doing that. A shrug isn't an answer."

He looked me in the eye. "Fine. You want an answer? I loved a girl a long time ago. I married her and she was going to have a child. I was the happiest man on earth."

"What happened?"

"What happened is that I was a goddamned idiot. She was three months pregnant with my best friend's child when I married her and I was stupid enough to believe her when she said she had miscalculated the birth."

"My God," I murmured.

"It gets better. She was still in love with him. And the only reason she married me was because he left her to marry Jude. I was an afterthought, a fallback plan."

"Did Jude know?"

"Not at first. But when my wife was giving birth it became apparent that this was no premature delivery. There were complications and she confessed everything to Tusker who told Jude and me. Tusker thought it was better the truth came out."

"And then she died?"

He gave a harsh laugh. "Not quite. She gave birth to a healthy ten-pound baby boy with my name and my best friend's eyes. Last I heard she had fallen on hard times and was running a brothel in Cairo."

"She broke your heart," I said softly.

"That she did. Put your ear to my chest and you could probably still hear the pieces rattling around."

I lifted my cup. "A toast to the broken ones, then."

He clinked his cup to mine and we drank. He said nothing for a minute but he was watching me closely.

"What is it, Ryder? Your silences are loud."

"I'm just wondering what your plans are."

"I don't have plans. I'm going home just as soon as I can."

"Not if you bring a case against Gates," he pointed out. "You'll have to stay for a trial to give evidence. Don't you want justice done?"

"That isn't fair," I argued, but the fight had gone out of me. "I'm tired, Ryder. I want to go home."

I looked out over the watering hole washed with new, pink light. "It seems a little odd for a grown man to have a tree house."

"It's where I sleep when the mosquitoes are bad." He said it simply, dropping the words like small stones into a pond. But I felt the heft of them. He had to avoid the mosquitoes because they could kill him. It was the closest he had come to telling me about the blackwater fever, and I waited, wondering if he would strip himself bare, throwing confidences like shed garments into my lap.

But the moment passed and he rose, putting out his hand. "Come on, Delilah. I'll take you home."

As he dropped me at the gate to Fairlight, he leaned across me to open my door. "I called in to the village before I came to get you. Moses is conscious and the *babu* says he will be fine."

"It isn't his time to go," I said, echoing Gideon with a small smile.

"It isn't yours either. Think about it."

The next morning Gideon came to tell me that Moses was markedly better, and I told him to make arrangements to come with me to Nairobi. He would serve as my witness for the incidents with Gates. He argued, as politely as Gideon would ever argue, but in the end I won. Omar packed us a basket of food and we set off in Ryder's appalling old truck. I managed to navigate the treacherous road to Nairobi with a little trouble and a great deal of flair. The result was that we arrived in record time, both of us covered in red dust. I had planned to take a room at the Norfolk to freshen up, but as soon as they sniffily told "my man" to wait outside, I turned on my heel and went straight to Government House. I could have gone to the police, but I thought more might be done if I initiated an investigation from the top down. Colonial police were most likely ill-equipped and underpaid and a case that would take them out into the bush would probably get shoved aside in favour of something easier. But they couldn't ignore a directive straight from Government House, and I wasn't about to take a refusal from a lowly clerk. That was a lesson I learned from my grandfather—never take a no from someone who doesn't have the authority to give you a yes.

I tidied myself as best as I could, then presented myself and Gideon at the reception desk and asked for Mr. Fraser. His secretary, the same rabbity-looking Bates who had escorted me there on my arrival, bolted from his seat to scurry into the inner office. After an unconscionably long period of time we were invited in. Mr. Fraser extended me the barest courtesy of a handshake. His necktie was askew and his hair was wild as if he'd been pulling at it. His desk was piled high with papers and maps and telegrams, and he didn't quite manage to repress a sigh as I sat. Gideon stood behind me.

"Miss Drummond, as you can see, I am quite busy. *Quite* busy. Can we make this very quick?"

"Of course," I said, smiling sweetly. "I wish to report an attempted murder."

His eyebrows jerked up and he gave a soundless whistle. "Yours?"

"Of course not! What makes you think someone would want to murder me?"

"It was the obvious answer," he muttered. He drew a notebook towards him and opened it, licking the tip of his pencil. "Very well. Who was the intended victim?"

"Moses, the cow herder who tends my cattle at Fairlight."

"A cow herder?" He paused, his pencil stilled. "You mean a native?"

"Masai," I replied, nodding towards Gideon. "This is Moses' brother, Gideon. He will serve as my witness to the events I will describe for you."

Fraser slammed the notebook shut. "No, he won't, because I won't be hearing them. Native disputes have nothing to do with us and should have nothing to do with you. I told you to stay out of these things."

I took a deep breath and tried again. "Mr. Fraser, this was not a native dispute. The guilty party is a man named Gates, a white man I dismissed from employment at Fairlight."

His brow furrowed and he rummaged on his desk through the papers until he found what he was looking for. "Are you aware he lodged a complaint with the police here in Nairobi against you? Said you fired a rifle at him. Twice."

"He was defrauding my stepfather and beating my cow herder," I replied calmly.

"Neither of which is sufficient justification for shooting a man with a rifle."

"I didn't shoot him. I shot *at* him," I corrected. "There's a difference."

He skimmed the rest of the report. "With a Rigby .416? You could have blown a hole in his chest the size of a dog if you'd missed."

"I didn't." I was indignant at the slur against my marksmanship.

He threw the paper onto his desk. "That is of no consequence. You recklessly discharged a firearm directly at this man with the intention of intimidating him. You might have killed him. If he chooses to prefer charges, there's little I can do."

"You must be joking. He trespassed onto my property, killed all of my chickens and cows, and attempted to kill my cow herder. And you intend to do nothing?"

"If I instruct the police to start an investigation, they will turn over everything, including your firing a rifle at Gates. They will determine that you started the entire matter, and you will be made to look ridiculous."

I rose. "I assure you, Mr. Fraser, I am not the one who looks ridiculous here. I know what justice is, and I thank you for showing me precisely what it costs in Kenya."

I turned smartly on my heel and he jumped to his feet. "Miss Drummond, do not do anything reckless. Leave this alone. Post guards at Fairlight if you feel threatened, and leave Gates strictly alone. These things almost always blow over."

"And when they don't?"

He shrugged. "Someone usually dies."

"It isn't going to be me," I told him before sweeping out.

In the truck, Gideon and I ate our sandwiches and drank cold tea. He had relaxed his rule about taking food from me, but he insisted upon sitting in the back. It felt absurd conversing with him through the small window, but he wouldn't hear of sitting alone with me in the truck. He was very conscious of appearances, and I realised then that Gideon operated under two different sets of rules, one for the bush where he knew his way and one for the city where he was of no more importance than the occasional warthog that crossed the road.

I fussed and fumed as we ate, dreaming up a dozen different petty vengeances for Gates, but none of them suited me. Gideon said nothing, chewing complacently at his food until I hit the window with the flat of my hand.

"You aren't helping, Gideon. I've spent the last

half an hour listing the ways I could make Gates suffer and you've said nothing."

"It is not for me to speak."

"Why not?"

"Such talk is poison. You must speak until you can speak no more. Then the poison is gone and you will be free of it."

I lapsed into silence, but he was right, of course. I knew he wanted Gates to pay for what he'd done to Moses, but his way was different. He would rely upon the lion or the cobra to act on his behalf, perhaps at the direction of the *laibon*. A Masai revenge would be a subtle thing.

But something seemed different about him, a subtle shift in his mood, and I wondered if leaving the bush had overwhelmed him.

"I'm sorry I made you come for nothing," I told him. "I thought it would be necessary, but I think it has upset you."

"I am concerned, but not because of the city."

"What, then?"

I turned in my seat and saw that his eyes were ringed with white. "Last night I killed the lioness who mated with the lion you killed, Delilah."

"But, I don't understand. What happened?"

"I had seen her many times since the day we hunted her mate. She always came quietly, low in the grass, but far away, and I was never near enough to throw my spear. Yesterday she came to the edge of the *boma*. She took one of the *babu*'s cows."

371

"But how do you know it was her? Surely there are thousands of lionesses in the bush," I argued, but Gideon was shaking his head pityingly.

"I know lions like you know dresses. You would not look at a purple dress and say it is the same as the blue one. This lioness was the mate. And I killed her."

"Why didn't you wait for Ryder? Or for me?"

"There was no time. She had already attacked once and would not leave the *boma*. The children were very frightened, and it was up to the *morani* to do their duty. My friend Samuel was very pleased to try to kill her, and he took up his spear to do this."

"And he failed?"

He nodded. "His spear only grazed her flank. She turned, very angry, and charged him. I had to throw my spear. I wanted only to stop her, so someone else's spear would be the one that took her life, but she turned again, and my spear struck her in the heart."

"The tenth lion," I said softly.

"And this is what I think about when I am silent. This will bring bad luck, Delilah, and it will be worse than the pinching man or the *rougarou*."

I threw the greaseproof paper back into the basket and turned the engine over. I gunned the engine, leaving the dust of Nairobi behind us as we headed back into the bush.

# 20

The house was quiet that night without Dodo. We hadn't been on good terms for a while, but I was always conscious of her, moving about, tidying and organising and patting things into place. Without her, I plumped cushions and changed the water in the flowers and dusted the picture frames myself. I even went outside and threw some toast for the tortoise, but it didn't bother to visit me either. The chores killed a little time, but in the end I was forced to wind up the gramophone to break the silence. I put on my jazziest recordings and danced with my shadow until the machine wound down and it was time to go to bed. And before I slid under the mosquito netting, I looked at the calendar and counted down the number of days until I could reasonably return to Paris. It would be a matter of a few months and then I could leave Africa behind me. Africa with its beauty and its wildness and its two sets of laws, one for white men and one for blacks. Africa with its hot breath and its blood-warm rivers that ran like veins through its heart. Africa with its sudden sunrises and sunsets so swift that darkness fell like a mourning veil. I hated the place, I told myself sharply. I hated it as you can only hate something that is a part of yourself, long forgotten and unremembered. I hated it with the force of a child's hate, unyielding and immovable. I hated it as I had never hated any place before.

And I cried long into the night at the thought of leaving her.

The next afternoon I consoled myself with a visit to Kit. His prospects were indeed improving. He'd gotten a much better gramophone, and a dozen new recordings which we spent the afternoon listening to while we sipped champagne—expensive stuff, not the swill he usually bought. He gave me caviar and toast points for lunch and when I asked if he'd sold a painting, he gave me a close-lipped smile and touched the side of his nose. I wasn't surprised he chose to keep silent. I recognised the gramophone as Helen's. She had apparently decided to tip the scales in her favour by giving him expensive presents, but she needn't have bothered. Kit was a diversion for me and nothing more. I was frankly more interested in how my portrait was coming along. It was almost finished, he told me. Only the edges left to complete, but still he wouldn't let me see it. He wanted it to be a surprise. That was Kit, I mused. Ever the child, he wanted the thrill of unveiling it at the opening. No doubt he expected gasps of admiration. But a grand gesture was a small thing to give him.

Later I remembered that afternoon. I forced myself to relive every caress, every word, every stroke and kiss and gasp. I wrote it down and tore it up. I dreamed it. I sat for hours on the sofa with a gin in one hand and a cigarette in the other, remembering it all. Did I know when he touched me it would be the last time? Did I have a premonition when he slid into me that never again would I feel the weight of his body on mine? I don't think so. But there was something sad about that last afternoon, a sense of something winding down, like a clock ticking past its last minutes, a phonograph offering up its last song.

I kissed him as he slept and gathered up my clothes and walked back to Fairlight. I ate alone and it was afterwards, when I sat alone on the dark veranda nursing a gin and tonic that I saw lights approaching. The car turned sharply up the drive and I stood as the car rolled to a stop. Rex alighted and walked slowly to the house, his eyes fixed on mine. I must have looked ghostly in the darkness, my dress pale against the black shadows.

He came near and he took my hand. "I'm so very sorry."

"What happened?" I asked in a voice I had not heard since I had buried Johnny.

"He was found this afternoon. Shot in the head. I'm so sorry," he repeated.

"Was it an accident? On safari?"

Rex held me by the shoulders. "Safari? What are you talking about? I'm not talking about Ryder.

It's Kit who has died, Delilah. It's Kit. Kit is dead."

He tightened his grip, but no matter how hard he held on, I knew I was slipping away as I fainted straight into his arms.

I came to on the sofa with Rex chafing my wrists. He had me propped against him, his arms holding me up. It felt blissful for a few minutes just to float there with nothing but his warmth tethering me to the earth. I knew there was something I did not want to remember, and I pushed everything aside except the feel of him. I was a shipwreck survivor, clinging to the only thing that could keep me afloat.

"Delilah," he said softly. And then I remembered.

I sat up, pushing away from him. "What happened to Kit?"

"There's no need to go into it just—"

"What happened?"

"He was shot. In his house. In bed. It was murder, but no one knows by whom."

In the same bed where I had slept with him only that afternoon. I went to the bathroom and heaved for several minutes. I felt better then. I washed out my mouth with eau de cologne and went back to the drawing room to find Rex with his face buried in his hands. I sat next to him, shoulder touching shoulder, soldiers together.

"Helen is grief-stricken, as you can imagine.

She was very fond of Kit. We all were. I will make the necessary arrangements. I don't suppose his family would care to."

"They'll have to be told."

"Of course. But they wouldn't have time to come out. We will have to stand as his family instead."

He rose and straightened, and I saw the force of Empire in him. "I will make sure an investigation is opened and the culprit is found. If it's the last thing I do, I promise you. I will make certain there is justice for Kit."

He left me with my unanswered questions, but I did not blame him. We could have circled around them like dogs snapping at a piece of meat and it wouldn't do any good. Not until the police had had their way, asking questions and turning over stones. I knew I didn't have long before they came to me. I sat smoking in the dark, knowing it would be the last peaceful evening for a very long time.

The next morning I was awake early, gritty-eyed and in a stupor. I thought Dora would have come back, but she didn't. Only Gideon came, but he seemed preoccupied and his smile was not in evidence. I worried Moses might have taken a turn for the worse, but when I taxed him with it, he merely shook his head.

"Moses does well, *Bibi*."

"You're supposed to call me Delilah," I snapped.

"I am sorry, Delilah," he returned, but there was

no gleam of amusement, no shared jokes. I took his hand.

"What is it, Gideon?"

"It is *Bwana Tausi*. The police have questioned me."

"Questioned you about Kit? What on earth for?"

His eyes slid from mine. "They think it is possible I may have done this terrible thing to *Bwana Tausi*."

His hand was like ice and I understood why. What sort of justice would a black man face in the murder of a white if there was evidence to connect him?

"Had you been to see him?"

"Not in many months. He painted my picture, but that was before the last rains."

"Don't you worry, Gideon. You had no reason to harm Kit. You have nothing to fear. I will take care of this."

He straightened to his full warrior's height. "It is not your place to take care of me, Delilah."

"Gideon, in the bush, I would trust you with my life if we were faced with a lion. There is no one I would rather have protecting me."

A proud smile touched his lips. "Thank you."

"But these are my lions. And it's my time to protect you."

That afternoon the police came. I was ready for them. I left off the riding breeches and Misha's shirts and put on a dress. It was white silk, light as a cloud, and designed to make me look fragile and vulnerable. I might have undone the effect by the red lipstick, but I had powdered well, making myself as pale as possible. I wanted them to remember I was not one of them, not a settler with skin browned and toughened to leather by seasons of equatorial sun. I came from a privileged place and privileged people who would use their influence to whatever end I wanted.

I received them in the drawing room and told Pierre to bring in tea and cakes. The inspector was athletic with a wiry build and a thatch of ginger hair he stroked constantly. He gave me a card that said his name was Gilchrist. He didn't bother to introduce his subordinates and instructed them to wait outside.

"No need to overwhelm the lady," he said with a small mournful nod in my direction. I gave him a wan smile in return and waved him to a sofa with a languid arm.

"Miss Drummond, I am very sorry to have to put you through this," he began.

I opened my eyes very wide. "But of course, Inspector. I understand perfectly. You must do your job," I finished.

That was the end of the pleasantries. For the next hour he hammered me, going over every inch of the same ground until he beat it flat. He explained that Kit had been killed most likely between five and six in the afternoon by a large-calibre revolver that belonged to him. The angle of the wound precluded suicide, and there had been no struggle. He covered my affair with Kit and everything else he thought might be pertinent. He was particularly insistent upon the point that this seemed to be a *crime passionnel.* Why were sex crimes always described in French terms, I wondered? Did it make them more palatable to Anglo-Saxon sensibilities? His eyes lit when he described what he thought might have happened.

"Is it not possible, Miss Drummond, that Mr. Parrymore was caught *in flagrante delicto* by a jealous spouse and was dispatched as a result of sexual jealousy?"

I decided to cut straight to the still-beating heart of the matter. "That is not possible, Inspector. I'm afraid Kit was not capable of pleasuring another woman yesterday afternoon."

"I beg your pardon, Miss Drummond?"

"Let us be frank, Inspector. Kit's talents in the bedroom were quite satisfactory, but he had his limitations. He had been with me twice between two and four-thirty. He would have been entirely incapable of rising to the challenge again."

The inspector flushed a little. "I am not quite certain I am—"

"Shall I speak even more plainly? Kit could not have achieved an erection then. After our time

380

together he would have slept heavily. He certainly didn't stir when I left, and I made no effort to be quiet. Whoever murdered him most likely snuck in when he was still sleeping and helped himself to Kit's gun. Kit wouldn't have heard anything."

The inspector hesitated. "Well, Mr. Parrymore's posture in death would indicate he had been surprised while in repose."

"Another hole in your *crime passionnel* theory," I added brutally.

The inspector gave me a thin smile. "As you say, Miss Drummond. But if Mr. Parrymore was killed as you suggest, by an intruder who came upon him as he slept, then this murder takes on an altogether more sinister cast."

"How so?"

"Premeditation, Miss Drummond. To kill a man when you have apprehended him making love to your wife is sometimes excusable. To kill a man with his own gun when he is sleeping is the foulest crime. Whoever did this will swing for it."

He paused. "Of course, premeditation speaks to resentment, deeply held emotion that has festered. Do you know of anyone who held a grudge against Mr. Parrymore?"

"No. The very notion is absurd. Kit is—was— the sort of man who glided through life, Inspector. He made friends easily, of both sexes. He had the gift of ease with people. Men liked investing in his art. Women liked investing in the man. I think they believed they could domesticate him."

"Did you?"

"I'm not looking for a husband. Kit suited me just as he was. I can't speak for other women."

"No, of course not. But was there anyone who might have rested their hopes upon Mr. Parrymore and found him a rather unreliable vessel?"

"Perhaps. But Kit and I never discussed such things. I assume he was sleeping with other women. In fact, I hoped he was. But who they were was of absolutely no interest to me." I didn't see the point in mentioning the others by name. If Gilchrist was any sort of investigator, he'd find them himself. And if he didn't? Well, that wasn't my problem.

The inspector paused in jotting his notes and gave me a slightly slack-jawed stare.

"How extraordinary," he murmured. "In my experience women tend to be curious about such things."

"You have no experience of me," I reminded him.

To my surprise, he flushed a little. "Quite," he said, his voice clipped. "You have no knowledge of who Mr. Parrymore's other special friends might have been. What about his politics?"

I shrugged. "The same as most colonists. He favoured independence."

His brows peaked. "Strongly?"

"I haven't the faintest. Kit and I seldom discussed such things when we were together. In fact, we didn't talk much at all."

This time the blush crept all the way to his neck and he tugged a little at his collar. "I see." He changed tactics then, and when he spoke, his voice was smooth as silk, suddenly warm and insinuating, as if he meant to coax a confidence. "I have heard that you are quite often seen in the company of one of the Masai. A fellow named Gideon."

I blinked slowly. "Oh, you mean Ryder White's tracker. Of course. He's a helpful fellow."

The inspector sat forward suddenly, angling his body so that his shoulders blocked me into the sofa. Why had I thought him slight? "Miss Drummond, I have reason to believe this Masai was there. I believe he was involved in Kit Parrymore's death. I want you to tell me why."

"I have no idea what you're talking about. It's madness."

"Is it? It wouldn't be the first time a woman has been the cause of trouble in this colony," he told me, his expression grim.

"You think Kit and Gideon quarreled? Over *me?* That's too absurd for words."

"I don't know what to think yet, but I know where to look and I know whom to ask. But right now, I want the story from you."

"I have no story to give you, Inspector. Gideon

is in Ryder White's employ and occasionally helps out here at Fairlight. Kit was my lover. As far as I knew, the two were barely acquainted. If you think I know anything else, I can only say you are barking up entirely the wrong tree."

"Am I?" I shifted and the white silk slipped a little off one shoulder, showing a bit of flesh that was every bit as smooth and white as the fabric itself. The inspector's eyes dropped to my skin. He leaned nearer still and I caught the smell of tobacco and bay rum and hair oil. "I want the truth. Are you and the Masai known as Gideon lovers?"

I miscalculated the slap a little. I wanted to hit him squarely on the cheekbone. If you aim it just right, you can actually split the skin on the ridge of the bone, leaving a spectacular mark. But I rushed it and caught his temple. My ring cut into his hairline and a bright line of blood appeared, marking the path of my hand like a river on a map. His head snapped back, but his body didn't move. He must have been expecting it, which was a dangerous thing. It meant he was far more experienced in these matters than I was and he was willing to risk a minor assault to get what he wanted.

He never took his eyes off mine. He reached into his pocket for a handkerchief as a few bright drops of his blood fell into my lap. I watched him press it to his temple as a slow smile crept over his face.

He rose then and took out a card. He dropped it on the table.

"I will be in touch, Miss Drummond."

When he left it was with a bit of a swagger, and I lit a fresh cigarette, wondering how much damage I had just done.

# 21

The next morning a council of war was held at Fairlight. I had sent out a summons, asking Tusker and Rex and Ryder and the Halliwells to come. Rex was in Nairobi making funeral arrangements for Kit, but Tusker and Ryder appeared with Jude in tow. Dora came with Mr. Halliwell, although Evelyn stayed behind to mind the school. Helen was there, looking older and more fragile, a damp handkerchief clutched in her hand. We convened in the drawing room to compare notes. Ryder was the last to arrive, hollow-eyed with fatigue and shaking dust out of his hair.

"Where's Gideon?" I asked him.

"In the barn. He couldn't stay in his village. The police have already been there again asking questions. We've been one step ahead of them for the last day and night. It's only a matter of time before they find him."

"We cannot let that happen," I said flatly. I turned to the others. "I wanted you to come because we must devise a plan to protect Gideon."

Helen spoke up, her voice sharp with emotion. "We can't take him. That's far too obvious. Ours will be one of the first farms they search, as will Nyama." Tusker nodded. Jude said nothing, and Halliwell frowned. Dora was busy passing out

386

sandwiches, although no one ate. I turned to Halliwell. "Can you keep him for a little while at the school?"

He gave me a sorrowful look. "I'm afraid not. He was a student there. It's only logical that they would search the place, and I cannot let that happen. I have the children to consider."

I thought of Helen pounding drinks back with both fists as Halliwell leered at her cleavage and I stared him down. "What about friends of yours? I know the mission has connections all over Africa. We could put him in touch with one of them and send him out of Kenya altogether."

He hesitated and I pushed forward. "We just need time. I talked to the inspector yesterday and I think he is fixed on Gideon because he's the easiest suspect. Once he finishes his inquiries and doesn't turn up another suspect, he'll stop looking. He will bring a case against Gideon and he will make certain Gideon hangs. Can you live with that? Because I can't."

Halliwell's eyes slipped away from mine as Ryder spoke up. "The inspector hasn't fixed on him because he is easy. He has evidence."

"What evidence?" I demanded.

"They found a bracelet at the scene, a Masai piece, and the colours indicate it came from Gideon's village."

I opened my mouth in astonishment, but before I could say a word, Jude broke in.

"I'll take him."

"The hell you will," Ryder cut in. "You heard what Helen said. Nyama is one of the first places they'll search. Besides, Anthony already thinks Gideon is guilty. If you take him home with you, Anthony will shoot him on sight."

"Not if—"

"Jude, leave it," Tusker instructed firmly. "Ryder is correct. Anthony would either shoot him or turn him in for the reward."

"What reward?" My voice was hollow and Ryder jumped to his feet swearing.

Helen wiped at her eyes again. "The news came out of Nairobi this morning. There's a reward for Gideon's capture. Every white and half the blacks in Kenya will be looking for him now."

"But it should have been days yet," I began. Tusker waved me away.

"Things can happen quite quickly out here when people have a mind to make them. It's a frontier, child. With frontier justice. Just be glad they specified he was to be taken alive."

Ryder swore again and I sat down. Even Dora put down the damned sandwiches and looked stricken. "There must be someone loyal enough to him to resist the money," she said quietly.

"There is," Ryder said. He exchanged a meaningful look with Tusker.

"Excellent plan, my boy. But you'll have to go with him to make sure he's protected."

"Of course."

"What are we talking about?" I demanded.

Ryder flicked a glance towards Halliwell. "Nothing I would care to get specific about."

Halliwell flushed. "Now see here—"

Dora cut in sharply. "He's right, Lawrence. It's best if none of us know." I raised a brow at her. Things must have gotten quite cozy at the Halliwell establishment if she was on a first-name basis with the master of the house.

He nodded. "As you say, Dora." Of course he would agree, I thought bitterly. The less he knew, the faster he could wash his hands of the whole thing. He was staring at Dora intently and she blushed a little. I thought with a pleasurable little shiver of how much I would enjoy telling her about his antics at Helen's last party.

"When will you go?" Tusker asked.

"Now. The sooner the better."

"I'm coming with you," Jude said. Her chin was set and Ryder nodded slowly.

"Jude," Tusker began, but Jude took a step forward, her fists balled.

"It's my decision, Tusker. If Ryder will have me, I'm going. I'm a better tracker than Ryder and a better shot than Gideon. They can use me."

I went to the rack over the door and took down the Rigby and handed it to her. "Take this. It's a better gun than yours."

She gave me a long, level gaze, then put out her hand. "Thank you."

"Just don't shoot it any more than you have to. Those bullets are damned expensive."

She gave me a faint smile and pocketed the ammunition. "One shot, one kill."

I followed Ryder and Jude to the barn. Dora had collected food and Ryder took all the extra ammunition he could carry. I helped, my head buzzing. I itched to go and look in my jewel box to see if my bracelet was still there, but there was no chance. They say in a crisis everything slows down, like when you hold your breath and walk underwater. But that wasn't true, not this time. Every moment was speeding by so fast, if I had stopped I would have fallen over from dizziness. So I kept on going, pushing through as things happened around me. My hands knew what to do even when my brain didn't. When we reached the barn door, Ryder turned and kissed me hard.

"You will come back," I told him. "That's not a question."

He kissed me a second time and unlocked the barn door. Gideon crept out of the shadows.

"*Bibi*?"

"I'm here, Gideon. You're going to go with Jude and Ryder. Somewhere safe."

He stood in front of me, tall and straight as a spear. "I understand." He put out his hand. "I would like to shake hands with you, *Bibi*."

I shook it, clasping that broad warm palm. I turned it over and looked at it. There was all of Africa in that palm. The line of the Mara River flowed across it, with the high plains where a man might be free and the deep ridge of the Rift where time stood still. I put the hand to my face and he held it there briefly before removing it.

"I cannot come back," he said, putting into words what I already knew.

"I will not forget you," I promised him. "As long as Africa endures, I will remember you, my friend."

I could hardly see him then. The tears obscured his face, and my last view of him was watery and insubstantial as a ghost. Already he was fading. I made to go, then turned back again. "What is your name, Gideon? I want to know your real name, not the one the white school gave you. I want the one your people gave you. The name God calls you."

He smiled. "I am Ole, Delilah."

"Ole," I said slowly. "Good. Because if I ever get to heaven, I want to know how to find you."

"This is a thing that I know—you are my friend, Delilah."

I turned then and walked to the door. But it was too late. The police had arrived.

The inspector emerged from his car with a selection of policemen and he smiled at me, lifting a piece of paper over his head. "I have a warrant for the arrest of the Masai known as Gideon. Where is he?"

"I don't know," I called out, "but you're just in time to see where the foreman Gates assaulted my cow herder. The blood has been scrubbed, but you can still make out traces. Would you like to investigate that?" I asked, stepping forward. Tusker and Jude closed ranks behind me as Ryder casually shut the barn door behind him. There were few places to hide inside, and we would buy him only a few minutes at best, but I could not stand by and let them take him, not on evidence that could have just as easily implicated me. Dora and Halliwell appeared on the veranda and Halliwell put his arm about her shoulders.

The inspector came nearer to me, and his men formed a wall behind him. He smiled again. "I have something more significant than the assault of a native boy on the docket today, Miss Drummond. Now, this will all go a great deal easier if you simply tell us where he's gone and let us get on with it."

"Get on with what?" Jude demanded. "Hanging an innocent man? Tell me, Inspector, what sort of trials do black men get in this country? I think we both know the answer to that."

His smile slipped a little. Bless her, I thought. Ryder had edged around to my left and I realised that between this action and Jude's theatrics, the police might just be diverted long enough for Gideon to effect an escape through the far side. He could hide in the *lugga* if we could just keep them occupied.

Jude started yelling then, stepping right up until she was toe-to-toe with the inspector. It was a step too far. As soon as she got within arm's length, the inspector shifted his attention to the barn itself. He signalled a pair of his men to take Jude and as soon as they moved forward, Ryder cocked his rifle.

"Try putting a hand on her," he told them. "I'm begging you."

They stood at a stalemate for a moment, the air charged as Jude refused to give ground and Ryder held the position at her back. The policemen drew their weapons, and all it would take was the slightest twitch and all hell would break loose.

"I did it." The words were out of my mouth before I even knew I was going to say them. Every single person on that farm turned to look at me, and I stepped forward again, squaring my shoulders. "I killed Kit Parrymore."

There was a moment of blessed, sacred silence before absolute pandemonium broke out.

Tusker started laughing, a deep belly laugh that was edged with hysteria. Dora collapsed straight into Halliwell's arms, and Jude swung around to look at me, colliding with Ryder. He was staring at me, his eyes locked on mine, and he under-stood.

I turned back to the inspector whose mouth had gone slack again. I held out my hands. "Did you bring handcuffs? Only mind you don't put them on too tightly. I bruise easily."

He shook his head. "Not so fast, Miss Drummond. I want a statement."

"Fine. Here's your statement—I went a little crazy and I shot Kit with his own revolver while he slept. I think I did. I mean, it's all so fuzzy in my head. I can't quite remember."

The inspector's eyes narrowed, and he gave me a smile as thin as paper. "I don't believe you."

I closed my eyes for a moment, letting the blackness wash over me. I heard the howling of the *rougarou*, and I felt the warmth of Gideon's hand in mind. I took one last deep breath and then I plunged.

"It wouldn't be the first time I went crazy," I said. I lifted my wrist and pulled off the black ribbon. "Do you see that scar? I did it with my husband's razor the day they brought what was left of him home from France."

There was a flash of hesitation in the inspector's eyes. Uncertainty was taking its first tentative steps. All it needed was a push.

"I spent three months locked up in an asylum in England. If you don't believe me, ask my cousin."

He turned his head to Dora. I didn't look at her.

394

It would be fatal to Gideon if Gilchrist suspected collusion. She had to tell him the truth, and I hoped she hated me just enough to do it.

"It's true," she said, almost inaudibly. She turned and buried herself in Halliwell's shoulder, weeping.

"I shall require a more extensive confession that that," Gilchrist said.

"Well, you're not getting one. Not until I'm in Nairobi with my lawyer present. Now take me in, gingernut."

I was gambling a little with that last bit, but as I expected, the belittling tone was enough to rattle him. He coloured to the roots of his red hair, then blanched as his men snickered. He took me by the wrists and towed me to his car. He opened the door and stepped back sharply to let me precede him. I turned back with a smile.

"Aren't you going to make certain I'm not armed?"

"I will take my chances," he said through gritted teeth.

I did not dare look back. I ducked into the car and settled myself in for the drive to Nairobi. Behind us I could hear the rest of the policemen piling into their cars and bringing up the rear of our little caravan. We drove slowly out the gates of Fairlight, and as the drive doubled back on itself I saw them all standing just as I had left them, a tableau in the morning light. I hoped

Gideon could see me through one of the chinks in the barn wall. I hoped he would get away and I hoped he would be safe. I hoped he would live a long and happy life. I hoped so many things during that long drive to Nairobi. I might have even prayed. Gideon needed a miracle to make it to safety and he would need a thousand more to keep him safe. But Gideon deserved a miracle. Even one I had to make with my own hands. It was a sloppy, untidy, makeshift little thing, my sad miracle, crooked and badly stitched, but it was all I had to offer him. I only hoped it would be enough.

I was taken directly to the police station for interrogation. We stopped once during the drive to Nairobi for the sharing out of a hamper of dry sandwiches and warm orange squash, but I refused. Anything I ate was likely to make an encore appearance, so I kept my mouth shut. We stopped twice more for punctures and mechanical trouble with the result that we arrived at the police station after dark, just as the first of the short rains was beginning to fall. I was hurried through a back entrance and put into a private holding cell. I glanced around, taking inventory. There was a narrow cot, one thin blanket, and unmentionable hygienic arrangements. I wrapped myself up and stretched out on the cot, closing my eyes. There were distant noises—voices, typewriters, the occasional ringing of the telephone, and once or twice the ominous clang as they locked another poor soul inside. I had seen Kilimani Prison on my first trip through Nairobi. It wasn't exactly the Crillon, and I crossed my fingers and said the rosary twice, hoping they wouldn't send me there. I was alone and separate from the holding cells of native Africans, something I pointed out to the inspector when he had me brought to an interrogation room some time later.

"I should have liked to have practiced my Swahili," I said brightly.

Gilchrist cleared his throat and one of his minions entered bearing a tea tray. "How civilized. And how very English," I murmured.

He gave me a thin smile and poured out a cup for me and laid a plate with sandwiches and cake. I lifted a brow and a slight flush touched his complexion.

"Eat it. It was sent over from the Norfolk Hotel." His voice was kinder than I had expected, all things considered.

I shrugged and helped myself. I had missed two meals and teatime, and if I was supposed to sit through an interrogation, I ought to keep my strength up.

He watched me and after a moment took one of the sandwiches himself, wolfing it down in a single bite.

"You'll give yourself indigestion."

He grimaced. "I have that already, largely thanks to you."

"You flatter me."

He sighed. "Miss Drummond—"

"Delilah, please. I suspect we're going to be spending quite a bit of time together."

"Delilah." He dropped his voice to something altogether softer than I had heard from him before. "I need your help. I don't believe you killed Kit Parrymore."

"Odd, then, that you should take me in so quickly."

He flushed again. "I let you goad me into that and I shouldn't have. I ought to have known right off that you were bluffing."

"Who says I was?"

He smiled, and to my surprise it was a genuine thing. "Where was he? In the kitchen? The storeroom?"

"The barn," I admitted. "But it wouldn't have done you any good to arrest an innocent man. I was doing you a favour."

"By confessing to a crime you didn't commit," he finished.

"Who says I didn't? I confessed. If you neglect that confession, I suspect the governor would be mightily put out. He's going to be under quite a bit of pressure to make sure this is solved quickly and discreetly. And I imagine if the governor is under pressure, so are you. I hear the Duke of York is planning an official visit next year. Just think what the king would say if you get this wrong! Why, I imagine, he might refuse permission for the duke to come at all. Such a perfect opportunity to showcase to Whitehall how much Kenya deserves self-governance, wasted! Yes, you are under pressure indeed, Inspector."

"You would not believe how much if I told you," he admitted. "But this absurd confession of yours—"

"It's not my fault if you don't believe it."

"Then help me to believe it. I must have facts, a motive."

"Oh, surely you can draw the inferences yourself. You're a clever man," I said, putting out my hand for another sandwich.

His hand clamped about my wrist. "Do you think I got this job by playing the fool? I will admit I swallowed your little bait like a good little fish, but I'm done with that. I've snapped the line and I will go my own way now. You no longer whistle the tune, Miss Drummond."

"You've rather mixed your metaphors there. And we agreed it was to be Delilah."

I slipped my arm from his grasp. He sat back, rubbing a hand over his temple.

"Headache? I always take a spoonful of bitters and lie down in a cool room with a compress. You might try it."

He gave a short laugh. "They warned me about

you. They told me you would twist me forty different ways. I could not imagine how, and yet here you are."

He forgot to be a policeman then. The cool efficiency dropped away and he sat, his hands clasped loosely in his lap, his expression resigned. He looked like a man who had just had his dearest illusions stripped away, and there was nothing left but need. It was a look I had seen before and not one I ever cared to be responsible for.

"Inspector," I said gently. "You ought to be asking me questions."

"I know. I just wish we could be honest with one another. The rest of it is exhausting. But if we could just have the truth . . ." He trailed off and leaned forward again, his eyes warm and coaxing.

I felt myself leaning nearer. "Inspector," I began, my voice a little tremulous.

He moved closer still, his lips parting expectantly. "Yes?"

I heard the frisson of expectation and I knew my instincts were correct.

I moved closer again. "I feel as though I could tell you anything. Anything at all."

"Go on," he urged, his eyes never leaving mine.

Closer still. I put a hand out to steady myself and felt the curve of his knee under my palm. "I will give you whatever you want," I said, tightening my grip. His leg flexed under my hand and his mouth curved slightly into a thin smile of triumph.

"Yes?"

"As soon as you get my lawyer. Until then, you can go hang yourself."

I sat back and laughed as he went brick-red and sat back as quickly as if I'd slapped him again.

"This isn't a game, Delilah."

"Of course it is. And you lost. Take it like a man. You thought you'd wheedle something out of me because I'm just a woman. Poor Gilchrist! I learned to turn men like you inside out before I could even walk. Now send me back to my cell and get my lawyer here. Quentin Harkness, Lincoln's Inn Fields, London. I'll wait."

"If you think I'm going to wait a fortnight for some spit-polished solicitor from London to make his way here, you are entirely mistaken."

"Language! And I think you will. Remember, Inspector, I'm not just a British citizen. I'm American. And I think my great-uncle, *Senator* L'Hommedieu, would be greatly interested if I were to be denied due process."

He wrote down Quentin's name and address, snapping off the pencil lead as he did so.

"What makes you so certain he'll even come?"

"He's my ex-husband."

Gilchrist laughed then, an unpleasant sound in the small room. "I'm surprised one got away alive. I rather thought you just bit off their heads and left them to die."

I had to give him credit. He had gone toe-to-toe with me and gotten the last word. It was more than most men did.

# 22

I spent the night in my cell running over every word from the interview and listening to the rain pattering on the roof. I hadn't mentioned the bracelet and neither had he. I think he meant to spring it on me and watch me fall like a house of cards. Little did he know the damned thing was most likely mine, and I had a witness who could prove it, so long as Bianca hadn't been too lit to forget that she'd commented on it at Helen's party. But the bracelet was a tricky card to play, and I wanted to save it for just the right moment. The next morning I was summoned bright and early for another interview with Gilchrist. This time he played to win, and I almost pitied him.

Almost. Instead, I waved my black ribbon in his face and fingered the butter knife, rubbing it against my wrist until he hollered for an officer and had me packed off back to my cell. That evening, after a surprisingly tasty meal sent over from the Norfolk, he came to my cell with two other officers, all dressed plainly. He brought me a simple black coat and told me to put it on.

"Well, it's not exactly Patou, but I suppose it will have to do," I commented acidly. I thrust my arms into the sleeves. "Where are we going, Inspector? Are you taking me out on the town?"

"Not precisely." He took me by the arm and hurried me to the back door of the police station. He propelled me through the door, holding an umbrella over my head as we hurried to a waiting car. The driver apparently knew where we were headed because he floored it before the other two had hardly gotten themselves settled.

Gilchrist sat next to me, his shoulder pressed companionably to mine.

"Come on," I said, batting my lashes. "I'm being winsome. The least you could do is tell me where we're going."

He sighed. "I suppose it wouldn't hurt to tell you. Arrangements have been made to hold you until your counsel arrives."

I steeled myself against the chill that went through me. "Kilimani, then?"

"Kilimani." The inspector was decidedly happy about it.

Kilimani Prison was not exactly summer camp. They put me into a special cell of my own and left me to rot as the rain continued to fall, relentless and grey, as soft and unfocused as I felt. I spent the next three weeks in my little cell, practicing my Swahili with the girl who brought my food and reading books loaned to me by the warden. He had an unnatural fondness for Dickens, but I managed. I made my way through most of them except *A Tale of Two Cities*. I got to the part where Carton is mounting the scaffold to give up his life in place of the husband of the woman he loves and I closed the book. "It is a far, far better thing that I do than I have ever done" just struck a little too close to home. But later I went back and underlined it and when that wasn't enough, I wrote it on the wall of my cell with a pencil.

I had visitors. Ryder didn't come, and for that I gave fervent thanks every day. Each day that passed was hopefully taking him and Gideon farther into the bush. Helen visited, but cried so incoherently she had to be escorted right back out. Rex came, and insisted upon seeing me privately in one of the prison offices. I was shocked that they let him dictate the arrangements, but I suppose it was a mark of how much influence he had in the colony. Gilchrist was obviously looking at him as the future president and he gave us ten minutes together. Rex held me gently and didn't say much. It felt glorious to have someone stroke my hair.

"I only wish you'd brought my hairbrush," I told him. "I'm sure I look a fright."

"You look wonderful," he replied. He kissed me on the cheek then and asked all sorts of penetrating questions about the legalities and whether my rights were being respected. He told me he'd been in touch with Quentin and he was on his way, but there was nothing more he could tell me, and the inspector tapped at the door while he was still talking.

"I'm afraid your ten minutes are up, sir," Gilchrist called.

Rex turned to me. "Is there anything I can send you?"

"A file?" I hazarded.

He smiled, but couldn't quite bring himself to laugh. "Steady on, dear girl. It will all be over soon."

"I hope so." He left me then, and Gilchrist had me escorted back to my cell where I marked another day off the wall in pencil.

My next visitor wasn't quite so diverting. Dora burst into lusty sobs the minute she saw me.

"Oh, for God's sake, Dodo," I muttered.

She blew noisily into her handkerchief. "I am sorry. I can't seem to stop."

"Were you able to get hold of Mossy? Did you explain the situation?"

"Not entirely," she said. "I cabled that there had been a little trouble but that you were just fine and you would write her with details when you were able."

"That's just swell, Dora! Why didn't you write her yourself? The story is bound to get picked up even by the London newspapers."

She nibbled at her lower lip. "I didn't know how much you wanted me to tell her. I didn't think about the newspapers. I suppose I've muddled things."

I sighed and folded my arms. "If I ever turn to a life of crime, you'll excuse me if you're not exactly my first choice for an accomplice."

She threw her hands into the air. "I'm sorry. I did my best, but it's all been so difficult. The funeral was—" She broke off and I wasn't sorry. I had read about it in the newspapers. The occasion had been attended by almost every white person in Kenya, as much for ghoulish curiosity as respect for the dead. I was glad I'd missed it. I hated funerals almost as much as I hated weddings.

She took out her handkerchief and sniffled into it.

"Stop sniveling, Dodo. It will all get sorted," I soothed. "I have been in worse scrapes."

"Scrapes? This isn't a scrape, Delilah. You have been taken in for questioning about the murder of Kit Parrymore. Do you even comprehend that? If you are tried, you will be hanged."

"Only if I'm convicted," I pointed out.

"How can you be so calm? You are not human!"

She burst into sobs again and I waited until she had soaked a second handkerchief.

"How's Lawrence?"

She snuffled and wiped her nose on her sleeve. "We're getting married."

"Congratulations. Do you want me to tell you now or later about his odd sexual proclivities?"

"He told me himself," she said sternly. "I don't care. He said when we're married we will go to a

407

new mission in Uganda, right away from here. And he doesn't mind that I'm not interested in that side of things. We will have a Josephite marriage."

"You're joking."

"I am not. Plenty of people do, you know. Particularly clergymen."

"For Christ's sake, Dora, there's no need to play Charlotte Lucas and throw yourself at some odious man just because you don't want to be an old maid."

"I'm not an old maid!" she cried. "I'm not a virgin, you know. There, does that shock you? I've had experiences. And I don't want them anymore. I'm finished with that sort of thing. I only want security, companionship. And so does Lawrence."

She wiped her eyes, and all the fight seemed to have gone out of her after her little outburst.

"How stupid I am," I murmured. "It was when I was off on safari, killing the lion that took the Kikuyu child, wasn't it? You changed after that. Was he going to paint you?"

She gave a bitter laugh. "No. Evelyn and I were supposed to have a lesson, but she had to stay behind at the school and I went anyway. I knew it would be just the two of us and I went anyway. I knew what would happen," she insisted. "I wasn't stupid or naïve. I knew he would try. And I knew I would let him."

"Why?"

She shrugged. "Because I am twenty-nine. Because after the age of nineteen virginity is a burden. Because it was time to let go of it. I just wanted to feel. All my life is neat and tidy and so orderly I wanted to scream. I just wanted to put it all aside and *feel* for once."

I said nothing and she went on, her voice calmer now. "It was different from what I expected. I've read books, plenty of them. But it was different. I thought it would hurt more. And I never realized . . . that is to say, when it was done, I think I understood you for the first time."

"How?"

"It isn't the pleasure you're after. It's the oblivion."

She was right. She did understand me better. It was indeed the oblivion that I craved, that moment of swimming in the sea that is the wide-open pupil of God's eye, where nothing exists but nothingness.

She went on. "I cleaned myself up and left him and I knew that would be the last time I ever did that. I thought I wanted it, that loss of control, that complete euphoria. But I was wrong. The feeling of things building up was quite pleasant. I shouldn't have minded if that were all. But then it kept going, it kept pushing and urging, and it took on a life of its own. It frightened me, that feeling. I would have done anything it demanded. I would have killed in that moment, I think. I would have thrown myself into a fire or drowned myself to finish it. I would have clawed the flesh off my own bones to be rid of it, to have that moment of completion. It was frightful. Honestly, Delilah, I don't know how you do it."

She lit a cigarette then with a deft gesture.

"You're taking on all my bad habits."

"Just this one. But you can have men, at least the ones that want something back. I haven't the stomach for it."

She blew out a ragged little smoke ring that dissolved into the air. "Remind me to teach you how to do that properly."

She smiled then and it was through her tears. She stubbed out the cigarette. "I'm marrying Lawrence this week. Then we're leaving for Uganda. The inspector isn't happy, but he has no grounds to ask us to stay. I won't be here to see this finished."

"I understand, Dodo. You've served your time. Godspeed."

She rose and brushed the ash off her skirts. "I always knew it would end in tears between us."

"I'm not crying."

"Yes, you are."

And so Dora left me. She had been my cousin, my companion, my chaperone, and I had become accustomed to her. Perhaps too much so. She had been my shadow, but shadows are insubstantial things, without depth or illumination, and Dora deserved better. I hoped she would be happy with Lawrence. Hoped it, but doubted it just the same. I heard through others that Evelyn was none too happy about Lawrence marrying and was devastated to leave her school. But Evelyn, like so many poor relations—like Dora, in fact—was at the mercy of her betters. She packed her bags and tagged along, the eternal third wheel. I hoped Kit had bedded her, too. God knew she'd have little enough to look back on with fondness at the end of her life if she kept on the way she was going.

I wrote letters to Dora and to Mossy and dozens of others, but there seemed little point in sending them. I tore them up instead and started a diary of sorts, writing down everything that had happened since that grey day in Paris when they had persuaded me to come to Africa. I didn't blame them. I was a problem to be solved, and Africa seemed as good a solution as any. I had been swept under the carpet, tidied up like any other unpleasantness. And then I had to ruin it all by getting involved with a man who went and got himself murdered. The irony almost choked me.

So I read books I couldn't remember and wrote letters I didn't send, and taught the guards how to play poker. My grandfather had learned in the Civil War and taught it to me. We'd always played for cash, and he never cared if he cleaned me out of every penny of my pocket money.

Apparently, the press had gotten hold of the

story in all its lurid detail and I had admirers. They flooded the place with gifts, including jewellery and liquor and proposals of marriage. They sent me Swiss linen handkerchiefs and Belgian lace collars, leather-bound books and boxes of marzipan fruits. I gave it all away. The other inmates had never owned such luxuries, and God knew I had little enough use for them.

But the result of my largesse was that I learned things. They paid me back in the only currency at their disposal—information. Every one of those girls knew someone or was related to someone who worked in a white household. I discovered the cannabis Gates had been growing at Fairlight had been a highly profitable operation for him and that he had sold to white settlers. I learned that Bianca's cocaine was smuggled into the country in boxes of Spanish talcum that went straight to Government House in diplomatic pouches. And I learned that some of the white settlers were stockpiling weapons. Opinion was running hot against the powers in London that had squashed the idea of independence for Kenya. Many believed an armed rebellion was only a matter of time, and that certainty had caused most of them to secure caches of arms, ammunition and food to withstand the siege.

I learned, too, about the smaller dramas that had been playing out around me. I learned that people with daughters under seventeen gave Bunny

Stevenson a wide berth, that Anthony Wickenden had moved off the ranch to live with a Masai woman who had given him the clap, and that Gervase had invested all of his money in a herd of Highland sheep that had fallen down dead in the heat. I also found out that the gallery owner in Nairobi had announced a posthumous showing of Kit's work once my trial was over.

"Bastard thinks I'm guilty," I muttered. I slipped the girl who told me that a box of violet creams from Charbonnel et Walker. I was still pondering the implications of an armed revolt when they removed me from my cell to meet with Quentin.

"You look like hell." It wasn't the nicest thing to have blurted out upon seeing him but it was true. His trousers were soaked to the knee and his hair was gleaming with raindrops.

He smiled ruefully. "Who knew it rained in Africa? And I wish I could say the same of you, my darling girl. You ought to at least have lost a little of your sleekness in prison."

I patted my hair. "A girl has to have standards." His smile faltered a little and I put up a hand. "Don't. Anything but pity, Quentin. You know I can't bear that."

He reached into his pocket. "I've brought a letter from your mother."

He held it out, but I hesitated. "I'm surprised the paper isn't smouldering."

Quentin smiled in spite of himself. "You might

be surprised. You always did say Mossy came through best in a crisis."

If she'd written to tell me off it would have been easier. But I suddenly couldn't bear the thought that she might understand, might be on my side. I put the letter away to read when I was alone and looked up at Quentin. He sighed.

"Jesus, Delilah," he said, subsiding heavily into a chair. "How did it come to this?"

"How does it ever? Wrong place, wrong man."

"You have a knack for that," he acknowledged. He leaned forward, and I could smell the familiar scent of his body, his cologne, the hair oil he used. "I have to ask. Did you do it?"

"I thought lawyers never wanted to know the truth."

"I am a solicitor."

I shrugged. "I never knew the difference."

"The difference is that I intend to make sure you get out. Now, tell me the truth."

I crossed my arms over my chest and looked him squarely in the eye. "No. I did not shoot Kit Parrymore. Happy?"

"Not entirely. You could be lying."

"To you, darling? Never." I bared my teeth in a smile.

"Delilah, you do understand this is serious? Murder is a hanging offense."

I gave him the same response I'd given Dora. "Only if you're convicted."

"Dammit, Delilah!" He thrust both hands into his hair, disrupting his careful combing.

"I'm sorry, Quentin. Yes, I understand this is serious, but I didn't do anything except lie to the police, and they deserved it."

"Now we're getting somewhere. What did you lie about and why?"

"I may have indicated that I killed Kit."

He blanched. "You confessed? To murder?"

"Well, yes. It put them in a rather difficult situation, you see, because I wouldn't make any further statements without my attorney. Now, they could have found one for me here in Nairobi, but all I had to do was wave my American passport and invoke the name of my senator uncle and they were happy to wait for you to arrive to question me further."

"You mean you haven't been charged?"

"No."

"Good God. And they've kept you in prison the entire time?"

"I think they said I was 'helping police with their inquiries.' Makes me sound quite eager, doesn't it?" He rubbed his face, and there were shadows under his eyes and around his mouth. "Poor Quentin. How long is it since you slept?"

"Days. I can't remember. I think I may have dozed on that god-awful train from Mombasa, but some fellow kept telling the most frightful stories of lions eating the railway workers."

"The lions of Tsavo. You ought to have listened. It's a fascinating tale." I thought back to the day I had tortured Dora with it. It seemed a lifetime ago.

"Be that as it may, I would rather keep to the matter at hand. The police inspector will be wanting a formal statement from you, and I would advise you to answer as fully as you can without revealing anything that might be prejudicial to your case."

"I don't even know what that means. Why don't I just tell the truth and we'll see where we are when we're finished?"

"It might be at the end of a hangman's noose," he replied brutally. "If you don't know if you ought to answer something or not, look at me. I will guide you."

"Fine."

"Are you ready?"

"As ready as I'll ever be."

It lasted seven hours with short breaks for lunch and tea. By the time we were done, the inspector lectured me thoroughly on the venality of making false statements and Quentin lectured him thoroughly about due process. It was a very thorough experience for everyone, and when it was finished, I was free to go. Inspector Gilchrist had arranged for me to leave from the back of the prison and he personally escorted us to the door. He opened it and I saw that the rains were still coming down in a soft grey curtain. Gilchrist turned to Quentin.

"Mr. Harkness, perhaps you will be good enough to make certain the car has arrived. I wouldn't like Miss Drummond to stand around outside and attract the attention of the press. No need to give the reporters anything else to write about," Gilchrist said, his lips twitching like a rabbit's. Quentin hurried out the back door leaving us alone for just a moment.

"Thank you," I said, tipping my head and smiling sweetly.

"Don't bother," he growled. "I ought to charge you with making false statements and hindering my investigation. You've cost me nearly three weeks."

"No, I didn't. I've had time to work it out, Inspector. You knew the first day you had me here that I didn't do it. And you knew Gideon didn't do it either. You wanted me in custody because as long as I was being held somewhere, you could claim to be doing your best to bring Kit's murderer to justice and you could keep Government House happy. And all the while, you gave an innocent man a chance to get to freedom."

His jaw hardened. "I don't know what you're talking about."

"Yes, you do." The inspector wasn't tall. I didn't have to stand on tiptoe to kiss him. I pressed my

417

lips to his and moved back just as he lifted his arms. "Thank you."

He reached into his pocket. "I believe this belongs to you."

He held out a Masai bracelet, blue and white, with a thin line of distinct green beads. I would still look in my jewel box when I went back to Fairlight, but it would be a formality. This was the one Moses had given me, the bracelet that had led Gilchrist to Gideon in the first place. The slight kink where I had stepped on it getting out of Ryder's truck was unmistakable.

I hesitated. "What makes you think that is mine?"

"Routine investigation. It does uncover most things eventually. You know, we'd have saved a great deal of time and trouble if you had just admitted that you lost it at Parrymore's during one of your trysts." But the inspector was wrong. I hadn't seen it since the night I had been with Ryder, the night I had tucked it into my jewel box for safekeeping. Gilchrist wasn't the only one to get it wrong, I realised as I took it from him. Gideon must have thought I had dropped it, too. He would have known it wasn't his, but he would not put me in danger by telling anyone it was mine. He had protected me with his silence.

I slipped it into my pocket and assumed a nonchalant smile.

"I wasn't sure you had mine. For all I knew it

might have been safely back at Fairlight sitting in my jewel box. Besides, I thought it might be more fun to spring it on you in court if you ever managed to get your hands on Gideon."

His expression was earnest. "He can't come back, you know. I've spent the past weeks persuading Government House that he's out of reach. If they so much as catch a rumour that he's back, they'll force me to take him in. I won't have a choice, and he will hang."

"I understand. Tell me one thing. How did you know he was innocent?"

"Because I know who did it. And that's all you will get from me."

He was as good as his word. He refused to tell me anything else, and when he handed me over to Quentin, he seemed happy to be rid of me. But I looked back once and I saw him standing alone, his eyes closed, his face pale, his hands clenched at his sides.

"That man looks anguished," Quentin said, smiling slightly. "You must have been hard on him."

"You have no idea."

# 23

Quentin and I retired to the Norfolk where he had checked us in under assumed names. Bathing arrangements had been almost nonexistent at the prison. It was heaven to scrub myself completely clean and I spent two hours in the bathtub, filling it over and over again until my skin was wrinkled as a raisin's and I smelled like lilies. Quentin was waiting in my room when I emerged.

"Feeling better?"

"Immensely. Is that dinner?"

"It is. I've ordered your favourites and three bottles of champagne."

"That's a start," I told him.

It was hours before we finished and when we did the table was littered with soiled dishes and ashes and the dregs of our champagne. We put out our cigarettes in the butter and danced in our bare feet until the manager came to complain. I poured him a glass of champagne and sent him off with a smile. Cables arrived and flowers, too, enormous bunches of them that filled the room with a thick perfume.

"It appears my incognita has been violated. And it smells like a funeral home in here," I told Quentin, peering at him through the bottom of a champagne bottle.

"Better than a wedding chapel," he retorted.

I laughed aloud. "Poor Quentin. Marriage hasn't treated you very kindly."

"Cornelia's pregnant. Again."

I waved my cigarette. "I should have a talk with that girl. Introduce her to the diaphragm."

"I wish you would," he said.

"Oh, God, Quentin. Don't be morose. You've money enough to take care of your brood, and I rather doubt you are even that bothered with them."

"I don't mind about me. I mind because of what it does to Cornelia. She changed when we had the twins. No conversation but nappies, no interests but gripe water and teething biscuits. It's only going to get worse with another baby. I married a lovely girl and ended up with my own grand-mother." He nodded to me. "That's not the smallest of your attractions, you know. You talk about things. You go places. And you're always lovely and slim and firm."

"Careful, old boy. You're leering now."

"Your robe has come open," he informed me.

"So it has." I didn't bother to adjust it. Quentin had seen it all before. He leaned close.

"What about it, my beauty? A bit of something warm to remember you by before I go back to cold Cornelia?"

I removed his hands from my body and placed them gently in his own lap. "This is all the something warm you'll be getting tonight. I'm very grateful to you, Quentin. But if you want payment for services rendered, you'll have to send me a bill."

His expression was one of frank astonishment. Then he laughed, a great hearty belly laugh that ended with him wiping his eyes on his sleeve. "My God. It's finally happened. You've fallen in love, haven't you?"

"No. I wouldn't know how. But I do know that my life is quite complicated enough just now without throwing yet another man into the mix."

He blinked. "Just how many men are we talking about?"

"Does it really matter? You know I've always been good at juggling."

"I don't know," he said coolly. "Sounds to me as if you're losing your touch."

He rose and I handed him his shoes. "Don't be sore, Quentin. I have to figure some things out and I can only do that with a clear head. If I sleep with you now, I'll only confuse myself more. You always were so good at making me forget everyone else."

That little piece of flattery did the trick. He gave me a contrite look and dropped a kiss to my cheek. "Darling Delilah. I was being a brute. Forgive me. I hope you manage to get it all sorted."

"So do I. Will you come to Fairlight?"

"Can't, I'm afraid. I have to hurry back to

England. I left things rather in a muddle when I dashed off to take care of you."

I put my hand to his cheek. "Dearest Quentin. How good you are to me."

"But not quite good enough," he said ruefully. He kissed me again and then he was gone.

That night, alone in my bed, I finally opened Mossy's letter. I read it over quickly, then twice more, savouring each word. She had a child's handwriting, loose and loopy, filling the pages with a hasty scribble of violet ink. She wrote that Granny Miette was holding a conjuring and had assured her I would be protected. Mossy related this in stilted words, and I could just picture the tight expression on her face. She claimed not to approve of such goings-on, saying they were backward and silly, but I had known her to ask for a bottle of Follow Me Water when she wanted to turn a man's head or a pinch of goofer dust to sprinkle in the footsteps of a rival. She went on to say that Granny had made a special trip into New Orleans to light a candle to Our Lady of Prompt Succour. I smiled when I read that and crossed myself quickly. "God bless you, Granny," I murmured. The Colonel hadn't taken matters quite so well. He'd cut me off for good, Mossy said. No more tidy allowances coming from the profits of the sugar plantation, and if I ever wanted to come back to Reveille to see Granny, I'd have to do it when he was elsewhere. I muttered a swearword or two as I turned the page. The rest of the letter was just random news of people we knew—who got married, who was getting divorced and who was the cause of it. It was Mossy's way of telling me that life went on and that this, too, would pass. She carried on in that vein until the last page.

> They said there was a curse on us and maybe there is. Maybe we were born under bad stars or maybe for us there's always a bad moon on the rise. But if it's true, if sorrow and loss follow us around like mean stray dogs, then that means somewhere, some fighting angel decided we were strong enough to take it. So shine up your dancing shoes and pinch your cheeks and lift your chin, child. Because if we're on the road to hell, we're going to dance the whole damn way and give them something to talk about when we're gone.

And below that, she had signed it, using a word that at her insistence hadn't crossed my lips since I was five years old.

*All my love, Mama*

I folded the letter and put it under my pillow and turned out the light. And in the darkness I heard it, the quiet green stillness that comes when the rains end and all the world is limp and soft and ready to begin again. I turned my face to the window where a slender new moon was rising and I slept.

I had nothing to pack, so I was empty-handed when I strolled down the main staircase of the Norfolk. My bill had been settled by Quentin, and I walked out to find Ryder's ancient battered truck idling at the curb. I ran to it and wrenched open the door.

"*Memsahib* Delilah! How good it is to see you! I have come to take you home." Mr. Patel was wearing his motoring goggles, as was his little monkey. The monkey hopped up onto a hamper and chattered angrily at me.

"Do not mind him, he does not like the city," Mr. Patel advised. "Come, come! Get in before the reporters realise I have come to take you away." He beckoned and I slid into the seat.

"How kind of you to come and get me," I murmured.

He ground the gears to powder and the truck lurched away. "Think nothing of it. The *sahib* sent word and told me to do this."

"You've heard from Ryder?"

Mr. Patel said nothing for several minutes as he negotiated his way out of the heavy traffic, weaving through ox carts and rickshaws and long, smooth touring cars. Finally, we turned onto the damp *murram* road out of Nairobi and he spoke.

"What was it that you asked me? Oh, yes, yes,

*Memsahib* Delilah. I have heard from him. He cables me to come to get you, and I am happy to do this thing."

"He cabled you?" There were few *dukas* farther out than Patel's and none were in the direction he was supposed to have taken Gideon. "From where?"

"Egypt."

"Egypt! What the devil is he doing there?"

"This I do not know. He says he has business and he will come when it is finished."

I hesitated. "Was there anything else?" I didn't dare ask about Gideon directly. I didn't know how much Ryder had told Patel and the fewer people who knew Ryder had taken him, the better.

Mr. Patel's brow furrowed. "No, *memsa*. All he spoke of was the package you had entrusted to him."

"What did he say about the package?"

"That it arrived safely and you were not to worry. He would tell you more about the package when he returns. This is all that I know."

The monkey began chattering again and it was impossible to talk. I slumped back against the seat, letting the weight of the last weeks roll away with each mile that unfurled over the thin red ribbon of road.

The drive was long and sticky and I was drooping with fatigue when we arrived. But the smell of the

426

earth after the short rains was intoxicating. Bushes were thick with green leaves and gladioli and wild orchids burst from ripe buds. Everything seemed heightened, the colours brighter, the sounds sharper. The scent of Africa hung in my nose and mouth, the tang of the freshly saturated earth, the green smell of new grass, woodsmoke and dung and that peculiar smell of Africa itself, unlike any other. It was evening when we arrived at Fairlight, and to my surprise, Mr. Patel stopped just inside the gate. He turned off the engine, and in the silence I heard it, a steady pounding, like a great beating heart within the land.

"What is that?"

He gestured for me to get out and I did. We walked the last quarter mile, and as we came around the curve where the jacarandas stood in full bloom, I saw them. From every tribe who crossed Fairlight—from the Masai, from the Samburu and the Kikuyu, from other, smaller tribes. They stood, shoulder to shoulder, some of them enemies from the womb, and yet there they were, stamping their rhythms into the soil of their common mother. They were dressed for cele-bration, wearing their finest skins or *kanjas*, decked in beads and bracelets, copper wires and necklaces. They lifted up their voices together, a mixture of tribal tongues and Swahili and English, a new Babel, but with one meaning. In every gesture, in every face, I saw the same emotion,

427

and I felt the weight of it so hard upon my shoulders, I almost fell to the ground.

I moved forward and the people gathered about me, closing around like a fist, fingers cradling something precious within the palm. They chanted and sang and stamped, and at length one figure broke forward. It was Gideon's *babu*, guided by a *moran*. He put his hand to my head and blessed me, and when he spoke in his high, reedy voice, it was loud enough to carry over the stamping of a thousand feet.

"*Nina mjukuu.*" It was Swahili, and his words were halting but I understood them. *I have a granddaughter.* He carried on, speaking and blessing, but I heard none of it after that first pronouncement. The chanting and stamping was a buzzing in my ears, as if a thousand bees had come home to nest. When he stopped, I took his hands in mine and acknowledged his blessing.

"*Nina babu,*" I replied to him. *I have a grandfather.* The people gave a great shout, and I saw that some of the women wept. They came forward then, these aunts and sisters of Gideon, and they enfolded me, smearing my clothes with the red ochre and the grease that they used to make themselves beautiful. They touched my face and hands and embraced me and called me sister. The men stood back, chanting a song of one who would not be forgotten, of loved ones lost and returned to the earth, and of the land itself which does not die but is always born anew with each fall of the long rains. They chanted of life, which is short as a spear of summer grass or long as the heart of the Rift itself, and of the silent land that waits beyond. They chanted of Africa.

They were still chanting when I began to crumple, long after night had fallen and long after the fires had been lit, and when they carried me to my bed and tucked me in as tenderly as a child and left me, it was this song of Africa that was my lullaby.

When I went to the window the next morning I saw that there was no sign of them save the bright green grass that had been trodden under their feet. After I had eaten a simple breakfast, the Africans came again, but this time it was the farmworkers, neglected after my stay in Nairobi. They came as if I had never left, bringing their wounds and ailments, offering up their pain. I applied ointments and powders, bandaged and gossiped, taking from them their suffering and their stories and giving them relief in return. They told me of two babies born while I was gone and an old man who had died and been given to the hyenas, his bones crunched to nothing in those powerful jaws. Africa had borne him and in the end, Africa had taken him back. There was nothing left to show he had been except the memories of those who knew him, and these they shared with me.

I traded them—salves for salvation because, as I worked, I felt peaceful for the first time in a long while. I gave them food and milk and when they left, I sat on the veranda for a long time, thinking of them and how little of the promise of Fairlight was actually fulfilled.

In the afternoon Ryder came, walking his slow-hipped walk, and I stood in stillness, watching him come near. He stopped a foot away from me.

"Let's go for a walk."

I followed him without a word, and he led the way out of Fairlight and onto the savannah. He took a different track, a path beaten hard into the earth and leading to a high rock outcropping. We climbed it together and he gave me his hand to bring me up the last few feet to where he stood. We settled down on the rock and he pointed across the savannah. There, on a termite mound, sat a cheetah, slender and watchful.

"He's beautiful," I murmured.

"She," he corrected quietly. "She just left her cubs two days ago and she's hunting for herself now."

"How do you know so much about her?"

She didn't move as she surveyed the savannah. Only the lightest of breezes ruffled her fur as it did the long grasses. A small herd of Thomson's gazelles grazed nearby, unaware of her presence.

"I've been keeping tabs on her for months."

"Why? You don't hunt cheetah."

"Because something that beautiful and dangerous is worth watching," he replied.

Just then she darted out, launching herself straight at a small patch of quivering grass. A young tommie huddled under the grass, waiting until the last possible moment to run. Too late, its mother saw the danger and circled back, bleating her distress and throwing herself between the cheetah and her young.

But the cheetah would not be diverted. She circled back, cutting sharply and seized the tommie, carrying it off in triumph. The mother sniffed the air and let out another soft cry before returning to her herd. The cheetah took her trophy back to her mound, suffocating it quickly and beginning to eat.

"She doesn't waste time," I observed.

"She can't afford to. She seems fierce but there are lots of things out here bigger and meaner than she is. Any one of them would take that tommie from her and go after her, too. She's a lot more vulnerable than she looks."

I sighed. "Did you bring me out here just to show me metaphors for my own life?"

A tiny smile tugged at the corner of his mouth. "No. I wanted to talk to you where we wouldn't be overheard."

I took a deep breath and let it out slowly onto the wind. "How is he?"

"Poor. I took him to one of the outlying villages

near the Ugandan border, too far for the officials in Nairobi to bother with. He has no cattle of his own and he can't claim his *babu*'s property when the old man dies. Without either of those, he can't take a wife. And he won't accept handouts from me."

"So I did it for nothing."

"He's alive." Ryder turned on me fiercely. "And that's all that matters right now. He will work hard and he will make his own way. Don't underestimate him, Delilah. He's stronger than you know, and right now he is walking on his own two legs—a free black man in a white man's Africa—because of what you did. Don't ever forget that."

I said nothing. Guilt was sitting too heavily on my shoulders to talk about it. I had acted impulsively, rashly, as I always had. And while it might have saved Gideon's life, it also made it impossible for him to have the life he wanted. Once again I had acted from the heart rather than the head, and there were consequences. Only this time someone else was bearing the weight of them.

"Have you thought about what you mean to do?"

I watched the cheetah tearing happily at the throat of the little tommie. Survival was a bloody business. "I mean to leave as soon as I can. Nothing's changed, Ryder."

He went very still, but I felt the change in him. Anger shimmered off him, sparking the air between us.

"I should have known. Tusker warned me not to rely on you. She swore you wouldn't stick it out, but I defended you. I told her she was wrong, that there was something fine in you, something that would see this place for what it was and be changed by it. But you won't change, and do you know why? Because you never stay anywhere or with anyone long enough to let them in."

I let out a ragged breath. "Do you know what a cicatrix is, Ryder? It's a scar, a place where you have been cut so deeply that what's left behind is something quite different. It doesn't heal, not really, because it isn't the same ever again. It's impenetrable and it's there forever, to protect you from hurting the same place again."

"You get maudlin when you philosophise."

"It isn't maudlin if it's true."

He grabbed my wrist, twisting it hard where the black ribbon bow folded on itself like a mourning flower.

"Can you feel that? Can you feel anything? Christ, Delilah, I thought I was damaged, but I have never in my life met anyone so afraid of feeling anything as you are."

"You know why," I said with a shrug.

"No, I don't. You told me what's happened to you, but guess what? Bad things happen to

433

everybody. I'll give you that. But you can't just shut down and refuse to keep living. Do you think that's what Johnny would have wanted? You might as well have jumped down into that grave with him and pulled the dirt over you like a blanket for all the real living you've done since then."

He turned and took my face in his hands. "Delilah, this may be the last chance you have to wake up. Life is giving you a new chance every goddamned day that you wake up and you're throwing it away. Wake up, Delilah. Wake up." He punctuated his words with his lips, pressing his mouth to my eyelids, my temples, my cheeks, my jaw, and with every touch he murmured, "Wake up.

"Wake up," he said. "Wake up, wake up, wake up." An invocation, an invitation, an incantation, but I pulled away from him and shook my head.

He dropped his hands. Silence stretched between us, heavy and thick. He settled back and pulled a cigarette from his case. Wordlessly he lit it and passed it to me before lighting another for himself. We smoked them in silence but I could feel him thinking, planning his next move. He was playing a chess game, trying to win, convinced he could keep me if he could just hit on the right strategy. He just didn't realise I wasn't playing the game.

He spoke quietly, weighing his words. "You

aren't like anyone I've ever met, Delilah. You are the most appallingly selfish person I have ever known. I thought once that there might be something good in you, something worth saving. But now I think there isn't, there can't be, if you could look at this place and how wretched it is and turn away. There is real good we could do here if you would only stop feeling sorry for yourself and have a care for anybody else. But you would rather dance off and leave it all behind, let someone else clear it up. Well, what if no one else will? What if you're the only one who could make a difference and you don't? It's sinful, that's what. And I don't use that word lightly. I'm barely religious. I hardly say my prayers and I almost never go to church, but I do believe in God and I believe some things are flying in his face. Walking away from here now is one of those things."

I opened my mouth to answer him, but I never got the chance. A cloud of dust was rising on the savannah, and as we rose and watched it started moving closer. Whatever it was, it spooked the tommies and they hurried on, dragging their gangly offspring with them. By the time the cheetah had left, picking her way delicately across the savannah, the apparition was almost upon us. It was the motorbike. Mr. Patel was riding it, his eyes shielded by his motoring goggles, his robes fluttering behind him like a knight's pennant. We descended from the rock as he skidded to a stop and jumped from the bike, heading straight for Ryder.

"This came and it was most urgent," he said, proffering a telegram. Ryder went to take it, but Mr. Patel shook his head. "For *Memsahib* Delilah," he corrected, nodding towards me.

I stepped forward and took the envelope. The ripping sounded unnaturally loud in the wide emptiness of the plain. Ryder had moved behind me, shielding me from Patel with his body. It was an exquisitely considerate gesture and a futile one. There is no such thing as privacy in Africa.

I read the lines twice, then three times.

"Who?" Ryder said quietly. I turned to him and he was staring at me intently. I don't know how he understood. Cables bring good news just as often as bad. But not this one.

"My stepfather, Nigel. He suffered a heart attack at his club in London. He died almost immediately."

Ryder said nothing. He opened his arms and I went into them. There was nothing in that embrace beyond what a parent might offer a grieving child. It was comfort and solace, and after a long moment he released me.

"Let's go."

"Where are we going?"

"I'm taking you home. To Fairlight."

But he was wrong. Fairlight was part of Nigel's estate. It belonged now to his eldest son, Edgar. It would never be my home again.

We made our way slowly back. There was nothing to hurry for. I could not make it to England for Nigel's funeral in any event. I sent cables via Mr. Patel to Mossy and to Edgar and turned my attention to the scenery itself. I did not expect to come this way again, and I found myself staring at the horizon, memorising Africa against the day when all I would have were my own sepia recollections.

We parted at Ryder's *boma*, each of us heading our separate ways and saying nothing. I stripped off my filthy clothes and tossed them in the corner, too tired to care. I barely washed before I fell into bed and down into a heavy sleep.

I awoke suddenly, startled by the screech of a monkey in the garden. A leopard must be roaming, I thought sleepily, but there was no familiar rasping cough. Instead, there was a strange, silken noise rustling in my ears and the smell of smoke in the air. I decided someone must be up early, starting a cooking fire against the morning chill, but even as I thought it, I knew it was wrong. It was the middle of the night, far too early for the hearth fires.

I sat bolt upright, throwing off the blanket and calling out. "Ryder!" I don't know why I shouted his name. He hadn't come home with me, but in that moment of horror, his was the name that I shouted.

I ran through the house and to the outbuildings, screaming for the men. The barn burned hot and high, and the harsh light against the western sky must have alerted Ryder at his *rondavel*. By the time he arrived, the barn was gone and the kitchen was fully engulfed. Pierre and Omar had rallied the men and they were passing leather buckets of water, but even as they worked I could see it was futile. The lake was full of water but there was no pump to bring it up, and so they worked as best they could, carrying the heavy buckets and passing them from hand to hand. Ryder soaked a handkerchief in water and tied it over his mouth before climbing up to the roof of the house, bucket in hand. He made the trip dozens of times, determined to save the house if nothing else. We worked all the rest of that night, and when the sun rose, it rose upon a battlefield. Two of the workers had fallen from the roof, breaking bones in the process, and several others had collapsed from the smoke and the exertion. Omar had burned his hand badly and Pierre's eyebrows were singed off. The barn was nothing but a charred ruin and the kitchen with all its stores had been utterly destroyed. The fences and half the garden burned as well, and the guest wing of the house had been gutted. Only the main living area remained, although the drawing room was heavily damaged by smoke.

I sat on what was left of the lawn, both of us muddy, stinking wrecks at that point. As I watched, the tortoise crawled out from under the veranda and made for what was left of the jacarandas, giving me a baleful look as he went. Ryder came to sit next to me, his hands blistered and raw from the night's work.

"At least no one died," he said drily.

"Leave it to you to find the silver lining." I fished in my pocket for a cigarette, but the case had been damaged. All that was left inside were sodden shards of loose tobacco and a few shreds of paper.

"I would have thought you'd have been cured of that after what you just went through," he said. I gave him an evil look and he smiled. "Cigarettes are in my truck. I would be the gentleman and get them, but if I stand up I'll probably fall over."

Soot was ground into his skin, but when he smiled the lines appeared, white and sharp, highlighting his good humour even at the worst of times. I fetched the cigarettes and a flask I found in the glove box. We each took a cigarette and a long pull from the flask before he passed it to the men who stood, shocked and exhausted, at the periphery of the garden. Their women had come to tend them, and for once I wasn't the one doing the mending and patching. The two with broken bones had been carried off to their homes. Until the swelling went down, the bones couldn't be set.

Pierre applied salve to Omar's burns and covered them loosely, and the others needed only rest and a good meal to put them right.

"Do you suppose this place is cursed?" I asked Ryder. "Was it built on an ancient Masai burial ground?"

"The Masai leave their dead out for the hyenas, princess. No, you're just unlucky all on your own."

"You mean Fairlight never had trouble until I came?"

"I mean you are trouble," he said. He took a deep drag from the cigarette and immediately started coughing. He spat black soot into the grass and ground out the cigarette on the sole of his boot before clearing his mouth with gin. "If you've ruined me for cigarettes I'll never forgive you."

I said nothing and he leaned over, pushing his shoulder firmly into mine. He lowered his head, his voice consoling. "You can always rebuild."

"I can't rebuild what isn't mine," I reminded him. "Fairlight belongs to Edgar now, and for all I know, he'll want the whole place torn down and the land sold."

"Pity," Ryder said lightly. "This place could be a real goer with the right hand at the helm."

He rose slowly to his feet and put out a hand to help me up. He winced a little as I grasped his blistered hand. "If the smoke gets to you, you can come stay with me."

"You don't have a guest bed," I reminded him.

He gave me a slow smile. "I know. That's why you would be sleeping out in the *boma*."

He bent and kissed me gently on the mouth, then walked away. I sat on the remains of the veranda, too tired to do anything else, until Moses appeared. He brought a bowl of corn gruel compliments of his *babu*, and motioned for me to eat while he sat next to me.

I forced down a few spoonfuls. "I'm happy to see you, Moses."

He gave me a smile, his broad, perfect smile. He sketched a few words onto the ground with his stick.

"You want to stay with me? But I have no cattle for you to tend, Moses."

He made a putting away gesture with his hand.

"You might think it doesn't matter, but you will miss the cows very much."

He put a finger to his chest, then to mine, hovering just over my heart.

"You are in my heart also, Moses."

My throat was too tight to swallow, so I handed him the bowl. He finished off the gruel happily.

Together we watched the giraffe come and drink at the far edge of Lake Wanyama. It was a small herd, just a few cows with their calves and a few adolescent males trailing behind. They were graceful and silent, bobbing their heads down at a ridiculous angle to get to the water. A crowned crane waded nearby, breaking the water into small ripples that flowed over to our edge, connecting us. And suddenly, the feeling Moses had conjured grew so strong and so deep I felt I could just float away on it. I was in love, really in love for the first time in a very long time, maybe the first time ever. And it was with this place, this Africa, as real to me as any man. The grey-green water of the Tana River was his blood and his pulse was the steady beat of the native drums. The red dust of his flesh smelled of sage from the blue stems of the *leleshwa* and sweetness from the jasmine and under it all the sharp copper tang of blood. In the heart of the Rift lay his heart, and his bones were the very rocks. Africa was lover, teacher and mentor, and I could not leave him.

I brushed the tears from my cheeks as I rose and put out my hand to Moses. "We're going to Nairobi."

He raised his hands palm up, questioning.

"Because I've been holding hands with ghosts for too long."

I motioned for him to get into the truck Ryder had left and we headed for the *duka*. Mr. Patel was sewing on his veranda, running up long lengths of sari silk.

"I am making curtains," he said, waving excitedly. "For Fairlight. To replace those which burned up. Only the best for *Memsahib* Delilah."

I didn't have the heart to tell him that I couldn't

pay for them. I couldn't even be sure Edgar would want them for what was left of Fairlight. But I smiled anyway. "Mr. Patel, I need to go to Nairobi. Have you seen Ryder? I want to take the truck, only I don't want to leave him without it if he needs it."

He waved a hand. "The *sahib* has already left on my motorcycle. He will have no need of the truck. If I see him, I will tell him you have taken it to the city."

I didn't stop to ask where Ryder had gone. I waved and floored it, heading as fast as I could to Nairobi. Unfortunately, I had a puncture and Moses proved as useless with machines as he was gifted with cattle. It took me more than an hour to wrestle the wheel off and patch it, and by the time we reached the city, the afternoon was sitting in long shadows.

I had given it some thought on the drive and it seemed to me my best chance was to head straight to the top. I hadn't bothered to wash or change my clothes and by the time I walked into Government House, I looked like something three days past death. My clothes were stiff with mud and sweat and my face was covered in streaks of soot. Mr. Fraser jumped to his feet as I strode into his office, Moses following close behind.

"Miss Drummond! What on earth—"

"I have a crime to report. Gates tried to burn down my farm."

Fraser looked pained. "Do you have evidence to this effect?"

"No, but who else would it have been? I have a witness that he threatened me when I discharged him." I jerked my head to Moses.

The lieutenant governor narrowed his eyes. "Is this the same boy that you reported Mr. Gates as having struck during the incident which caused you to discharge him?"

"Yes, but I hardly see—"

The inspector, who hadn't even opened his notebook, rose and gave me a pitying look. "I understand your frustrations, Miss Drummond, but I'm afraid this matter is at an end."

"At an end? Did you even hear what I said? The man tried to burn down the farm where I live."

"Was anyone killed?"

"No, but that's—"

"Was anyone materially injured?"

"Two with broken bones and one with a burned hand," I recited. "Still, I hardly think—"

He gave me a cool look. "Miss Drummond. Africa is a difficult place. Too difficult for some. Now, I suggest you book passage back to England or New York or wherever it is that you came from and forget all about this."

"That's it? That's all the Kenyan colonial government can offer? I am patted on the head and told to go home like a good little girl?"

"As I said, Africa is a dangerous and difficult

place to live. This colony demands a very specific type of temperament to thrive here. One must be resourceful and strong and able to withstand anything. Very few people manage to live here happily." He gave me a smile that didn't reach his eyes. "I think it has become quite apparent that you, Miss Drummond, are not one of those people. And in light of this most recent development, I feel I ought to warn you that steps will be taken."

"Just what does that mean?"

"It means that you will be asked to leave the colony. I'm afraid your time here is at an end."

Moses' hand crept into mine, and I tightened my fingers around it. "You can't do that."

"I think you will find that I can. The governor is indisposed with an attack of malaria and not expected to resume his duties here for at least a month. In his absence, all trivial matters are being handled by me. And you, Miss Drummond, are a trivial matter."

"But I have permission," I said, my voice hollow.

"Permission that may be rescinded at any time by this office. I did warn you of that when you arrived," he said, a trifle more kindly. "But it would seem you have made a habit of trouble, and you have overstayed your welcome here. You may return to Fairlight to collect your things. Passage will be booked for you on the steamer leaving out of Mombasa in a fortnight. That should give you ample time to say your farewells."

I wouldn't give him the satisfaction of seeing me beaten. I gave him as dazzling a smile as I could muster, the one that got me the best room at the Hotel de Crillon even when I was skint. "I've learned a lot from my time in Africa, Mr. Fraser, a lot about how to survive here. And one of the first things I learned is that before you count your kill, you better make damn sure you've done the job. Because something you've only wounded will have just enough fight left in her to make her dangerous. Come on, Moses. We're leaving now."

# 24

I went straight to the nearest telegraph office and cabled London. I had to do something, anything, and my only hope lay with Edgar. I explained, as briefly as I could, that Fairlight had been badly damaged by fire and that I wanted to buy the place. I cabled Quentin to offer him a business deal and to discover whether or not it was legal for Fraser to kick me out of Kenya. I bought Moses and myself each a stalk of sugar cane and we sat on the steps of the telegraph office to wait for the replies.

"Do you like Nairobi?" I asked him. I sucked at the cane, tasting a thousand memories of Reveille. Each year, the Colonel would take me out to the field to cut the first cane of the harvest, testing it for sweetness. He always cut a piece for me, peeling back the skin to offer me the pale flesh. It seemed impossible that the same taste was on my lips in Africa of all places.

Moses nodded excitedly then dampened his finger with juice from the cane to write on the step. "London."

"You want to go to London?"

He nodded again. He occupied himself drawing pictures with the end of the cane while I ticked off the minutes.

Finally, as the sun dropped below the horizon and the brief evening turned sharply to night, the proprietor emerged with two pieces of paper. He put them into my hands and I thanked him, holding them up to the paraffin lantern to make out the words.

The first was from Quentin, assuring me that the lieutenant governor did indeed have the power to revoke my permission and have me chucked out. He promised to get on to one of his influential friends to sort it out, but that could take weeks, and by then I would have been bundled onto a steamer out of Mombasa. He also agreed to a proposition I had made him, and I felt my spirits rising as I tore into the next telegram, the one from Edgar. I read it over twice then three times before crumpling it up in my fist.

"Let's go, Moses. There's no reason to stay."

I didn't dare the drive all the way back to Fairlight in the dark. I stopped a little distance outside Nairobi and Moses and I slept in the truck. Hyenas kept up a racket during the night, and long before the sun was fully up we were on our way. We arrived back at Fairlight by lunchtime. The place looked sad and tattered and a little embarrassed as the acrid smell of smoke still hung in the air.

"Nothing hard work and some paint can't fix." Ryder emerged from the house as we arrived.

"Sorry I took your truck without asking."

He shrugged. "I didn't need it."

"I went to Nairobi," I started, but he held up a hand.

"First things first. I need to take Moses home."

"Moses has gotten himself to and from his village a hundred times without help," I snapped. I was tired and cross and all I wanted was a stiff drink and a proper sleep.

"Not this time," Ryder told me. He motioned to Moses and they set off. I threw up my hands and followed them. We struck out on the path that we always took, but even before we reached the village, I knew something had changed. There was no gentle droning buzz of activity, no smell of woodsmoke and milling cattle. The village was empty of life, and the gates all stood open to the savanna beyond.

"What happened?"

Ryder turned to me. "The Masai will leave a place when they feel it's time. His village has moved on, and I know where they've gone. His *babu* asked me to bring him when I could."

He headed us into the bush and I felt my anger growing with each step. Half an hour's walk past where the village had been, the Masai were building a new settlement. The women had staked out new homes and were busy plastering fresh mud on the walls while the men constructed sturdy *bomas* to hold the stock. I stopped at a distance and nodded to Moses, telling him to go on. He waved at me and I turned back to the path, walking as fast as I could.

Ryder stayed to chat with the *babu* a moment, but caught up to me quickly.

"You don't have a weapon," he said lightly. "Did you forget everything I taught you?"

"Shut up," I told him. "Just shut up. I don't want to talk."

"Fine. I won't tell you you're about to step in an ant-bear hole."

I dodged it and dashed my hand across my eyes. Ryder caught at my hand but I shook him off.

"Leave me alone before you catch it," I muttered, but his hearing was good.

"Catch what?"

"Whatever damned curse it is that's following me around." I strode off again, and Ryder followed more slowly, walking behind me until we reached the ruined garden at Fairlight. He took my arm, hard this time so I couldn't pull loose.

"Want to explain that now?"

"No," I said, but he didn't move, and I realised he was prepared to stand there all night, holding my arm.

"Everything is ruined. Everything I've done since I came here is wrecked. Everyone I cared about has been damaged."

"That is quite a curse," he said solemnly.

"Don't you dare laugh," I warned him. "I will slap you so hard your grandchildren will be looking for your teeth."

"I don't doubt it," he said, but his lips still twitched.

I raised my hand, and he took it, pressing it close to his chest. I could feel his heart beating, slow and steady, and I shook my head. "Don't. Don't be nice either. It's just too hard."

"What is?"

"Saying goodbye to you. To this, to Africa."

"So don't go."

"I have to," I told him. "Fraser is rescinding my permission. I have to leave within a fortnight. He's booking my passage back to England."

"And you don't want to go?"

"Of course I don't want to go!" I said it as though it were the most obvious truth, the truest thing that anybody ever said, as I said the words aloud for the first time. "I don't want to go," I repeated. "I tried to buy Fairlight today."

"Did you?"

"Oh, go on and laugh! I know it's funny. Everything I do is a goddamned joke. But I wanted this place. I wanted it so much I cabled Edgar and asked him to sell it to me."

"And did he?"

"No. He said it wasn't for sale. And even if he would sell, the price he named was so high, there's no way I could have managed it."

"I thought you had some expensive Russian jewellery tucked away for a rainy day."

His hand was still flat over mine and mine was still pressed against his heart.

"They're paste. The Volkonsky jewels are nothing but pretty glass. That's why I wouldn't turn them over to the relative who is making a claim on my husband's estate. I didn't want anyone to know that Misha had been broke when he died. It would have embarrassed him so much to have people know that everything was gone. I promised him on his deathbed not to tell."

"So you're broke."

"Near enough. I sold my car to Quentin, but that only got me nine thousand pounds."

"Nine thousand?" He dropped my arm and rubbed at his chin. He hadn't shaved, and the sun glinted gold in the shadow on his jaw. "That will do."

"For what?"

"Fairlight. I thought you wanted to buy it."

I stared at him, wondering if the heat had given me some sort of sickness. "I don't understand."

He spoke slowly. "Nine thousand pounds. It's a fair price. For that I'll let you have the house and gardens and a few acres for a *shamba*, but no more. I have plans for the rest of the land."

I balled up my fist and hit him hard on the shoulder. "Stop talking nonsense and tell me what you mean right now."

He caught my fist and held it. "Edgar couldn't sell you Fairlight because he already sold it to me. I want the land, and I'll keep it. But you can have the house and the property around it."

"Why do you want it?" I asked, seizing on the least important question of the dozen that had sprung to mind.

"Because I'm establishing a nature preserve. If I mean to do something meaningful out here, I'd damned well better start. I'm not getting any younger, you know," he said.

"I don't believe this," I said. "I need to sit down." He slid an arm around my waist.

"Better?" he said into my hair.

I pushed him away. "No, worse, actually. But we're both forgetting that I can't actually buy property here. I'm an undesirable immigrant, according to Mr. Fraser. I was a fool to think they'd let me stay."

He shrugged. "They will if we tell them you're my fiancée." I reeled a little, but he kept talking. "It's a small lie, and by the time they figure out that it's not true, Kendall will be back at his desk. Believe me, Fraser is using his absence as a chance to get rid of you, but if you stand your ground, you should be able to pull it off."

"You want a fake engagement?"

"Is there a better kind?" His expression was cool and unreadable.

"I don't know," I started, but he put up a hand.

"Don't decide now. I have to go up to Narok and look at a plane that a friend of mine is willing to sell. There's been a lot of talk about how useful planes could be in running safaris, and if that's true, they'll be doubly useful in conservancy efforts. If you decide to buy the place, just cable me there and let me know. If not, then I'll see you around, princess."

He put out his hand and I shook it slowly.

"Safe travels, then," I told him.

He started towards me then stepped back sharply, as if he'd just won a war with himself. He lifted a hand in farewell and for just an instant he stood at the end of the garden, silhouetted against the trees. Then he was gone, and I was alone at Fairlight.

I was alone for all of that week at Fairlight until Tusker came. She brought tinned peaches and we ate them with new bread by the side of the lake. A lazy hippo was bathing on the other bank, rolling over slowly from side to side in the mud to cool herself.

"I hear you're leaving us," she said.

"Word travels," I replied, smiling.

"You're an idiot. And so is he."

"Thanks for that. You're the one who told me not to get involved with him at all, remember? Or was that just a tidy piece of reverse psychology to push us together? I know you told him I wasn't a stayer. Was that another bit of manipulation to get him to fight to keep me? Never mind. It doesn't matter now. None of it does."

She shook her head angrily and seemed about to change the subject then decided to plow on. "You'll be miserable in London or Paris or New York. Have you thought of that? You'll be standing on some stupid street in a stupid city wearing a stupid frock and you'll be struck straight to the heart, wondering what is happening here, what we're doing then. And you'll be sick over it, sick as a parrot."

"That's quite a picture you paint," I said lightly.

"It's the truth."

"Things are complicated," I told her. "And they'll be less so if I leave."

"Why?" she demanded. "Because loving hurts? Grow up, Delilah. *Life* hurts. It's only the strong who survive. It's only the gamblers who aren't afraid of rolling the dice who really live."

I sighed. "It's no good, Tusker. I can't stay here for crumbs. I thought he wanted me, but all he offered was a sham engagement. He's far more concerned about his conservancy. I'm only ever going to be an afterthought for him. And to continue your gambling metaphor, if I were going to stay, it would have to be for a man who was willing to go all in."

"I don't even know what that means," she said, flapping a hand irritably at a bug.

"It's a poker term. It means when you are so sure of what you're holding that you risk everything. You put every last bit you have on the line because you are that sure you're going to win."

She let out a little scream and tugged at her hair. "Oh, you impossible little wretch! Don't you even realise that's what he's done?"

"What are you talking about?"

*"He has gone all in.* The day he went to Nairobi it wasn't just to buy Fairlight. It was to sell everything else he owns in order to raise the money. The coast house in Lamu, the *dukas*, his cane fields. It's all gone."

My mouth went dry. "Don't be stupid. Ryder already has money. His father made a fortune in the gold fields in the Yukon."

"And squandered it in a year! Everything Ryder has, he earned. And he sold it all to buy Fairlight, not for some stupid conservancy project, but for you, you little fool."

"Why didn't he tell me?"

She rolled her eyes. "I have horses with more wit than you, girl. Because he didn't want you to feel beholden. He wants you here because you *want* to be here, because you want him and this life enough to give the rest of it up. Why do you think he's willing to go along with the preposterous lie about you being his fiancée? Because he's hoping one day it will happen."

She finished with an air of triumph. I put down my peaches.

"He can't marry me. His wife is—" I broke off.

"In Cairo," she finished smugly. "Where he went when you were sitting in jail in Nairobi. It cost him a fortune, but he got his divorce. The minute you stepped in to save Gideon, he knew he'd have to get rid of that slut wife of his so he'd be free to take care of you. It was only a matter of time before Government House bowed to pressure and chucked you out of the country. He wanted to be free to offer you marriage to keep you here."

"But he didn't—"

She shrieked again. "What man would? Good God, you're the most footloose woman he's ever met. He knew if he proposed sincerely you'd bolt for Mombasa. He's figuring if he can just keep you here, eventually you'll come around and realise he's worth twenty of any other man you've ever known."

I shook my head. "Stop it. Stop saying things like that. You're confusing me."

"Why? It should be crystal clear to you. He is as desperately in love with you as any man has ever been with any woman. You want poetry and heartfelt declarations? He has sold everything he owned, everything he ever worked for, just for the possibility of keeping you close enough to see you once in a while. He's willing to wait for you until the crack of doom, biding his time and eating out his own heart because all he wants is for you to love him back. So do it," she said, her eyes bright. "Do it, Delilah. Love him back. He deserves that."

She scrabbled at her eyes. "I'm an old fool, but I'm not wrong." She rose heavily to her feet. "By the way, Gates is dead. Thought you'd like to know."

The change of subject was so fast it gave me whiplash.

"What? How?"

"Fell off a ridge while he was poaching and broke his leg. Hyenas got to him."

I shuddered, but only part of it was in horror. There was a tiny sliver of satisfaction that was so primitive and so savage, I ought to have been afraid of it. I remembered then my thoughts on the subtlety of a Masai revenge, of the *laibon* and of what Granny Miette had taught me about magic, the light and the dark, the healing and the harming, both sides of the same thin coin.

"So Fairlight is safe now."

She smiled thinly. "Africa takes care of its own."

After she left, I spent the rest of that afternoon sitting by the lake, watching the sun dipping lower, casting long shadows. I went to bed just as the moon rose. I could see a faint shape through the mosquito netting, a man hovering near the door, his features smudged as I looked out of the tail of my eye. When I turned to look at him directly, he vanished, and I knew that this time he was gone for good.

The next morning I walked to Patel's and sent a telegram to Narok. That evening was Kit's gallery opening in Nairobi, and I packed a bag with the things I had salvaged in order to spend the night. I had just locked the case when Helen arrived. She hugged me and pulled back to look at my face.

"My poor darling! Africa hasn't been very kind to you, has it?"

"It's had its moments. Let's sit on the veranda and have a drink."

I poured and Helen carried them out, exclaiming as she looked at Lake Wanyama. The light was glittering on the blue-green water, and in the shallows a marabou stork waded with stately intention. "Such a beautiful view! I think it might almost be better than ours." Her tone was light, as if she hadn't a care in the world, but I wondered if she were in pain. The sunlight wasn't kind to her. It highlighted every line on her face. She had fought a hard battle against getting old or ugly, but time and disease were winning.

I chose my words carefully. "Rex said the same thing. He seems quite fond of the property."

"He is," she replied in the same cautious tone. "In fact, I thought it best you hear it from one of us. He's making an offer on Fairlight. It's a generous one," she hurried on, "you needn't worry that we'll try to take advantage of your stepfather's family. In fact, I think they'll be pleased. Rex wants to rebuild the place. It's always been such a fine house, and he's always pictured himself living here on the lake."

It seemed damnably cruel to talk about a future that Helen most likely wouldn't share, but I didn't have a choice.

"I'm surprised you want to leave the farm. I know how proud you are of what you've built there."

She gave a short laugh and turned her head to me. "We can keep fencing if you like, but I think it's best if we speak plainly. It's time for you to leave Africa, my dear."

There was nothing malicious in her voice, no new coldness in her tone. It was said as sweetly as if she'd been inviting me to a garden party. But I knew better.

"Is that why you burned Fairlight down? To get rid of me? Because you're worried that Rex might be getting too fond of me?"

Her peal of laughter startled the stork. It launched itself with an irritable flap of the wings. "Oh, my darling child, is that really what you think? You must believe me when I tell you that so long as we live, Rex and I belong to each other. It doesn't matter what else we get up to, we are partners. Our loyalty is only to each other.

You just don't matter enough for me to bother with."

Oddly, I believed her. "Then why the push to get rid of me? Was it Kit? Did you resent the fact that he preferred me?"

She lifted a hand and studied her nails with lazy interest. "Did he? I always thought Kit was like a tomcat—only interested in what was right under his nose at any given moment."

"You're probably right. So what was it? What turned you against me? What made you so eager to frame me for Kit's murder?"

Her hand stilled. "Do you know or is that a shot in the dark?"

"Oh, definitely a shot in the dark. Most of this is. But I had a lot of time to think it over in prison and I believe I'm right. You decided Kit had to die and you were happy for me to swing for it. And now you'd like me to leave Africa because I'm the one person who knows you killed Kit. I'd just like to know why."

The laughter pealed again. "So many shots and so few of them true! Where shall I begin, pet? You and I both had our fun with Kit. Oh, it stung when he first started seeing you, I admit. He didn't have as much time for me, and I didn't like that. But it wasn't long before I realised Kit wasn't going anywhere. He liked variety too much, and that's my specialty," she said, stretching her legs out in front of her. "He was a lovely boy, don't you think? But venal, with a very small heart, always grasping at what didn't belong to him."

"Is that why you gave him presents?"

She lifted one foot, balancing the heel carefully on the toes of her other foot. "I didn't give those to him. Rex did."

"Why on earth—"

She flapped a hand at me. "Can't you guess? Blackmail! Kit discovered that Rex had been stockpiling weapons at a little fishing cabin he keeps up at one of the lakes. He threatened to go to the authorities with what he'd seen if Rex didn't come across with some money. Rex gave him what cash he could lay his hands on, but Kit wasn't terribly particular. He was just as happy with the wristwatch and the gramophone."

"But most of the settlers are stockpiling weapons. Why would the government care if Rex is?"

She gave me a narrow smile. "Because most of the settlers aren't contemplating kidnapping the Duke and Duchess of York to make their point."

"You're joking."

"Not a bit of it. Rex had thought of abducting the governor, but as soon as he heard about the proposed royal visit, he realised how much better this would be! So much publicity for the cause of independence."

"It's madness."

She shrugged. "Well, of course it is. But you

know men and politics. Listen, I've been married for the better part of two decades. I know exactly how to manage Rex. All I had to do was go along with his idea and tell him how brilliant it was, and somehow in the year between now and the Yorks' visit, I would have figured out a way to change his mind."

"But then Kit happened."

Her mouth turned grim. "Kit happened. He began making demands on Rex and Rex panicked. Believe it or not, Rex isn't half as strong as he pretends to be. He relies on me—more than anyone ever realises. We are each other's support, and he needs me."

I wasn't sure if she was trying to convince me or herself, but it made an odd sort of sense. Most men wouldn't have tolerated Helen's blatant catting around. Rex almost seemed to take a strange sort of pride in it.

"So Kit threatened to expose him and demanded money," I prompted.

"And truth be told, there isn't much, not after building the house and furnishing it and importing all of Rex's breeding stock. Besides, I knew Kit. He wouldn't stop until he'd bled us dry. He had to be taken care of."

It was a sinister phrase, gentle and nonspecific, but lethal.

"You decided together to take care of the problem?"

"No, the idea was mine. The best ideas always are," she added with a ghost of a smile. "All Rex had to do was pull the trigger and leave the rest to me. I knew Kit slept heavily after an afternoon in bed. We just needed to wait until the two of you had been together and then seize the moment."

I thought back to the evening she and I had spent together—the long moments she had been alone in my rooms, powdering her nose and pilfering my jewel case.

"Did Rex know you intended to frame me?"

She rolled her eyes. "I told you—too many shots in the dark and most of them were misses. No one ever intended to frame you. I took that bracelet because it was Masai. I thought the authorities would centre their investigation on the natives instead of the whites. I was horrified when they identified the bracelet as yours."

I wasn't sure if I believed it or not, but she had no reason to lie to me now. In fact, she seemed to be enjoying herself. I told her as much.

She nodded. "It's cathartic. Rather like the confessional except none of those boring churchmen to set you a penance." She paused then looked me squarely in the eye. "We had a plan to save you, you know. Rex was keeping careful tabs on the situation in Nairobi. If they had charged you, I would have made a confession to killing Kit myself."

"Why you if Rex pulled the trigger?"

Her smile turned beatific. "Because I'm the one with a life to give. There isn't much of it left, but it would have done the trick." She raised her glass in a salute and drained it down. Her mood turned brisk. "Any more questions?"

"I'm sure I'll think of some after you leave, but I don't expect I'll get a chance to ask them."

She rose and I followed suit. "Then I take it you're heading back to civilisation like a good girl?" Her tone was arch but not entirely unfriendly.

I didn't answer her directly. "Tell Rex he isn't getting Fairlight. I made an offer myself this morning, but I was too late. It's already been sold."

Her eyes widened. "But who—"

"It belongs to Ryder."

She laughed in spite of herself and threw up her hands. "I might have known. That man always does manage to get what he wants."

I walked her down the veranda to the steps. "I don't know where I'm going yet, Helen. But I know this—you took the life of someone who might not have been perfect, but who didn't deserve to die. And you ruined the life of an innocent man who was my friend. I know I can't go to the authorities. They'd laugh me right out of Government House. So you and Rex are safe from the law. But you aren't safe from me. For as long as you draw breath, I will remember what you did to those two men, and I will pray you burn for it. And when you die, wherever I am in the world, I will remember and I will go on, Helen. Rex and Gideon and Africa and everything you love and everything you hate will go on without you. And we will all be the better for it. That is a thing I know for sure."

I turned on my heel and went into the house and closed the door softly behind me.

# 25

That evening I was in Nairobi. It was the opening of Kit's show at the gallery, and the owner had requested my presence. I dreaded it. The press would be there, asking ghoulish questions and sticking their noses into everybody's business. But it was Kit's last hurrah, and I felt I owed him at least that.

I had gone straight to the Norfolk to check in. They gave me the tiniest room imaginable, no doubt to discourage me from coming back, but I didn't mind. It was for Kit. I bathed and dusted myself with rice powder to whiten my skin. I brushed a tiny bit of jasmine oil into my hair to make it gleam, and painted on a deep crimson mouth to match my nails. The white silk dress I had worn to my first party in Africa had burned, but I found another in a little shop near the hotel and I bought it for Kit. He had always liked me in white. I fastened a tiny sprig of stephanotis at each earlobe in place of earrings and tied the black silk ribbon around my wrist.

When I was ready, I took a cab to the gallery and found the place already in full crush. So many flashbulbs popped when I stepped out of the taxi I was nearly blinded, but Mr. Hillenbrank rushed out to escort me in.

"Miss Drummond! It is such a pleasure to have you here tonight for the unveiling. I was hoping you might do the honours?"

I murmured something appropriate and let him take charge of me. He towed me around the room, introducing me to various people. I was only half listening to the names and the faces were a blur. I hadn't had an answer to the cable I sent Ryder, and I kept thinking of the contents. Just three short words, a scrap of language, but I had thought it enough to bind him to me.

MARRY ME. STOP.

A hundred things could have happened. The cable could have gone awry. They could have crossed, the cable arriving in Narok after he had left. Or Tusker could have exaggerated, I thought with a chill. She could have declared things he didn't really feel. I pushed that thought aside and walked the gallery, looking at Kit's paintings. There was one of Gideon, tall and proud, and I felt my heart roll up into my throat as I looked at my friend. I swallowed it down, hard, and it sat like a lump.

Just then a shadow fell over my shoulder. "Enjoying the show, Miss Drummond?"

I turned. "Inspector Gilchrist. I am surprised."

"Why? Aren't policemen permitted hobbies?" He peered at the painting. "Is it a good likeness?"

"The best." I took a deep breath. "Inspector, I know—"

"No, you don't," he said firmly. "And whatever you think you know, forget it. He has friends in very high places, Miss Drummond. Very high places. You got lucky this time. But if you cross him again . . . well, don't, is my advice."

I opened my mouth to tell him about Helen then closed it again. What was the point? She was guilty of something dark and terrible—and very soon she would pay for it. As to Rex, at least Gilchrist knew to be watchful of him, and I suspected that without Helen's careful planning, he would slip up one day, too badly for any of his connections to save him. Africa would take care of her own.

I smiled at Gilchrist. "Very well. But I have friends, too, Inspector. And I hope you're one of them."

He put out his hand to shake it. "I think if I were going to back a horse, I would always back you, Miss Drummond. You might be a long shot, but I suspect you always come through."

With that he bent and kissed my hand and melted away into the crowd.

I was happy to see how many of the paintings bore tiny cards stating that the work had been sold and identifying the buyers.

After a few more toasts and a dozen more introductions, Mr. Hillenbrank moved to the centre of the gallery, bringing me with him. He made a lengthy speech about Kit, his enormous

469

talent, his zest for life. At this last bit, several ladies in the crowd tittered and several more lifted discreet handkerchiefs to dab away a tear or two.

Mr. Hillenbrank carried on as if he heard nothing. "But Kit Parrymore was more than just a talented artist. He was an artist of tremendous potential—potential he only came close to unlocking with his very last work. Around you are hung samples of his youth, his exuberance. But with this painting, he came very close to maturity. With the help of its subject, I give you *Delilah Drummond.*"

At his signal, I reached for the cord. It hesitated at first, and I had to tug quite sharply to make it move. Then all at once it fell away, a puddle of crimson velvet on the floor at my feet. There was an audible gasp from the crowd. I turned to look at the painting.

Kit had captured me, all of me. I was child and woman, fully present and already gone, entirely his and no man's at all. My painted self held every contradiction, and it held them in such perfect harmony it was like seeing a symphony spelled out note for note on the canvas.

My glance moved to the card pinned to the wall beside the painting. *Delilah Drummond.* And neatly typed below it in bold letters on a clean white card, PROPERTY OF J. RYDER WHITE.

Mr. Hillenbrank was at my elbow. "I am

470

particularly pleased to have sold that piece before the show," he said with a quiet air of satisfaction.

"Is he here?"

"No, but we received a cable only an hour ago from Narok. The gentleman was most particular about the wording on the card. He must be quite an ardent collector."

I reached up and kissed him on the cheek, leaving a scarlet impression of lipstick behind. He coughed and looked immensely pleased.

"He is not a collector at all, Mr. Hillenbrank. But he is a hell of a stayer."

With that, I stepped aside then as the crowd moved forward to get a better look. I walked straight out of the gallery and into the street. Around me Nairobi heaved and swelled and parted, like the vast rushing waters of a river in spate. Women carried baskets on their heads and a group of children ran laughing as a baboon chased them for their fruit. Men roasted sweet corn to sell and called out their peddler's wares in high, piping voices. A dozen languages met and mingled on that street, and the air smelled of spices and smoke and the warm flesh of the African earth. A high, droning noise sounded far overhead. I shaded my eyes and looked up to see a small plane silhouetted against the sun. I took the black ribbon from my wrist and waved it high overhead, signalling. Ryder was coming home.

# Acknowledgments

This book, more than any other I have written, owes everything to the kindness of friends and strangers. I am most grateful to:

The stylish and generous Dianne Moggy and her husband, David, for sharing safari photos so spectacular I could almost believe I was in Kenya.

Becky at Busch Gardens Tampa for answering endless questions and giving me a behind-the-scenes tour of the facility—including access to Kasi, a handsome young cheetah who listened politely while we talked.

Jill Martin and Jackie Ogden for arranging access to Gary Noble and Steve Metzler, Disney wildlife experts who graciously shared their time and expertise at Animal Kingdom and the Animal Kingdom Lodge. Heartfelt thanks for the thrill of standing ten feet in front of a roaring lion—an experience I will never forget. Particular gratitude to our safari tour guides at Animal Kingdom, most especially Mark, for making us forget for just a little while that we weren't actually in Africa. (It was a true delight to return home and find out after the fact that Mark just happened to be a fan of Lady Julia and Brisbane.)

Vee Romero for her passion for Africa and its wildlife.

Dr. Ross Fuller, my dentist, who made endless trips to his office far more bearable by sharing his wealth of knowledge on the subject of historic double-barreled British rifles, specifically the .416 Rigby.

Jana Angelucci and Gail Sauer for their Georgian hospitality and willingness to play chauffeur. Also, to Kim Caudell and Blake Richardson Leyers for providing research that has not made it into this book but will certainly prove too delicious not to use in the future. Many thanks to Gayatri Khosla and Rati Badahur Madan for their contributions regarding the character of Raj Patel and their delightful enthusiasm.

Alecia Hawkes for transcribing by hand the narration of BBC documentaries on the history of safari which I could not access from the U.S. *Generous* is not a strong enough word to describe her contributions.

The entire Harlequin MIRA team—art department, sales, PR, marketing, editorial and support— all the many hands that labour willingly and with such flair to make my books the best they can be. Particular thanks to Michael Rehder for giving me the breathtaking cover of my dreams. I am especially grateful to the beautiful cover model who graciously allowed her hair to be cut to truly embody Delilah Drummond.

The immensely talented Miranda Indrigo for an elegant, featherlight line edit that has elevated this book beyond what I could have done alone, and to Laura McCallen and Michelle Venditti for their eagle-eyed attention to detail.

My writer friends for encouragement, laughter and perspective. Most especially to Joshilyn Jackson for inspiring me to write fearlessly and to Lauren Willig for her generosity and enthusiasm when we realised we were both writing 1920s Africa books with characters named Dodo!

Chobani for fueling me, Nicole Hunt Sardinas for posting TOTO's "Africa" video, and Jomie Wilding for providing cupcakes during the home stretch. Frivolity is sometimes an essential component of creativity.

Librarians, booksellers, bloggers and readers who come to events, buy books, sell books, send emails, tweet and kindly share their appreciation with others.

My staggeringly supportive agent, Pam Hopkins, for innumerable kindnesses.

As ever, my family. Without my parents, my daughter and, most of all, my beloved, I would write, but poorly.

And to the people of New Orleans for showing me exactly where Delilah comes from and who she is.

# Questions of Discussion

1. Delilah Drummond is a unique and not always likable heroine. How do the different characters in the book view her—as a friend or adversary? What was your reaction to her? How does Delilah change over the course of the book?

2. Ryder White is a larger-than-life character. What traits make him appealing?

3. How does the political climate of colonial Kenya influence the characters and their response to their environment? How does Dodo display attitudes typical of the colonial English? In contrast, the Farradays are representative of a particular type of scandalous settler notorious in Kenya between the 1920s and 1950s. How do you think each of these characters views Africa?

4. Gideon and his younger brother, Moses, both touch something within Delilah. What does this relationship seem to fulfill for each of them? Delilah makes a tremendous sacrifice for Gideon. Why? Was she right to do it?

5. Delilah is very comfortable with her sexuality and with the effect she has on men. How do sexual relationships drive the action of the book? How is Delilah's sexual relationship with Kit different from that with Ryder? How does Dodo's experience with sex change her plans?

6. Africa is as much a character in the book as any of the people. How does Africa itself play a role in the story?

7. Ryder makes tremendous sacrifices to keep Delilah in Africa. Was he right to do so?

8. What is Delilah and Ryder's potential for a happy ending?